THE CURSE OF ARKADY

THE MAGICKERS #2

THE CURSE OF ARKADY

THE MAGICKERS #2

EMILY DRAKE

DAW BOOKS, INC.

DONALD A. WOLLHEIM, FOUNDER

375 Hudson Street, New York, NY 10014

ELIZABETH R. WOLLHEIM
SHEILA E. GILBERT
PUBLISHERS

http://www.dawbooks.com

First printing, June 2002
1 2 3 4 5 6 7 8 9

DAW TRADEMARK REGISTERED
U.S. PAT. OFF. AND FOREIGN COUNTRIES
—MARCA REGISTRADA
HECHO EN U.S.A.

PRINTED IN THE U.S.A.

Dedicated to wishers and dreamers everywhere,
and especially my children,
James, Jessica, Aaron, and Maureen.

Contents

1   Alarms   *1*

2   Curses   *11*

3   Charmed, I'm Sure   *20*

4   A Little English   *29*

5   Good News and Bad News   *38*

6   Dirty Deeds   *45*

7   Semper Fi   *55*

8   Howling Like a Banshee   *69*

9   In the Glooming   *76*

10   The Honor of Your Presence   *79*

11   Two Wrongs and a Wright   *87*

12   Can't Bear these Changes   *101*

13   Spooky Old Houses   *112*

14   Coinkydinks   *119*

15   The Game's Afoot   *125*

16   Strange Thing in the Night   *131*

17   On the Other Hand   *139*

18 Dragon Magic 149

19 Warm Fuzzies 155

20 Button, Button 163

21 Oooops 170

22 Anchors Away 180

23 Surprised Party 186

24 Truth or Dare 194

25 Moonstruck 202

26 Game Plan 209

27 The Dark Hand Closes 216

28 Secrets 225

29 The Hidden 233

30 Gates 245

31 Tiger, Tiger, Burning Bright 253

32 No I in Team 263

33 Oh, Henry 270

34 Rescue 280

35 Come into My Parlor 286

36 Charge! 293

37 Lucky Guess 301

THE CURSE OF ARKADY

THE MAGICKERS #2

Alarms

H E'D been there before. But this time, in his dreamwalk, he'd already been through the shifting sands on the beach below, and through the cemetery that wrapped about the castle ruins like a moat guarding it. He'd already tripped the dragon-head lock that held the gates shut and would spout flame if opened improperly. He had already gone into the ruins and fallen downstairs into the catacombs beneath.

He'd done all that, time and again. This once, Jason seemed to be starting where he'd always finished before. Maybe it was because now he knew how important a dreamwalk could be, as it had been explained by Tomaz Crowfeather. Maybe it was be-cause he was different now. Trouble was, it made the dream more dangerous, not easier to escape.

A cool wind from nowhere sent chills along the back of his neck. He looked down. The cuffs of his jeans and his sneakers dripped with sea water from his trip across the beach. His toes felt like icicles and he squooshed when he took a step, but he had to keep moving down here. Silvery moonlight rayed through the broken castle roof and fell in spidery lines across the tunnel. It left behind shadows sharper than the night itself. Jason took a deep breath and strode forth. Although unsure exactly where he was going, he knew his journey led past the catacombs and he had to get there, had to get *through*.

Behind him, the wind picked up, keening, its voice beginning to howl. Jason paused, listening intently, his head tilted. No! Those *were* howls. Echoing eerily along the walls of the tunnels, faint but getting closer. Wolfjackals, racing down the stone pathways, after him! He couldn't be caught, not now, not here.

He threw caution to the wind. He put his lean body into a run, through the turning tunnels, no need to remember the way if he had to go back, because going back would lead him right into the eager jaws of the pursuers. Jason knotted his fists, pumping his arms to drive his body forward. His left hand ached as though he'd caught it on something, but it was an old injury, one he knew well. The catacomb turned sharply to the right and he with it, and then it suddenly opened into a large cavern room, dark with shadows.

He plowed to a halt, seeing no passage out of the cavern. He knew this room, too! His heart pounded heavily in his chest at the sight of the carved tomb, with the still figure resting atop it. Anyplace but here! Jason looked around wildly, but the scant moonlight filtering down from above gave little illumination. The shadows seemed to leap at him, and he swerved away instinctively, bumping into the sarcophagus itself, rapping his leg sharply and throwing his weight over it. He scrambled back, but his shirt caught on the sharp edges of the tomb, capturing him. No matter how hard he pulled, the fabric only stretched and refused to come loose.

Jason braced himself and yanked. The howling wolfjackals sounded closer, far too close. The sarcophagus refused to yield.

He had two choices: remove his shirt or stay and face the wolf-jackals.

The cold figure on the tomb moved. An icy hand reached out and grabbed his wrist, gripping him tightly with fingers that felt like marble.

Make that three choices!

Netted between shirt and hand, Jason froze, his heart drumming loudly in his chest. He twisted his wrist till his skin burned but the tombstone hand stayed fast around him. It pulled him down, nearer and nearer to the finely carved face with its curled dark hair. It wanted him. He could feel it . . . inhaling him. Drawing him in. He would sink into that figure until he was part of it!

In sheer panic, Jason fought, thrashing, his wrist growing bloodied and his shirt finally ripping free, though it did him no good. He remained captured, as if a steel trap held him, and he was as eager to be free as any wild animal. He fought till he couldn't struggle anymore, exhausted, shivering—and he realized the wolfjackals had stopped howling. He turned on one heel, and saw them, eager feral faces with eyes glowing green in the darkness, blocking the tunnel out.

The hand pulled him close. He bucked and battled against it, feeling the warmth being sucked right out of him by the icy fingers, his sneakers slipping and sliding against the gritty flooring. He could feel the heat in his body rushing out of him. In moments he would be as cold as the figure that gripped him!

"No!" Jason's voice echoed sharply back at him, and the wolfjackals bunched up, growling and snapping at the sound. Their eyes let out green sparks as they watched him. He braced his feet against the base of the tomb and pulled with all his might. No use!

Dream world or not, he was falling! Jason felt his body go limp and icy, unable to stand and slumping over the sarcophagus. The hand about his wrist tightened even more till he wanted to cry out in pain, the crescent scar livid and pulsing. Spread-eagled over the tomb, he knew he would never leave unless he did something desperate, and NOW. He dug his free hand into his pocket to grip his crystal tightly, focusing his thoughts into the red alarm beacon that was one of the last lessons he'd gotten from Gavan Rainwater, Magicker extraordinaire.

He could feel the very last shard of his warmth spearheading into that thought as he collapsed. In his mind's eye, he could see himself like an arrow shooting away. . . .

Gavan Rainwater's office at Ravenwyng was just as he re-membered it. Cluttered, with a massive desk of scarred wood, and a huge, somewhat battered high back chair behind it. It was empty of all but a clutter of old books and papers spilling out of a corner bookcase, cascading down a dented metal file cabinet, and covering (more or less) the top of the desk. Odd lumps of quartz and semiprecious rocks, some polished and shaped and others not, were lying about haphazardly wherever they seemed to have been tossed. One massive golden topaz stood like a proud lantern, its rays catching the beams of an unseeable moon or sun and spreading the light throughout the musty office.

His shout for help came blood-red through the topaz, a sin-gle crimson ray of alarm. It pierced the quiet disorder of the office, but there was no one there to take notice of it. Jason himself saw it blearily as his eyelids began to close. A dark shadow fell across his vision, clouding the golden topaz.

Blacker than the shadows of the office, a raven hopped upon the desk. With a ker-aaack! it investigated the topaz, clacking its beak against the massive gemstone. It eyed the red beam and then, with another clack-clack of its sharp beak, spread its wings and launched into a low, lazy flight from Rainwater's of-fice. He sensed its glide through the corridors of the empty Gathering Hall and then into the night, sailing over the lake waters, silhouetted by the low hanging moon. Was it going for help? Was there anyone at all who could help him now?

He had no more time to wonder!

The wolfjackals trotted into the cavern chamber now and raced once around the stone-and-marble tomb, then surrounded it, growling, crouched low on their paws. He could smell their heated breath and drool, like putrid steam upon the icy air. The leader paced forward, his tail making one slow wag of triumph.

He opened his sharp-toothed lined jowls, hunching his neck and shoulders in the painful effort to speak like a human. "You are *mine*," he reminded Jason, and ran his scalding raspy tongue over the throbbing hurt that Jason's left hand had become.

The pain of it jolted him. So shocking was it, that he flinched wildly, throwing himself off the tomb. He smashed onto the floor. The wolfjackals scattered as he landed, and the pain of hitting the stone with his cold brittle body shattered his dream into a thousand sharp pieces and he . . .

Came awake.

Jason lifted his face from the lined paper under his hand. A string of drool followed him, and he wiped it away quickly. His notebook lay across his desk, open, and he'd been working on homework. WHAT I DID ON MY SUMMER VACATION. Under it he had written: Found out I was a Magicker. And then he crossed that out. Learned to use crystals for Magick. Scribbled across that. Made new friends in summer camp. That had stayed. Was bitten by a wolfjackal and fought off the Dark Hand of Brennard. . . . His pencil lay over that line, as if he hadn't quite got a chance to blacken through it before he'd fallen asleep.

He lifted his other hand, stretching. From his attic bedroom, he could hear the normal, comforting sounds of the McIntires down below in the entertainment room, laughing at something on television. The hearty bellow of William "the Dozer's" big laugh, echoed by the more delicate tones of both Joanna and Alicia sounded faintly to his ears, ever so much better than the eerie wailing of wolfjackals. He took several breaths.

The porthole window of his attic bedroom stood open to the night breeze, which had grown very cold, and he leaned over, closing it. He knocked down his latest Mercedes Lackey book while doing so, and the unicorn bookmark in it fell out. Jason left it lying there on the carpeted corner near his bookcase. No one would bother it. This was his part of the world and nothing uninvited ever pulled down the trapdoor stair to come in. He liked it like that.

Jason tore the paper out of his notebook and wadded it up. With serious thoughts in mind, he pushed his dream away, and began to craft an essay that would make his Honors English teacher happy and not mark him as a candidate for a strait-jacket. His room gained some warmth as he wrote of bright summer days and campfires and friends like Bailey with her twisted sayings and the pack rat she'd captured for a pet after it had pilfered many shiny items from her cabin. The words flew across the pages. Not once did he say anything that would jeopardize any of his comrades as Magickers in a world that knew nothing about them.

He came to a stop as he tried to finish the paper. What he had really done on his summer vacation was learned a lot about himself, as well as making new friends. But how much of it did he dare reveal? He tapped his pencil point on the desktop, pondering. Tap, tap. Although the time spent at Camp Raven-wyng was weeks in the past, his thoughts seemed to be stalled back there.

TAP, TAP.

Jason jumped in his chair.

TAP.

He stood up, glaring at his window. A black shape winged

past it, and Jason threw himself at the pane, to catch a glimpse of it as it flew past. Raven, again!

He opened his stair and clattered down them, determined to catch a glimpse of the bird, if he could. He grabbed the trash from the kitchen as he went, it was his night anyway, and could serve as a cover. Then he headed out the back door, into the night-darkened backyard and driveway where the Dozer had the trash cans lined up like solemn soldiers. He tossed his bag in the appropriate can . . . not "Papers Only," or "Yard Cuttings!," but the one marked "Plain Old Garbage," then ducked across the yard, where he could see the yellow moon glowing through the eucalyptus and slippery elm trees.

The darker-than-night bird wheeled over him, gliding as silently through the sky as an owl. He knew it! He knew that had been no crow . . . that was a raven, and undoubtedly one of Tomaz Crowfeather's. It had been too quiet in the weeks since summer camp's abrupt ending. Far, far too quiet. He hadn't had a Tomb dream in all that time either. Something was up! But what?

He raised his hand, rather like a falconer, as he'd seen Tomaz do. The Native American had struck a far different figure than he did . . . a grown man, with a face lined by the sun, hair banded at the nape of his neck, always in comfortable blue jeans and vest and shirt, hammered silver disks and turquoise stone jewelry studding his waist, his wrists, his neck. But Jason stood there expectantly, anyway.

The raven circled above him. It dove at his hand, passing it, the wind from its wings slapping his open palm. Then, with a cry, the bird dropped something into the dewed grass and disappeared into the darkness.

He picked it out of a tangled spiderweb in the corner, strands holding it tightly for him, keeping the paper from being carried off by the faint night breeze. He tucked it into his pocket and hurried back into the house. His step on the stair caught Joanna's attention, and she called out from the TV room, "Jason?"

"Yes, Mom. I just took the trash out so I wouldn't forget it. I'm almost finished with my homework."

"Good!" Although he couldn't see her, he could hear the pleased smile in her voice.

Without further interruption, he hurried back to his attic bedroom, pulled the stair up and secured it. Then, and only then, did he take the paper out and flatten it to be readable.

Greetings, young Magicker, from Headmaster Gavan Rainwater and staff.
Be diligent in your studies and beware the Curse of Arkady!

He knew it! There *was* danger lurking nearby. "What on Earth is the Curse of Arkady?"

"A thing to be feared and watched out for, it seems."

Jason whirled around in his chair. "Gavan!"

The headmaster of Camp Ravenwyng leaned against his porthole window, his unexpected presence filling the room. "You rang?"

"In my dream—"

Gavan frowned slightly. He straightened up, drawing his cape about him, and bringing his wolfhead cane up to look into the crystal held by the pewter creature's wide jaws. "You set off the alarm beacon through your dreams? That's power, Jason. Good and bad." He rubbed his palm over his cane as if communing with his crystal. "I think I'll have Tomaz visit you again, give you some more instruction on dreamwalking. Yours seem to be very potent, and yet you have to be able to read and control them."

"What more can he tell me?"

"I'm not sure." Gavan gave him a lopsided grin. "Tomaz is a man of infinite depths. His knowledge of other ways of magic is vast, and I'm still learning about it myself. But this I know." Gavan Rainwater stared into his face with eyes of crystal clear freshwater blue. "We can't afford to have you scared, Jason. A Gatekeeper has to be strong and curious, ready to explore, and wary enough to handle what he finds. I've a friend, Fizziwig, who will be training you for that, but in the meantime, we have to help you find a balance."

"I'm not scared."

Gavan reached out and put a hand on Jason's shoulder. "No?"

"Not that scared anyway."

"Good. If you were that scared, you couldn't think, and we need you to keep your wits about you. We are spread thin, Jason, watching over all of you, and there will be times when none of us can come to your aid, despite the alarm beacon."

Jason tapped his note. "Then that's why Tomaz sent this. A warning to keep us ready."

"What is that?"

Jason passed it over. Gavan scanned it, and handed it back with a sigh. "He dares what he shouldn't, and in all of our names. The Council will be furious over this, but perhaps he's right. We debated this, and the Council voted not to frighten everyone unduly. Tomaz and I disagreed, but we were outvoted. Evidently, Tomaz took the warning upon himself." Gavan rubbed his jaw. "If I can't stop the Council from bickering, we're not going to be able to face Brennard. You should all know there are risks out there now, of being found and attacked and not just by the Dark Hand."

"So there is a curse."

Gavan nodded slowly. "A curse that can be dark and deadly. Gather the others, and warn them if they haven't been already, and learn to guard yourselves. Take care of each other, Jason." He tapped the head of his cane, and his very body seemed to grow thin and disappear. His voice lingered after he'd vanished, saying, "Do all that is within your power to do!"

"I will!" pledged Jason, and the Magicker was gone. It was only then that Jason realized Gavan hadn't told him what the Curse of Arkady was.

Curses

"WHEN are we seven met again?" asked Bailey, her voice hollow and thready, pitched to send echoes through the air and raise the fine hairs at the back of everyone's neck.

Trent wadded up a piece of paper and threw it at her. It bounced off her freckled nose and into the pocket of her shirt. "We're in my backyard and we're only here till my dad gets home!" he snorted, unimpressed.

The pocket rippled and bumped and squeaked, and the paper wad was abruptly ejected, followed by the whiskered and curious face of the pocket's occupant. Lacey let out an indignant chirp, cleaned her pack rat face with tiny paws, and dove back into Bailey's pocket, leaving only her tufted tail hanging out. Grinning, Bailey tucked that back in, as well.

"Sounded good, though!"

Ting smiled slightly as she smoothed a dark wing of hair from her oval face, her almond-shaped eyes lighting with a quiet humor. "You always sound good, Bailey. It's the mind behind the words. . . ." Her sentence trailed off. She folded her hands in her lap and bumped her shoulder against her friend's as if to emphasize the tease.

"Yeah, yeah." Rich and Stefan had been playing cards, as usual. Stefan gathered them into his big, chunky hands as he turned his attention to the meeting. "I got football practice in thirty minutes. This had better be good."

Getting them all together at one time was no small feat, and Jason could only thank a slow Saturday morning for the timing. He'd sent a summons by crystal, but it had taken days to get them together here. He fished out the raven-delivered paper. "Anyone besides me get this from Tomaz?"

Bailey's hand shot up. Ting frowned, then shook her head. Rich grunted and both the redhead and his chunky pal nodded. Danno's answer was to pull out a similar piece of paper from inside his jacket. Trent shook his head in the negative. "What's up?"

"It's a warning."

"Trouble?" Trent's eyes lit up. "And they're worried we might get into it?"

"I think," said Danno quietly, "we've got enough problems with the Dark Hand. Fair warning against anyone or anything else is good." He wrapped his arms about his legs, darker Latino face a contrast to the cream color of his shirt.

"But no one's been bothered, have they? School's been going, days and weeks are passing. I think it's all a bunch of hooey cooked up to keep us quiet."

Stefan echoed Rich's scoff. "Yeah. Like homework."

"Homework is cooked up to help us learn," remarked Ting. She stared at her slender hands in her lap.

Jason sat down on a big rock that occupied most of the corner of Trent's small patch of yard. "I think," he offered, "that we can expect the Dark Hand, just like the Magickers, to be recovering from the battle at Ravenwyng. First we defeated their spy Jonnard, and then the others. They've probably been catching their breath, and now they're getting ready to strike again. I don't think they'll have wolfjackals to help them, but they could be anyone, anywhere, tracking us."

"Why no wolfjackals?"

Jason shrugged. "They need a lot of mana. My guess is they stay close to Havens and Gates. But members of the Hand are just like anyone."

Rich rolled his eyes. "Like they can find us. There's only how many million people in the country now?"

Trent shot him a look. "You think they couldn't?"

"I think," Rich said, tilting his head in Trent's direction, "that we're small fish to them."

"Not so small," Bailey muttered. "Remember what Jon did to Henry Squibb!"

They all sat in silence for a moment thinking of round-faced, funny, and smart Henry who'd had his newly found Magicker powers destroyed by the traitor Jonnard. The discovery that Jon had been a thief, traitor, and destroyer had shocked them all. Ting let out a little sigh. "I see Henry sometimes," she said. "At our dentist. I can't tell if he remembers me or not."

The Magickers had ways of protecting their existence, and one of them had been used on Henry after the disastrous theft of his fledgling powers. It had sent him home in a baffled, cheerful, totally clueless state. Not that Henry had been all that different, but . . . well, he *had* been magickal. "You don't think he does?"

She shook her head. "I don't think so."

Trent said quietly, "I miss Henry."

"Me, too." Danno scratched his hand through thick, dark hair. "Think we'd get in trouble with . . . them . . . if we said hi or something?"

"I don't think we'd get in trouble, but would it be fair to Henry? Seems to me, he's better off not knowing what he lost. Ignorance is bliss and all that."

Bailey glanced at Trent. "I thought it was 'Ignorance is best,'" she said. Trent nudged her. "You would!" acknowledging that Bailey seemed to have a bottomless source for her slightly twisted sayings.

"I think," Jason said slowly, "that being a Magicker—past, present, or future—is too important to forget. I won't forget Henry, and I hope someday he'll have a chance to remember just who all of us are. Ting, if you do see him, tell him I'd like to talk to him sometime. Maybe over the computer, he'd like that." Jason rolled his paper into a scroll and popped it back into a vest pocket. "We're the only ones left from camp with crystals and our full memories of what happened." Silence fell over all of them as they remembered the dreadful storm of power called mana that brought wild Magick as well as torrential rain and thunder and lightning, nearly destroying Ravenwyng. Their summer of learning the mysteries of Magick had come to a sudden ending, but Ravenwyng had survived, with their help. Jason took a deep breath. "I called us all together to . . . well, to make sure everyone was all right, and to see if we could set up a ring, to keep tabs on each other, to help out."

"We've got the alarm beacons if something goes wrong," Danno said. He watched Jason's face. "The last thing they taught us."

"What if it's not enough?" Jason looked around at all of them sprawled on Trent's back lawn. He did not want to discuss his dreams and what Gavan had said, but the foreboding it had left him with was like a bad taste in his mouth that wouldn't go away.

"What did you have in mind? We can't meet like this all the time." Trent studied the crystal in his hand, saying nothing else, but Jason knew his inner thoughts. They'd used their crystals to step through, but that ability was new and rather untried with them, not to be misused or used often. They all needed far more training. Destinations could be rocky, even dangerous without it. The elder Magickers were busy trying to ready a training program that would make up the gaps, but until then, they had to be very careful what they did.

Trent, of all of them, was in the most jeopardy. Only Jason knew his secret. Trent had no power. Not even the elder Magickers had seen through the powerful screen of wit and knowledge he'd thrown about himself. His quick mind and deep wealth of reading knowledge had kept him from being discovered, and his love of magick made him eager to be a Magicker in any way he could.

"Most of us have access to computers. I was thinking, an e-mail ring. Just a daily check on how we all are, if we've seen anything odd or felt anything."

Stefan grunted. His thick, square face reflected the bear being he could abruptly shapeshift into. "I could do that," he said.

"Me, too." Bailey and Ting answered almost at once.

"That would work for me," Danno agreed. "Getting away to meet in person is a lot trickier. Especially since my dad's company may be transferring him overseas for at least a year, and if that happens, we're all going." Rich shrugged. "Whatever," he said, as if supremely bored.

"I think it'll work. Better than phoning and trying to explain the charges." Trent crossed his arms over his lean figure.

"E-mail," Bailey added, looking about at all of them, her golden-brown ponytail bouncing as she did, "could be faked. I suggest a password. Just to identify it's really us."

"Finally something cool." Rich smiled slowly.

"How about Excalibur?" said Trent.

"How about freakazoid," countered Stefan. He clambered to his feet, shifting his weight back and forth restlessly. The backpack on his shoulder held his football gear, lumpy pads and helmet and all.

"How about something serious," said Jason. "Like what Tomaz warned us about, the curse. How about Arkady?"

Each of the seven thought about it briefly, then nodded in turn. "Done, then. Every day, when you can, send a note. We'll take down each other's addresses and we're finished."

Ting nibbled on one fingertip as she wrote out the e-mail lists for everyone, looking as if there were something she wanted to say.

"What is it, Ting?"

"Should we include Jennifer?"

Jason thought about the older girl, blonde and willowy, who had been Ting's and Bailey's cabinmate and counselor. "Well . . . I don't know . . ."

Ting fidgeted.

"What do you think?"

The pencil wobbled in Ting's hand. "I heard . . ." she said softly. "She's avoiding all of us. She has a boyfriend. She's different from last summer."

"A boyfriend? Oh, mannnnn." Trent frowned. He'd always had a kind of interest in Jennifer, Jason remembered. Not that he'd ever own up to it.

"Maybe it's best we don't, then. Till she makes up her mind and everything?"

"All right." Ting nodded, and her expression calmed as she returned to writing out copies of the lists.

It only took a few moments, and then Ting and Bailey had their crystals out. They focused and disappeared in a soft shimmer. Stefan fished his out with his great, clumsy paw of a hand, yet held his gem with a kind of tenderness as he looked into it. Rich followed him like a shadow at Stefan's heels. Danno winked at them, before focusing on his crystal and vanishing. Soon only Trent and Jason remained. Trent slapped his hand against Jason's shoulder.

"There's another reason we can't meet like this too often,

besides needing more practice. We could be leaving a trail the Dark Hand might pick up on."

Jason thought. "Not if we went into the Haven."

"You're the only one who's really been there, Jason. And I couldn't get there without you."

"It's something to think about, though. The Haven is out of time and place. It could be the perfect spot for us to go to if there's trouble. I need to look into it."

"Meanwhile, how about I find out, if I can, who this Arkady is and what this curse might be? I wonder why Tomaz or Gavan couldn't just tell us what the curse is."

Jason nodded in agreement. Books and knowledge were Trent's great asset. He knew all the myths and fables, and what he didn't know, he could track down almost immediately with his expertise on the Internet and libraries. "I think," he said slowly, "we need to know as soon as possible. A warning isn't enough. We need to know what to look out for."

"Something you didn't tell us?" It was a question Trent looked like he really didn't need answered.

"Like that line from Ray Bradbury," Jason said, quoting one of his favorite books. "'By the pricking of my thumbs, something wicked this way comes.'"

Trent grinned. "Actually, I think that started with Shakespeare, but I get your meaning. And forewarned is definitely forearmed in this case. I'll let you know whatever I find."

"And I," answered Jason, "hope you don't find anything, but we both know better!" He rubbed the back of his left hand, where the scar of the wolfjackal bite looked healed and yet still remained tender. It would never go away, that mark, and there were times when it was just as fresh and painful as if newly made, despite all the months of healing. He thought of the night he'd gotten it, the very first night of summer camp, before he'd even been told he had been born with Magick in his blood. With a shudder, he recalled the snarling ambush of the beastly wolfjackal and the ripping of his skin as he'd fought it off. *You're mine!* the beast had snarled at him before slinking off into the darkness.

After a moment's hesitation, he added, "This is serious business, Trent."

"I know."

"You could be the easiest one for the Dark Hand to get to."

"Or the hardest. I can't leave a Magick trail, can I? Besides, we don't really know what Brennard is up to, if anything. Supposedly, both he and Gregory the Gray haven't been seen in a couple hundred years. His followers are pretty much on their own."

"That doesn't seem to have stopped them, and anyone who can make Gavan or Tomaz worried is gonna scare me." He thought. "I think they can move throughout our world pretty much at will. They're more organized than the others."

"It comes of *not* having a Council, I think."

That made Jason smile. "No long arguments about how to do things, right?"

"You've got the idea." Trent leaned against the back railing of the yard deck.

Jason hesitated for a long moment, but Trent seemed to be waiting for him to say something else, so he composed his words. "I still get dreams."

"Still? I thought those got pretty well squelched at camp."

"Maybe for everyone else, but not me." Jason rubbed his chin. "Why me?"

"Think you're the weak link in the chain?"

"I hope not. I don't want to, but—sometimes—I wonder."

Trent considered it, then shook his head vigorously. "Nah. It has to be more than that. If Brennard was looking for the weak ones, he'd have come after me. Or Henry. Or Rich, maybe. I think he's drawn by strong talent, and that means you, bud."

Jason shifted uneasily. He did not think of himself as being any more gifted than any other Magicker. If anything, he'd been cursed. He rubbed his scarred hand again. The only way of knowing for sure if the wolfjackal had marked him as Brennard's own was a way he did not wish to try, and that was to let Brennard tell him face-to-face. "I don't want to meet either Brennard or Jonnard again."

"One thing you have to consider is that Tomaz sent the note. I'll do all the research and digging I can, but he's the one you ought to talk to. And, with those dreams, you can't wait to do it."

"Think so?"

"I know so. Look. We're all hanging out here, and we're brand new. It's like driving in rush hour right after you get your learner's permit! You're crazy if you don't ask for help."

"You're right." Jason's head bobbed in reluctant agreement. "I'll get hold of him as soon as I can, and let you know what happens. But you've gotta let me know if anything starts happening to you!"

"Look. I'm going to worry about you, and you're going to worry about me. That's what friends are for. I promise you," and he marked his finger over his chest. "Anything weird and you'll hear about it."

"Right back at you." He cupped his crystal. "Time to bail, then."

With a wave to Trent, he looked into his crystal, focused on a doorway back to his own place with total concentration, and then stepped through.

Charmed, I'm Sure

"GOD help me if I ever agree to another Council meeting," Gavan Rainwater muttered to himself, and rubbed his temple with the cool pewter wolfhead that adorned his cane. The massage failed to alleviate the dull, pounding throb of a headache as he tried to listen to the droning words of Macabiah Allenby, who was most strenuously protesting the warning Tomaz Crowfeather had sent to those new Magickers his Talents could find. At this table in the Ravenwyng meeting hall sat some of the most powerful Magickers alive—and there were few enough of those, unfortunately—and Gavan knew that they were not here because they were happy.

They should be happy. Because of the efforts of his staff, the camp had successful been drawn beyond the borders of the Iron Gate, and now rested temporally in a Haven, a pocket of magickal mana that put it outside of the time stream of the world. Gavan was now concentrating his efforts on anchoring Ravenwyng in the small dell dominated by the Iron Mountain Range. Anchoring it and warding it against ricocheting back into place.

That was why he'd agreed to a Council meeting in the hope of securing the aid of a few more Magickers in getting those wards set. But he would not get it from the six who'd come in to join his own staff. Instead, he was facing an inquisition of his actions and plans.

Tomaz, on the other hand, seemed to be amused by Allenby. The Native American was leaning forward on the long conference table, his elbows firmly planted on the table's edge and his chin resting on the steeple of his fingers. The deeply weathered lines of his face curved in an otherwise neutral expression.

Allenby, as bald as an egg except for a white fringe of hair that ran around the circle of his head, and then descended about the edges of his lower face in a wispy beard, sucked in an enormous breath and launched into what one could only hope was the summation of his speech. Gavan wove and locked his fingers together. They sounded like old women, all of them, old women gathered at the laundry vats, to argue and gossip and vent old spites. He'd come forward in time, most of them had, yet these six seemed mired in centuries long past. He sighed heavily. If anyone else at the table heard him, they made no sign, except that Tomaz looked at him briefly, with humor dancing in his dark eyes.

"And furthermore,"Allenby wheezed, "the usage of such familiars as Crowfeather's ravens ought to be deplored, if not totally banned, in the future. Movement of that sort might attract the Dark Hand's attention, and put us all in jeopardy!" He stopped suddenly, as if finally out of words or breath, or both.

Tomaz waited a long moment as if making sure Allenby had finished. The Council member sat back in his chair, took out a neatly folded handkerchief and mopped first his face, and then his bald head.

"Now then," Tomaz said mildly. "The movement of natural creatures is far less likely to attract the attention of Brennard's people than any other method we could use. I also hope you don't suggest that we leave the children in the dark, uninformed. Yes, it might be said we failed in our attempt to educate so many in such a short time. We live and learn. They *lived and learned*. And a remarkable handful stayed by our sides to combat the wild Magick of a mana storm and the attack of the Dark Hand through it. I call that an amazingly successful failure." Tomaz smiled, slowly, the expression dawning on his face like the sun coming up on a desert landscape.

"Here, here!" cried Eleanora softly. Lace framed her face and the dark ringlets of hair about it, although tiny dark circles of fatigue outlined her eyes. Her musician's hands were folded gracefully upon the table.

Dr. Anita Patel, however, shook her head sadly. "We found too many. More than we can train or protect. When we disassembled the camp, we had to take their crystals and the memories of all but this handful. We had good intentions and not nearly enough resources to do what we wanted to. This is a disservice. I, for one, am not in favor of moving forward on the Academy. Not yet. It is too soon."

"What?" Her words brought Gavan leaping to his feet. "You can't mean that! I'll sit here all day and listen to bantering about quills versus ballpoint pens when writing out spells and incantations, but I will not argue about whether the Academy goes forward. It has to. There is no other way!"

"SILENCE!" roared Aunt Freyah, as she brought down her gavel sharply. "Points of order, ladies and gentlemen! You are all out of turn except for Master Crowfeather here!" Her dark eyes snapped, and the soft halo of her silvery hair fairly shimmered in her anger. "Shall we keep to parliamentary rules of procedure?" Her voice rose with every word.

Wincing, Gavan seated himself. He folded his arms across his chest and hoped he did not look as if he were sulking.

That he did not succeed was obvious when Aunt Freyah rapped the table sharply again, shattering his thoughts.

"Ow!" He sank back and looked at her reproachfully.

She twirled the gavel in her veined hands. "And we will keep to our seats at all times! We are not heathens, nor is this a brawl."

He looked at her. "It will be a brawl if it comes to a fight over the Academy, Auntie. There is not a Magicker alive who can stop me from opening its doors to take in our future and see that training is done properly." He rubbed his brow that now rang from her fervor to restore order as well as the headache he'd developed from Allenby's speechmaking.

"I don't think that's really the question at the moment, Gavan," Eleanora said quietly. "We'll have a school open, but will there be any students who will be able to attend?"

"Preeeeecisely," said Allenby.

She curved her lips into a smile. "Without warnings such as Tomaz sent out, there can't be. Even with warnings, we have to face issues like Jonnard." Her face paled at the mention of the traitor who had nearly sabotaged all their efforts.

Tomaz tapped his turquoise-and-silver watchband. "We have not been able to track him. He hasn't gone back to his home, and traces there of him seem to have vanished." He gave a rueful expression. "Computers are remarkably easy to hack, it appears."

"He was trained for nearly a year before camp opened. Anita, you recruited him, didn't you?" Soft, accented words from Isabella Ruelle who sat quietly near the table's end, her dark blonde hair pulled back from a face dominated by a hawk-like nose, marring beauty into handsomeness. She wore a lacy mantilla about her shoulders, her dress of deep maroon brocade both contemporary and stylish and yet speaking of her Spanish heritage. She was seldom seen outside of Europe since the awakening, and Gavan knew he ought to be pleased by her attendance.

He was not. Despite her soft voice, Isabella trained the Leucators, the inner force of the Magickers that bore a resemblance to the Inquisition, and Gavan was prepared to swear Isabella enjoyed it.

The East Indian doctor nodded slowly. She adjusted her sari about her slender figure, and the belled anklet she wore from time to time chimed slightly. She had a tattooed bracelet of henna about one wrist that she glanced at before speaking. "Yes, myself and Hercule Fizziwig. He seemed a raw but likely candidate. He had a lot of charm. I can hardly believe . . . well, as it appears now, he recruited us."

"Where is Fizziwig anyway?" Gavan pondered.

Freyah looked about the table, waggling the gavel in her hands. "Let's see . . . he . . ." She scrunched her face up. "Ah, yes. He went off to celebrate Cinco de Mayo."

Concern ran around the conference table except for Tomaz Crowfeather, who turned in his chair to look at Aunt Freyah. "That," he said flatly, "was in early May."

"No one has heard from Fizziwig since early May?" repeated Gavan.

"Some things are provident," Freyah answered. "You don't question them, you just accept them."

Hercule Fizziwig had not been among the more trackable of the Council. Everyone was used, more or less, to his unannounced journeys and research forays. She pointed the gavel at Rainwater. "You haven't exactly been asking for him either."

"True, but—" Gavan sat back in his chair. "I can't believe no one's said, 'Where's old Fizziwig?' No one?" He glanced at each of his fellow Magickers.

"Afraid not."

"Considering Jonnard, we will have to try to find Hercule as soon as possible. If there is one traitor among us, there well may be more." Isabella tapped her fan on the tabletop. "Or I could assign a Leucator . . ."

A shudder ran around the room at the thought of a shadow

mage from beyond the Havens, a dark, hungry mirror image which would not stop till it found and attempted to join with the Light image who had spawned it. Yes, it would find its quarry, but if allowed to join, all would be horribly corrupted. It took an iron will to control a Leucator. She smiled, her lips outlined in brilliant crimson lipstick. "That *would* be rather drastic. Perhaps called for later."

Sousa, who'd been sitting at the far end of the table, his long tapered fingers fiddling with the battered cornet in front of him, said quietly, "More likely the Dark Hand has done him in." A man who rarely spoke out at meetings such as this, preferring to let his music speak for him, Sousa lapsed back into silence.

"Neither is beyond consideration. By his name alone, in hindsight, one might believe Jonnard to be related to Brennard. There were many rumors Antoine had a son, long before there were rumors he'd gone over to the Dark. We don't know how old such a son could have been." Eleanora put one hand to the back of her neck and rubbed slightly, as if in some pain. "An heir he had no intention of letting Gregory 'taint' with his teachings." She winced faintly again, and did not see the worried look Gavan gave her or the glances traded between Freyah and Tomaz.

"We were all fools. Too eager to find new students." Allenby took his handkerchief, and wiped his shiny pate. He then refolded the damp cloth square many times before stowing it back in a vest pocket.

"They were all children," Anita Patel protested slightly. "How could we not trust them?"

"Most of us wouldn't be here today if we had trusted like that." Freyah tsked in emphasis, while the doctor's flush darkened her already deep complexion and she looked away. "However, if he is related to Brennard, I don't think anyone here can dispute the fact that charming, or rather, charmed, would explain how the boy managed to endear himself to us. Jonnard

Albrite." She made a scoffing noise. "Albrite, the son of the Dark One. They must be laughing at us still!" The gavel whirled in her hands.

Gavan straightened in his chair. "Laughing—but defeated. And they'll stay that way, if I have anything to say about it. If we can put that aside, the one question I have has yet to be answered. Are we going to be able to get help with warding Ravenwyng?"

All eyes turned toward the massive, silent man who sat at the far end of the table, cloaked in a dark, hooded garment that hid his features uncannily well. But Gavan did not need to see him to know what the Moor looked like. Known only as Khalil, and as ancient as Brennard or Gregory, the towering man carried a presence as vast as it was aged and powerful. Had he slept through into modern times or lived it? No one knew, and Khalil was not telling.

Khalil reached up with both hands and dropped his hood. A face carved by harsh sun and sharp desert winds looked back at all of them. "At this time," he said, "the Warding of Ravenwyng is left in your hands alone."

Gavan's mouth twisted. Nicely put, to make it sound as if the elders had declined to meddle in his affairs. The two stared at one another for a long moment, but Khalil said nothing further.

"All right, then." Gavan tapped his cane on the floor, working his fingers about the wolfhead handle. "Allenby, I put you in charge of tracking down old Fizziwig and seeing what he's up to, and, please, remind him what is going on. And, while we're sitting here, I will let you all know that I haven't forgotten I am neither the wisest nor the most talented among us. But I have the drive. The will. And there will be an Academy at Iron Mountain, come hell or high water. Since you all came prepared to wrangle, but not to give aid," he stood, "this Council is dismissed." He turned abruptly and strode off, leaving Freyah with her mouth open, and the gavel hanging from her fingertips.

In bursts of crystal color, most of the others left. Eleanora put out her hand and caught Freyah's wrist. "Stay for a moment."

"Of course, dear. What is it?" Freyah settled back in the chair. Her bright blue eyes sparkled with delight. She'd always been one for a spirited discussion, Eleanora thought fondly, and smiled.

"You've always been one to help, so I can't understand why you're holding back now." Eleanora gazed into those brilliant blue eyes. "Your Haven would be perfect for the Academy."

"It's too small," answered Freyah firmly.

"You know that with our help it can be enlarged. We wouldn't need much more . . . two or three acres."

Freyah shook her head so vigorously, her silver curls bounced about her face. "No. No, you'll stretch it too thin and destroy everything. Eleanora," she took Eleanora's hand in both of hers, "I worked hard for that tiny niche when it seemed no other Magickers had survived. I worked for it, and I made it. There's no great Gate to protect it. All it has is me, and it's all I've got. So I will keep it mine and I will protect it from foe or friend as fiercely as I can!"

"But . . ."

"No buts. I like it the way it is, and that's the way it shall stay. When you are ready, I'll be there for Iron Mountain Academy, but you've a long way to go, haven't you? Too many cooks spoil the broth. You don't need my energy, and my Haven does. There I'll spend it till the need is clear."

Eleanora tried to keep her mouth from curving unhappily and failed. "We need you now, Aunt Freyah."

"No, dear. You just think you do." Freyah quietly put Eleanora's hand on her knee, and stood up. "I know you think I'm a selfish old woman, but I have my reasons and my ways."

"It would save everyone so much trouble and strife . . ."

"No!" Freyah's word cracked like a whip. "Someday you may understand, but trust me now. My Haven stays as it is, or there will be nothing *but* trouble. And I'll not explain. We're both adults, and you should know to trust me."

"Oh, I do. Still . . ." Eleanora had not quite given up, and she had refrained from saying "but."

Freyah wagged an index finger at her. "No 'stills' either! Not another word." She tapped the great crystal in her necklace and disappeared in a shower of color, like a sprite into a burst of firework sparks.

Eleanora waited until she was certain the air was entirely empty, and then let out a great sigh.

A Little English

"YOU know," Alicia said, watching Jason, her long legs crossed in soft violet pedal pushers that matched her T-shirt, her hairbrush in hand. She perched on the edge of her rosebud-pink canopied bed. The whole room gave him the heebie-jeebies because it was so sickeningly feminine, with pink and lace everywhere. He'd had a look at Bailey's room once, cheerfully tossed and rumpled and haphazard like his own. He felt like an alien in Alicia's room, not to mention what he had to give up in privileges to come in and use her computer. "Dad would get you your own computer if you asked him to," she continued smoothly, and gave him an innocent smile.

He wasn't sure he wanted one. He said so, even as he sat over her keyboard, pecking out the letters for his e-mail.

"For one thing, it would help you with your homework. You'd learn keyboarding, and everyone has to know the computer sooner or later, for writing reports."

"Maybe."

"And you could play games on them. *Dungeons and Dragons* and stuff."

Jason stopped typing and gave her a glance. "I'd rather read books."

"Well, of course," she agreed. She ran her brush through her hair. "But you wouldn't have to borrow mine, and you could research, and your account would be private."

He stopped typing again. "Private?" She'd given him a screen name to use on her main mail account, and he had his own password and everything.

She tilted her head. "Jason, if it's on my computer, I can get to it."

"But—"

"Trust me," she said quietly. "And doesn't your camp friend Trent have a computer? He can show you all the ins and outs. There's a lot you can find on the Net much faster than in a library. I record stuff on mine, like a diary." She smiled again. "Only I know how to make sure it stays locked."

He highlighted a sentence to delete it on his mail, then sent the letter. The idea of Alicia pawing through his e-mail drove a cold shudder right through him. "Think he would?"

She shrugged, and moved past him to the desk, where she stood, waiting to sit down. "Ask him."

He couldn't get out of her room fast enough for either of them.

On the way back from the kitchen with a peanut butter and jelly sandwich and a glass of milk, he paused at the room used for the Dozer's work study. McIntire was on the phone, frowning, and tapping his heavy fingers on his desktop impatiently.

"Yes, I know the house sits on prime cliffside property. And yes, I know what it's worth as a project to all of us. But, the McHenry house is still occupied by a McHenry, and he's made it quite clear he's not selling." His fingers drummed. Jason hesitated to enter the office during a business call, one that obviously had the Dozer on edge.

"No, I'm not going to put pressure on him. That's not my job, and it's not one I want. Look, we've done some nice projects together, clean deals. Let's keep it that way. No, I don't think I misunderstood what you meant. Look, you can bring it up before the board if you want, but like I said, McHenry doesn't want to sell. All right, then. Talk to you later." His voice sounded a teensy bit calmer when he hung up and picked up a magazine, leaning back in his creaking leather chair. He spread the golfing magazine out between his two thick hands.

Jason wanted to ask, then changed his mind, but he wasn't fast enough. McIntire looked up and caught him as he started to walk past the open doorway.

"Something wrong, son?"

"Not really."

His stepfather smiled at him, his big hands practically obscuring the magazine. "Sure? How's that ankle holding up?"

"Fine! Just great, doesn't bother me at all."

"Think you'll make the first lineup?"

"I should! Another week of practice and tryouts, and the coach will post the teams." Jason hesitated, and even as the Dozer said, "Excellent, excellent!" he raised an eyebrow.

"Want to come in and have a seat? Man to man?"

"Well . . . um . . . okay."

It was not that the McIntires didn't act as if they loved and accepted him, they did. But they were equally as kind to telephone solicitors and dirty stray cats, and he often wondered if he were just a charity case. You know, the boy whose mother died and then several years after he remarried, his father died, and no one else was able to take him. He just didn't trust the cheerful good nature that William, Joanna, and Alicia flung his way every day. Were they just enduring him until he could find a better home? He never wanted to do anything that would test it. Asking for a computer might.

"What's on your mind, son? Everything all right?"

"Everything," Jason said with conviction, "is just fine."

"Good! Just a question or two, then? Something I can help you with, maybe?" William McIntire kept his booming voice down inside the house, used as he was to shouting across vast construction sites. For that, Jason could only be thankful. Someday he might want to ask a question about something personal. He fidgeted a bit on the study chair as he steadied his sandwich and milk.

"How's business?" he started. Then he wanted to kick himself for asking.

"Great, couldn't be better! Tear 'em down and build 'em up bigger and better." The Dozer's eyes twinkled with cheer at Jason's interest. "Come out to the site with me some weekend."

"I'd like that." And he would, except that his stepfather was always going just for an hour to check on something and finally trailing home a full workday later. He'd have to find a way to bail if he did go. Luckily, the McHenry thing, whatever it was, didn't seem to bother the Dozer all that much. He took a bite of his sandwich and chewed, and managed to get out, "Do you think I could get a computer of my own?"

"What?" McIntire frowned, then smiled. "Oh! Your own computer. What did you have in mind? Something fancy? Fastest speed, all the bells and whistles?"

"No. Just something basic. I'd like to be able to get on the Internet, but . . ."

His stepfather nodded. "Homework and things like that?"

"Yes, sir."

"Well." McIntire reared back in his chair. "I don't think that will be a problem. Let me look into it, see what I can find. A lot of nice bargains out there in computers right now. Good solid manufacture, at good prices." He beamed and reached for his golf magazine again.

Equally relieved, Jason blurted out, "Thank you!" grabbed his snack and retreated from the study. Upstairs he sat for a moment or two before eating. That had almost been easy. But it

THE CURSE OF ARKADY

wasn't easy to ask for things, it had never been, as anxious as the McIntires seemed to be to give them. Well, it wasn't a done deal yet. As Bailey would say, seeing is almost as good as holding. He'd believe it when he had a computer sitting on his desk.

Jason trotted along the soccer field lines, the grass crushing beneath his cleats with the smell of being newly mown. Far off at the main field he could hear the whistles and grunts and noise of the football team practicing, but here, on the junior varsity field, bordered by shrubbery and one warped wooden bleacher, they were all alone except for the two practice teams. He tried not to feel anxious as he jogged into position for another kickoff and glanced at the score cards being held on the sidelines. 1–1. Not good enough! No Magick. He couldn't use Magick no matter how much he wanted to. He inhaled and exhaled a few times, and dangled his arms to lose tension. Think of something besides soccer and making the team. Or Magick.

Not only was it forbidden, but could he be any more of a freak? He didn't even want to try. It would be fun to tell Sam . . . heck, he wondered if Sam had Talent or if he could get Mrs. Cowling to test Sam the way she had the others . . . then they'd be a real team. Then he wouldn't be a freak, not really, 'cause he wouldn't have to keep the truth from Sam any more. Maybe she could be convinced to test him somehow. He could just talk to her after school sometime. . . .

The coach trotted along the sidelines, whistle in his hand, watching Jason closely.

"Don't get offside," he warned, his white legs moving quickly to keep in step with the teams. Jason had only a moment to wonder how the coach managed to never get tan even though he wore shorts day in and day out, when the soccer ball came his way. The black-and-white orb shot toward him as the passer's instep met it squarely. With scarcely a pause, Jason passed it back and ran upfield. The sagging net goals waited,

but he wasn't nearly close enough to catch the pass cleanly. The
defender caught up with him and the two wheeled around each
other, Jason breaking free.

He felt good. He'd played three quarters and he still had legs,
and the breath whistling through his lungs felt clean and sharp.
The old injury that had kept him out of soccer camp for the
summer had long since healed.

"Coming your way!" Sam yelled, and with a grin, he passed
the ball to Jason who had an almost perfect lineup for the goal.

Except for Canby, solid and mean-looking, determined to
defend it.

We're on the same side, thought Jason, except, of course, for
this game they weren't, and Canby didn't particularly care if
Jason made it onto the first squad. It had been Canby, with a
sliding tackle, who'd changed his whole plans for the summer.
This time though, Jason saw him coming. He zigzagged away
and heard Canby let out a faint grunt of frustration as he easily
outran the other. The wind skirled about him as he dribbled the
ball downfield toward the goal net. Sam kept pace with him
from the other side, and as Martin Brinkford closed in, his pale
blond hair flying as the older boy outran Jason with his long
strides, Jason passed it off.

As he outdistanced his pursuer, Sam let out a shout and sent
the ball back his way yet again. It shot toward him, with the
coach yelling, "Shoot, Jason! Cut it! Put some English on it!"

He would have to get the angle to even get close to the goal
from where he'd caught the ball. Gathering himself, Jason
paused a moment, breathed a faint prayer, and kicked the ball
. . . *hard.* It sailed from the instep of his soccer shoe toward the
net! With a grunt, and a swing of his square body, Canby lunged
in defense. He and the ball collided, and the black-and-white
soccer ball abruptly shot off in another direction out of bounds
and deep into the wild shrubbery bordering the field's end.

Jason stopped, his mouth hanging open. He hadn't . . . heard

. . . the ball cry out "Ooof!" and then, a faint "Oh, my!" as it disappeared into the greenery . . . had he? He couldn't have. Still . . . the voice sounded vaguely familiar.

"I'll get it!" he shouted and barreled into the bushes after the soccer ball. There were shouts behind him, as the coach told each and every one of the players how they'd done so far, and he felt the greenery close like a curtain behind him. The soccer ball lay in a nest of old leaves and grass. He picked it up cautiously.

"What an experience!" it said.

He almost dropped it, but instead turned the ball about till he could see a face pushing slightly out of the black-and-white leather. Jason stared. "Mrs. Cowling!" What had he done? Just by thinking about her?

"Jason! Do shut your mouth. You look like a carp at feeding time." His English teacher sounded a bit peevish.

"Yes, ma'am." His jaw snapped shut. But he could not help staring at the animated face looking back at him. Eyes snapping with vigor and soft curly hair in a halo about her aging face. "How did—are you—I mean—" He hardly knew what to say. "I'm so sorry. Are you all right?"

"How exhilarating!" Mrs. Cowling beamed at him. "As for how, well, I assume you Magicked me in here. Do Magick me out as soon as we make a goal, I've papers to grade."

"I didn't mean to. I was just thinking about errh, you know, the testing and stuff." He tried to keep his mouth firmly shut between words. "But . . . doesn't it . . . *hurt?*"

"Goodness no! I'm not the ball. I'm just a passenger, as it were."

"Oh." He held the soccer ball between his palms.

"JAAAAAson!" bellowed from the field hidden behind him.

Mrs. Cowling gave him a flashing smile. "Show time!" she said gleefully.

"Ummm . . . right." He tucked the ball under his arm and

trotted back to the field. Making a goal was now not the only immediate problem he had. Getting Mrs. Cowling Magicked back where she belonged suddenly became extremely important. If only he knew how. . . . He touched the crystal pendant tucked inside his shirt. Ting had made a brass wire cage to hold his crystal loosely, and had shown him the secret way to open it and slip his focus out when he needed it. But it would do him no good if he didn't know what he'd done, and how to undo it.

The thought of Mrs. Cowling's head bouncing down the soccer field endlessly for another thirty minutes or so of practice unnerved him. Could anyone else see her? Hear her? And was she really all right? She'd always been a little . . . well . . . odd. But then, she was a Magicker, too, or at least, had come of Magicker blood. He should have asked her for help!

Sam grabbed the ball from him. "Get in there, I'll do the throw-in!" His best friend, well, one of his best friends, grinned at him, his wiry body tensed at the edge of the powdery white line.

"Right." Jason's lips felt cotton dry as he turned away and got into position, jostled by the other players, his eyes intent on the soccer ball. Sam didn't seem to notice anything unusual, his dark eyes scanning the crowd. He made a tiny movement with his chin. Jason caught it and moved to the signal as Sam threw it in. He caught it on his chest and let it drop, dead at his feet, with no one near him but the goal. He drew his foot back, then hesitated.

He only had seconds. Jason swallowed tightly, then kicked the ball as hard as he could, arcing it toward the net, and it lifted off the grass as it flew. He heard a happy "Wheeee!" as it went, then sailed past the goalee's blocking hands right square into the goal. He tapped his crystal, thinking, *Done!*

The coach fetched the ball out of the net, smiling. "Good shot, Jason."

Canby snickered as he trotted past to line up for the kickoff.

"Whee!" he said mockingly, and Brinkford joined him, the two laughing as they got into position. Jason's face warmed, but he had other fish to fry. He fell in with the coach, trying to get a look at the soccer ball. He could have sworn he saw a wink, and then Mrs. Cowling's face faded into plain old black-and-white leather diamonds.

Jason let out a sigh of relief. Sam punched his shoulder. "Nice job!"

"Thanks."

It did little good, in the end. The other team got two more goals, but by the time they all left the field, tired, sore and winded, the coach looked pleased. "We're going to have a great team this year," he remarked. "Good depth in all positions. I'll be posting Monday after school."

Sam danced around Jason. "We made it, I betcha."

"Maybe." Suddenly the soccer team didn't seem quite as vital as it had. He'd worked Magick, unknowingly, and against another Magicker. That could be big trouble.

But how big?

Good News and Bad News

SAM'S finger eagerly stabbed at the sheet of paper duct-taped to the gym's main door. "We made it!" He bounced once for emphasis. "First string! Well, you're first string, I'm first string alternate! How cool is that?"

Jason felt himself grinning ear to ear. "It's very cool," he said. He read the list for himself a second time, scarcely able to believe it. A heavy hand descended on his shoulder with a thump.

"Move it, Adrian. Other people want to read the list," snorted George Canby in his ear.

Other players jostled him aside. The hand on his shoulder thumped him a second time. Jason turned about, frowning as Canby gave him a grin that was anything but friendly, then added, "Made the team, too? Good."

"What's that supposed to mean?" Jason answered uneasily.

"It means," the other boy said, "I'd rather play with you than against you. And if you don't do a good job, I still get to level you." Still grinning, Canby lifted his heavy hand and moved away. The other boys scattered to let his broad body through as if he were Moses parting the Red Sea. Was it Jason's imagination or did the whole breezeway outside the gym shake as he passed through it? Jason stifled a sigh. His silver lining had a cloud named Canby.

"This means extra practice. First year first stringers and alternates go to both practices." Sam fell in with him as they headed for first bell. "I don't mind, do you?"

Jason shook his head emphatically. "Are you kidding? At least the coach is giving us a chance!"

"Yeah, and my dad can quit ragging me about the money he spent on soccer camp." Sam let out a pleased grunt punctuated by the warning bell for first class sessions.

With good news under his belt and the start of a brand new day, Jason felt ready for anything. Even as he thought it, the hairs prickled at the back of his neck.

Almost.

Was he prepared for the Curse of Arkady?

Not that he'd had any chance to be. No one had uncovered anything yet. Even Trent, with his knowledge of computers and search engines that devoured information from the Internet and spit it back out at incredible rates of speed, hadn't been able to find a reference. Truthfully, he hadn't expected there would be any. Magickers were sworn to an oath of silence about themselves and their abilities. None of the elders but Tomaz had even breathed a hint.

Jason thought he knew why, but he hadn't discussed it with anyone yet. He called it the Churchill Axiom, based on the famous quote by the World War II British leader: "The only thing we have to fear is fear itself." Grandma McIntire was good for something, he supposed. She'd taught him that one, explaining that the imagination could trap you worse than reality. The adult Magickers hadn't warned their new recruits about the curse to prevent the students from inviting it simply by worrying about it.

Tomaz Crowfeather, though, was different. Not just in that he was Native American, and dressed in comfortable faded jeans and vest over a soft white shirt that might one day be embroidered with a laughing coyote or the next day with a coal-winged raven, or that he wore hammered silver and turquoise jewelry on his wrists and belting his waist. Not in that his view of Magick was a little different from that of Gavan Rainwater or Eleanora Andarielle or any of the others. But he himself was different in his Magick. His was the longest unbroken line of Magickers since the fallout between Gregory the Gray and Brennard, which had outright killed many and sent the others, shocked, either into a deep sleep or hurtling through time. Centuries ago Crowfeather's ancestors had absorbed the British Magicker blood into their own shaman line, and taught the talents accordingly. His Magick could be traced all the way back to Gregory the Gray and even earlier, if he wished to do so.

Tomaz didn't. He wasn't the type to stand on ceremony. He revered his ancestors, but he felt that he must stand on his own two feet and his own proven ability. Each man, he had told them during the summer, was responsible for his own footprint upon the earth. His Magick, strong in its own way, was a blend of Talent that the others understood, and and even more power that they did not. Perhaps that was why Tomaz had answered his own conscience and sent them all a warning. Whatever the curse was, it was dangerous enough that Crowfeather had defied the Council. An involuntary shiver ran down Jason's back. If it worried Tomaz, it sure as heck would scare the beans out of him!

Sam peered at him. "You okay?"

"Yeah. I just got the creeps for a second."

"Canby is enough to give Hannibal Lechter the creeps." Sam waved as he veered away to his morning home room class, and

Jason ducked his head and trotted to his own. He wouldn't let the burly boy cloud the day if he could help it. He'd made the team!

At home, the Dozer and Joanna seemed suitably impressed, although his stepmother wore a slight frown. "More tackles?" she asked, referring to the accident which had sprained his ankle badly at summer's beginning.

McIntire patted his wife's hand. "Now, Joanna," he said. "Boys need to be boys. Besides, Jason has speed and agility. He should be able to outrun most trouble. When are the games, son?" He inhaled deeply, puffing out his massive chest.

"After school most days. And practice on others."

"You'll be busy, then." He tapped the bowl of his pipe. "Make sure those homework grades don't suffer!"

"No, sir. They won't."

"Good. Good." He rumbled a bit, then cleared his throat. "Bit of a mess upstairs by your room. See you get it cleaned up before dinner!"

He hadn't been upstairs yet. Puzzled, Jason nodded and left the kitchen nook where Joanna and the Dozer were having an afternoon iced tea, he home surprisingly early. Alicia was nowhere to be seen, but she had an after-school Young Filmmakers class at the High School for the Gifted which she attended. Just as well. She wasn't the easiest stepsister in the world to get along with, almost as much of a pain as a real sister. He almost thought she couldn't help being perfect.

She'd spent her summer at a camp in Colorado aimed at the arts and had made a short film there which had promptly won an award for outstanding merit at camp's end. She returned home with an enthusiasm for moviemaking. Not that he was into competition, but the fact he had helped save Eleanora and FireAnn and Gavan and all the others from the Dark Hand of Brennard could hardly be talked about, and he'd gotten no award

but the satisfaction. Finding out he had a Talent for opening
Gates as well . . . well, if he so much as opened his mouth about
it, his family would think he'd gone crazy. Still . . . a pennant
with "Hero" stitched across it or something would have gone
nicely on his attic bedroom walls!

Jason plowed to a halt in the upstairs hallway right where
his trapdoor ladder could be dropped out of the ceiling. A clutter
of boxes filled the corridor. He took a long, slow look, then
couldn't help grinning. A computer! In box after box. . . . lying
in the hallway, waiting for him to open his bedroom and take it
up. And not just any computer. This was state of the art. As fast
as chips could make it go, these days. Awed, he let out a whoop
and then stood and stared. From down below, he could hear the
pleased, rumbling laughter of the Dozer.

Alicia peeked out of her room. So she was home, after all.
She wrinkled her nose. "Got it, huh?"

"Wow," was all he could manage before pulling his ladder
down and eagerly beginning to haul the boxes up. His willowy
blonde stepsister emerged from her own room long enough to
hand boxes up to him and wish him luck.

It was even easier than it looked, and since McIntire had
made sure his home was cable ready, all Jason he had to do was
plug in, and he was connected to the Internet. He found himself
writing Trent. His friend's name flashed on and, in surprise,
messaged him.

**Hey! What are you doing on-line? I thought the great
Alicia wouldn't let you till after dinner!** typed Trent.

She doesn't. I got a new computer. You like?

No kidding? Tell me about it.

And so Jason did, prompted by a few comments from Trent.
They typed back and forth, just like talking face to face, only
taking a little longer because Jason wasn't very quick at typing
yet. Trent seemed impressed by his computer, but more impor-
tantly, it made communication wide open for them now. The

telephone had long distance charges and people could pick up on the line. This way, they could share anything and everything they wanted. Trent showed him how to set up the computer with a password so that only Jason himself could get in. Jason found himself sitting back in his chair, still grinning broadly. He'd missed Trent and the others more than he could say. They were Magickers. They were family.

They traded news. He'd made the soccer team, Trent had made the cross-country team. Trent loved his history teacher, Jason had doubts about his math teacher. Trent told him that Stefan had made his school's first line football team, promoted from the junior varsity team. That surprised neither of them. The great hulking Magicker was a shapechanger from human to bear . . . often unpredictably. In either form, he was big and bulky. And they talked about Jennifer, slim and pretty and older than either Bailey or Ting. Trent had a thing for her which he'd kept pretty quiet all summer, but Jason could see it creeping out as they worried about where she was and why she was pulling back.

Being a Magicker is not the easiest thing in the world, he commented.

Are you kidding? Trent shot back. **It's about the only thing in the world!**

Maybe she's worried her family would never accept it. Jason sat back, watching his computer screen for Trent's response. Heck, *he* worried about that.

Trent came back with a written shrug. They talked about other stuff, then Trent had to go, to finish chores and start dinner before his dad came home from work.

Jason took some time to set up his e-mail ring for everyone before signing off. Then he clattered down his trapdoor ladder and downstairs, bursting in on McIntire and Joanna. "Wow! It's great!"

"You have everything set up, then?"

"No problem. Thank you! It's terrific."

Dozer nodded in satisfaction. "I'm glad it worked out. I want it used sensibly, though. No late hours. Don't do anything to make me have to ground you."

"No, sir, I won't." He started out of the kitchen, paused and turned. He looked at them. "I really mean it . . . thank you!"

"We're pleased," Joanna said, smiling. She held her arms out, and he hugged her, and the Dozer slapped him on the back with his great, callused hand. The moment passed, and he tugged away. His heart was filled with warmth, but it was quickly emptied by the faint sound of Joanna's voice as he retreated.

"Do you think that's wise?"

"Wise?"

"There's so much on the Net he could be exposed to . . ."

"Ah." William McIntire grunted. "My dear, if he wanted it that badly, he'd find it anywhere. I once had a friend who underlined every dirty word in the Bible. Took so much work he lost interest."

His face red, Jason returned upstairs to collect all the empty boxes and clean his room up for dinner. She'd be watching him, he knew. She worried a lot about being a good mother. Sometimes it was a real pain. Sometimes it produced a real pain, like Alicia. With a sigh, he began to put his room in order. He'd have to be careful. Very careful.

Dirty Deeds

THE lid of the trash bin clattered down resoundingly, its BOOM echoing around them. Sam muttered, "This is getting old."

Papers and assorted trash crinkled around Jason as he got to his feet and listened for silence outside. He nudged Sam. "Yeah, but this time, it's our teammates who did it. It's an initiation!"

"Bah." Sam leaped to his feet and grunted as he tried to budge the lid over their heads. "I hate the smell. I hate being shut in!" He pounded his fists on their cell. "I hate the dark!" He pounded harder in growing panic.

Every movement drummed through the old metal bin and sent a thick, foul odor rippling through the stuffy air. Jason heard nothing further outside and put his arms up, determined to get them out before school officials noticed their being canned. "Take it easy," he said. He cupped his crystal in his hand, but the rock stayed cold instead of answering his focus. Baffled, Jason carefully pulled it partway out of his pocket. It wouldn't do to drop and lose it in all the trash around his feet!

He rubbed his fingers over it. Lantern light or maybe even a bit of levitation, he thought. The hard, faceted surface of his crystal met his fingers. The welcome flare of a bonded crystal acknowledging his touch did not happen. Jason bit his lip. Arkady's curse at work? Shoving the rock back into the deep recesses of his pocket, he decided he'd have to rely on hard work. "Help me shove," he said, as he braced himself to push.

The two of them pushed and heaved, with sweat running down their faces before they finally got the lid banged open and could clamber out. Suddenly his crystal flared out, with a bright sunlit ray, but Sam had turned away and did not see it. A golden aura settled around them as Jason choked in surprise. Quickly, he brushed his hand over it, squelching it. The warm rock settled back into its inert coolness while he stretched in relief. Welcome fresh air washed over them, and as they did a little victory dance, a cough sounded. They turned around slowly. Jason felt his face go warm.

Vice Principal Murphy stood waiting, arms crossed over his chest. "Again?"

Jason shrugged. "It happens."

"Any particular reason? Did you see who did it?"

Both boys shook their heads. Murphy sighed. He pointed a finger at Sam. "You can go, son, but you—" He pointed a finger at Jason. "You need to stay. You seem to attract trouble, Adrian. Weren't you the boy who had his clock cleaned by Canby last spring? Wound up with his leg in a splint?"

"That was me," he admitted reluctantly.

"You're on my list, then," said Murphy.

"List?"

Friday afternoon had all but cleared the school out, and so Sam hiked up his backpack, giving Jason a look of apology before heading off. Jason dusted himself off, giving the vice principal his attention. "List?" he repeated.

"My list of trouble just waiting to happen. Let's head to my office," Murphy answered. "This will be short and sweet. We all want to go home."

Jason trotted after the man, somewhat curious, and glad to be in the open air again, shedding the smell of the trash bin as he followed. Murphy was a nice enough guy, always dressed in a suit, looked like he could have been a banker or something but instead he was chief enforcer at the school. He was young, Jason supposed, and had a picture of a nice wife with freckles across her nose and two small kids, who both shared the same freckles, on his desk. This was his first year at the middle school.

"Sit down," he said, pointing in the general direction of several chairs.

"Sure." Jason settled down, feeling vaguely uneasy. Had Murphy seen anything? He gazed at the picture of his wife and two kids. Nice family. He decided to count freckles to take his mind off Murphy's expression.

"Middle school," Murphy said, "can be really demanding. It's a time in your life when you're not a child, but you're not quite a teenager yet either."

Jason throttled back a sigh. Not one of *those* lectures? He tried not to squirm in the chair.

"That's why," Murphy continued, as he steepled his hands and swung around in his chair, staring at his wall full of cheerful posters and interesting looking credentials hung in frames, "we have middle school. We have it to bridge those few years when you are in between, to help you through. As I said, you're on my list. We don't want feuds, Jason, and I'm here to intervene."

"I'm not feuding." His voice came out sulky, and he shut his mouth, deciding it was better not to talk. Jason waited. Sooner or later, Murphy was going to ask why he'd been in a cloud of golden, glowing light . . . wasn't he? How could he not have seen it? He tried to think of a logical explanation, and couldn't. The only thing he could do then, was convince the vice principal that he *hadn't* seen it. Or maybe to forget he'd seen it. He had a few options . . .

". . . and that is why I think you'll find this program beneficial."

"Program?" Jason glanced up from his tumbling thoughts, to find Murphy now staring at him. He'd obviously missed something.

"It's nothing to be embarrassed about," Murphy said. "And, of course, we'll have to discuss it formally with your parents, but since today is Mr. Finch's first day, I thought you could meet him and get things rolling. We brought him in as a kind of prevention force. Get to the problem before it really happens, you see."

It sounded to Jason as though things were already dangerously out of control. "Ummm," he said, fishing for a useful thought.

Murphy stood. "Come on, it's just down the hall. He's waiting."

He didn't seem to have much choice, so he joined Murphy again for a short trip through the school's administration office. They seemed to be heading for a tiny cubbyhole at the far end of the farthest offices. Boring beige walls led into an even more bland cubicle of an office.

"Statler," Murphy said warmly. "It was good of you to wait. Jason Adrian, this is Statler Finch. He's our new counselor, brought in for special programs. Finch, this is Jason Adrian. Excellent student, good athlete, has a bit of trouble with peer acceptance. He's on the early warning list we discussed." He put his hand on Jason's shoulder and drew him inside the doorway.

"Peer acceptance?" Jason looked at both of them warily.

"Bullying," said Finch, standing, with an expression that could be taken as a smile or a glare. "You could call it bullying."

Peer acceptance? Jason thought. This was about the bullying? "Then why are you hauling *me* in? I'm the victim."

"Only because you attract and allow it. But I'm here to change all that."

Statler Finch stood behind the cluttered desk which was overlaid with books and files, and boxes still half-opened, their packing leaking out onto the desktop. He was tall, thin, wore glasses perched high on a prominent nose, had pale skin, and his body teetered on the brink of clumsiness. If anyone was made to suffer smirks and bullying, it would have to be Statler Finch.

He turned, nearly pitching headfirst over the arm of his desk chair. Grabbing frantically, he righted it and himself and sat down with a thunk. Neither he nor Murphy seemed to have noticed anything, but Jason pinched his own leg, hard, to keep from laughing.

The impulse stopped dead when Finch settled his dark brown eyes on him. Eyes dark and hard as flint, without any light to them.

"Thank you, Mr. Murphy," the man said. "I'll just be a few minutes, then we can all go."

The vice principal left, with Jason quelling an urge to call out after him, not to leave him with Statler Finch. But he did not, and the two of them stared at each other.

"That name give you trouble?" Finch smiled thinly.

"Jason? No."

"Adrian. It is rather like a girl's name, isn't it?"

Jason looked over the counselor's shoulder to a single framed object hanging on the wall. There were other nails, waiting, but this was the only one that had been utilized yet. It stated that one Statler A. Finch had graduated, with honors, with his doctorate in Psychology. "People will make fun of anything," he said. "I don't worry about it."

"But you don't stop it either?"

Sitting there, with the faint reek of the trash bin still clinging to him, there wasn't much Jason could say. "It's not important."

"It isn't?"

"No."

"What is important?" Finch smiled thinly. It didn't reach his flint-hard eyes. There was no way Jason was ever going to tell him anything remotely personal or important. There was no way he'd ever admit to being a Magicker or share what was important in his life. Silence stretched between them.

"Can I go home now?" Jason finally asked.

"In a moment. You see, the school hired me to help fellows like you. Bullied around, mistreated. A lot of harm can happen. Anger driven inward. People need to know how to assert themselves, how to express that anger . . . safely. Or there can be tremendous problems later."

Great. The school thought *he* was the problem, not the idiots who did the bullying. Jason kept his silence, afraid that anything he said would be remembered and used against him.

"That's where I come in." Statler Finch leaned over his desktop, across the clutter, his thin body clenched with intensity. "I'll work with you and your family until you can handle these situations on your own. I'll . . . defuse you."

Jason had a mental image of his skull being opened from the top, his brain being defused, and his head being snapped shut again. He barely kept from shuddering. "I don't think I need a program," he said finally.

"We'll see. I'll make an appointment to talk with your parents. I am sure I can share a few insights that will help everything." Statler rustled his thin, bony hands through the paperwork on his desk. "The first evening free, I'll be there." He stood. "Thank you for stopping by, Jason."

Jason darted to his feet. Finch stopped him in the doorway. "I'll be seeing you. Soon."

Jason did not run till he hit the school's front doors. Then he bolted as if he could outrun the memory of Finch's cold stare.

Jennifer Logan frowned as the sky grew darker. Although that meant fall was coming into its prime and Halloween drawing near, she didn't like losing the sun so early. She turned the watchband on her wrist, bringing it around so the caged charm fell into her palm, and her crystal flared with a soft, welcoming light. Before homework for high school, and before a promised phone call from Matthew Douglas, before anything else, she had exercises to practice.

She stood outside in the cooling air of late afternoon, and looked about to make sure no one in the neighborhood noticed her as she walked the perimeter of her house, trying to ward it as she'd been taught. Once she'd learned it well enough, she could lend her abilities to help ward the Havens. There were other Talents, but she really had no desire to develop any yet. There were days when she wanted, more than anything, just to be invisible. Of course, if she were invisible, then Matthew Douglas would never have noticed her. If not invisible, then, just . . . normal. That was it. Normal. Normal enough to fit in with the crowd at school and not have to worry about her Magick popping out at weird times.

Stepping carefully around her home and yard, she began to gather power from the natural ley lines in the ground itself, lines of energy from the elements of the Earth, and weave it together for a protection. She could not get a ward to last longer than a night, but even that took all the will she had, and every day it grew stronger. Jennifer felt a tiny spark of pride as she walked and thought, and gathered and wove.

The last element to gather was the night itself, dark and cold in her mind as she touched it. She hesitated, as always. She'd been deathly afraid of the dark when she was little, something about having been scared one night, and although she was all grown up now . . . well, nearly, next summer she'd get her learner's permit to drive! . . . the night could still make her uneasy.

Jennifer swallowed tightly. Her fingers twitched as if she actually held ribbons in her hands to gather and braid and knot together, but it all flowed through her mind. She'd seen Aunt Freyah and Eleanora and FireAnn do this many times before. *Their* hands had never twitched. Practice! Practice makes perfect.

She needed to do this now, for herself and her family, and later she would be able to do it for all Magickers, something important, something needed.

Jennifer shuddered as the dark ribbons she held turned slimy, fighting her, fighting her will to knot them to the ley lines of bright, powerful goodness running through the earth surrounding her house. Like a snake, the ribbons seemed to want to twist and turn and writhe in her hands. Their touch made her skin crawl and her stomach turn, and her fingers twitched and danced in distaste until her crystal rattled in its cage, threatening to shake loose.

Jennifer frowned and tossed her head, shaking her long fine locks of blonde hair away from her eyes so that she could concentrate. She wanted to finish, in a hurry now, as nighttime fell and the promise of Matthew's call nagged at her. Homecoming was just around the corner, and Harvest Dance, and even though she was only a freshman and Matthew was a junior, there was a chance . . . just a glimmer of a chance, he might ask her! But if she didn't hurry and finish, she'd miss his call. She only hoped that if she did, the answering machine and not her parents would pick it up.

Impatiently, Jennifer worked at the ribbons she'd called to her, trying to force the inky lines of night into her pattern. Then, suddenly, the reluctant streams answered her, gathering and flowing around her, pouring in as though she'd broken a dam.

Jennifer could hardly breathe as it began to flood around her, swirling, rising in a black cloud around her. She'd drown in it! She began to work feverishly at her wards, unknotting, letting this line drop, then that, but still the night poured in.

She looked in panic about her backyard, but there was no one around, no one she could cry out to, no one who would understand. She tried to focus for the beacon, but everything got so cloudy, she didn't know if she could get through or not.

And then it began to devour her from the inside out. Jennifer tried to scream and couldn't. She would be lost! She poured everything she had into her crystal to save herself. It flared hotly in her hands and then exploded into a thousand pieces, and rained over her like dust from a spent firework.

The night took her. Covered from head to toe, stifled, blind, numb, she fell, all thoughts gone from her head, only knowing that she fell because there was a brief jar of pain as she landed, and then the growing dampness of a night-dewed lawn beneath her.

Jennifer closed her eyes, weeping silently.

That was how Eleanora found her. She lifted Jennifer up and held her, and crooned a small bit of a song she knew from years past, and wrapped her arms around the girl tightly till the warmth came back, and Jennifer stopped weeping, and opened her eyes.

Only then did Eleanora dare ask, "What happened, lass?"

"W–w–warding, or trying to."

"Overexerted yourself and fainted?" She smoothed Jennifer's honey hair from her face, noted her pale, pale complexion, and felt the erratic pulse of her heartbeat.

"No. It turned on me. The night—" Jennifer's eyes brimmed again.

"Jennifer, dear, I don't understand. A ward is a simple thing, just a weaving of the natural elements around you, and your own strength to tie them. There is nothing evil or unnatural here. It all comes from you and your awareness, dear."

Jennifer shuddered. She said dully, "Then something in me is very, very dark and evil. I can't risk letting it out! I can't! I can't! I couldn't control it. My crystal shattered. I'm nothing anymore!"

"Now, now. I'm here. You'll be fine." Eleanora smoothed back her hair again. But her brows knit tightly as she leaned over the girl. Shattered crystals meant that Jennifer had nearly lost herself, and they her. If Jennifer could even bond to a crystal again, it might be months before she was well enough to try it. This was a dreadful setback for the young Magicker.

The girl wrapped both of her arms about Eleanora. "Save me," she begged.

"I'll try," said Eleanora quietly.

Semper Fi

BAILEY'S mother leaned close and gave her a quick kiss on the forehead before pausing at the apartment door. "Now remember, if I'm late, you two take the bus. But if you miss the bus, I don't want you walking down to the next bus stop."

"I won't," Bailey agreed.

"If you're late to school this morning, just have them call me." Rebecca Landau lingered for another minute, her briefcase in one hand and purse in the other.

"I will." Bailey sat, her cereal spoon suspended in midair, waiting.

Her mother sighed. "All right, then. Everything is all set with Jiao. She'll drive Ting over to school, and then I'll see you and Ting tonight. Tomorrow we'll hit the matinee after the school festival, then home she goes."

"Great!" Bailey grinned gleefully.

Her mother waved and bolted out the door. Even as it shut, she could hear the hurried footsteps running down the corridor. Bailey waited a moment longer, then put her spoon in her mouth and crunched away. She hurried to finish her own breakfast, clear away the dishes, settle Lacey down in her pack rat habitat, and grab her backpack. Lacey wrapped her dark-tufted tail about her body, buried her face, and went to sleep in a nest of cedar shavings and toilet paper, quite unconcerned about Bailey going. She chirped reassuringly at the pack rat anyway. Lacey's tail twitched as though perturbed at being disturbed in her morning nap. Bailey wrinkled her nose.

She checked the time as she turned down the thermostat for the day, and pitched herself out the door. She was late! And, clattering down the stairs and bursting out of the apartment building, she could see the bus pulling away from the stop even as she burst into the morning sunlight.

Grumbling, she hiked her backpack on one shoulder. If she briskly walked the three blocks to the main avenue, she could catch any number of buses headed toward school. Of course, she'd been told not to. But . . . Bailey cast a look at the brisk autumn day. Blue sky, light wind, no clouds. A good day to walk. She hesitated. It wasn't the exercise that bothered her mother. It was the used car lot on the third block, where a very large and frothing dog sat inside the gates, on perpetual guard. He was heavy and mean, and the gates were wobbly. Her mother was of the opinion it was only a matter of time till Ulysses broke free and hurt someone.

Being late to school, on the other hand, was more of a problem than her mom seemed to think. Bailey broke into a trot, her ponytail bouncing in time to her stride. If she didn't look at Ulysses, perhaps he'd not notice her going by. Better safe than silly, as her grandma always said.

By the time she neared that feared last block, however, Ulysses was already at the diamond-shaped wires, barking energetically at a much older and taller passerby when he spun around to see Bailey approaching.

"GAR-woof! Woof! Woof!" he trumpeted, lunging at the

fencing. It bounced and chimed as his thick brown body hit it. Spittle went flying from his flapping jowls.

"Ewwww," Bailey muttered, dodging past the flying globs. She looked at the metal signs rattling against the fence with every bounce of the madly barking dog. G & S Fine Used Cars and Marine Sales. Then a second sign, hanging below it. Beware of Dog. And, written in marking pen under the word dog, someone had penned, Ulysses S. Grunt.

Bailey grinned. That last was her handwriting but the owners of G & S had yet to wipe it off. Maybe they liked it. There was no sign of what Ulysses thought about it, unless it was in the red curl of his tongue and the snap of his white jaws.

Ulysses launched himself at the gate, his great thick head pounding into the back of the sign. It rang like a gong. He fell to the ground, frothing and growling. Then he gathered himself and stood, panting and snarling, on sturdy if bowed legs. She did not wait to see what else he would do. She took to her heels, scurrying past, as the loosely chained gates quivered and wobbled and as he tried to thrust his massive head through the gap.

Both she and a city bus arrived at the corner at the same time. With a quick look at the routing, she climbed aboard hastily, presenting her bus pass. She sat down, slightly out of breath, as the bus pulled away and Ulysses S. Grunt bounced up and down on the other side of the car lot as if knowing she had made her getaway. She wouldn't tell her mother, but if the festival's meeting ran late, they might well miss the last bus and she might have to confront the Grunt twice in one day. And that was tempting fate!

Bailey spent the rest of her short bus ride contemplating various plans to keep herself and Ting out of trouble on the way home, but she knew there wasn't a lot she could do. Ting, as quiet and slender in her American Asian way as anyone could be, had one fault she couldn't seem to overcome. She was late. Always, continually late. And she was so quiet and unassuming that even when she arrived somewhere, she was so often not noticed that it made her seem even later!

It was glorious, though, having her summer roommate just across town. At summer camp's too quick ending, she thought they'd all be flung to the wind like autumn leaves, only to discover that Ting lived just across town from her, as did Henry Squibb. It was a big town, with a population of over 500,000 people. Still, once a month, she and Ting had an overnight. Besides having a friend who didn't think she was *totally* weird, they could share what they'd learned about their crystals in practice, talk about school, families . . . well, in Bailey's case, she only had her mom and grandmother . . . but Ting had become her best friend.

They could giggle and watch DVDs and work on the charms that Ting had started making. She had a Talent, it seemed, for infusing small bits of crystal with a charm spell, mild and not very long lasting, but it was fun to experiment with. They both thought that, eventually, this was how the elder Magickers could make powerful warding stones. Ting seemed very pleased that she might have an ability which later would grow into something really useful. They were going to sell the charms at the All School Fall Festival tomorrow, which was one reason they were getting together tonight, to attend the last planning meeting and to get ready.

As for Bailey, well, she wasn't sure what she could do that was special. Oh, she'd disappeared for a while when she first got her crystal, but it wasn't a matter of being invisible or anything great. And she had Lacey, of course, and there was that afternoon a pondful of frogs decided to follow her around. She wasn't worried, though. Being a Magicker had been incredible so far, and she knew someday something special would trip and fall over her. She had absolutely no doubt. And it would be an adventure to discover it!

The bus came to a halt at the corner near the school. Bailey jumped up and was down the stairs almost before the doors finished opening. She just had time before the bell rang to visit her locker and switch a book or two. Today would be a great day, absolutely. It always was.

That was, of course, before she got bumped in the hallway and dropped her backpack, causing her papers to be scattered everywhere. And before the cafeteria ran out of pizza slices and she had to settle for chicken nuggets. And before they decided to play field hockey instead of getting onto the courts and playing volleyball. And before the English teacher assigned a five page essay. Of course, into every life a little rain must puddle. Nothing momentous to ruin her high spirits with a Friday night sleepover, and a Saturday movie to look forward to.

Of course, when the last bell rang, and the school parking lot cleared out, and Ting still wasn't there for the meeting, Bailey began to feel a little disgruntled. She sat on the brick planter outside the office, swinging her sneakered feet, and waited. It being the last day of the school week, no one lingered besides those who were there for the last planning session and to get the booths set up. Not the teachers, not even the janitor, and certainly not the students! The wind picked up a little, with just an edge of chill to it. She wondered what the weather would be like for Halloween next month. *Please don't let it rain like it did last year!* she begged silently. She then wondered if Ting could make a weather charm. Now *that* would be something to see. Imagine a Magicker strong enough to charm away storms!

That thought brought a small sigh. She'd be happy for Ting, of course, but . . . what lay ahead for her? Anything? Surely a vast world of possibilities, but of what kind? Perhaps as many possibilities as there were types of people, since the Magickers felt that all Talents came from within. So who was she, and what could she do?

She took her crystal out from under the neckline of her shirt and pulled it off over her head, a brilliantly purple amethyst on a pretty, twisted silver chain, and stared into it for a moment as it rested in her palm. Some Magickers could focus their crystals just by touching them, but she was still new at it, and found it worked best when she held her crystal nestled in her palm. The slant of the late afternoon sun played into the amethyst, bringing a glow to its faceted sides. Many crystals were common quartzes, but not all, and hers was as valuable as it was beautiful, but that wasn't why she'd chosen it. It had called her, somehow, to touch it and bond with it. From the moment she'd touched it, it had warmed to her and even now lay in her palm with a faint welcoming tingle. It was a beautiful gem, and all hers.

Bailey crossed her legs, studying her crystal, wondering how it was she'd managed to stare into the amethyst and get lost in it the very first time she'd held it. Could it ever happen again . . . ?

"Bailey! I'm here!"

Ting's soft high voice carried over the noise of a car pulling up and the door opening and shutting, yanking Bailey out of her thoughts and putting a welcoming smile on her face. She bounced to her feet, shoving her amethyst deep into her pocket chain and all as Ting swung her overnight satchel over one shoulder and they hugged.

Ting's mother leaned out. Jiao Chuu smiled although she looked faintly tired and worried. "See you tomorrow night, honey!"

"Okay!"

"Remember," Bailey added. "My mom will drive her home!"

Jiao smiled, her soft wings of shining dark hair pulled back from her round face. Ting had told Bailey that Jiao had several meanings in Chinese, charming and tender and lovely. Bailey thought Jiao was easily all of those. "Thank you, Bailey. You girls have a good time." The car pulled away slowly. Ting heaved a sigh.

"Wassamatter?"

"Grandmother isn't doing well. We may have to go up to San Francisco for a few weeks."

"You, too? What about school? You're staying tomorrow, right?"

"Mom says she can home school me for a few weeks or I can even transfer for a month or two, if we have to stay that long. My dad will take us up, then come back for work and to take care of my sisters." Ting had an older and a younger sister. Bailey sometimes thought she was so quiet because she'd been sandwiched in the middle.

Bailey looked at her in dismay. "Months?"

Ting nodded. "Mom's pretty worried about things. She won't tell me everything, but it's what she's *not* saying that bothers me." She paused. "Grandmother may be dying, I don't know."

"Oh, Ting! Don't think it."

"I can't help it. You know how you know things are really serious, but nobody will tell you? It's like that whenever they talk about my grandmother. All I catch are whispers."

The two of them fell into step, heading for the conference hall.

"They do it to protect us."

"I know, but wondering is worse. I mean, I keep wondering if she's got cancer or what." Ting shivered slightly, and Bailey hooked her arm through her friend's in warming comfort.

"If you go, what will I do? We just got the computer ring set up, too."

"We'll take my brother's laptop. She already told me that. I can't be on it long, but I can talk to you every night. She says it's easier than everyone phoning everyone. She can talk to my dad and uncles, too."

"That's not so bad, then. Maybe your grandmother just needs some help for a while?"

"I hope so. I'm going to try and make a health charm. Want to help me?"

"Sure! Two heads are better than one, if all those extra hands and feet don't get in the way!"

Ting laughed then. "Bailey!"

"What?"

"Oh, nothing." But Ting was still smiling widely as they ducked into the big gymnasium.

Decorators had already been at work on it, and harvest wreaths and banners hung everywhere. Piles of dried gourds and newly picked pumpkins lay by the door, and the immense hall had been cleared except for a few large round tables. Cardboard booths were being assembled as fast as the older students could get them together, and Mr. Nicholas, the music director, was orchestrating everyone as cheerfully as he did the school band. They got in line for their booth assignment, and Mrs. Nicholas, his wife, looking only slightly less cheerful and a trifle more harried, smiled at them as she sorted through a deck of cards.

"Ah. From different schools but sharing the same booth! That's the spirit! That's what we're all here for. And who are you rooting for in the big game tomorrow?"

Ting stared at Bailey and Bailey stared back at Ting. Neither of them had really wanted to stay for the football game; they were doing the matinee instead. They both shrugged.

Mrs. Nicholas laughed and hugged them both. "Just smile and pretend you like football if anyone asks."

Bailey took their placards and tucked them under one arm. "We need to finish setting up the booth," she explained.

"Of course. Oh, and your mother called, Bailey. She said she was going to be at the office for another hour, and you'll have to take the bus home. Is that going to be a problem for you girls?"

"Nah." Bailey shook her head. "I do it all the time. Working mom, you know?"

"I know," smiled Mrs. Nicholas. "Take your pick of any of the garlands and banners. Tomorrow, there should be squash for everyone, too."

"Just what I want! A squash!" Bailey laughed and waved at Mrs. Nicholas. Ting hurried after.

"You know," Ting said thoughtfully as they found their booth (already assembled!) in the corner. "Maybe we should go to the game. Isn't Stefan a tackle on the Midford team?"

"Yup, he made the Midford Bears all right." Bailey smothered a laugh. "And I think Rich is a trainer or something."

"Rich?" Without missing a beat, Ting took the placards from her and taped them neatly to the front of the booth.

"You know the most physical thing he does is trot after Stefan and hope Stef doesn't shapeshift when anyone else can see. And he'd make a great trainer, he's such a hypochondriac. He knows how to do anything for anyone who might be ill or hurt." Bailey talked quietly, although the din in the hall was so loud, it was doubtful anyone could hear them. Still, you never knew. And this was Magicker business, and had to be taken seriously.

"Think we should go to the game?"

"And miss the movie? I've been waiting months for it!"

"Well, me, too. It's settled, then. We'll stay with the movie." Ting tossed her long dark hair back over her shoulder before bending down to make sure their signs were securely fastened to the various booth sides.

Bailey went and found a harvest garland and began twining it about the wooden boards that formed the booth's window. She hurried, aware of the tick of time. It only took a few more minutes and they were all squared away. Bailey stepped back.

CHARMS and TALISMANS for Luck and Fortune. She smiled. "Looks good!"

"Think we'll sell any?"

"I hope so, the school funds need it. And no one is doing anything like it, although my mom's probably right . . . food will sell the best. She says boys our age do nothing but eat." She frowned slightly. "Do you think it's right?"

"What?"

"Well." Bailey shifted her weight slightly. She lowered her voice even more. "Selling Magick."

"No one will know it's Magick. I mean, real Magick."

"They'll think it's just for fun, right?" Bailey wrinkled her nose dubiously.

Ting nodded, her dark hair swinging about her face. "Exactly! It can't be traced back to us. And besides, it fades after a week or so. I can't seem to put any strength into the charms. All they'll have left is a pretty bit of jewelry. It's only for fun, Bailey."

"Still . . ."

"Look," said Ting with a firmness not usually found in her soft voice. "Across the hall they're reading Tarot cards and they're selling fortune cookies. So . . . what could we be doing wrong?"

"It's not like anyone is going to know," repeated Bailey.

"Right."

"As long as it's not trouble. I get into enough on my own!" Bailey flashed a grin, then, tossing her head.

They went back to Mrs. Nicholas and confirmed they'd be back at ten in the morning for the festival, grabbed their things, and scurried out to the bus stop just as the bus pulled up. They settled on adjoining seats, and chattered about things in the ordinary world like school, boys, movies, and clothes. The blocks flew by and then their transfer stop came up. Both of them tumbled off the bus, looking for the next one that would head down Bailey's street. As they straightened and shouldered their bags, Bailey caught sight of the bus they wanted just pulling away. She bolted after it, shouting to Ting, "Come on!"

They sprinted down the block, sneakers thundering, backpacks and satchels bouncing, but the city bus pulled farther and farther away. Ting wobbled to a halt and bent over, catching her breath. Bailey slowed down, circled, and trotted back. "I'm sorry."

Ting giggled. "Like it's your fault. Anyway, it's not far, let's walk it."

Bailey hesitated. She dug the toe of her sneaker into the sidewalk. "Mom asked me not to walk."

Ting considered her with almond eyes. "Because of the dog?"

"Ulysses S. Grunt." Bailey nodded. "It's like tempting fate."

"Well . . ." A rapidly cooling afternoon wind skittered around them. Ting shivered a bit. She dug around in her satchel, then let out an exasperated sound. "I forgot my jacket!"

"You can borrow one of mine, but we have to get home first. We'll just have to walk fast. We'll keep warmer that way, and maybe Ulysses won't notice us."

Ting swung her long curtain of dark hair over her shoulder. "Maybe he just *looks* mean."

"As long as it's not one of those 'if looks could kill' situations." Bailey tossed her head. Ting matched long, hurried steps with her. "I think it's awful that someone takes a puppy and trains 'em to be mean and nasty."

"I don't see how you can train 'em to just be . . . well . . . stern if they've got to protect something. Some jobs call for nasty."

"I don't know. It just doesn't seem fair to the dog. They all start out as warm, squirmy little bundles of fur."

Ting grinned. "Only you, Bailey."

"What?"

"Nothing." Anything further she might have said was interrupted as they approached the chain-link fencing of the used car lot and marine supplies yard, and Ulysses came bounding out, in full voice. *Thieves!* he barked. *Burglars! Trespassers!* He bounced on stiff legs, hackles raised all over his neck and shoulders, jowls rippling with each bark.

He hit the fence with a clang of enthusiasm and warning. The structure trembled and rang like a gong as he slammed his thick, square body into it again and again. Bailey muttered, "Oh, shush, Ulysses. I walked by this morning and didn't touch a thing!" She put her nose in the air and walked faster, Ting scurrying to keep up. The sidewalk was broken here, in spots, with tiny clumps of wilting crab grass growing out of it, and fractured lines where the concrete mysteriously bulged up, but whatever tree roots might have caused it could no longer be seen.

Ulysses bellowed more dog warnings and curses at them. He began to sound out of breath.

"He'll huff and puff till he blows the fence down," noted Ting, almost as breathless as the dog.

Both of them shivered. They were more than halfway past the long car and boat lot now, and the dog seemed more determined than ever. The chained front gate with its signs rattled and clanged as Ulysses hit them. Bailey thought she saw the wobbly gate give way. She pushed at Ting. "Run!"

They both did, pelting across the sidewalk, but Bailey's sneaker hit a wide crack. She yelped as she fell. She went sprawling to her hands and knees, backpack flying off and skidding a few feet in front of her. Ulysses charged down the other side of the fence.

Her hands and knees burned fiercely, and her ears rang from Ulysses' loud barking. She turned her face and for a moment, was nearly nose to nose with the slobbering dog. His hot breath felt like steam across her freckled nose. His jaws opened and he charged at the bottom of the fence where it gapped.

"Oh, boy!" cried Ting. She pulled at Bailey's elbow. "Get up, get up!"

Bailey scrambled to her feet and grabbed her backpack. The outer door of the office building, a rather long trailerlike structure at the back of the car lot, opened and shut with a loud BANG!

"Ulysses!" a man bellowed. The dog paid no heed. He pawed frantically at the bottom of the fence as if he could dig a hole big enough to force his body through.

"Come on," Ting pleaded, yanking on Bailey's arm. They skittered away from the fence and down the street as Ulysses continued his tirade at the fence corner.

Bailey tried to dust herself off as they moved.

"Are you all right?"

"Yeah, yeah. What's a few scrapes and bruises if I've still got my face." Bailey grinned at her.

Ting ventured a look back. "He really is mean," she said slowly.

"He didn't start off that way," Bailey muttered. She checked the strap on her backpack. Things had started to work free, books and papers, and she shoved them back in place as they hurriedly walked along. They got to the corner and crossed quickly, before slowing down a bit. The wind nipped at their bare legs and arms.

"I can fix hot chocolate when we get home."

"That sounds great! Marshmallows?"

"Maybe. They might be a little stale."

"Stale marshmallows melt slower in hot chocolate," Ting said with delight.

By the time they got to Bailey's building, the two of them had planned a snack that included graham crackers spread with chunky peanut butter and fresh bananas on top. Bailey could hardly wait to get her key in the apartment door lock. Her mom wouldn't mind her cooking a little bit as long as they cleaned up.

Long moments later, they sat in the chairs surrounding a small table in the kitchen nook, swinging their legs and contentedly looking for a few last crumbs. Ting took out her crystal. It was a soft daffodil-yellow color.

"Did you get that polished?"

"A little. I wanted to be sure I couldn't . . . you know . . . hurt it somehow."

Bailey smiled at her. Ting's first crystal, a pinkish quartz, had gone to pieces on her. She was very careful with the second one bonded to her at summer camp. She'd kept all the shattered pieces from the first, occasionally making one of the glowing bits into a pretty piece of jewelry. Bailey eyed the quartz. "Looks cool. I wonder if I should get my amethyst polished."

She reached for her crystal. She patted her pockets.

Bailey blinked.

She pulled her backpack to her and rummaged through it. Then she held it upside down over the table and watched everything shower out of it.

Everything but her crystal.

She reached in her pocket again and finally, finally, fished out the chain. Snapped in two, the pretty twisted silver chain lay across her hand, empty.

Bailey sat back in her chair.

"What is it?" asked Ting slowly, as if afraid she already knew the answer.

"It's gone." She closed her eyes in thought a moment, remembering the dog pawing frantically at the pavement. "It's gone! And we've gotta go back and get it."

Howling Like a Banshee

TING'S face paled. "You can't mean that!"

"I have to have my crystal. I have to. You know what happened last time I lost it." She searched frantically through her backpack, coming up empty-handed. "I bet it fell out when I dropped the pack. The chain must have snapped." Bailey frowned and then rubbed between her brows, erasing the mark as she often saw her mom and grandma do. She thought the faint wrinkles made her grandmother interesting, but they seemed to feel differently. "Rub that line out," they were always lecturing her. It hadn't worked on them, but who knew? "We've got to go get it."

"It's almost dark. Your mom will be off work soon. Can't we go back with her?" Ting watched her, worry all over her slender face.

Bailey shook her head emphatically, her ponytail bouncing from side to side. "She'd never understand." The two stopped talking and looked at each other for a moment.

"That's the hardest thing, isn't it," Ting said slowly. "My mom is so cool, and I can't tell her. I can't tell her anything."

Bailey nodded, wordlessly. As close as she was to her mother, not a word could she say about being a Magicker. If she could have, her mom would have understood about going for the crystal. As it was, there would be no excuse for what they were about to do. With a sigh, she got up from the table and went to the tiny hall closet by the apartment front door. It was crammed with jackets and coats and odds and ends. She managed to pull out two Bailey-sized jackets and gave one to Ting. "We've gotta hurry," she said finally.

With a resigned sigh, Ting nodded and followed her out the door. The shadows had lengthened and pooled under the trees, and night was very near. Bailey cast a look down the street, then took a long breath, pulling Ting along after her. Car headlights were already on as they came down the street slowly, in ever growing numbers as vast numbers of people got off work and headed home. She had to hurry before her mom showed up and caught her blatantly disobeying. They skittered down the sidewalks like fallen leaves in the evening breeze, shivering more from worry about what they were going to face, than the sudden cold.

The sidewalks, too, were crowded but suddenly, no one seemed to be nearby as they drew close to the car and boat lot. In the twilight, the looming shadowy bodies of cars, boats, and trucks looked like great, dark beasts hunkered down and waiting. The office in the back had no lights and seemed very quiet and still. The chain-link fence rattled eerily in the near dark as the wind shook it. It seemed terribly fragile. Bailey slowed and Ting stopped altogether, standing on one foot and then another.

"Maybe it's not here at all," she said.

"No." Bailey shook her head vigorously, ponytail bobbing. "I can feel it!" She reached out and took Ting's hand in hers, startled to find it was icy cold! "Hey, zip that jacket up. We can't have fun tomorrow if you're sick." She paused. "I bet I can light it up."

"Without holding it?" Ting stared at her.

"I think so. Sure would make it easier to find. I've gotta get closer, though."

They were not close enough yet for Ulysses to perceive them as a threat. Another few feet, though, and his sharp ears and nose would catch them trespassing on his sidewalk, in front of his yard. Both girls took a deep breath and began to tiptoe closer.

A car swept past with blazing lights, dazzling them. Bailey blinked a few times, then whispered, "Okay." She squeezed Ting's hand a little to comfort her. Closing her eyes, she concentrated on the amethyst as if she had it in her hand, remembering the glowing spell that would evoke a soft, sure light from it. If it worked, it would surely be visible in the twilight, wherever it was. Thinking hard about what it felt like in her hand, Bailey remembered its edges and ridges and rich purple color. . . .

Bailey jumped. A soft white light flared from the corner of the fencing, then fluttered out. "There!"

"What? I didn't see anything." Ting cast her gaze about. Although her hand felt warmer in Bailey's grip, she shivered.

"There!" Bailey darted forward, dragging Ting with her. She slid into the metal fence, reaching forward into an even darker corner of the yard, filled with old wrappers and crackled leaves and other debris, caught and held by the twisted wire prongs at the fence's bottom edge.

Alarm! Ulysses bounced to his feet. WOOF! He spun around, button nose wrinkling. WOOF! Trespassers! Robbers! Another bounce and he was after them, head down, barreling at the corner of the fence where Bailey shoved her hand through. She began to fish around wildly. The rough links caught at her wrist and jacket. She combed her fingers through the leaves quickly, finding pebbles and harsh sticks . . . nothing. She pushed through, leaning her shoulder into the fence, felt it sag a little under her weight. Then . . . something. She reached for it, stretching, even as Ulysses charged down on her. Alarm! Alarm! Burglars! He woofed.

The hard edge of her crystal teased her fingertips. Bailey leaned into the fence, trying to wriggle her thin arm through farther. "Almost . . . got it," she said, with a grunt.

"Bailey!" shrieked Ting, as Ulysses tore toward them. His jowls flapped and spittle flew as he tried to growl and bark simultaneously.

Bailey found something angular and hard. She closed her hand about it triumphantly. "Got it!"

Ting jerked on her other hand. "Come on! *Run!*"

She tried to pull her arm out. The fence clamped down around her. She was stuck, and stuck fast! She could feel Ulysses' hot and heavy breath on her as her ears rang from his loud protests.

AWOOF! Woof!

He snatched at her, sliding to a stop in a shower of gravel and dirt and leaves. His teeth clamped down on the hand holding the crystal, and he froze, growling, eyes narrowed.

Ting let go of her other hand and screamed, but covered her mouth, so it came out a strangled, thin noise.

Bailey stared into Ulysses S. Grunt's beady eyes. His ivory teeth held her tightly, and hot drool ran over her knuckles. He would not let go, but neither had he actually bitten her, his great jaws simply holding around her. She took a shaky breath.

"Let go," she whispered.

Ulysses stared at her. He braced his thick, stumpy body, ready for tug-of-war. She had no doubt he would win.

Her crystal warmed slightly in her fingers. If she'd let go, she probably could have pulled her arm and hand back through the fence, but then—what would the point be? It was the crystal she needed! What to do?

It seemed as if her summer flashed by. Dark-haired Eleanora, floating gracefully across the ground, lecturing on the power of naming. Bailey tried to breathe. It didn't seem to be working.

Then she got it out, her voice tight and squeaky. "Ulysses S. Grunt. Let me go."

The dog flinched. His jaw worked a bit on her hand and crystal, mouthing her. He almost let go, but then Ting started tugging frantically on the back of Bailey's jacket.

"Someone's coming," hissed her friend. "The office lights just came on!"

"You don't want to do this!" Bailey told the dog. Ulysses S. Grunt made a stubborn noise and planted his thick body even more firmly.

He left her no choice. She'd have to bespell him. Words rattled out of her with hardly a thought.

> *"Your life as a bad dog must end.*
> *You were born to be man's best friend.*
> *From here on out, be a happy pooch*
> *Who only wants to love and smooch!"*

Ting groaned. "Bailey, that's awful!"

"It's all I could think of on short notice."

Ulysses S. Grunt stared at her. Then, he let out a low whine. He went to his belly, jowls quivering. But he didn't let go. Instead, he seemed intent on imprisoning her hand so that he could lick it to pieces! Heavy footsteps came their way. Ting tugged on her jacket again.

"Let go!" Bailey commanded the dog.

Ulysses snuffled. He let go and rolled over onto his back, begging. She pulled her hand free, crystal still in her palm. He watched her mournfully. She took a step away from the fence, and he let out a forlorn howl. It echoed sadly about the lot.

"Good grief."

The dog rolled over, got to his feet, and lifted his head, howling again. She stuck her arm through and patted him. "Quiet down!"

He snuffled her fingers happily. Bailey pulled her hand out. Ulysses howled.

She stuck her hand back in, and he grunted in contentment.

"You've created a monster!" Ting accused. She danced up and down in real discomfort from the cold. "I'm going to freeze out here and someone's coming. Let's go!"

Bailey pulled her hand back and straightened.

Aoooooooo!

"Hey . . . you kids! Stop teasing my dog!" Light gleamed as a flashlight snapped on, and a great, hulking man lumbered over to the dog, glaring at Bailey and Ting.

Ting froze. Bailey backed up and felt her friend as stiff as a post stuck into the sidewalk. She wasn't going anywhere unless it was in drag mode. Words ran through her mind but failed to tumble out of her mouth. "Umm . . . ummm . . . We were just making friends."

Ulysses rolled over onto the thick boot of the man. Startled, the man looked down. Ulysses drooled happily. "He was just howling up a storm."

"L–lonely, I think," Ting managed to say.

The man, who more than slightly resembled the dog, frowned heavily at them. "You do anything to him?"

"Ummm . . . no," said Bailey. She shoved her crystal into the pocket of her jacket.

The man reached down and rumpled the dog's ear. "Wow. Maybe he's beginning to come around! We got him from a rescue. He was mistreated. We've been working with him, my brother and I." A slow smile spread across the man's face. He thumped his leg. "Come on, Ulysess! Dinnertime!" The dog gave a doggy snort, bumped his muzzle against his owner's leg and, after one longing look at Bailey, trotted off happily.

"Lucky," said Ting.

"Yeah," answered Bailey, more than a little amazed at Ulysses' transformation.

"That's your Talent, Bailey, it has to be. You're . . . some kind of animal tamer."

Bailey wrinkled her nose.

"Look," said Ting earnestly. "Lacey came to you. Even the wild animals at camp would come close to you."

"You don't think . . ."

"I do."

"Wow," said Bailey, thinking. "Maybe. Or maybe not. Maybe it's just luck . . . and we're going to need a lot of that if we don't get home right away!"

They ran.

In the Glooming

FRESH from sleep, the man sat straight up in his narrow bed. He put both hands out, palms down, to the white silken sheets around him, and took a deep breath, remembering his troubled dreams. One Gate open and another being rattled. The movement in the forces of Magick troubled him. It felt like being caught in a maelstrom unaware at first, then growing ever more certain you were being pulled to your death by drowning.

His chamber filled with a handful of followers alerted by his stirring. One helped him to his feet while another straightened his robes and brought him shoes and a longer, heavier robe against the chill. Another brought him a tray holding a carafe of dark, bitter coffee scented heavily with cinnamon, accompanied by a small pitcher of fresh cream, and an empty mug. He poured the coffee and liberally doused it with cream, then took a long draft of the steaming brew. Its heat went through him like a lightning bolt.

If he could not stop Gates from being opened, perhaps he could find some advantage in the energies released by the happening.

"Even in my sleep," he said to his silent followers, "I have set in motion a plan. Your parts will require accurate and prompt execution."

"Your will is as good as done," they answered in unison, bowing deeply. It pleased him because he knew they did not obey blindly. They obeyed because they respected his intelligence and power and foresight. He had gathered them because of that. Mindless obedience did no one any good. Here, he had the most powerful Magickers left in the lands, and their abilities and Talents were his. He smiled to himself at the thought.

"Tell us our part," said a soft, gentle voice at his elbow. "And did you rest well?"

Resting was extremely important to him right now, as he gained strength, gained stamina, returning to his old self. He shook his head slightly. "The boy invades my dreams," he said, "as I suppose I invade his." He frowned then. "In addition to what I propose we do . . . I want the boy. He must be brought to me."

"Your will is done," they answered, the chamber caught in echoes of their voices.

He smiled tightly. "Far easier said than done," he replied. "Trust me." Then he drained his coffee mug dry. "Listen well."

When he had finished detailing his plans and thoughts, he dismissed them, saying, "Send in Jonnard."

The young man came in quietly. He brought in a tray filled with two fresh mugs of coffee, cream, sugar, and biscuits, although they were far too sweet and soft for Brennard's taste. Cookies. American cookies. Something cloying with melted bits of chocolate in them. Brennard took one, leaving the others for Jonnard. The lad was not so grown up that he did not crave sweet biscuits.

Brennard sat back. He waited for the other to finish half the offering in front of him before snapping, "Progress?"

"Slow." Jonnard shifted uneasily. Dark shadows lined his

cheekbones with bruises of fatigue under his eyes. "I am failing."

"Never. You took on an unknown opponent, and nearly beat him. That is not failure. The drain . . ." Brennard set down his coffee cup. "We can handle that, if and when we have to, if rest doesn't restore you."

Jonnard fisted a hand. "I should have taken him down!"

"He is more, and less, than a Gatekeeper. We had no idea of that till your encounter, and although your defeat smarts, there's no shame in it."

Jonnard stood. "He had no training!"

"True, true. But he picked it up from you almost instantly, did he not? No one could have predicted that, but now that we know it, we can and will know how to face him. How Gavan located him, I don't know, but we need to find that out, as well. Are there more of him, lost in these states of America? Around the world?" Brennard leaned forward intently. "Untrained, they will squander the mana. They endanger us all. Use them or stop them."

"I will stop Jason Adrian."

Brennard considered the other: young, so steadfast in his anger that he practically shook, his fisted hand growing white-knuckled. "Good. But first I suggest you channel that energy into recovery. I need you to be prepared."

Jonnard put his fist over his heart then, as had gladiators of old saluting their emperor, and murmured, "As you wish."

10

The Honor Of Your Presence

JASON backed away from the computer, smiling after read-ing his mail. Only Bailey could get into trouble like she did. He remembered the troop of frogs which had followed her around camp one day, ribbiting in worshipful chorus, while she tried in vain to drive them away. Big frogs, little ones, even tiny ones who hopped in high leaps about her, chirping had carpeted her every step. Campers had stood around making comments about kissing the right one to break the spell. She'd been morti-fied until Tomaz Crowfeather had taken her aside and helped.

The early Saturday morning held its misty gray chill as he slipped out, heading for the park. He'd left a note behind to remind everyone that he and Sam were going to meet and prac-tice, then have lunch at Sam's house. He shrugged inside his sweatshirt, hunching his shoulders as if he could keep his ears warm that way, and slow jogged to the park to get his legs going. Bailey hadn't said if Ting had talked with Henry Squibb yet, but he hoped so. Friendly, klutzy, round as an owl, Henry hadn't deserved to lose his powers and, worse, to be enchanted to forget the summer they'd shared. It wasn't right, and Jason had been horrified when Gavan Rainwater and the others had insisted. His protests went unheard. Even though it was to protect him from being further harmed by the Dark Hand of Brennard, it hadn't been an easy thing to see Henry change before them. The others wouldn't talk about him after that, but Jason couldn't forget him. How could anyone?

As earnest as he was bumbling, as cheerful as he was determined, Henry had spent the summer in the cabin across from Jason and Trent. There had never been any doubt that Henry was Talented, it was his control that had always been . . . well . . . inept. Sometimes too much Magick, and at the end, not enough. The scary thing was, it could have happened to any of them, any that the traitorous Jon Albrite had chosen to attack with his training from the Dark Hand.

The street curved gracefully into the treed grove of the park, with its neatly groomed open grass areas beyond, the mecca of weekend soccer games and frisbee tournaments, picnics and other leisurely pursuits. A circuit of jogging and bicycle paths wrapped around the huge park, and the groves of elm, eucalyptus, and evergreens wove throughout. He and Sam liked to practice at the far end, where the field was lined by shrubbery and a little isolated from the rest of the park, and from the main fields.

There was no sign of Sam as Jason scanned the area. He slowed, and did some stretches. He wiggled out of his sweatshirt and tied it around his waist. It was Sam's turn to bring the practice ball, so he concentrated on keeping warmed up, jogging around the boundary of the area. A lone crow flew against the dark gray sky of the morning, circling overhead, coasting on unseen air currents. He took it for a good omen.

He swerved too close to a shrub, and it whipped against his hand and arm as he passed. The sting of it echoed through the small, crescent-shaped scar on the back of his left hand. It

pinged as if the scar were fresh, sore and bruised, even though
it had healed to a thin white line. It throbbed as he slowed to a
walk and examined it. It was not tremendously imposing, as
scars went. It did not reflect the great, ivory teeth that had left
it, ripping at his skin. Nor the hurt of being impaled on the open
jaw, with the heat of the growl rolling down his wrist, and the
vicious glow of triumphant eyes in the dark. It did not show the
pain underlying its supposedly healed surface, as if a thorn were
pushed under his skin. Sometimes he wondered if he had a
sliver of a tooth caught there.

Jason prodded his hand gingerly. Pain lanced through him
as if he'd stuck himself with a needle, and he danced from one
foot to the other, trying to hold back a yell. It throbbed hotly
while he tried to catch his breath. It was hardly ever this
painful!

Suddenly, he looked up, and around the section of park he
was in. Thickly wooded, very quiet on an early Saturday morning, and far from the street.

And he seemed to be alone in it.

Jason reached for his crystal and began to trot toward the
curve of the park where at least the street might be seen. Something rattled in the brush behind him. Without turning, he
cupped his gemstone and began to form the spell he needed for
a shield. His mind stumbled. Rushed! He couldn't remember!
He'd done this every day, and now his mind was empty.

The trees and shrubbery crackled as something pushed
through, running after him. He picked up speed, glancing back
over his shoulder. It exploded through a hedge, crashing onto
the grass and racing after him. It growled low and harshly, ivory
fangs slashing at the air, huge silvery body poised to catch him.
Wolfjackal!

Impossible! In the real world, here, now, and after him! He
could hardly breathe at that thought. Wolfjackals came from

the netherlands, borne on Magicker mana . . . how could they be so strong here, so far away from the Gates and Havens?

Jason had no doubt they would be as deadly here as they'd been at Camp Ravenwyng. He bolted.

A second unseen thing thrashed through the undergrowth as well. Jason cut back, as if defending himself on a soccer field, and the beast closing on him slipped on the still morning wet grass and went rolling. It gnashed its great jaws and leaped back onto all fours, glowering. Sun glinted in its green eyes, and it narrowed its gaze as though far more used to darkness. The wolfjackal slunk low, stalking, because Jason had halted, backing up to a great tree trunk. He could not expect to outrun it anyway. Either of them, wherever the second one was. They would both have to face him if they wanted him now, the massive old California oak tree guarding his back.

He cupped his crystal and tried for a shield again, a cover of light, and the crystal flared. He pushed all his thoughts and hope into it. He could feel an answering warmth from the rock he held as it answered, and for a moment, an immense shield enveloped both Jason and the tree! It shimmered brightly in the thin morning light and then popped like a bubble. His ears felt the pressure as it shattered and he staggered against the rough bark of the oak as it blew. His knees went wobbly.

The beast shivered as it watched him, more jackal than wolf and yet oddly similar to a wolf with its black-and-silver coat. It might even be handsome if it were not so obviously a hunter, a tearer of flesh. His left hand ached, and sharp, jabbing pains stabbed across it as if sent by lightning. The wolfjackal's tongue lolled, bright pink, from its toothy jaws and it crawled forward, eyes gleaming in bright anticipation. Jason gulped. Even if he could sound the alarm through his crystal, there was no time for an answer!

The wolfjackal turned its head slightly, with a welcoming growl, as the other readied to join it.

The brush rattled again, and the second of Jason's pursuers stepped out on two feet. He locked eyes with Jason and smiled slowly. Tall, with dark russet hair, and a band of freckles across his nose that belied his solemn look, he wore black pants, and a long black duster coat over a white T-shirt, dressing like someone out of the *Matrix* movie series. Pitch-black sunglasses hid the color of his eyes. He dropped a hand to the wolfjackal's ruff, and rubbed the ferocious creature gently. The wolfjackal growled and leaned against the man's knee.

"Running seems out of the question."

"Giving in definitely is." Jason looked at the other. "Who are you?"

The man's smile thinned. "Now that," he answered, "would be telling, wouldn't it? But I know who you are. Come along with me and save us both the trouble." He extended his free hand, the cuff of his sleeve falling back, revealing a bronze wrist-cuff shaped like a hand gripping his arm. Jason looked at it, then quickly looked away. This was more than a simpler follower of the renegade wizard Brennard. This was a member of the Dark Hand itself, and he knew he should be afraid. They were assassins, not apprentices.

He might be if he had time to stop and think. His gaze swept the park behind the man and animal. The sounds of cars sweeping now and then along the outer border of the area could be heard but no vehicles could be seen. Sam should be along any minute now, but he'd be on foot and alone, too . . . no match for the rogue Magicker facing Jason. Still, any distraction might help.

The Dark Hand noticed his gaze and followed it before turning back quickly to Jason. "No help to be had?" he said. "What a pity." He took a step forward and the wolfjackal bounded to its feet, following. "As they say . . . we can do this the easy way or the hard way."

Jason tightened his jaw.

The other noticed, and nodded. "The hard way, then." He snapped his fingers and the wolfjackal strained forward, snarling louder. "I thought perhaps an intelligent lad like you might realize there are two sides to every story."

"Probably more than that, even," Jason responded.

"Yes. All I wish to do is extend an invitation."

"Delivered by wolfjackal?"

The man paused, then laughed faintly, coldly. The sunglasses hid his eyes, but Jason doubted if the laugh crinkled or warmed them in any way. "Got your attention, as they say." He kept his hand buried in the loose skin of the creature's ruff, holding him back but without much control if the beast decided to lunge at Jason. "Come visit with me. Give me some of your time and that intense attention you hold for Magicking, and find out the rest of the story."

He heard a car slow down beyond the edge of the park, and a car door slam. Jogger being dropped off? Sam? Anyone? "Do I have to believe what you tell me?"

That took the man aback for a moment. Then he showed his teeth, much like the beast growling and snarling at his side. "Regardless of what you think, young Jason, none of us can force you to believe anything. But there are differences, important differences. Differences urgent enough to war over. I don't expect you to make a choice in a day, but you can't make any choice at all without listening. Without *knowing*. Come with me and exercise some of that independence you think is so important." He held his hand out again.

Instinctively, Jason moved away, or tried to, but the oak held him fast. Whatever would his stepmother Joanna think about his refusing a polite invitation? She was always getting them, to one charity event or another, and she would sit at the table and read them aloud to the Dozer. "The honor of your presence is requested at this year's Gala Sunbright Dance and Auction for the ailing children at Hospital Sunflower. . . ." At which point, William McIntire would looked up, with a twinkle in his eyes, and say, "Presents? Are they asking for presents again? I thought we just gave them a bagful!" To which Jason's stepmother would respond by putting down the invitation, and giving her husband an exceedingly fond look.

Somehow, Jason didn't think this invitation was to anything nearly as fun or noble as a charity dance and auction.

"Come with me now, or regret it later." The Dark Hand looked at him, almost mournfully, in his somber dark duster and black clothing, and pale skin.

"Jaaaaaaaason!" came a faraway call.

He straightened. "It'll have to be later, then. I'm busy." He pushed himself away from the tree at a dead run, leaped over the startled wolfjackal, and took off across the green field as if the devil itself were after him. A muffled curse and snapping growl echoed after him, but he did not look back. He ran toward the faint sound of Sam's call, shouting, "Over here, Sam!"

He sprinted as if the coach's shrill whistle drove him, as if the wind itself were under his heels, as if a gold medal awaited him beyond the curve of the grass and eucalyptus trees. He thought he felt hot breath across the backs of his legs and the sound of the panting wolfjackal hounding him. The only invitation the beast had in mind was one for dinner!

Sam came trotting through the shrubs at the path's end, a wide grin across his face, and there was a snap behind him. It was as though a door opened and closed, taking the wolfjackal and the Dark Hand with it. He could feel their sudden absence. Slowing, he looked over his shoulder . . . and saw nothing.

Sam hiked up his duffel bag and paused on the jogging trail. "Hey, I'm sorry I'm late—" He looked at Jason. "What is it?"

Jason grinned. "Nothing," he said. "Just that I'm really glad to see you. Really, really glad to see you."

Sam laughed. "No kidding? Well, wait till after we do line sprints, and then tell me how glad you are!" He tugged on the referee's whistle around his neck. "Just like the coach!" He blew a sharp blast, and added, "Adrian! Give me ten!"

Jason dropped to the grass but instead of doing push-ups, toppled over to catch his breath.

"What are you waiting for?" Sam demanded, mock angry.

Jason grinned. "I'm thinking of all the different things I can tell you to do with that whistle!"

Two Wrongs and a Wright

A
N hour or so later, with the sun hotly dappling the grass
and towels around their necks, Sam and Jason readied to
head home. Muscles stretched and lungs full of morning air,
they paced each other returning to the main areas of the boule-
vard park. He caught the sound of something moving through
the underbrush followed them. Branches rustled heavily and
gravel skittered.

"Did you hear something?"

Sam leaped over a patch of dried leaves and crashed into
another, crunching and scattering them. "Hear what?"

"I don't know. Something." Jason looked back over his
shoulder. He swerved along the pathway. He didn't know what
Sam would do if a wolfjackal sprang on them. For that matter,
he didn't know what *he* would do this time, given that his crystal had failed to shield him. How could he explain a frothing,
growling, powerful beast that was neither wolf nor jackal but
both, a creature not from their own dimension? But more than
having to explain a wolfjackal to his buddy, he wanted to be

able to tell him what *he* was. What he did. What he could do, with Magick. Who he was, a Magicker.

He could not. The Oath of Binding kept his jaws glued shut, but could not block his curiosity. How would Sam react? Would he treat Jason as he always had? And what if Sam had Talent of his own? Could Jason tell that? He'd been warned that the Binding would stop him in his tracks, that it could not be by-passed, but—was it true, or would it work that way only because he believed it would?

Could he risk their friendship and maybe even their lives by trying to show Sam the truth?

He heard no more noise but those of the thoughts wheeling around in his head. And while he thought, Sam jogged along-side him, talking about the soccer team and the schools they would be facing and making plans for defense and offense and extra training, his face intent on what he was saying, not even noticing Jason only half listened. Distracted, both of them ran onto the bicycle path without looking. There was a moment when he realized something zoomed head on at them and then they both wheeled about and dove into the bushes. A screech and clatter followed.

Jason sat up, to look at a cyclist righting himself and his bicycle. The scrawny figure seemed vaguely familiar, Jason thought, as he rose and helped Sam to his feet. The cyclist reached up to pull his helmet off, saying, "Everyone okay?"

He looked at Statler Finch. Sam picked up their gear bags, shaking dust and old leaves off them. He dusted himself off. "We're fine . . . I think."

"A lot of running. You two boys look like you're being chased. Any trouble?" Finch's cold eyes watched him. Judged him.

"No, sir," Jason said, finally. His hand itched to curl around his crystal, for comfort if nothing else, but he resisted. This was one man who must never, ever, find out what he was made of.

This was a man who might believe in Magick for all the wrong reasons and try to turn Jason inside out over it. He said carefully, "We're just out getting some extra practice."

"Cross-country? Track team?" Finch's gaze stayed on him. "Exercise is as good for the mind as it is for the body."

Jason shifted uneasily. The man knew what team he was on. Why ask?

"Soccer," offered Sam. "Sorry we didn't see you. Hardly anyone bicycles here."

"It *is* a bicycle path." Finch stood, mountain cycle in hand, with scrawny legs looking as if they'd never heard of a tan, let alone had one, sticking out from his bicycle shorts and bicycling shoes on his feet.

"Yeah, I know," Sam agreed. He did a cooling off stretch.

"Everyone all right, then? You both seemed in a big hurry."

"Yes, sir, and yes, sir. Breakfast is waiting at home!" Jason put on what he hoped was a starving look. He didn't like having the fellow watching them. His left hand twitched and he put his right hand over the crescent scar for a moment. Nor did he want Statler to see him twitching.

"Hard work gets you what you want." The man smiled at both of them, but the contortion of his lips did nothing to warm his eyes. They stayed cold and dark, and Jason couldn't look at him for long. Finch made him feel like a formaldahyde frog in bio lab.

Finch put his helmet back on, distracted by having to cinch the straps down again tightly. "Well, I won't keep you boys. I remember the days when one breakfast hardly seemed enough!" He laughed, again without warmth and without caring that neither Jason nor Sam laughed with him. He straddled his gleaming vehicle, hands encased by trendy biker's gloves. He kicked off, and began to pedal away, his thin calves knotted with the effort.

Sam watched him cycle around the curve and disappear. He scratched his head. "He's creepy. Who is that?"

"The new school psych I told you about."

"Ick." Sam shuddered. "I wouldn't even tell him my name, if I could help it."

Jason stared thoughtfully after the disappearing man. "I may not have any choice," he answered. "School has decided it's not bullies who are a problem, but the victims. But I'm not telling him anything." The scar under his fingers gave a single, painful throb.

"You have to go see him?"

"Looks like. Unless my parents say no." Somehow, he didn't think that would happen. They were very anxious he be all right . . . sometimes too anxious even though he wasn't theirs. What he did need, he wasn't sure. Maybe a little more trust on their part. He sighed.

"Okay, now that's crazy. We're the bad guys 'cause we're getting trash canned?"

"Something like that." Jason's stomach growled faintly, as if the mention of food did indeed wake up hunger pangs.

"That's just wrong." Sam did another stretch before flashing a grin. "Race you home?"

"You got it!" They bolted like streaks across the pathways and out of the park, toward Sam's neighborhood.

Bailey adjusted the brilliant gold, red, and brown harvest garland at the corner of their booth. She peered across the gym. "Wow, a lot of people already. Looks like they picked a good day for this."

Ting straightened her outfit a bit nervously, flinging her black hair over her shoulder as she sat down and brought out her tray of charms and talismans. She and Bailey had been working on them all morning. Bailey perched on the stool beside her.

"Don't worry, Ting, our stuff is going to sell like hot muffins."

Ting giggled. "Hotcakes!" she corrected.

"Better than that. You can't eat hotcakes with your hands, but you can muffins." Bailey tossed her head, ponytail swinging. She look over the tray of simple jewelry they'd made up. Small bluish crystals and quartz in the wellness area, pink for friendship, clear for studies and wisdom, hanging in simple twisted wire cages for necklaces or attached to clips for charms. The cages—free-form and pretty—were harder to make than they looked.

Ting had been very patient showing her how to twist and bend the wire after warming it a little. Ting had bought several crystals and broken them into shards, and then they were put into the settings once she had worked her Talent on them, filling them with a soft glow, giving them luck. Just like rabbit's feet, although heaven knows she'd never thought a three-legged rabbit could really be lucky!

Canned music began to play through the hall, country style, and Bailey wrinkled her nose. At least it wasn't too loud. She leaned over the Lucky in Study tray and stirred the charms about a bit. In the hall's light, they didn't sparkle as much as they would outside or in stronger light, but they still had a nice glimmer to them, catching the eye. She saw a group of girls survey the hall, and then their gazes fell on the signs she and Ting had made to decorate the booth.

"Ooooh," they breathed as one and headed toward them.

"Brace yourself," Bailey said to Ting. "I think it's the Barbie clones."

Ting laughed, then she whispered, "I think they're just customers!" She offered a welcoming smile as the girls came to the booth's counter.

The tanned blonde girl with very, very short hair bounced on her toes. "Jewelry," she exclaimed, and beamed.

"Earrings? Toe rings?"

"Charms," said Ting quietly, almost shyly.

Bailey stood up. "Three kinds," she explained brightly. "One for friends, one for learning, one for happiness."

"Friends?" said the blonde's number one clone, her yellow hair done in braids. She had dark brown eyes and a nice smile, and had not been born with blonde hair. She picked up one of the friendship charms. She looked at Ting. "How about . . . special friends?"

"A love potion?" chirped Barbie wannabe number three.

"Well . . . um . . ." Ting's face flushed a little and she threw an uncertain glance at Bailey.

Bailey leaned over, and lowered her voice a bit, drawing the three closer to hear her. "It can't be a Love Potion," she said, "because it's not a drink, it's a crystal. Think of it as a concentrate." And she nodded sagely.

Ting kicked her ankle under the booth counter, not hard, but Bailey distinctly felt it. She paid no attention. "The charm's purpose," and she lowered her voice yet again, after looking side to side, as if revealing a great secret, "is to make sure your friend remembers and thinks of you. A lot."

All three blondes bounced. Giggles erupted, which they fought back, and looked around to see if they were getting noticed.

"I'll take one."

"And me!

"Me, too!" They all spoke nearly as one and for a few moments, she and Ting were very, very busy picking out just the right charm for each, taking money, and bagging the jewelry.

Bailey handed the money box to Ting after they left. "See? Was that so hard?"

"Love charms?" Ting practically stuttered.

"Well . . . not exactly . . . but kinda. Luck is mostly in the perception anyway." Bailey leaned on her elbows. She watched the Barbie clones drifting across the hall, where they converged into another group and disappeared in a frenzy of greetings and hugs and bounces. "Uh-oh."

"What? What is it?"

"I think we're about to be swamped." Bailey watched the flurry of conversation across the hall, punctuated by looks and hands pointed in their direction. As one, the larger group started their way.

Within moments, Ting and Bailey sold more than half the jewelry they had made and brought. The two of them could hardly keep up with the chattering questions and orders, hands and fingers flying across the trays, gathering up two and three of the various charms at a time.

"After all," said one of the last customers as she left, smiling happily, "You can't have too much luck!"

Bailey and Ting sat back exhausted on their stools. "Wow," remarked Ting quietly. "We may not have enough to stay the whole afternoon." She looked at the picked-over trays, reaching under the counter to take out the lunch bags with the few extras they had made and spread them out where they belonged. "That's all of them."

"This is going to help the benefit a lot," Bailey said with pride. Half their proceeds went to the fund, and the other half would just cover what Ting spent for crystals and jewelry wire and chain, with maybe enough left for an ice cream sundae each. Still, it was an unspoken Magicker creed, or seemed to be, that their Talents could not be used for profit, or at least not vast amounts of it.

A shadow fell across the gleaming charms, accompanied by a deep snicker. "Selling Lucky Charms? Where's the marshmallow treats?"

She didn't have to look up to recognize Stefan and Rich. Stefan had a certain odor that, while not entirely offensive, definitely didn't come out of a cologne jar. She sat back on the stool as Ting piped up, "Hello, Rich, Hello, Stef. Ready for the game later?"

Even knowing who she was going to see, Bailey still blinked with surprise when she did look up. Stef had bulked up, standing square and big in front of her. "You could be a football team," she blurted.

He grinned. He ran his hand over his flat top haircut that made his head look like a big, mean square. "You think?"

Rich, his thin, wiry, red-haired friend, rolled his eyes. "You look like a tank," he said. "Okay?"

Stefan grinned. He hiked up his jeans and tapped his T-shirt with a big number 31 on it. "That's me."

"Cool," said Bailey. "I mean it, really. Good luck."

"You guys coming? Your team is gonna get thrashed, Bailey."

"Nah, I don't think so. We've been wanting to go to this movie for weeks, and today's our last chance, practically, before it comes out on DVD. I hear it should be a good game, though."

"I had three solo tackles last week."

"Four," corrected Rich.

Stef look at him. "Four?" Another slow grin spread across his face. "Coolio."

Rich also wore a T-shirt, but his had a zero on it. Ting tilted her head. "What do you play?"

"I'm the stats manager and I help the trainer. I get to tape wrists and ankles and stuff. And look after him." Rich gave his friend a look that was only half scornful, the other half one of genuine concern.

"Has he ever . . ." Bailey lowered her voice. "You know."

Rich shook his head quickly, a blaze of red across his pale skin. "Nope. Not without warning. Just twice since we got home."

Stef grunted. Both girls looked at him, seeing the bear he could become in their memories. Not just any bear, but a gruff and roly-poly cub, one that listened to them like Stefan would, then went off and did whatever his own stubborn bearish mind wanted.

Ting let out a small sigh of relief. "Well, that's good."

"That's training," said Stefan. He patted his pocket, then took out his crystal and held it for a moment. "My parents don't even know."

"They'll be at the game," Rich added. "Along with mine." He tugged on Stefan's elbow. "You need to chow some lunch down now or you'll get sick." He looked at the girls. "Football stuff. Can't play on a full stomach."

"Riiiight," said Bailey. She didn't grin till the two had trudged off. Then she looked at Ting. "Who'd a thunk Rich would make a good mother hen?"

Ting chuckled. A family stopped at the booth, and Ting explained the blue wellness charms along with the clear crystal study charms to the mother who had an entire flock of small ones hanging onto her. After a few moments of consideration, the harried woman chose the most peaceful blue talisman she could find on the tray and bought it.

"Don't forget to put it to your forehead when you meditate," Ting called softly after her. The woman nodded, amidst the chatter and crying of the little ones tugging on her and begging to go to the popcorn booth.

Bailey just stared and tried to hide a shudder.

Ting nudged her. "Just 'cause you don't have brothers or sisters!"

"That was a lot, though. Like a . . . a . . . pack."

"Oh, they weren't all hers, I'm sure." Ting looked after them, a sympathetic expression on her face.

The day slowed down. They ate their tuna salad sandwiches in the booth, and customers came by occasionally, but most people were more interested in the many food booths scattered around the hall. Food was clearly the fastest way to a teenager's spending money, Bailey observed. She brightened, though, when a familiar, owl-shaped face crowned by unruly brown hair came toward them, spectacles sliding down his nose.

"Henry! Henry Squibb!" she called out, and waved her arm.

The former Magicker turned slightly, and looked at them both closely. He had his arm full of squirming toddler, a girl in a frilly dress with a matching ruffled panty, kicking her dimpled bare toes against her brother's hip. He came over to the booth, a slightly curious and anxious expression on his face, which washed away when he said, "Oh, yes. I remember you. From camp. How are you?"

Sadly, he didn't really remember them the way they had been, having washed out dramatically from Ravenwyng. Bailey smiled cheerfully at him anyway. "Fine, and you? Remember Jason and Trent? Jason has a computer now, he could use help with. He wants you to e-mail him."

"Oh. Really." Henry looked slightly baffled again, then brightened slightly. "Jason and Trent had the cabin across from me, right?"

"That's it!"

Ting took a piece of paper and wrote down the e-mail addresses for both Jason and Trent, and passed it to Henry. The owlish Henry had to grab it quickly before his sister squealed and captured it instead. A tiny piece of paper hung from the corner of her mouth already, the same color as one of the dance flyers someone had been passing out earlier.

Henry flushed slightly. "Abbie likes to eat paper," he explained.

"Don't we all?" Bailey grinned at him, and they laughed.

He bounced the toddler in his arms. "I'm just watching her for my mom . . . she's around here somewhere."

"Playing big brother, huh?"

"Trying to. It's not always much fun, but she's being good today. I guess the paper tastes great." Henry grinned then, like the old Henry who'd gone to camp with them and had a crystal and had done wondrous things. Not like the Henry who'd taken the Draft of Forgetfulness and forgotten all about having been a Magicker.

"Henry! Henry?"

He turned. "That's Mom. Gotta go. Thanks for the addresses. I'll try to write 'em, if I don't forget." Waving, he moved off across the crowd and disappeared.

Ting let out a sad sigh.

"I know," said Bailey. "I know." They finished their lunch in silence, then each sat alone as the other took a break and came back. Selling the charms didn't seem nearly as neat as it had earlier. The day wore on.

A girl came toward them across the hall, as if homing in on a beacon, letting nothing in her way slow her down. She reached them, and gripped the counter with both hands.

"I need a love charm."

"Well, we have friendship charms," answered Ting slowly, pointing out the tray.

"Noooo. No. I was told you had love charms." The girl was older, like their friend Jennifer, probably fifteen or so. She was pretty in a natural kind of way, but her eyes looked a little red as if she might have been crying.

Ting gave her a troubled glance.

"Not exactly. I mean . . ." Bailey shifted from one foot to the other.

"You *have* to. You don't understand. She's trying to steal him from me, and . . . and . . ." The girl's voice broke. She had a tissue wrapped around the fingers of her left hand, and it looked like it couldn't take too much more damage as she brought it up to her nose.

Ting got out a pink pendant and pressed it into the girl's hand. "It's only luck. Like a reminder. That's all."

"But . . . but . . . they said . . . you said . . ." Her face began to crumple.

Ting squeezed her hand closed around the pendant. "It's just a crystal. But it'll like, absorb your feelings, and when you give it to him, he'll think of you." She smiled hopefully.

"It'll help, then?" Their customer sniffled.

"Couldn't hurt. But in the end, you're the important one. He either likes you or he doesn't. Do you see?"

"Well. All right, then."

Ting patted her hand. "Good luck," she said. A moment of concentration passed over her face, and Bailey knew instantly that she was putting extra into the crystal before it left her hand entirely.

She waited until the girl wandered off, her hands clutched together.

"That was nice of you."

Ting shook her head. "Someday," she answered, "you and I might be like that."

"I hope not!" Bailey stared across the hall in a brief moment of terror. They leaned against each other. There were days when growing up looked like it might be unbearable.

All in all, they sold out early and had time to sit and enjoy some fresh handspun cotton candy before Bailey's mom showed up to get them. She came into the hall in a crisp shirt and blue jean shorts and running shoes, looking ever so much like an adult version of Bailey that Ting was amused. She found them after just a moment of looking over the milling crowd at all the booths.

"There you are!" She waved and trotted over. "How did it go?"

"Fine," answered Ting as Bailey cried out, "Wonderful! They've already asked us back for the Spring Fling."

"Really? That's quite a compliment. Maybe you two have a

future as custom jewelers." She checked her watch. "We can just make the last matinee. Ready to go?"

There was a moment of silence in the great hall, as if everyone had stopped talking. Rare, but it happens. And into that moment stumbled their desperate customer followed by a tall, rather ordinary looking boy, a silver chain dangling from his hand. It caught both Ting's and Bailey's attention, and it seemed, everyone else's.

"Caroline Wright, I adore you!"

She put her tissue up to her nose. "What were you doing in his locker? You weren't even supposed to *touch* that!" She cast her glance around, as if searching urgently for someone. Both Ting and Bailey ducked.

"I had to get Brian's books for him. But what does Brian matter? I'm the one whose heart you've captured!" The youth stopped, and pressed his hand to his chest, totally unaware of the attention he was gathering.

"Oh . . . oh . . . go away!" Caroline blew her nose on her tattered tissue. "Now, Franklin. Now!"

He looked at the floor. "As you wish." He began to move away, through the crowd, dejected. Then he thrust his fist into the air, their charm grasped tightly in it. "But I'll not give up! Not until you see me as the one who cannot stop thinking of you!"

"Right pew," Bailey muttered. "Wrong church."

Caroline let out an annoyed shriek as he turned and left the hall, still crying out, "I adore Caroline Wright!"

Bailey bolted to her feet. "Now," she said firmly, tugging on her mom's arm, "is a really good time to go."

She and Ting beat her out to the parking lot, still looking over their shoulders fearfully for Miss Wright who seemed stuck with Mr. Wrong.

"It'll wear off," Ting repeated several times. "It'll wear off."

Bailey's mother looked at her in concern as they piled into the car. "Are you all right, dear? What will wear off?"

"Calories," answered Bailey firmly for Ting, who seemed in a bit of shock as they buckled their seat belts. "From the cotton candy. Just . . . calories."

"In that case," Bailey's mom said thoughtfully, "we'll get our popcorn unbuttered." She started the car and off they went.

Can't Bear these Changes

RICH looked at his friend with grudging admiration. "All suited up? Ready to go?"

Stef grunted, his helmet dangling from one hand. His uniform, which his mother had worked very hard on to launder away grass stains from the last game, sparkled, and his shoulders bulked so high with his new pads and gear that his neck nearly disappeared. He shifted from one foot to the other as the locker room cleared and everyone ran out to the field, metal door clanging shut after them. He could hear the dim sound from the bleachers, the roar of students from schools all over the city here for this game. And he was going to be in it! Varsity. Not bad for his second year in middle school. He'd worked hard for this, though, eating right, training, memorizing the playbook, waiting for his third game.

Rich pounded and tugged on his pads a little, making sure they sat exactly right. His red hair stood out under his baseball cap in unruly shocks. "Now," he repeated. "Don't be drinking the red gatorade if it's out there. It gives you headaches, all right? Just head for the water cooler."

"Right." Stef shifted his weight uneasily. "I gotta go, Rich. My parents are in the stands and everything." He could feel the heat through his buzz cut, even with his helmet off. The backs of his ears felt itchy.

"Okay, okay." His friend stood a moment. Stef was keenly aware that Rich had tried out for football, too. He hadn't even made the lowest team, his body too thin and wiry and a little clumsy. But sharp. Rich could think circles around him. Rich pounded him into place one last time. "Okay!" He turned away and trotted out of the locker room. Stef moved to follow, then stopped, dizzy.

The feeling of something wrong swept him. Everything felt tight. His shoes hurt. Stef stared down and then gave a low groan. Oh, no. Not now. Not *now!* He patted his tight football pants down. Nothing. Nothing at all . . . his crystal was in the locker. Letting out a yell for Rich, he kicked off his athletic shoes and shuffled toward his locker. Hands going thick and clumsy, he managed to paw it open. He grabbed his crystal between his palms and held it tightly, reciting the words Tomaz had taught him, which always seemed to help.

Nothing.

He mumbled the words again, trying to focus. All he could think about was his stomach rumbling. He was hungry!

Stef threw the crystal back into the locker and began to shed his uniform as quickly as he could before it was ruined. His football dreams, his whole life, fell to the floor around him and he lifted his head and let out a bawl. It echoed through the empty locker room. A heavy metal door opened and closed.

"Hey, Stef! Coach is waiting and he's mad."

Stefan-bear dropped to all fours and bawled again, frightened and very unhappy. Rich came around the corner of the lockers and stopped dead in his tracks.

"Oh, boy," he said. Then added, "Oh, bear," unable to think of anything else.

The young bear sat down miserably on his haunches and looked at him, pawing at his nose unhappily.

Bending over, Rich quickly gathered up all the gear and thrust it back into Stef's locker which gaped open, stuff falling out of it as if it had burst. He looked at the crystal on the top shelf. Stef must have been trying to get it. Too late for that now. Too late for anything except to figure out what to do with one overgrown cub. How was he going to sneak Stef-bear out of the area without being seen? He stared at the ceiling in exasperation where the great golden bear of the school's seal stared back.

No. It couldn't be that easy . . . could it?

Rich pivoted on his heel. In the trainer's stall, extra jerseys hung. He grabbed one with a great double zero on the front and tugged it over the bear cub's head. Stef-bear licked him, long pink tongue raspy and harsh. "Cut that out. You've gotta wear this. And mind me. Really, really focus, Stef, okay?"

The bear cub stared at him, nose wrinkling. It pawed at the football jersey.

"Stef! I mean it! Listen to me. This is bad stuff. You want to be thrown in a zoo or something worse? Like a . . . a . . . a lab? So people could poke at you and try to figure out what happens? No way! Now you just focus on me and try to do what I tell you to!"

The bear cub let out a bawl, just like a frightened toddler. Rich sighed and threw his arm around the burly animal's neck.

"I won't let 'em get you. And if they do, I'm going, too. You won't be alone, okay? But I can get us out of this . . . I think. Just keep that jersey on." Rich hugged the bear cub tightly. "And . . . ermmm . . . take a bath sometime soon when this is all done. You stink." His face squinched together at the odor of the furry beast who was clumsily trying to hug him back. He pushed the cub away. "Jeez. That's enough of that."

The metal door clanged open. "Olson! Hawkins! Get out here!" The assistant coach filled the doorway as he bellowed.

Rich put both hands around the bear cub's muzzle, muffling the surprised noise from the animal. It came out like a throaty retch, sounding just awful. He called back. "That's Olson, sir! Just nervous about the game. He's ralphing. I'll have him out when he's done!"

The coach grumbled, then the door slammed shut. Rich let go as Stef-bear pulled his lips back from white teeth and shook his head uncomfortably. He made a bleating sound of protest, curled up, and went to sleep.

"Oh, man." Rich sat down on the bench. Sometimes Stef changed in his sleep. If that happened, they'd both be out of trouble. But if it didn't . . . muffled shouts from the football arena drifted to them. Rich sighed and pulled out a worn-out paperback novel and began to read. He'd wait it out . . . for now.

After fifty very long minutes, the cub rolled over and sat up, bawling, pawing at his eyes, and making hungry noises. Rich groaned and looked at him.

"Don't look at me like that." Rich straightened. "Okay, here's the plan . . . we go out to the old softball field and—"

The bear reared back on his haunches, both paws waving frantically.

"Nnnno, no, no, no. Don't worry. You're the mascot, see? If anyone sees us, which they won't, but just in case." Rich tugged the football jersey back into place, and pulled Stef's duffel out of the locker. "I've got your clothes and stuff in here . . . jeez, Stef, get some clean socks, will ya? Anyway, when you change back, you're all set. We just duck in the bushes and wait for you to return. Got that?"

The bear cub mournfully shook his head.

"Don't worry. I'll repeat it later. Follow me." He couldn't be positive, but he was pretty sure the bear cub was nearsighted with a real knack for falling into prickly bushes and scratchy stuff. Luckily, there wasn't too much of that around the school athletic fields. He tugged on the cub's thick neck, pulling the shapechanger after him. He grunted as he hauled the animal's stubborn weight behind him. He stopped and looked the bear right in the eyes. "This is the only way. Just stay calm. They're not looking at us, everyone will be looking at the game!"

Stef-bear rolled beady brown eyes, then began to lumber toward the locker room door. He stopped at the end of the locker row, and swung his head about, nose sniffing vigorously. Rich patted his shoulder. "Come on, come on!"

The bear ignored him. He began pawing at one of the locker doors in determination until the dented locker swung open. Bawling in satisfaction, Stef-bear reached in and pawed out a big package of sweet honeybuns. Wrapper and all, he crunched contentedly.

All Rich could do was watch as the bear ate up the honey and cinnamon pastries grunting happily and spitting out shreds of cellophane here and there. He cleaned up the mess but there was nothing he could do about the sprung locker. It had been kicked shut many a time, and now had passed the point of no return. He closed it and taped it with a few inches of bandaging tape, and began to urge Stef-bear outside with him again.

Having eaten and with the tantalizing flavor of honey inside rather than outside, the bear cub seemed ever so much more willing to go along with Rich. He leaned heavily against Rich's denim legs as they walked around the back of the roaring stadium and the sound of whistles and thuds and heavy grunts of football battle. Rich put his hand down on his friend's furry head. Stef was in there, somewhere, sometimes in charge and sometimes buried under animal instinct. Tomaz had told them both how to keep Stef in charge as much as possible through his crystal; otherwise he'd be a great danger to himself and others. He didn't know how much either of them was in charge right now.

He grabbed one of the cub's round ears. "Stay with me, now," he said, as they moved into the shadow of their bleachers. A great roar went out as they did, and his friend pressed hard against his knee. The slanted cement structure over them rumbled with stomping and noise. "Just a little farther."

They might have made it safely, but Rich forgot two critical factors. One . . . restrooms. Two . . . small children who had to use the restroom frequently. Oh . . . and three . . . the restrooms were under the bleachers.

He froze as a harried woman with a youngster in tow came at them. "Momma, look. It's a bear in a shirt!"

Without looking, she tugged on his hand, "No, dear, it's just someone dressed up." Like a freighter on high tide, she plowed toward them, child in her wake.

"No, it's not! Lookie, lookie! It's real. It's a baby bear!"

"Matthew, of course it's not—" She paused. Her nose wrinkled. She turned even as Rich pulled on the bear cub's ear, hard, to hurry him past the two. Matthew hung on his mother's hand, his own grubby fingers outstretched and reaching. "What *is* that smell?" She frowned at Rich and Stef-bear.

Matthew grabbed a handful of fur and pulled it loose as Rich tried to haul Stef-bear past. The cub let out a bawl of pain and bolted, nearly knocking both mother and son on their backsides. Rich cried out and lunged after as, head down and paws churning, Stef-bear headed straight for the football arena! Rich skidded after in hot pursuit.

The crowd roared. Stef-bear bawled. As he galloped onto the field, players scattered and referees began to blow their whistles like steam engine trains.

"What the heck is that?"

"How cute! It's got a football shirt on!"

A kid leaned over the bleacher rail, waving his arm, trying to grab at them. "Mommy! I want one!"

"Now, honey . . . that's real. We can buy you a stuffed bear at half time." His mother placidly knotted her hand in his jacket and pulled him back onto the bench next to her.

Stef-bear came to a wary stop, head up and swinging about. Rich stopped, too, and tried to sneak closer. Both coaches turned and stared at Rich.

"Mascot," Rich said.

"Good lord, that's real."

The assistant coach shaded his eyes with his clipboard. "That a guy in a suit? Isn't it?"

"No, sir, it's a real bear. A cub. I can only have him here a little while, then the owners are gonna pick him up. He . . . he's an orphan and they're training him for movies and commercials and stuff." Rich stood uneasily. His friend reared on his haunches, weaving a little, pawing the air, uncertain whether to bolt again or drop to all fours and go to Rich. He held his breath. Both bleachers on both sides were filled completely and he blinked in the sunlight. It suddenly seemed like not such a good idea to have Stefan out here.

The scoreboard turned numbers, and they were behind 13–6.

The crowd roared as the other quarterback fired a long pass. Their coaches groaned, stalking up and down the sideline in frustration. And then, the pass popped out of the receiver's hand as the tackle hit him. The brown ball headed right at Rich and Stef-bear, squibbing across the grass, people diving right and left at it. The bear let out a loud bleating sound and bounded onto the field after the ball.

Darting between players and across the game line, Stef-bear went after the ball as if it were something to eat. Reflecting on it later, Rich decided it did resemble a beehive, a little. Who knew how well bears saw? All he knew was that the bear cub was off and running wild!

He pushed his way through the standing players to see Stef-bear pounce on the rolling football. He shook off two tackles as he took the ball in his jaws and munched. It deflated with a loud pop, but the bear hung on and began a field-long scramble toward the goal posts. Half the players ran from the scampering cub, the other half tried to ward him off.

By the time the whistles stopped blowing, Stef-bear sat happily in the end zone, flattened football hugged to his chest. The jersey was in shreds around him from missed grabs and tackles.

The coach turned around and bellowed at the stunned players, "By George, if the mascot can make a touchdown, so can you!"

Rich caught up with Stef-bear and took the ruined football away from him. It hung limp from his hand as the refs and equipment manager caught up with him. He handed it over, his face warm with the embarrassment of it. The equipment guy just laughed and gave it back. "Maybe he can like chew on it or something."

Coach Dumbowski waved energetically at him. "Get that critter off the field! This isn't a zoo, Hawkins. Where's Olson? I know he's in on this. Hiding in the locker room won't help!"

"He . . . he'll be out in a few, Coach. He really is sick. He . . . ah . . . he ate a bear snack!" Rich held tightly onto the bear cub's ear and it bawled in protest at his pinching fingers.

"A football field is no place for animals," the coach bellowed, although they were scant feet away. He was louder than the referees who'd just announced the touchdown was "no good!" "Get him out of here, and next time, get permission from me before pulling a stunt like that! And find me Olson!"

"Yessir. Thank you, sir!" Rich tugged on Stef-bear, *hard*.

The buzzer rang for half time and the band came marching out. Whatever nerve the bear cub had left broke as tubas and trumpets blared and drums thundered. He raced out of the stadium and Rich, gear bag in hand, took chase again, puffing and muttering.

There was no sign of the creature. Rich slapped his forehead. He cast around and shook his head.

"Oh, man." All he could do now was wander about, hoping his friend would stay hidden if he transformed back. Rich grumbled to himself as he crossed the different athletic fields, heading back to the farthest corner practice field. People would think him some kind of pervert wandering around till he found someone leaning from the bushes, going, "Psssst!"

He took out his own crystal and sat down on the ground, leaning into the sagging backstop of this little used soccer/softball field. Cupping it in his hands, he tried as hard as he could to focus on his friend and the creature he turned into. He didn't know what else he could do. Maybe in the quartz's depth, he could possibly see him or something. Feel him.

Like a magnet, the crystal whipped around in his hands, and he lost his grip. It went sailing over the backstop and into the shrubs. A moment later he heard an aggrieved bear cub grunt; it rolled over into a more irritated human grunt.

"Hey, buddy," Rich said and went to retrieve both. "You made a touchdown! And we've gotta get out of here!"

After long moments, Stefan got hold of himself and emerged, pale and shaking. He sat down and began to pull his clothes out of the gear bag. "Oh, man. Oh, man. My parents are out there, wondering what's going on. What if I turn again?"

"Just keep in control, Stef. Just do it."

Stefan finally stood, clad head to toe in Milford football splendor, but his face looked as if he could throw up any second, just as Rich had been telling the coach he'd been doing. "I can't do it."

"It's your choice." Rich listened. "Sounds like half time is over." He crossed his arms over his chest. "I'm just a trainer, but

I think I'm gonna go join the team for the second half. Maybe I can be of some help or something." He picked up his gear bag.

"You can't just leave me here."

"Sure I can. Look, Stef, you wanted to be on this team. You gotta know there's gonna be moments when you turn, and you've gotta learn how to handle them, especially if there's something you want. Dumbowski is looking for you, and you're gonna blow it, big time, if you don't show. Not to mention your parents." Rich turned and started to walk back.

"Rich!"

Stefan's voice sounded high and really frightened. Rich turned back around slowly.

"You'll keep an eye on me?"

"You know it. You just keep focused. I've got your crystal here in my bag. Anytime you're on the sidelines, come by and hold it for a few."

Stef rolled his eyes, then gave an agreeing grunt and fell into step with him.

The coaches were standing by the sidelines and Dumbowski glared at Stef. "Where have you been?"

"Sick, sir."

"You look white as a sheet. You up to this?"

Stef gripped his helmet tightly, then pulled it on, to hide the paleness of his fear. "Yessir!"

Coach shook his head, stepping back. "I want no more antics like that last one. Any more and you're cut, got it? No wild animals, no getting sick on game day."

"Yessir," the two echoed.

"All right, then. Get in there." Coach pointed his pencil at the bench. "Next play, you're in the rotation. Rich, I've got one ankle somewhere needs taping. Find him and take care of it." Both nodded.

"Good." Dumbowski smiled slightly. "Only thing worse than a sick football player is a disappointed parent." He tilted his head and looked up into the stands, where Rich saw Stefan's parents stand up and bounce up and down, screaming, as he stepped onto the field's edge and sat on the players' bench.

Rich let out a sound of relief before turning away. Like a first down, they'd missed catastrophe by a bear's breadth.

Spooky Old Houses

MCINTIRE came to Sam's to pick him up after lunch, which had not been planned, but the Dozer had an appointment that drove him past the neighborhood, so Jason rode with him. He liked driving with the Dozer in his business truck. It rode higher than other cars on the road, and it had a kind of solid comfort about it. It didn't matter if he was sweaty and dirty from practice either, as long as he didn't eat or spill something in the cab. Conversation with McIntire was at a minimum except for every now and then when a development he'd built got pointed out, or interesting and helpful tidbits of advice would be offered. Sometimes the advice could be deadly dull, but often it would be something interesting or offbeat. Today McIntire was quiet, and that meant he had a lot on his mind.

Jason had a lot on his mind, too. What was the Curse of Arkady and had it infected his crystal, rendering it nearly useless? If it had, would his crystal ever regain its power, or would he have to search and bond a new one? And if a curse was not the reason his crystal had not protected him in the park . . . what was?

What was it that could make him fail so terribly at something that had become as natural to him as drawing breath? Was this how Henry Squibb had felt? Would it stay? But he wasn't empty, he could feel it inside him, filling him. He just couldn't rely on it. It was like not being able to trust himself.

Jason shivered slightly, and forced his thoughts to other things, such as their destination.

"Where are we going?"

"Place up on the bluffs. An estate, actually. I may be doing some work there."

Jason thought he knew where, remembering the talk from a few weeks ago and a few mutterings recently. "The McHenry house?"

"Mmmm," answered the Dozer. "Looks like it. Sudden death in the family leaves it available to sell. There's probate and business for them to deal with, but they want me to look at it in advance." His big hands tightened on the steering wheel till the knuckles went white, and then he forced his hands to relax. Jason decided that silence might be the way to go, so he looked out the window and enjoyed the drive.

And it was a bit of a drive, past the boundaries of town, off the main freeway onto a side road that wound into the bluffs overlooking the ocean. A little two-lane blacktop took them along a hidden coast. The homes built among the eucalyptus and California oaks were scattered, all custom, with acres between them. He wondered what kind of development someone wanted to build here. Homes? Condos? Apartments? A center of some kind? They'd gone miles without passing a grocery store or fast food stand. He rather liked that, though. This was country, and open, and although the rains hadn't come yet and it was dry, it was pretty. He liked it like this. He got the feeling the Dozer did, too. Some places, he told Jason once, need more buildings. Others don't. Men ought to be smart enough to know the difference.

They took a corner and a sparkling cove dominated by a

wide, sweeping bluff came into view. The water drew his eyes naturally, the tide going out in curls of white foam, the wide Pacific beyond pulling it back into its vast steely blue depths. There was a nice spill of beach, looking private and untouched. Then Jason tilted his head to look up the bluff, and his heart nearly stopped.

The stuff of nightmares, he thought, looking at the dark, brooding house. *His* nightmares. His blood went cold and stayed that way, as his hand froze on the edge of the car window. His senses whirled about him as he looked up at what could only be described as some sort of fortress, gated and overlooking the bay like some gargoyle of an estate. He could almost see the power tumbling about it, chaotic and wild, as if the building were caught in its own storm of mana, and it hurt to look at it.

"Wha–what is this place?"

"This is the McHenry estate."

He'd known it, somehow. Maybe it was the telltale fact that the road seemed to lead right inside the coal-black gates, or the fact that McIntire was driving right up the hillside toward it, or even just the fact that he was here, now, and the fortress of his nightmares yawned in front of him. He gripped the door handle tightly. A small sound escaped his clenched lips.

"It's something, isn't it? I don't agree with his taste, and it doesn't look like any castle I've ever seen, but word is, it was taken from a famous old fortress in Wales. They also say he had every board and stone shipped over to build it. Back in the day when Huntington and other bankers and railroad men were building their homes near Los Angeles, McHenry was building his here. Been here over a hundred years now, and someone wants to tear it down."

"Will they? Will you?"

"I don't know the answers, Jason. Yet. Want to come in with me or sit and wait?"

He wanted to sit. He never wanted to set foot on the paved driveway, but he knew he should. He should see the difference between reality and his nightmare. The road gate, for one, was already vastly different. No dragonhead lock, no quest to pass this far, not even a security buzzer to press so that it might open. It hung open as though locking it were out of the question, yet as they drove through, pain battered his skull for a moment. His head snapped back in surprise at the sharpness of it. Jason sank down in the seat, blinking, his ears ringing.

Gatekeeper. Of all the thoughts that used to run through his mind when considering Magick and all its uses, that had never been one. Yet it had been he who had found the gateway between Camp Ravenwyng and an alternate domain, shaky though the passage might be. Now Gavan Rainwater and all the elders were working their Talents to try and make both planes steady, with an open doorway between them, so that the camp could be a sanctuary for those with Talent the real world might exploit or condemn. Efforts had not yet been successful. Jason was the only Magicker who could reliably enter the valley he'd found beyond the old rusted back gate of the summer camp. Other tries sometimes brought success, other times left Gavan or Tomaz wandering around in a blind canyon for hours, going in circles.

He was the Gatekeeper, like it or not.

He put one hand to his temple as McIntire eased his vehicle into the sweeping, circular driveway of the McHenry estate. His head felt as though it could throb hard enough to burst, and then, suddenly, all was still. He sat up on the truck seat. McIntire had parked and turned the engine off without Jason even noticing. He looked back and saw the gate swinging slightly in the wind. It wasn't a Gate, not by any means. More like a two by four to slam someone in the head with for trespassing through the real Gate.

McIntire seemed unaware of Jason's reaction. He got out

and looked over an older white Mercedes already sitting in the driveway, then glanced over his shoulder at Jason.

"Getting out? This old place might be fun to look at."

He slid out gingerly as if the gate might try to bludgeon him again, but nothing happened. He could smell the sea salt spray from below, and hear the cry of gulls as they wheeled and hung in the air over the gulf for long moments of time, then plunged down to the ocean to dip and skim. He could almost feel the dizzying drop in his own gut as they fell, but they had outspread wings to catch them. Jason ran a few steps to keep up with McIntire's long stride, and they both reached the carved double front doors at the same time. Jason wasn't surprised to see that a great, bronze door knocker with a grotesquely twisted gargoyle face hung in the center of the main door.

Jason nearly winced as the Dozer grabbed the ring and thumped it, hard, three times. The noise reverberated inside the building as if he'd struck an immense Chinese gong. For a moment, he thought he caught the huge, lumpy nose of the gargoyle twitching in time with the brazen echo. The estate seemed to groan in answer, but his stepfather apparently noted none of the fuss as he released the door knocker and shifted his weight, waiting impatiently. They heard footsteps long before the door actually opened, and as it did, Jason leaned with it, to peer inside.

A huge cavernous entryway met his gaze. No wonder everything echoed. It looked like a massive concert hall, with room to hold his school's marching band. Doors at the far end stood open, leading to the north, west, and south. The individual who held the entry door, however, looked like a butler, formal suit, cravat, vest, and all, and wings of graying hair combed back into dark full hair, a strong Roman nose, and disdainful eyes as he gazed down at them.

"May I help you?"

"I am William McIntire, builder. I have an appointment."

"Ah. Yes." The butler looked down at Jason. "Your apprentice?" One eyebrow rose in disapproval at Jason's attire and state of appearance.

"My son. He'll be fine." McIntire managed to look a bit insulted, as if the butler insinuated that Jason would be difficult to tolerate.

"Follow me, then," the tall man said quietly. He strode off, with a slight lean to his left, one shoulder a tiny bit higher than the other, as though he walked into a strong wind and had to forge his way through it. He wore ankle boots and the heels drummed solidly on the gleaming wooden floor as he trod it, the planks creaked as they all crossed over it. For a moment, Jason stared downward, as if he could discern the hollow levels below, just waiting for the boards to give way and open up, just as in his nightmares, though these boards had not been dry-rotted by time and neglect.

Even the Dozer glanced down once as if pondering what lay under the flooring. That reassured Jason only in that it wasn't his imagination, but made him worry more about the soundness of the structure. The complaints of the boards sounded much louder under McIntire's heavier footfalls. Only the butler seemed not to notice or care as he led the way through the northern door at the foyer's far end.

While the entry had been somewhat recognizable from his dreams of the place, nothing beyond the northern door was. Understandable, as he usually fell through into the catacombs below long before getting very far in his exploration. Jason looked about warily. It was, in many ways, a very imposing fortress or castle, even in these times. It also seemed nearly empty, what furniture there was pushed to the walls, with wooden crates lying about, either nearly filled or already hammered shut and stenciled. He tried to read the wording as they were hurried past, but it seemed to be in a language other than English or something equally baffling.

McIntire let out some words of appreciation as they were led into a great library, its built-in shelves still full of books and other wonders, lined by empty crates on the floor, the wood paneling gleaming with polish and care and beauty. A great ox-blood leather sofa lined one half wall, and a sprawling desk of golden oak held court in the center of the room. Three gentle-men were seated at it, two behind and one in front. His vision blurred as a fraction of the power that had hammered at him earlier, struck at him now. For a few moments, he could hardly see or stay on his feet.

Jason scrubbed at his eyes. One of the men got to his feet smoothly and left through a door in the side paneling, but not before Jason caught a blurred and fleeting glimpse of his face. He stumbled over an edge of fringed Persian carpet lining the floor and when he looked up, the man had completely disap-peared from sight.

Jason righted himself quietly, and stood by McIntire in near shock. It looked like . . . but surely couldn't have been . . . the man who had attacked him in the park that morning.

Coinkydinks

H E wanted to hide behind McIntire's burly frame, but he knew he couldn't. It wouldn't help any, and he'd just be that much more conspicuous. All the same, it was trouble just being here. He didn't believe in coincidences anymore. The Hand was behind this, somehow, and drawing his family in. Magick forbidden or not, he would do what he had to.

From beside McIntire's elbow, Jason watched the procedures warily.

"This is a fine old home," William McIntire said, as he leaned forward and offered one of his great hands to shake.

"It is a liability on the current market, but I agree it was made well years ago. Upkeep, however . . ." The man leaning forward to connect with McIntire was tall and thin, with graying red hair and a small sprinkling of freckles over his face. He was older but not old, slender, and held more power in his voice than in his bones. He shook swiftly and straightened, tapping a portfolio stuffed with papers that lay on the desk.

"I understand you're the one to do the work."

"I am, if it's the project I've been sent permits and drawings on. It's an ambitious project and one I think would utilize many efforts. I take it you are spearheading the holding company, and the sale on this place has gone through?"

"Yes, and nearly. We're trying to get a head start, so if we need any loans or funding, we can point out our many strengths. Having you as head of construction would certainly be an asset."

McIntire smiled only a little. He wasn't easily flattered, Jason knew. In fact, he tended to distrust flattery, preferring to earn praise after a job was done, not before it. Jason moved a little, trying to get comfortable, his legs slightly stiff after the morning's runs, and was instantly sorry as attention shifted abruptly to him.

"Brought your son along?"

"Yes, but he knows this is business. He'll keep quiet and not repeat anything."

"A good lad, then." The redheaded man studied Jason a moment, then lost interest as Jason did his best not to look noticeable.

"What do you think, McIntire? Is this a project you'd be interested in? Think you might like to come on board?"

McIntire chuckled. The deep noise reverbrated throughout his hefty frame. "We'd need to talk time, crew, and salary, of course." He looked around. "I'd hate to tear down a place like this. Maybe you could consider making it your anchor. Break it into artists' lofts upstairs and a restaurant and a few nice shops or offices down here. I know an interior decorator that would give her eyeteeth to have this room as her studio."

The other looked about, too, as if seeing the room for the first time. McIntire's finger jabbed the air. "Those are good woods, some excellent carpentry in those bookcases, the paneling."

"Yesss . . ." the other answered slowly. "We hadn't considered it really. An anchor for the development, you say?"

"A bit of class. Never hurts."

"True. We've plenty of grounds left to do what we want. Hmmm. This place is immense, you know. A good seventy-five acres."

"I think that leaves you room to be generous here. Consider it. Despite my reputation, I hate destroying to develop. This is a solid, good building with ambience and craftsmanship, and it would be a shame to pull it down."

"We have our reasons, but I'll put your ideas out. May I tell them you're interested?"

"Work up an offer to put on the table, and we'll talk again."

"Done, then." The red-haired man smiled faintly, and picked up his portfolio. "I've got a flight out, but I'll be back soon and perhaps we can do lunch then. I promise I'll have an offer to put on the table that will make it worth your while."

"Do that." They shook hands firmly and when McIntire let go, stepping back and dropping his hand to his stepson's shoulder, Jason thought he felt a creepy-crawly tingle. It had to be his imagination. Had to be.

"Can you find your way out or do I need to . . ."

"We're fine," McIntire rumbled. He turned Jason about and guided him out the library door and back down the way they'd come in. He did not say a word till they were buckled into the truck and easing out the entry gates. Then he let out a low, heavy sigh. "I don't know if it's the place or the people," he said, "but it makes me uneasy."

Jason gave a nervous laugh. "Do you really think anyone would want to have shops or stuff in there?"

"Not sure, really. The McHenry place has some historical significance, and it really shouldn't be leveled, but as far as going to a restaurant in there or anything else, I dunno. Made the hair on the back of my neck stick up."

"Me, too!" Jason put a hand back there and scratched a moment.

The Dozer laughed at him. He patted his shoulder again. "Nice thing about my job right now is that I don't have to work with people who make me feel like that! He could put all the money in the world under my nose, and I could say no if I wanted to." McIntire looked in his rearview mirror as they drove down the winding roads and could smell the ocean. "If I wanted to," he repeated slowly.

"But you're not sure yet."

"No. Not quite yet. If that bluff is developed, it ought to be done . . . how can I say it? Gently? Without disturbing the area around it, and without putting a great stucco eyesore on the face of the earth. It would be a challenge." McIntire trailed off, lost in thought. He shook himself. "Need to get you home. Showered. Homework this weekend, no doubt, and other stuff, right?"

"Right." Jason settled into the seat as the truck bumped softly over the country lane roadworks. McIntire guided the truck off a side road, and Jason realized they were leaving by a different route. They descended the cliffs and reached town in less than half the time by not following the shore but cutting straight through the bluffs.

His stepfather let out a soft sigh as they drove into town. "That's the way to cut the road," he said, as he turned down their block.

"It's much faster and shorter."

"That it is, and even though it's through the foothills, in the long run, the environmental impact on the land and the neighbors will be better. We can put in two lanes either way, do a bit of terraforming, and it'll actually be better for the watershed and wildfire danger." Then McIntire smiled at him. "Always business."

For once, Jason felt like he understood his stepfather completely. He had business at home, Magicker business.

"Jason?" Dr. Patel's soft voice sounded more in his forehead than his ears, as he gripped his crystal. "May I come in?"

He sent through a "yes," and in a moment, her petite, sari-wrapped form stepped out of nothingness and into his attic bedroom. She smiled as she removed a damp bath towel from a corner of his bed and sat down. "Trouble, you said?"

He plopped down in his desk chair facing her. His hair was still wet from his shower, and his clothes smelled fresh from the dryer. The red dot on her forehead looked like a small jewel. "Big trouble. I was chased by wolfjackals this morning."

"What? Here in your town? Tell me everything." She folded her hands in her lap, frowning, and prepared to listen. He spilled out everything he could remember, and with a gentle question or two, thought of even more, including the McHenry house and the fact his crystal had failed in providing either a shield or awakening the beacon.

"That is not good," she said quietly when he'd finished. "Our only hope in keeping you safe is that the beacon works. It did in trials. I cannot understand it, but Gavan and Tomaz need to be informed immediately. I'll handle that. I am pleased to see your wits kept you safe." She paused, tucking a strand of dark brown hair behind her ear. "Jason, may I see your hand again?"

"Well, um . . . sure." He put his left hand out and she took it in both of hers, leaning over it and peering closely at the scar along the back of it.

"I have long wondered," Dr. Patel said, "if there was a tooth splinter or something lodged beneath that marked you. It remains sore, though it appears healed, and you've told me it twinges from time to time." She looked up, into his worried expression. "Does it pull on you?"

"Pull?"

"Do you sometimes feel as if you want to do something you shouldn't do? Or . . ."

"Come over to the dark side?" he started to crack, and then stopped. Suddenly, it wasn't all that funny. He'd wondered, too, if the wolfjackal had really marked him. It said it had, but he'd decided that the beast had only been trying to psych him out.

"Yes," she answered.

He shook his head vigorously.

"Good. Well, then, I'll leave you to . . ." Her gaze swept his bedroom, and she smiled. "Clean your bedroom and work on homework?"

He blushed. The doctor nodded, still smiling. "I'll meet with Gavan and Tomaz as soon as possible. This is serious business for us." She gave him a quick hug before standing, putting a hand to her pendant, and then disappearing with a slight waver and whoosh, leaving behind only a faint aroma of sandalwood, her favorite perfume.

Jason rubbed his hand. Her probing fingers had set off a dull throb, as though the scar were freshly bruised. Again. He sighed. He hadn't told her about the Magicker at the McHenry house or any of that, and wondered if that had been a good or bad thing. But he didn't want to seem a coward or anything, and he wasn't sure how he felt about it. Had he seen the Magicker? He wasn't sure. And if he was wrong, it could bring even more trouble, which he certainly didn't need.

The Game's Afoot

H E checked his watch. Dinner was a good hour off, even if his stomach was rumbling in protest. He grabbed some emergency rations from his desk drawer (granola bar) and sat down, munching happily, careful to eat nowhere near his keyboard. Even as he watched the screen, mail came up and he dusted his hands off quickly so he could see who it might be.

It came from HobbitHenry, and for a second, he had no idea who that could possibly be. Then he cried, "Henry Squibb!" and pounced on the mail to open it. And, yes, it was from Henry, dear owl-faced Henry with his unruly hair and innocent eyes, and he could practically hear the voice leaping out at him through the words.

Dear Jason! How are you? Have any more wicked popcorn fights? My sleeping bag still explodes every now and then in the storage part of my closet. I can't seem to keep it tied tightly enough. I saw Bailey and Ting, and they gave me your new computer address. Welcome to the 21st century! <g> I heard you and Trent play D & D. Always

wanted to try that. Well, I've gotta babysit while Mom goes grocery shopping. C U Later!

Jason sat back in his chair, smiling. Henry sounded nearly like his old self, as far as Jason could tell, except that he'd no memories of his brief time as a Magicker during their summer together. The Henry who'd been led off after drinking the Draft of Forgetfulness had been a quiet, humble boy embarrassed at having caused trouble and being sent home early. It had broken Jason's heart to see him like that even though he knew it was necessary and Eleanora had assured him that it wouldn't hurt Henry in the long run.

He'd have to remember to tell Eleanora that Henry was back to his talkative, if bumbling self. Then he fired off a letter to Trent, in hopes that Trent would agree to let Henry into a D & D session. Not only did he want to stay close friends with Henry, but Jason had some small hope that Jonnard Albrite had not permanently damaged Henry by stealing his powers. Trent didn't come up as being on-line, and Jason squirmed in his desk chair with disappointment.

In the meantime, he opened up other e-mail that was waiting for him, and began to frown, reading in some alarm, and some amusement. Leave it to Bailey and Ting to set the rummage sale on its ear, but what had happened to Stefan, through Rich's account, could only be bad.

And, Rich added at the bottom of his mail,

It's all I can do to convince Stef not to join a circus! I don't blame him, he's afraid of being caught and taken apart to see what makes him tick.

Jason wrote back a quick, encouraging letter that the Magickers were aware of the mishaps and increased danger, and included his own stalking, and warned everyone to take care and practice their shielding. He paused as he wrote that. Even though his had failed momentarily, he had to have faith in it. Had to! His crystal was bonded to him, and as much a part of him as . . . well . . . a hand or a foot. To think of having to give it up and get another sent chills down the back of his neck.

His stomach rumbled again, reminding him that one small, crumbly sweet granola bar was hardly a whole dinner. Like it or not, he was going to have to raid the kitchen. Maybe Joanna would let him have an apple or something. He was starving!

Jason pushed away from his computer and dropped the trapdoor to his room in a hurry. No one answered his entry into the kitchen, although the oven was on and the timer ticking away. He grabbed a big shiny Red Delicious apple and bit down into it, savoring the sweet juices as he heard voices and trotted toward them in the living room. At the last possible second, he recognized oily tones and tried to swerve away, but Joanna's sharp ears heard him in the hallway.

"Jason! Come in, come in." He was backing out, but her voice hooked him and reeled him in like a gaping fish, all the way into the living room where she sat. McIntire ruled the great armchair, and the school psychologist perched at one end of the couch and smiled at him.

Of all the places in all the world, Statler had to find his way into Jason's living room.

He stopped dead in his tracks to gather his wits.

"Wasn't it nice of your counselor to stop by and visit with us?" Joanna smiled brightly at him. Statler had evidently interrupted her cooking, for she still wore her apron appliqued with big yellow sunflowers and small blue butterflies.

Jason wondered who on Earth would want to claim Statler? He looked as pasty white as ever and, even though he'd cleaned up and changed into Dockers and a soft gray shirt, he still looked unwholesome somehow. "Umm . . . well, yes. He's not exactly mine, though. I mean, he's there for the whole school, you know?"

"Ah, but, Jason. As you know well, my concern at the school is the welfare of youngsters like you who need help coping with the school yard bully. The bully is an age-old problem and not likely to go away, so we've decided to work at the other end . . . with his victims."

Joanna blinked, and her careful air of cheerfulness fell away. "Jason?" She looked at him. "Are you having trouble at school that I don't know about?"

He shifted uneasily. "Not really."

McIntire leaned his bulk back onto the armchair cushions, and the entire piece of furniture groaned and swayed a bit as he did so. "You'd know who to come to if you did, right?"

"Yes, sir."

"Actually," Statler Finch said, and he leaned forward, putting his hands on his knees, looking into Joanna McIntire's face. "Jason's already had a bit of trouble on a regular basis, and I've been asked to intervene by the vice principal. You see, it's the school of thought among administrators now, as a result of several tragedies around the country, that it's the bullied ones who need watching, and skill coaching, or they . . ." He paused. He turned one hand over and gestured through the air. "Or they snap."

The only snap he felt like would have done a wolfjackal justice. Jason clenched his jaws in case he felt himself slip.

"Oh, Jason," cried Joanna in dismay, as if she had failed him in some fatal way. She buried one hand in her apron pocket and knotted it.

"It's nothing, Mom, really. It happens to everyone once in a while." He shrugged.

"Denial," murmured Statler, his dark eyes glistening as if in sympathy.

"I can deal with it."

"I've failed you."

He kept from rolling his eyes at Joanna. "I'm fine. I can handle it!"

"Self-delusion." The counselor's eyes brimmed.

"Look. If the vice principal who is supposed to be the enforcer can't handle him, I can," said Jason firmly, then promptly regretted it as Statler cried out, "Shifting of blame!"

He stifled a groan away from Joanna who winced with every proclamation of his mental instability from Statler, and looked desperately at McIntire. His stepfather rumbled, "I think we can work this out fairly quickly, Statler. Jason's a good lad, if quiet. How can we help and what do you suggest we do?"

A look of triumph flashed across Statler's face, one which he quickly squelched. "I think it would do him a lot of good to work with me once a week, after school, say, for an hour or two, and then monthly meetings with all of us."

Joanna seemed to relax a bit. "Oh, I think we can arrange that!"

"Mom . . ."

McIntire frowned. "I might not always be able to make a monthly meeting. Business is booming right now, and it looks like I might have another development coming up. Unless it would be all right to just meet with one parent now and then?"

"The world is full of single parents, and they do their job wonderfully," gushed Statler. "I'm sure we can do without your presence now and then, just as long as we have your support in the program I'm going to lay out for Jason."

"Mom . . ." he tried again, shifting, but her attention was avidly fixed on Statler. Did mice stare at a snake before they were gobbled?

"What about my daughter? Should she be part of the family meetings?"

"She's Jason's . . . half sister?"

"Step."

"Yes. By all means . . ." Statler's eyebrows waggled in furious thought patterns before he said happily, "Yes, we can work on a number of difficulties in Jason's life. I recommend we bring her in on the second family meeting."

Joanna exhaled happily. "Oh, good."

"Mom!"

Joanna looked at him, surprised. "Yes, Jason?"

"Mom, I have soccer after school, every day, until the season ends. I can't miss practices for counseling. They'll throw me off the team for missing."

Her hand moved inside the apron pocket, clutching and unclutching whatever it was she had hidden in there. A tissue or handkerchief, no doubt. "I think," she commented slowly, "that we need to look at the whole picture, and that is dealing with your problems now. There will always be soccer later."

"But I'm on the first team *now*." He stared incredulously. How could this be happening to him? "Next year is . . . well, it's next year! I worked hard for this. And you promised after last summer . . ." His voice trailed away. He couldn't complain too much about missing soccer camp last summer, and discovering he was a Magicker instead. Still . . . losing soccer now? How unfair could things get!

McIntire cleared his throat, sounding like approaching thunder. "I'll have a talk with your coach. Maybe something can be arranged. It's for your own good, son." He stood. "I'll make sure it's arranged. Sports and learning should be balanced, and you're right, you worked hard for this. I'll do what I can to make sure you're kept on the team. But you have to promise to work with Mr. Statler here."

A thin smile touched the counselor's lips.

That sounded like a deal, and one which he really did not want to make. He looked from McIntire to Joanna and back to McIntire. "All right," he agreed reluctantly. The last thing he wanted was Statler poking around in his brain! He'd have to make the counselor think he'd cured him, and quickly.

If he couldn't, he was cursed. Absolutely cursed, and he was beginning to think it was no coincidence.

Strange Thing in the Night

TRENT scratched his temple for a moment. *You enter the room,* he typed, *and find . . . what? What do we find? Whose perception is highest? This would be a very bad room to get killed in.*

There was a tiny lag while both Henry and Jason received and pondered his thoughts. The dungeon game room stayed on pause, tiny avatars showing the positions of their characters at the threshold of the area. Various intriguing items appeared to be awaiting them, just like chessmen on a chessboard. They could be idle but a moment or two, then they would draw monsters and the room, sought as sanctuary, would no longer be safe. Trent had his own ideas as to how they should proceed, but this was a committee decision, and so he waited to throw his suggestions out until the others spoke up.

He sat back in his chair, folding his hands behind his head, and stared for a moment at his *Lord of the Rings* wall calendar. The realization of how close it was to Halloween struck him. The days had been flying by, so busy was he in school and in trying to figure out the Magicker lore to see if there was any way, any way at all, he could catch up. If it wasn't in the blood, maybe it was in a book. Something, somewhere. So far, he hadn't found one. But then, he was the only one who hadn't been hit with the Curse yet either. Maybe there were some advantages to not being a novice magician.

The thought of not having any Talent at all ran through him like a deep wound, though. Seeing the others with their crystals doing wondrous things and hoping to learn more . . . well, it hurt. Keeping up the bluff that he was doing what they were, only they were too busy doing their own thing to catch him, or his crystal was drained, or he was joined to Jason and Jason was handling it . . . well, it was an ugly pack of lies and likely to get much, much uglier. And, sooner or later, one of the elders was bound to notice it, too. He didn't know how they hadn't, so far. Henry's misfortunes had been his good luck, he supposed. Even when a Magicker, Henry's Talent had been wild and unpredictable.

Trent grinned as he remembered how they'd been taught to fill their crystals with light, so they could act as lanterns, and Henry's had gone up in a spout of flame. For a few days after, he'd handled his focus with a big oven mitt covering his burned hand! With Henry pulling stunts like that . . . his perpetually exploding down sleeping bag and out-of-control crystal . . . who'd notice Trent?

Only Jason knew his secret and that he'd revealed only when they'd had to face down a storm of uncontrolled magical power called mana, and the fiercesome beasts of the Dark Hand as well as the dark Magickers themselves. And Jason never demanded a thing of him. Not that he tell the truth or resign or anything else. To Jason, Trent was as much a Magicker as anyone else.

If only.

*   *   *

Message windows began to pop up. Jason wanted to investigate the perimeter of the room cautiously. But Henry said, and Trent read it a second time to make sure . . . he wanted to use the natural thieving ability of his halfling character to scan the room and detect any traps, mechanical or magical, awaiting them. Interesting. Very interesting that in the D & D campaign they'd begun, Henry relied more and more on magical type abilities, almost as if his subconscious mind was nagging at his conscious mind to remember. Jason claimed he could see more and more signs of it; Trent had been more naturally skeptical. This game, though. Henry had been quick to choose a character with natural abilities and an affinity to magic, if perhaps a bit chaotic . . . well, maybe Jason was right.

Jason quickly sided with the other two after Trent presented the option to him, and they proceeded but not before Henry's clever character tripped an immense trap by releasing a djinn from a clay jar . . . but it all turned to the good as the djinn granted each of them a wish to be used in the future. All too soon their gaming time came to a halt and they had to stop, saving their progress in this labyrinth of adventure. Henry left after a quick, excited note, saying he had to help take care of his little sister before bedtime, but Jason lingered to talk with Trent a bit.

I think you're right. Looks like Henry's recovering some of his memory and some of his abilities!

Jason fired right back at him eagerly. **I know. This means a lot of things change. One . . . the Hand could go after Henry again, without his even knowing it, to drain those powers again. So he's gotta be protected till the elders decide if he can or should be taught again. And two . . . any of us can be drained over and over for the use of the Hand. That can't be good.**

Trent rocked back in his chair. Shades of the *Matrix!* Being used over and over to fuel the bad guys? He didn't like the sound of that at all. And it was clear that Jason had been considering all the ramifications for a few days.

He helped Jason mull over the problem of the school counselor, too. Both decided that it was best not to do anything, make it look like Jason was cooperating completely, and try to make the school officials think so, too, until Finch and the vice principal decided their idea had either 1) worked or 2) was worthless. They talked a minute or two longer about what to do, then his father knocked softly on the door, reminding him it was bedtime. Obediently, he said good night to Jason and signed off. As he was crawling under his blankets, the door swung open a crack, his father leaning in.

"Everything all right?"

"Everything is fine!" Trent punched his pillow and then pulled his comforter up. His dad half smiled. He missed the days when his father gave his famous ear-to-ear big grins, but those times were gone. They'd left when his mother died, and he wondered if they would ever come back. He knew *he* didn't feel much like it except for those rare moments when Bailey cracked him up or Jason made him feel good about having friends and hanging out again.

His dad stepped in, which he rarely did, and tucked the comforter around him tighter. "Getting on toward winter," his father said. "And while there aren't winters here like I had back home as a kid, you still need to keep warm." He paused, his hand on Trent's head a moment. Then, without another word, he turned and left.

The bedroom door stayed open the barest of a slant, golden light from the living room raying in from the lamps there until his father turned those out, too, as he went to his bedroom. Trent waited a moment or two, then snuggled in deeper and felt himself drop off to sleep.

* * *

Jason found himself back at the mansion. Only this time, as moonlight silvered across cold and crackling sand, and he approached it with all the wariness he could, Jason knew it was the McHenry house. Naming it didn't make it feel any safer or nicer than it had before. His skin crawled. Yet he could not keep himself from entering the gate and beginning the walk across the curved driveway to the massive wooden doors. He was saved, at least, from entry through the old family cemetery with its unexpected potholes as rotting caskets and catacombed grounds gave way at the slightest step!

He put his palm upon the burnished golden oak door. The wood felt warm, almost hot to his touch, yet it continued to send shivers down his back. He didn't want to go through that door, but he had to. He was drawn as if he were a piece of metal and a powerful magnet lay beyond the door, but also his own curiosity and need to know drove him along. With hands that grew colder by the minute, he finally moved to the great door latch and lifted it. The doors swung inward with a great creaking, not of rusting hinges, but of heavy weighted wood, as if a massive barrier gave way. The knowledge and sound sent chills down his back. The McHenry house didn't have a latch, it had a knob like any other door he usually used . . . and it had opened out.

He had already known he was dreaming. But not why. He never knew why he dreamed what he did . . . if he was reliving the past or anticipating a future. Jason only knew that there were these moments in his dreams he had to endure. All he could do was watch, and remember, and hope to learn something later.

He pushed the heavy doors open with a grunt. A draft of air blasted him in the face, nearly gusting him out of the threshold . . . hot, smoldering air that stung his eyes and immediately dried his nostrils and lips. He coughed and put his hand up to shade his face.

Before he could see anything or take another step, from the dull and red glowing interior of the darkened hall, a furred shape growled and leaped at him. Jason fell back and scrambled out from under the wolfjackal, his free hand instantly wrapped around his crystal.

His shield flared to surround him, and the beast tumbled away, snarling, ivory fangs clashing angrily at empty air. Jason kicked out, catching its sleek wolfish body and sending it skidding back into the McHenry house. He slammed the doors after it.

He'd enter when he was ready, and prepared, and not before.

Jason woke, panting and sweating lightly in spite of the cooler night air, and he lay for a while until his heart stopped drumming so loudly and he thought he could sleep without wolfjackals prowling his dreams.

Bailey woke to the sound of the teakettle whistling from the kitchen. For a moment she thought of FireAnn, with her fire-red, naturally curly hair pulled back into a kerchief, her voice with a mild Irish lilt, fixing cuppas for those who wanted it while she got busy sorting herbs and recipes for the day's cooking. But it wasn't FireAnn. It was her mom, and Bailey grinned. Even better!

She threw herself out of bed, waking up Lacey who chittered sleepily from her cage before diving back into a nest of colorful bits of tissue. Bailey grabbed her robe before popping into the kitchen. Sure enough, her mom had a big china pot waiting to brew tea, and a plate of sweet rolls ready to be warmed in the microwave.

"Wow. Party?"

"Mmmmm," her mother said, not quite looking at her as she picked up the kettle from the stove and filled the teapot. Almost instantly, the smell of jasmine and oolong tea filled the kitchen as steam issued from the neck of the china pot. It had to steep for a few minutes to really taste good, so her mom straddled the kitchen stool across from the counter. She looked at Bailey. "Hon. We need to talk."

The good mood dropped from her. Bailey hadn't heard her mom sound like that since . . . well, since the divorce. As it hadn't been easy news then, she didn't think it would be anything easy now!

Her mom fixed her mug of tea with a squeeze of lemon and a heaping teaspoon of sugar just like Bailey liked it, before sliding it over. Bailey immediately wrapped her suddenly cold hands around it, and waited.

Her mom sat down, and tried to smile. "I talked to Ting's mother early this morning," she said.

Bailey's throat got very tight. "What's wrong with Ting?" The words barely squeaked out.

"Nothing, hon!" Her mom reached over, and patted her hand. "But it's not good news. Her grandmother is very ill right now, and Jiao is going up to San Francisco to be with her for the next few months while she undergoes chemo and radiation therapy, and she's taking Ting with her. Ting will be going to school up there."

"Wow. Is everything going to be all right?"

"They hope so, but the treatment can be . . . well, it's not easy. So Ting's mom thought it best she be there and that this would be an opportunity for Ting to get to know that part of her family better and to experience the culture up there. San Francisco has a very large Chinese community, you know." Her mother sipped at her mug of tea. "It's not like you're losing her, after all. There're phone calls and the Internet."

And crystal. "Yeah, I know," muttered Bailey. She picked up the spoon and clattered it around inside her mug. "I mean, she has to go, and I understand, but I'll miss her. And she's gonna miss Thanksgiving and Christmas and New Year's . . . we had stuff planned."

"I know, honey."

Bailey tossed her head. "We'll just have to make the best of it, right?"

Her mother smiled. "Right."

On the Other Hand

"**S**LACKER!" said the coach, practically frothing at the mouth. "The one thing I won't have on any of my teams is a slacker!"

"Yes, sir," Jason mumbled.

The coach stabbed a finger through the air. "My office, after practice! Now get your buns out there and do drills with the rest of the team!"

"Yessir!" Jason bolted.

He joined the line for sprints, and then danced in place with Sam to keep warm on this chilly, gray afternoon while waiting for his turn.

"That went well," Sam commented dryly.

Jason nodded. The two of them had figured he'd ground Jason right then and there for even being given the note that Joanna and McIntire had sent to school. Instead, he'd studied it, turned red in the face, and ordered Jason to his office after a few well chosen words on athletics building character and commitment to the team and hard work and effort. Thirty minutes of the old, "There is no I in team" lecture.

He windmilled his arms around. The last thing he wanted
was for the coach to think of him as either a troublemaker or a
weasel, and the sooner he could look him in the eye and convince him of that, the better he'd feel. In the meantime, he
could look forward to being worked twice as hard. He took a
deep breath. Whatever Coach threw at him, it would be better
than sitting in Finch's office, waiting to be dissected.

Sam dug his elbow into Jason's side. "Look who's
watching."

Jason twisted about and saw a spindly figure sitting in the
dilapidated bleachers that ran alongside the fields. He seemed
to be taking notes. Jason groaned. Statler Finch himself.

Sam flashed him a look. "Don't worry. Coach won't let him
stay."

"Hope not." Jason had no time to say anything further as he
was barked at, and he lunged into movement, down the pow-
dered white lines and withered grass, weaving a running line
between bright orange cones. When he got back, sure he'd
beaten his best time, Coach merely looked at the stopwatch in
his hands, frowned, and made a circular motion with his hand.

"Again."

Jason inhaled. He dashed off without another sound, frowning, his arms and legs moving with controlled speed, cornering
and slaloming through the cones as if he were a downhill skier.
He finished, a little out of breath, and slowed going by the
coach.

Coach frowned. He jerked a thumb. "Again."

Jason had it in him, but there was the rest of practice and
maybe a short game ahead of them yet. He took a deep breath
and set off again. This time, to save his legs, he took it slower.
Because he was tired and without a break, he'd begun to wobble
a bit. All he needed was five or ten minutes, but Coach wasn't
giving him that. So . . . rather than touch a dreaded cone, or
worse, knock one over, he had to slow down. Be careful. Treat

the cones as if they were opponents to be wary of, another team to outfox. It took him minutes longer, and when he trotted back to his coach, he did so with every intention of stopping this time and gathering a few minutes' break, at least.

Coach looked him over. "A bit slower that time."

Jason nodded wordlessly. Deep breathing felt good.

"What did you learn?"

Jason, his hands on his knees to rest, looked up in surprise. "Learn?"

"Learn." Coach jabbed a thumb out to the field. "Those cones are the enemy. What did you learn?"

Puzzled, he thought about it and then warily offered, "Not to give the enemy a break, even when I'm not feeling my strongest. I took it as fast as I could and still be careful."

"Good. Take a breather, then go up and join the others." Coach turned his back on him, clipboard in hand, eyes already downfield on another player.

Surprised, Jason fell back and got a small cup of water from the big water cooler at the field's edge, washed his mouth out, and then went over to join Sam and the others. He mulled over what he had said that had pleased the coach, even if only in some small way.

The coach didn't stay pleased. By the time Jason plopped down on a spare chair in his office and waited for the man to appear, he was drenched in sweat, scratched from two falls in the bushes and brambles that cornered the practice field, and wondering if he had enough strength to walk home. He had about two seconds of peace before his coach walked in, coffee cup in hand, and muttering.

"I'll make this short. Finch and I have had a talk. If you've got problems," and he stared hard at Jason, with a piercing gaze, "I don't want to see them on the soccer field. Since this is school business, I'll allow you the one day. Once. But if you want regular counseling, then you either do it before school, in the early morning . . . or you quit the team. Got it? No slacking. None."

"But, sir, this isn't my idea."

"I don't know if it is or if it isn't. Vice Principal Murphy has been working to institute some new things here at school, most of which I support. As to this counseling . . ." Coach grunted before continuing, "All I know is that you asked to be part of a team, and that team deserves your commitment and focus. You show promise, Adrian, as an individual player, and as a team asset. I expect you to live up to it, but the team deserves to come first."

"Yes, sir." Jason stared down at the corner of the desk.

"Well? Doesn't it?"

"Yes, sir, it does. I want to play soccer more than anything!" Well, nearly. But he wasn't about to discuss Magicking with a soccer coach whose style consisted of that of a drill sergeant, even if the oath of Binding would let him. Which, thankfully, it wouldn't. Supposedly. He had no intention of putting the oath to work. The thought of sitting in front of the coach, his jaws fixed and voice frozen was, well, unthinkable!

"Then let me put it to you this way, Jason. In another year or so, you'll be in high school. An honors curriculum there means classes before and after the regular schedule. Zero hour and so forth. It's early, but students who want to get ahead work for it. If you want to stay on this soccer team, you're going to have to work for it, too. Not just on the field now, but off it. If Finch wants you to come in for counseling, tell him it's before school, not after. After school, you belong to me! Got that?"

There was no way not to get it. Jason nodded.

"All right, then. Shower and go." The coach set his coffee cup on the desk and began flipping through his clipboard.

Jason stood, then hesitated a moment. He cleared his throat. "You'll . . . ah . . . mention this to Mr. Finch, too? Kinda back me up?"

Coach looked up, and drilled him with his dark, unblinking eyes. Then he nodded. "I'll suggest it to him as well. But it's your job to make the arrangements."

"Yessir!" Jason bolted for the door before anything else befell him.

Absolutely cursed, no doubt about it. Not a one.

Words interrupted a tomblike silence. Brennard's hand gestured fitfully in impatience.

"I asked if all was in place."

The disciple bowed before his master, and remained quiet for a moment, staring down. "The beginnings of the trap are in motion, Brennard. The bait has been offered. I think all shall take it. And we are poised, waiting."

Brennard thoughtfully brushed his dark hair off his forehead. "We don't want any mistakes this time."

"No, sir."

He leaned back in his chair, one arm over the back of it, turned sideways for better support as if his tall, seemingly young body still needed the strength of the furniture. And, thought his disciple, perhaps it did. Brennard had nearly died, after all. "The problem is," Brennard said slowly, as if thinking aloud, "there are too many for us as well as for them. The nets are flung too far to catch all these little fishes, and so we need to concentrate on the ones who shine brightest. We will start here, and make an end here if we can. You have the teeth? The other items I prescribed?"

"I do." The disciple took out a small cloth sack and laid it on Brennard's knee.

"Excellent. Modern times are quite remarkable, actually, but also, it means that we all must take care, very very great care about what we are doing. Being revealed now would make our situation extremely precarious. Until that time when we have secured the Havens for ourselves, we are as vulnerable as Gregory's motley lot is, a fact I am not quite certain they have fully realized. If they have realized, they have not acted upon it. That becomes our advantage. I am not afraid to make use of anyone's weakness."

"And what of the dreams?"

Brennard frowned. More than an expression, the atmosphere about him seemed to fray and discharge irritably, tiny sparks zapping through the air. "They are but dreams."

"Not omens."

"Memories, at best."

"You are certain?"

Brennard stood then, looming over his disciple. He did not care to discuss the disturbing dreams he had, nor the ones he sent out. "As certain as I care to be, for the moment. Unless you would care to be divorced from your body and soul for a while, and explore that metaphysical plane?"

"N–no. No, sir. Thank you for the opportunity, but I am not prepared." The disciple bowed, quite deeply, and did not look up for a very long moment, until he heard Brennard's breathing return to normal. His glance flicked up then, and he saw Brennard sit back down, gathering up the small cloth sack he'd delivered. Then and only then, did the disciple hazard to straighten up, although he took a wary step backward. Truth be told, there was nowhere on this world he would be out of Brennard's reach. Those were the ties between them, the pledges and vows chaining him, in return for his favored disciple status. Gladly, he'd given them then. Now, he was not so certain.

"Then," remarked Brennard almost mildly, "do not question me."

"Master." He inclined his head. "I don't question you, but myself." He sighed. "It is not a matter of dedication, but confidence, I suppose."

"Working with me will dispel that. There are great things to come. Many, many great things. This is a world of vast possibilities now, with many struggling countries just waiting for strong and guiding hands. We will do well. Trust me." Brennard smiled then, drawing his cloth sack closer and cradling it for a moment against his chest. "We will do very well indeed."

Rich sat down in his backyard, almost hidden amid the long purple shadows, facing the back screen door on his porch, although he did not expect his parents to come through. They were spectacularly uninterested in him with the exception of his grades, and he made sure he always got decently high grades without having to study endlessly. Still, he didn't want anything that he, Stefan, and Tomaz Crowfeather were going to say or do to be noted. The very thought of it, or perhaps something else, sent a chill down his back. "Gad," he muttered, and shivered. "I hate that."

"What?" Stefan looked at him, dumbfounded.

"Chills down the back of my neck. Like somebody was walking on my grave."

"Ugh." Stef shuddered in disgust.

"It's just an expression," the quiet adult sitting with them said, smiling reassuringly. Tomaz Crowfeather sat cross-legged on the ground as the last shreds of the day were obscured by a pink-and-gray sunset, and he held up something in his hands, so that it caught the very last beams of sun raying through the clouds. He lowered it, and gave the small muslin bag to Stefan.

"What is it?"

"As long as you wear that," Tomaz said quietly, "you will not change skins."

"You're kidding me?" Stefan held the bag in his big, square, chubby hands and then turned the fetish bag over and over in his palms.

Rich felt the coldness in the ground through his jeans and shifted uncomfortably. "You can keep him from doing that?"

Tomaz nodded solemnly. He dropped his hands to his knees, big heavy turquoise stone bracelets rattling, and rested, watching the two of them.

"No shit." Stefan quickly tied the smallish bag to the chain he wore about his neck.

"If you could really do that," remarked Rich slowly, "why didn't you do it a lot earlier and save me . . . us . . . a lot of trouble?"

"Yeah." Stefan looked Tomaz over. "Not to mention even more trouble."

Tomaz gave a slight smile. "It is not wise."

Stef grunted and began to fidget. "I don't get it."

"Okay . . . shifting into a bear in front of a football stadium full of people is wise?" Rich put in quickly.

"Nor that." Tomaz considered Stefan calmly, then looked at Rich who'd asked the question. "But it is not good to suppress that which is meant to be. Talent needs to be trained, shaped, and nurtured, not bottled up and hidden. Tell me. Would you rather deal with a Stefan-bear you've known all along and trained with—or a full-grown, frightened, and confused beast who suddenly erupts into the world?"

Both boys rocked back slightly. Stef's thick face showed a fragment of surprise, while Rich paled at the implications.

Stefan let out a grudging exhale. "Since you put it that way."

Tomaz nodded. "I do."

"So . . . if that's my Talent . . . what happens now?"

"Until you understand the Curse, he'll stay suppressed, for a short while. And if we can't keep it under control, then . . ." Tomaz's voice trailed off.

"Then what?" Rich shifted.

Stefan rubbed his nose, grumbling.

"Well, in the old days, we'd move out where the Talent wouldn't be a problem. Now, we don't have as many options."

"So I'm stuck until I just explode?"

"Hopefully not." Tomaz got to his feet. "But, in the mean-time, you won't be changing skins unless you want to."

"That's good, I guess."

Crowfeather nodded. He pulled the watch chain from the pocket of his denim vest, and an arrowhead-shaped crystal fell into his weathered hands. "Until we meet again," he said quietly, moved one hand over his crystal, and disappeared.

Stefan's hand went to his neck. He gripped the bag of herbs and magicks tightly, as if clutching a lifeline.

Rich patted his friend's shoulder and stared off into the gathering night. Magick used to seem fun. Even when it was bothersome. Now it seemed downright dangerous.

. . . **And**, typed Bailey quickly, **she's leaving Saturday night and I won't see her for months and months!**

Have you talked to her yet? And you can't be like that, Bailey, we've got the crystals and the computers. We'll be in touch with her constantly. She may even be better off up there, out of the Curse's reach. Jason pondered that. Did the Curse have a circle that it affected, and could it be escaped from? Like a field or area of infection?

Or she could be in worse trouble, with none of us around to help!

Jason stared at his computer screen. For a second he wondered if Bailey would be able to communicate at all if they took the exclamation key off her keyboard. The thought made him grin. **She'll be fine,** he told Bailey. **Do you think Gavan or Eleanora would let anything happen to her?** On the other hand . . . and Jason stared at his left hand splayed over the keyboard, his scar meeting his inspection. On the other hand, they hadn't prevented *that*, or the attack a few days ago. And without a beacon working reliably, could the elders help any of them?

Or were they on their own with only each other to depend upon?

Don't worry. Ting will be fine.

Bailey shot back at him—how fast did she type, anyway? Faster than she talked, which was like a bullet. **I want to get together Saturday to say good-bye. All of us, if we can.**

That might be a little risky. Crystal travel was something they hadn't quite mastered, but he didn't want Bailey any more upset than she already was. So he answered, carefully, **Sounds like fun. I'll see what I can arrange.**

She signed off after telling him a quick joke, and the computer was suddenly very still. Funny how Bailey could just fill up a place, even when she wasn't actually in it. He turned off his computer, pushed the keyboard aside, and pulled over his algebra book, his thoughts churning round and round as if he were still doing laps around a soccer field. Whatever the Curse of Arkady was, they had all better start working on a cure.

Dragon Magic

"HOUSE of the Flower Dragon," Ting repeated slowly.

Jiao Chuu smiled and teased her daughter gently. "As many times as you have visited my mother's house and you never noticed it was so named?" She took a sweater and folded it softly into the suitcase spread open on the bed as Ting sorted through keepsakes she wanted to take or leave behind.

Ting shook her head. "I only remembered the dragon along the roof. I don't think I ever bothered to look much closer." She studied the photo taken of her, her mother, and her grandmother a year ago last summer, all of them standing in front of her grandmother's San Francisco home. Behind them, a long, serpentine dragon coiled upon the roof tiles.

Chinese dragons were so different from European dragons, from the kind that Jason and Trent talked about facing in their D & D games. Far from looking like some kind of dinosaur, Chinese dragons were long and thin and incredibly agile, a source of great wisdom and knowledge, as well as fierceness and honor. She had always known their dragon was a protector and

guardian, but she had never before noticed the bright chrysanthemums he carried or wore sometimes in a garland about his
neck. The bronze flower petals had been cloisonne enameled a
brilliant orange-red. She looked at the picture of her grandmother's home again. "Can I scan this and send it to Bailey? I
want to tell her she's got Lacey, but I've got a dragon!"

Jiao laughed gently. "Perhaps when we get settled in. Your
father already has the computer boxed up."

Ting nodded, and put aside the photo to pack. She looked
up at her mother, who was beautiful in many ways, but who
seemed tired and a little sad this day. "You had something you
wanted to tell me?"

Jiao sat down next to her daughter. "Plans have changed yet
again. We'll be flying up early Saturday instead of driving on
Sunday."

Oh, no! Ting flinched at her words, but said nothing. All of
this was hard enough on her mother without her making it
worse, but she'd miss their gathering! What would Bailey
think? And all the others?

"I'm sorry," continued Jiao. "I know you had plans to go for
pizza with everyone, but Father thought it would be easier and
safer for us to fly up and we'll be with Grandmother that much
more quickly."

That was, after all, what was important. Ting nodded, soft
black wings of hair tickling the sides of her face as she did. "I'll
call and explain," she said. "And they'll understand. That's
what friends are for."

Her mother stood without another word except to hug her
quickly before moving off to finish her own packing. Her out-
wardly calm face, as usual, hid her true emotions, but Ting
knew the worry in her eyes would not leave till Grandmother
was well again.

Ting tapped the crystal on her homemade bracelet. She'd
miss everyone, and especially the shenanigans Bailey had

planned, but there was no helping it. Anyway, a short flight would be much easier on everyone than a long drive. Bailey and Jason would have to wait. It's not like she was going away forever or had no way to see them again. She had Magick now.

Already pulled out of school, she waited until afternoon to call Jason so he could pass the word around, not wanting to hear the disappointment in Bailey's voice.

"Hello, McIntire residence."

Ting recognized the cool tones of Jason's older stepsister Alicia. "Hello, Alicia, it's Ting. Is Jason home yet?"

"Doesn't seem to be. May I take a message?"

"Please, if you would. I won't be able to meet everyone at Trevi's Pizza tomorrow. We're flying up to San Francisco early. Tell him I'm sorry, but I'll send e-mail as soon as my computer arrives and gets all set up."

"Will do. Sorry to hear about your grandmother."

"She will be all right, I think. It's just going to take a while. Thank you," answered Ting softly before hanging up the phone.

Alicia hung up the kitchen phone and looked around. Breakfast dishes were supposed to be done by Jason before he went to school, but the kitchen looked a mess. She'd have to clean up before everyone else got home. Alicia wrinkled her forehead, then let out a huffy little snort. Funny how messages could be forgotten over kitchen messes!

Statler Finch looked at Jason over a cup holder filled with pens and pencils, all with wicked, sharp points. "Since it's been requested, I will make myself available in the early morning for our sessions, Jason, but only if you can assure me you will be here."

"Once a week."

"For now. Depending on my findings, I may need to see you more often."

Jason managed a wry grin. "Depending on how screwed up I am, huh?"

Statler did not smile back. Something cold glinted in his eyes. "Something like that." He leaned back in his office chair which let out a low squeak. "So. I understand you and your friend get trash-canned every few weeks."

"Something like that."

Statler made notes on his yellow legal pad and did not seem to notice the faint echo and irony in Jason's voice. Without looking up, he said, "Tell me how you feel about that."

"Smelly. And, you know, hassled."

"Hassled? How?"

Jason thought it should be obvious. He shrugged. "Late for class or soccer workouts. That sort of thing."

"What sort of thing?" A thin smile snaked over Statler's lips.
"Trouble."

"How does trouble make you feel? Anxious? Angry perhaps?"

"It makes me feel a little angry that guys like him get away with it, and I'm the one who gets yelled at. But it's not really all that much, so I don't think about it."

"You push it aside, then?"

Jason felt the hard chair seat under his thighs and the early morning chill of the school office and tried not to squirm. "Not really. I forget about it because it's not important."

"What do you mean by that?" Without looking up, Finch skritched lines of notes across his paper pad, the pencil lead dragging with an irritating noise over the yellow lined paper.

"I mean what I said. This time next month or the month after, it's not going to matter. It's not one of the things in life that's important." At least, that's what he tried to tell himself while he was figuring out how to peel yesterday's old hamburgers off today's book report.

"So you don't have to deal with it?"

"I didn't say that. I have to deal with it every time they do it, but . . . it's not going to matter in the long run as long as I keep my cool. Dozer says it's important to know when to pick your battles and when not to."

The counselor looked up sharply. "So this is a battle, then?" The pencil lead creaked and scratched furiously.

Jason suppressed a wince. "Not really. I think my stepdad means choosing when you're going to stand and when you're going to give way. Settle." For a second there, something had flickered in Statler Finch's eyes, and Jason didn't like the looks of it. He reminded himself to choose his words very carefully.

"Tell me about your dreams, Jason."

There was no way he was going to do that. He looked down at his shoes quickly, in case the defiance showed in his eyes. He shrugged. "Usual stuff, don't remember most of 'em."

"Any dreams about school?"

"Sometimes. You know. Forget the locker combination, or late to a test. My stepmom says not to worry, those are just anxiety dreams. She says almost everyone gets those." There was no way on Earth Statler would get him to talk about his nightmares, though. He told no one about those, because he knew that, twisted and dark as they were, they dealt with Magick.

"Perhaps," Finch responded, making another note.

Jason stared uneasily for a moment, wondering if other people really did have those kinds of dreams or if Joanna was just trying to soften life for him, as she often did.

Before he had the thought finished though, the ten minute warning buzzer sounded for late honors, and he was free, his time up. If he triple hurried, he might make the last of soccer practice. He bolted to his feet.

"Very well, then. Try to have a good weekend and week and I'll see you . . . early . . . next Friday morning."

"Yes, sir." Jason lunged for the door and as far away from Statler Finch as his quick feet would carry him.

He was right, he had missed all but the last thirty minutes of soccer and it seemed the coach had saved wind sprints and laps for last today, just for him. Sam was puffing and sweating as he joined him and grinned. Jason didn't mind.

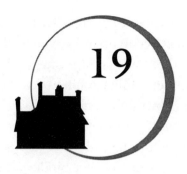

Warm Fuzzies

BAILEY fidgeted on the kitchen chair, pushing her books away from her. Homework, homework. Normally she loved homework, odd as that was, but thinking about losing Ting, seeing her go so far away, and being worried about her friend's grandmother all made her very restless today. Ting had to go, there was no doubt about that; the family needed Jiao Chuu and Ting, but that also left Bailey behind. And who could she share with now? Who would understand what she meant when she worried about things? Her mother didn't, couldn't, know. She shared everything with her mom, but Magicking was one thing she couldn't. Not only did the Oath of Binding keep her jaws wired shut, but just the thought of it kept Bailey from saying anything. It was hard enough being a single mom . . . being a single mom to someone who was learning Magick and could be taken away? Locked up forever while being examined to find out why she was a freak? And what if her father found out and decided it was all her mom's fault and tried to get custody? No. She couldn't put her mom through that!

They could giggle over rock stars with torn jeans and belly buttons showing, teachers who fell asleep in class during home-work session, cars that belched blue smoke, boys who said one thing then did another while tripping over their big, sneakered feet . . . but not this. Although, admittedly, Ting was more fun to talk boys with, too . . . sometimes her mom would get this worried expression on her face. As if boys meant anything!

Bailey tapped her pencil on her binder and tried to concen-trate on the assignment at hand. She'd actually already done this assignment once, but now that the rest of the class was catching up, she needed to go over it and make sure that she'd been correct. Boring stuff. She decided to chew on her pencil instead.

Lacey chittered from her cage. Bailey checked the kitchen clock. Late autumn meant the sky went dark early, but it was still too early for her to be up. She grinned. Why not take advan-tage of her usually nocturnal pet? She could use a furry snuggle.

Bailey slid her chair over to the corner bookcase that held the cage and other odds and ends pertaining to the pack rat's care. Lacey sat outside her nest, which consisted of a cardboard toilet paper roll and various fluffs of tissue and newspaper, all chewed up and about the roll inside and out for comfort and warmth. Her little black tufted tail lay curled on a wad of nose tissue, in pale yellows and pinks. Her whiskers twitched. She groomed her face, then looked up expectantly as Bailey removed the lid to reach in for her.

The room spun for a moment. Ceiling seemed to swap places with floor. Bailey had this disconcerting vision of being very small with something large reaching down for her. Everything whirled about Bailey, round and round, and she froze in place, her stomach sickened by the sudden jolting amusement park ride view of her kitchen! Sink and refrigerator and cabinets spun past in a dizzying march. Walls revolved around and around and then came to a clanking halt with a thud that made her eyeballs feel as if they were bouncing for a moment. She closed her eyes tightly, every sense revolting.

She felt a tickling in her outstretched fingers as Lacey scrambled up into her palm. Opening her eyes gingerly, she pulled her hand out of the cage, leaving the lid open as she brought Lacey out. The room seemed to have jolted back into normal gear, but she wasn't too sure it would stay that way! She rubbed her pet's head gently with her thumb. Lacey nuzzled back affectionately. They weren't exactly owner and pet, the pack rat was, after all, an animal born in the wild and hardly considered tame to anyone but Bailey.

Yet there was definitely a bond between them and there had been since they first touched, since that day when Tomaz had pried open a loose board in their summer camp floor and found the pack rat and her nest of shiny, stolen objects. Lacey chittered mournfully as if remembering that day, too, and her lost treasures.

"Awww." Bailey reached back and pulled off her hair band. It was one of twisted silvery tinsel and looked very bright and shiny. Lacey took it in her paws with a happy chirp and dove off Bailey's hand back into her cage, tissue bits flying everywhere. The inside of the cage looked like a snowstorm of color as Lacey dug, her paws sending the tissue confetti every which way, until she had finally eased the silver band into a safe spot and covered it up. Not until Lacey was done making sure the treasure was hidden, did she return and squeak up at Bailey to be picked up again.

Bailey reached inside a second time, and that awful whirling sensation hit her again, like a hammer right between the eyes. She let out a groan as her world went topsy-turvy. She clutched the edge of the kitchen table as her body threatened to slide out of the chair, unable to tell up from down, and gravity laughed at her. Lacey ran up her arm, squeaking in alarm, and buried herself in Bailey's hair and collar, her warm body burrowing against Bailey's neck. She closed her eyes until the spinning went away, and then opened them slowly.

The kitchen stayed put. She hardly dared to look at it to see if it would stay that way. Bailey put her elbows on the table and held her head in her hands, very very still for long minutes.

Click, click, click.

She listened. Something was in the hallway, in the corridor outside the apartment. Something at her apartment door.

Bailey held her breath. She thought she could hear a wet snuffling at the door. An animal. A dog? Not likely; this was pretty much a No Pets building, except for the legally blind guy who lived upstairs with his service dog, but they went to work every day.

Yet when he walked by with his dog, she would hear that same click of the dog's nails on the tiled corridor. But surely they were still at work.

Bailey slid a hand up to her neck and stroked Lacey's silken fur, listening, thinking. Nothing. Nothing but her own breathing, her own heart beating fast. She inhaled deeply. Scaredy cat! There was nothing to fear but herself. And getting horribly dizzy again. What homework she'd done would be ruined if she threw up all over it. Bailey gulped. She reached for her pencil and decided that even boring schoolwork was better than sitting on the edge of her chair, petrified. She had barely put lead to paper when . . .

Click. Click. Click.

A muffled noise at the door as if something heavy leaned or pressed against it. A definite snuffle as if something sniffed at the bottom edge of the threshold. She couldn't be imagining this. Bailey stared out across the kitchen table and down the short hallway to the apartment door. Its deadbolts were closed as was the heavy chain lock, yet somehow she did not feel safe. Lacey gave a tiny squeak at her chin.

She thought of the wolfjackals which had pursued Jason. Could there be one here? Now? Tracking her at her door?

The wet snuffling reminded her of . . . well, Ulysses S. Grunt who still eagerly greeted her at the junkyard fence every time she went by. Could he have tracked her home? She knew she had nothing to worry about if it was indeed Ulysses although she'd have to get him back to the junkyard as soon as possible. Good dog or bad wolfjackal? Who paced outside her apartment door?

There was only one way to find out, and that would be to open that door, and there was no way Bailey was going to be stupid enough to do that. She listened intently. Did she hear a snarling underlining the snuffles? A low, rumbling growl? Wolfjackal! Did she imagine it? Did she hear?

On the other hand, she wasn't about to just sit there and be terrified.

Bailey shot to her feet. She rummaged around the kitchen till she got out the cutting board, the paring knife, and the fresh garlic. Quickly she pulled off a clove of the fragrant herb and chopped it into slivers. The pungent smell filled the kitchen. Raw garlic could be very very strong. No wonder vampires didn't like it! She scooped up the slivers and tiptoed to the front door, then quickly scattered the slivers at the base of the door and its tiny crack. Then she moved back against the wall, and waited.

Click. Click.

Silence.

Then, a wet snuffle just scant feet away from her, on the other side of the door. And the low vibration of a growl. Lacey's small paws dug at her neck and hair as the frightened creature tried to hide better. Bailey stared at the door waiting.

Snuffle.

Then, a sharp sneeze. And another. Bailey put her hand over her mouth to keep from laughing.

Another sneeze, followed by a low whine. Then a rapid click click click as whatever it was trotted away.

She held her breath for a bit, to be sure. Lacey shivered against her neck. Nothing but silence.

Bailey let out a cheer. Then she wrinkled her nose. "Oh," she said to Lacey. "This is going to stink for a long time." She'd have to chop some lemon to clear away the smell. She thought of something else she had to do, right away, and pulled out her crystal.

Eleanora glided across the floor, and wrinkled her nose slightly. Ever defiant of her petite size, she had a habit of levitating a few inches, the hem of her long skirts concealing the fact that she hovered in the air. "You . . . put garlic in your tea?" she asked softly, as Bailey took the whistling pot off the stove and carefully poured very hot water into their best china teapot. The smell of lemon slices and jasmine tea wafted up from the steaming pot as Bailey blushed.

"Ummm . . . no," Bailey answered. "That's repellent."

"Very effective." Smiling, Eleanora sat down at the table, in long skirt and long sleeved ruffled blouse, and waited for her tea to be poured. She watched Bailey. "When someone activates the alarm beacon, I would gather it's for more than tea. I expected to find trouble." She extended one slender hand from her ruffled sleeve, tapping her fingers on the table as Bailey poured out two cups and sat down.

Bailey took the chair opposite Eleanora who showed no surprise as Lacey ran down her arm and grabbed a cookie crumb before retreating back up to a perch on Bailey's shoulder. She dunked her cookie and enjoyed the satisfying sweetness before answering. "I'm not sure if we had trouble or not. Making sure would have led to more trouble, I think. Like sending a cheese to find a cheese."

Eleanora opened a pink packet of sweetener to dose her tea.

"I see. I think. There was something here but you didn't investigate what?"

"I think I had a wolfjackal at the door."

"And no way of finding out for sure unless you opened it to look?"

Bailey nodded. "The peephole wouldn't let me see something that was low and up against the door."

"So . . . you put down garlic at the threshold?"

"Something kept walking by and sniffing. At first I thought it was the guide dog upstairs, but they're usually at work now. I couldn't think of anything to do, except that."

"Ingenuous! Apparently it worked." Eleanora cupped her pendant, a distant look on her face. "There is nothing I sense in the corridor now. However . . ." She frowned, closed her eyes a moment, then opened them and looked at Bailey. "I'm afraid you might have been right. There is a taint there, and it's not raw garlic." She smiled slightly. "They were bold to have struck here, where they can be observed. They won't be back. They will try other, more shadowy methods next time. You're going to have to be awfully careful, Bailey."

Bailey shivered. The hairs on the back of her neck and along her arms stood up. She rubbed at her arms. "But I'm safe here, at least for now? They won't try to get us? My mom and I?"

"I can't guarantee that, but the Dark Hand is successful because it doesn't leave itself open to discovery. They know you know that they have located you here, and you can't be taken without a fight, a struggle they want to avoid for now." Eleanora reached over and grasped her hand. "We'll do everything we can to make sure they stay discouraged!"

Bailey shook her head slowly. "I don't know what I could have done. They had some sort of spell. It made me very, very dizzy. I could hardly sit up, let alone stand and fight, Eleanora."

"A spell? Describe it."

"It was awful. I got sick to my stomach. It was like being on one of those rides that spin you backward, then turn you upside down." Bailey paled just at the memory. "The whole kitchen just went round and round."

Eleanora looked baffled. "I don't understand, hon. There's nothing I can throw that would cause that. Which is, of course, not to say that Brennard hasn't been researching and trying to create new spells . . . but I haven't heard of that one. Tell me again exactly what happened, and don't leave anything out!" She sat back, teacup in hand, watching and sipping as Bailey began to recite the afternoon over again.

". . . and then I called for help." Bailey dunked and slurped up the next to last cookie. Lemon melts, slightly stale and gone very hard, which made them perfect for dunking. Bailey wiped her hands up very thoroughly.

Eleanora sat with an extremely thoughtful look on her face. "Tell me," she said, "what you would see if you were in Lacey's place and someone reached in for you."

"What?" Bailey felt her face wrinkle in total surprise. "But . . ."

"Just imagine. Lean back and imagine you are a wee, tiny kangaroo rat in the corner of that cage, and someone reaches in and plucks you up, turning your world upside down and around and around?"

Bailey narrowed her eyes, thinking. Then she bolted out of her chair. "Oh no! I'm turning into a shapeshifter! I'm going to be a pack rat!"

Button, Button

"I'M cursed," wailed Bailey. "Cursed to become a pack rat!"

"Hmmm," murmured Eleanora in obvious amusement as she watched Bailey dart around the kitchen. "After having seen your bedroom, I'm not so sure that's incorrect, but it is. You, my dear, are not a shapeshifter."

Bailey stopped and stared. "But what, then?"

"You merely saw the world for a few moments through Lacey's eyes."

"No way!"

Eleanora nodded sagely. "Way," she countered.

"That's impossible."

"Think about it. And trust me, with your Talent, you may well find strong bonds with an animal or two. Stories of witches and cats come out of real life happenings, only distorted by those who don't understand. I know Tomaz has been wanting to work with you on this, but he's been a little busy with Stefan's problem."

"No kidding." Bailey thumped into a chair. It made a little

sense, though. The impression of being reached for just before all the dizziness started. "So Lacey and I have a bond."

"Don't you think so?"

"Oh, yeah." Bailey smiled and put her hand to her shoulder to stroke the tiny furred ball. "That was pretty awful, though. If I make her that dizzy every time I pick her up . . ."

"Once again, think about it. No doubt there was some dizziness and some problem with your mind trying to handle two sources of sensory input." Eleanora looked a little smug. "If I may retreat into the scientific for a bit."

Bailey grinned. "Well done! Pretty soon you'll believe in satellite TV and cell phones!"

"Never." Eleanora turned pink and shook her head. "Demon technology." She smiled at Bailey across the teapot. "The important thing, Bailey, is that you not let Lacey overrun your thoughts, your control. She is, after all, only a wee animal and not as smart as you are, although sometimes we may think she's terribly clever."

"Tell me what to do."

"Think of that part of your Talent as a door. It's always shut. Lacey must knock on it and get permission to enter. Use your meditation exercises on your crystal that you've been doing . . ." If Eleanora noticed the embarrassed and slightly guilty look on Bailey's face at this last, she ignored it and cruised right by. "Those exercises will help you build a framework of contact. Otherwise your mind will have a tiny creature running about in its thoughts nonstop, and that won't be good for either of you."

"No," muttered Bailey. "It certainly wouldn't be." Her hand absently reached out for the last cookie, but Eleanora beat her to it, taking it up demurely and placing it in her tea saucer.

"There are advantages, of course," the Magicker continued smoothly. "Lacey can get in and out of places very quickly that you can't. That could be very useful, if she is trained." She broke her cookie in half precisely and devoured part.

"Wow." Bailey tugged thoughtfully on her ponytail. "Can she be trained? Is she smart enough?"

The beast in question let out a tiny snort as if making fun of Bailey's words. Eleanora laughed.

"She'll do. Let me show you a training exercise that should be fun for both of you. When I was young, we used to play a game called 'Button, Button.'" She smiled slightly. "Buttons were very expensive in my youth. Rather like playing with a silver or gold coin." Eleanora fished around in the cloth purse attached to her slender wrist and brought out a pretty carved bright red button. "Take this and let her see it, then hide it in plain sight. Always reward her when she finds it." Eleanora tapped her cookie. "I think a crumb or two of this would make her very happy. Soon, she'll be able to find the button even when it's well hidden!

Bailey took the button from her. "That's it?"

"For starters, till Tomaz has time to work with you both. Don't expect too much of her, Bailey. She is very smart in her way, although limited, but she trusts and loves you and will give everything she's got to please you. It is your role, as her protector, not to abuse that devotion."

"I'll be careful," vowed Bailey.

"Good. 'Cause if you send her out to see if a wolfjackal stands there, she'll be eaten in one gulp."

Bailey gasped.

Eleanora stood, nodding. "Don't forget that."

"I . . . won't!" Bailey had to force herself to breathe in the middle of her words. She held the button tightly.

"In the meantime, I'll be listening for you. We also seem to be attuned." Eleanora smiled. She glided round the kitchen table and kissed Bailey's brow gently. "Take care and call when you need me." She tapped Bailey's crystal. She slid her fingertips over the pendant at the hollow of her throat, nearly hidden by the ruffled neckline of her blouse, and disappeared.

Bailey cuddled Lacey gently in the palm of her hand. "Have I got a game for you," she said softly, and pictured the cookie reward in her thoughts.

Give a mouse a cookie! typed Trent and Jason could almost hear the dry laugh accompanying it. Grinning, Jason typed back, **Elephants work for peanuts, but pack rats have even crumbier wages.**

Hey, guys! I worked really hard and so did Lacey. In fact, afterward she slept all day and all night!

Jason laughed harder. The thought of a poor exhausted Lacey curled up in her shredded paper nest with even her tail tucked in beside her was too funny to take seriously. That, coupled with the thought of Bailey shapeshifting into another pack rat, whiskers trembling and bright eyes looking for sparklies, made him laugh till he nearly snorted.

Bailey must have sensed their combined mirth because she typed **Hmppph!**, added a smiley face with its tongue sticking out, and signed off the Internet messenger.

Which was too bad because Jason wanted to talk with her about the dangers of the wolfjackal lurking, but Eleanora had undoubtedly found a way to ward the Landau apartment or she wouldn't have been so certain Bailey would be safe there. Outside, however, was another matter. Bailey could be brash, but she would never be mistaken for stupid, so he had to hope for the best.

Trent sent a message to him, though, that stopped all his thoughts about Bailey. He blinked and read the screen twice to make sure he understood.

Henry wrote me and asked if I were afraid of Jon, too.

His brain stampeded. Jonnard Albrite, tall, thin, older, somewhat worldly even, a camp counselor of sorts, and cabinmate of Henry Squibb. Jon, a plant from the Dark Hand of Brennard, who leeched Henry's powers from him and tried to do the same to Jason! Of course they were afraid of Jon, but Henry wasn't to remember that! **When was this? How did Jonnard even get mentioned?**

He didn't. Henry just popped up with it yesterday, after our DR session. You had to leave and help Alicia with chores.

No kidding. He asked you that? What did you say?

I said that camp seemed a long time ago, and Jon was your (Henry's) roommate, not mine.

Did he drop it, then?

No. He said he had dreams, sometimes, of camp, of things that he knew were impossible. Then he stopped.

Oh, man. He couldn't be remembering . . . could he? Jason stared for long moments at his computer screen, trying to think of what to say or do. Finally, Trent sent another message.

Think about it, Jason. We shouldn't have been able to discuss this with him. Not unless he were a Magicker, because of the Binding.

Jason sat back. Trent was implying that Henry was still a Magicker, even without power. Because Trent was? He couldn't be sure. There might be an even more awesome answer. Before he could respond, Trent typed again, insistently.

He might be getting his memory back. And his power. We should find a way to test this. If he is, he'll draw the Dark Hand to him, and he'll be worse off than any of us. Weak, untrained.

What about Ting's farewell party? He knows Ting.

Good idea. A party and a test.

They both signed off then.

Jason climbed into bed, but sat with his legs drawn up. He reached for a book and began to lose himself in it, in its own magic and mysteries, when he felt a familiar tingle and lifted his head. Tomaz Crowfeather appeared in a brief, rainbow shimmer. He lifted one hand in greeting, an open handshake without the shake.

"Good or bad time, Jason?"

"Good, I think." He dog-earred the corner of the page to mark it, then closed his book. "Gavan told you?"

Tomaz drew up his desk chair and straddled it, sitting backward and crossing his arms across its back. "He did. We had all hoped the dreams were gone, but it appears not. Are they frequent?"

Jason considered that. He dreamed every night, vividly, but not that dream. Every handful of weeks, perhaps. He shrugged and said as much.

Tomaz nodded. He scratched the side of his jaw with a blunt thumb, the beaten silver disks on his turquoise bracelet rattling gently as he did so. "Are you using the techniques we talked about?"

"I'm trying to. Deep breathing before I sleep, imaging, the other stuff you mentioned."

"Good. Good. Without a lodge or sweathouse, it is difficult to concentrate as you should, but there are two things you must always be keenly aware of." Tomaz leaned over the chair back. "You must always be aware of whether it is your dream you are walking in, or another's. If it is your dream, you are in control, but you must take care, for there is much for you to learn within it. If it is another's . . ." He frowned. His bronzed skin wrinkled deeply about his eyes. "It will be difficult, Jason."

"How? To leave? Will I be trapped in there?"

"Possibly, but it goes beyond that. You must tell if it is friend or foe. And, either way, there still may be something valuable to learn."

Jason felt very cold. He drew the blankets of his bed up over his pajamas for warmth. "How do I do that?"

"Again, that is difficult. Dreamwalking is not reality. We see things symbolically, and according to our own backgrounds. A coyote for me means one thing, for you, most likely another." Tomaz nodded as if to emphasize that.

"Then what do I do? How do I know?"

"You must reach even deeper within yourself and test for the truth. Even a dreamwalk meant to show or warn you of lies will ring of the truth. And you must learn to do it quickly, Jason, or else you could be trapped by another. In all other ways, your Magick and Talent can help you. In a dreamwalk, it could prove deadly."

He went icy. Even the blankets and comforters on his bed no longer helped. "Deadly?"

"You are very vulnerable to your dreams. You can be hurt both physically and mentally. So. You must think of every dreamwalk as a challenge, a race if you will, to determine what it is made of, what it can give and take away from you. You cannot hesitate either way, Jason."

"If I'm in someone else's dream, then . . . what do I do?"

"For the moment, till we've had time to train you more, you get out. Any way you can, as fast as you can." Tomaz reached out and patted Jason's knee. "Let me show you a path that works for me. Again, our dreams reflect who we are, our heritage and our culture, so your path will be different for you." He talked to Jason a while longer, his voice low and soothing. Then Tomaz reached out and covered him up as he lay down sleepily, still listening, and was still in the room talking as Jason realized he'd drifted off to sleep.

Οσσps

H E dreamed of the McHenry house again. As used as he
was to this dream, it did not strike him as odd that it had
changed, changed as he realized and grew within his knowledge of what Magick was and what being a Magicker meant.
He understood the Gate now and how he opened it, and what
it meant that he did. He even understood the catacombs and
the deathly still figure lying on the cold stone tomb waiting for
him and trying to draw him close.

What he did not understand was why he dreamed it over
and over. Was he supposed to understand and vanquish every
speck of it before he could move on and grow? As Tomaz had
told him, it could be his dream or someone else's. He thought it
was his dream. His Path. He had to learn its lessons. If not,
would this specter of Brennard haunt him as long as his days in
Magicking went on? Was this a war for his right to be what he
was, or even more serious, a struggle for his very soul?

If it was, how could he hope to protect others like Henry and
Trent who hadn't the skill? Was he meant to open a Gate where

the nightmare reach of Brennard and his Dark Hand could not go? Was he the one, and the only one, who could find a way to safety?

Jason paused at the vast paneled doors to the old estate. They stood closed, foreboding and massive. If he was intended to find a safe way, this was not it. The doors crackled with energy, sinister and draining. He hesitated to touch the entry but knew he had to, his hand resting over the dark gold wood and feeling a heat generating from it. Every hair on his body stood on end. Every fiber that he had within him told him not to do it, not to go farther, not to touch the cursed door! But he had to. He knew he had to.

He ran his palm over the door's surface, an inch or so away, without actually touching the wood. Tiny sparks of energy flared and flashed as he did. Every now and then one actually zapped his skin like static electricity. He jumped when it zapped him; he couldn't help it. Clenching his teeth, he shoved his hand out to the door and pushed it inward.

They opened soundlessly, both great doors pushing in at once. Moonlight flooded in over his shoulder, a wide silvery beam cutting through the darkness of the old estate, splaying across the interior. For a moment as he stepped inside, he almost felt as if caught in a spotlight. His shadow cut a jagged black figure within the moonbeam.

He crossed the foyer quickly, the floor creaking dangerously under him. Jason did not want to plummet downward as he often did, crashing through into the chambers below. He had a mission tonight, and it drew him, and so his movements were deft and sure. He crossed into the inner room.

As he opened that door, the moonlight gave way to golden, electrical lights, and the pleasant heat of a lit fireplace with logs burning brightly and the feeling of being in a real room somewhere, a welcoming. There were chairs and other upholstered pieces scattered about, all facing the fireplace. There were cardboard boxes against the walls, and cabinets open, their contents spilled outward and into some of the boxes. There was a sense of leaving, of packing here. Jason stopped and looked around.

"Come in, Jason. We haven't long here, as you can see." Unlike the room, the voice was cold and unfeeling.

Jason turned and saw the chair closest to the fireplace swing about slightly. There was a man sitting in it, quiet and still; brunette hair curled to his shoulders and his face had the pallor of marble. The man was dressed in a dark suit, with a soft white silken shirt. There was an unearthly aura to his entire being. He looked at Jason, unsmiling, dark eyes seeming to pierce right through him.

"Got off the tomb, I see," Jason commented. He was used to seeing this figure lying atop that cold sarcophagus.

The man laughed. None of the mirth reached his eyes or voice, or colored his skin with a pleasant blush. There was no humor in him at all as he leveled his gaze on Jason's face. "It was an effort I made," Brennard said. "No thanks to you."

Jason had no more intention of coming near Brennard now than he would have if the man were still atop his cold stone tomb below and reaching out for help. "What are you doing here?"

A thin, chill smile. "Don't you mean . . . what am *I* doing here?"

"Either way. What are either of us doing here?"

"I know," said Brennard. "I might tell you. Or I might not. It depends."

For a dizzying moment, Jason wondered if he were really in a dream or if Brennard had crafted a way to meet, to trap him. If he blinked, would he wake up, or would he lose everything by being caught? He ought to be able to wake if he had to, to escape. If this *were* a dream. And if it wasn't . . .

A shiver ran down his back, icy cold fingers trailing along his spine.

Still, given his choices, he'd rather be here facing Brennard than Statler Finch. The odd comparison ran through his thoughts, startling him for a moment, and he took a step backward because it really wouldn't do to be facing Brennard off-balance. Nor keeping half his mind, half an ear, out for his unprotected back. His left hand ached a bit, but he did not rub it. He would not touch that scar in front of his enemy. Why, he was not sure, but he thought it might not be a good thing to let Brennard know he had any edge against Jason.

"Come closer. Let me have a look at you in the light."

Jason took two steps forward, not really carrying him all that much closer, but enough to be polite. Look him over, Brennard did, the dark eyes of the Magicker examining him from head to toe.

"Strange clothes," Brennard commented dryly, "But I am told that I should get used to them. Some things are better. Some are not. Much is greatly changed." The elder, who did not look in years to be much older than Gavan Rainwater, shifted in his chair, large slender hands moving restlessly. "You've a focus, I presume?"

"It's not what makes me a Magicker, but yes." Jason fought the need to put his hand on his crystal, to take it out and check it, make sure it was safe against this man. The more he wanted to do it, the more he felt that it was because Brennard was somehow making him want to do it, and therefore he would not.

Brennard frowned slightly. "You lack much training."

"And yet I elude you." Jason put his chin up.

"Here, yes. For the moment." Brennard gestured. "Out there, yes." He smiled thinly again. "For the moment."

"You expect things to change? I expect to get stronger."

"Do you?" Brennard leaned forward, his expression intent. "What Gregory and I fought about was nothing less than the essence of Magick itself. What if they are wrong and I am right?

How can they possibly train you? How can you possibly grow into your potential and protect yourself, and your friends, from the world we have today? What if they are all wrong, and I am right? Ask yourself that."

"If you are right, why do you pursue me with nightmares and wolfjackals?"

"They are not mine. They are a . . ." Brennard sat back, and his hands made a pass through the air. "They are a negative aspect to the positive forces of the mana. A balance, if you will. For every light, there must be a dark."

Jason did not wholly believe him for a second. If the wolf-jackals weren't his, he did not hesitate to use them, nor did any of his Dark Hand!

"I admit," said Brennard quietly, "what I offer is not appeal-ing. It would be wonderful to think that Magick is unlimited, that it is flowing everywhere and we can just reach out . . . and hold it. But think, Jason. Is there any resource in your world that is unlimited? The sun? It will burn out. Perhaps a thousand thousand years, perhaps sooner, perhaps later, but it consumes itself. Our water? As we dirty it, there is less and less available. The earth itself? Wind and pollution eat away at it. What then? Nothing. Why should Magick be any different?"

The golden lights illuminating the room flickered. Brennard did not seem to notice it, but Jason did. And the one thing he desperately wanted was *not* to be left alone in the dark with this man. His words made a kind of sense, but there was a catch to them, and Jason knew he would find that catch, if he had a moment or two to himself to think. Here and now, though, was not the time to examine Brennard's teachings.

In fact, it was time to go, Jason decided. He took a step back.

"Don't go, lad. Stay. Perhaps there is something I can teach you, some little thing you will have of me, that might convince you later." Brennard looked upon Jason, and in his gaze the boy caught a glimpse of power and knowledge.

Jason didn't think staying was an option.

"Your friends aren't nearly so good at denying me," Brennard stated.

"They're as strong as I am."

"You think so? I know better. I'll have them, too, perhaps even before I have you."

He took another step back and sensed the doors right behind him. Once through those doors, he would be in the dark and hotly pursued again. Jason paused. He looked around the room. Why had he felt so much heat at the front doors?

As he looked toward Brennard, and the fireplace, he sensed a curtain of fire behind them, consuming that end of the room, like a wildfire out of control. It danced and wavered like a heat vision mirage, flames licking upon the walls and up toward the ceiling. A cold illusion, Jason thought, but not one which Brennard seemed to even be aware of. What did those flames strive to tell him?

"Good-bye," said Jason abruptly as he turned and bolted back through the doors he entered by.

Brennard snarled an oath and sprang after him, or so Jason thought because he heard the heavy chair tumble to the floor as he dove into darkness. The moon's singular beam seemed very thin and inadequate, but he'd left the front door open, and raced for it knowing that the end of his dream awaited.

He would reach it this time. He wondered if there would come a time in his nightmares when he did not—and what would happen then?

That worry still haunted him when Trent's dad drove by and dropped Trent off for the day. Trent shouldered his backpack as he leaped out of the car, shouting, "I'll call you when I'm ready to be picked up!"

Trent's dad grunted a reply through the rolled-up car window as he pulled away. The two boys sparred a bit, happy to actually see each other. "He doesn't mind your staying out late?"

"Nah. He's got sales projections for next year to work on, said he wouldn't be much company anyway. He doesn't mind driving back tonight, though he said I could stay over if that works out better."

"Cool. Have you got that stuff for Henry?"

"Sure do. It didn't take much time at all, with the computer and stuff." Trent tapped his backpack, grinning widely.

"Good, 'cause I need to know how much trouble Henry might be in."

"Oh? What's up?" Trent trotted up the walkway toward the back door and kitchen, matching Jason's steps.

"I think we're all under attack, in one way or another. I'm not so sure they want to do away with us . . . I think maybe he wants us corraled. Brought in. So we can be used in one way or another." Jason paused, his hand on the back doorknob. "And I don't think the Magickers can protect us."

Trent followed him in, looking about to make sure that part of the house was quiet and unoccupied, before whistling softly. "That's pretty heavy, Jason."

He went to the stove and checked the teakettle to make sure it was full before turning on the heat under it. Then he arranged two mugs and poured hot chocolate packets into each before answering, "I know. But the facts are in front of us. The beacon rarely works. Whether something is interfering with it, or they can't monitor it as they'd like, or whatever. And, face it—we won't use a beacon unless we're under attack. By then, it's too late. We're already in trouble, and we're not trained enough to be able to face all the Dark Hand can throw at us."

"So what's the solution?"

Jason shrugged. "We need a place of our own. Someplace to be safe and to study."

"Hogwarts."

Jason grinned at the fictional reference. "Well, doubt if we could find anywhere so neat, but . . . yeah."

"Ravenwyng."

"They're working on that one. I've been thinking that what I need to do is find us a Gate or two, for safety. Like a shadow we can slip into, if we need to."

"Through the crystals."

"Yes."

Trent watched him solemnly. "That'll do for you guys. What about me?"

"I'm thinking I can fix a crystal with a . . . a swinging door. One that anyone can push open or shut."

"Neat, if you can do it. Dangerous, too . . . what if you can do it, and I drop the crystal?"

"You wouldn't."

"What if I did?"

"No one else would know how to use it."

Trent squirmed a bit on the kitchen chair. "It's tempting," he said slowly, "if you could do it."

"I'm the Gatekeeper. If anyone can, I can."

Trent watched him as he poured water into the mugs, making frothy cups of hot chocolate, plopped two big marshmallows into each, and brought them to the kitchen table. "Just because you can, doesn't mean you should."

"We have to be safe."

Jason knew Trent couldn't argue with that, and he didn't. Instead he concentrated on sinking his melting marshmallow, pushing it under with the bowl of the spoon and watching it plop! back up onto the surface. "Why can't we just pop in through the Iron Gate to Ravenwyng?"

"First of all, Gavan and the others are working in there, when they can. Council meetings and stuff. And when they're not there . . ." Jason considered. "I don't know, it worries me. Like the alarm beacon. It should work, but frequently it doesn't.

I think Brennard has found a way to interfere with Ravenwyng, at least until Gavan gets it settled and locked beyond Iron Gate. Secondly, the Dark Hand knows about it just as much as we do. No, we need a Gate of our own."

"So you just open one?"

Jason rubbed the back of his neck. He looked at Trent across the table. The smell of the rich chocolate drinks in front of them scented the whole kitchen, and he pulled his mug closer and sipped at the dark froth cautiously. "Well. It's not that easy, I'll admit that. But I can feel one, close by, and it's getting . . . I dunno . . . closer?"

"Feel it?"

Jason nodded. "It's like having itchy palms and you know you're going to get unexpected money or something. It's twitching at me. I know it's there, somewhere."

"So that's what we're going to do before everything else starts happening? Find a Gate and just pop through?"

"If you'll help."

Trent looked at him, a chocolate-and-marshmallow mustache riding his upper lip, which he licked off looking quite satisfied and catlike. "What do I do?"

"I need an anchor. Someone on this side."

"I can do that." He sank his second marshmallow. "What if there's trouble?"

"Yank me back. Just like . . . just like pulling me by the arm."

Trent nodded. "I can do that, too." He lifted his mug, gulped down half his remaining drink, and sat back. "I can't let you make me a swinging door, though."

"And why not?"

"It's too dangerous. Anything could go in, or come out. Think about it, Jason. It won't work. I'm on my own, unless I'm with one of you, and I'm only as safe as you guys are. Which only means I have to do everything I can to make sure everyone else is okay, so you guys will be able to save *my* bacon when I need it!" He drummed his fingertips on the tabletop, always listening to an inner music no one else could hear. "All right then, let's rock and roll."

Jason grinned. "Soon as I'm ready."

Later, he thought he'd never be ready for this. Not really. Cupping his crystal in his hand, Jason stood with the early morning sun slanting across his back, Trent with an arm linked through his, and the tickle of a Gate growing stronger and stronger until he knew all he had to do was *Push* and it would swing open. What sort of Gate it was, he had no real idea and there was a tiny, nagging thought at the back of his mind that it could be a trap of Brennard's, but that was why he had Trent here. Like a safety ground for an electrical current, Trent would keep him tied to his own world, no matter what he found on the other side of the Gate.

He took a deep breath. "Okay," he said. "Here I go." He rubbed his crystal, looking deep into it, seeing a shadowy plane he wished to open and going through.

The Gate swung in. He stood for a moment, then swirling color hit him, and howling winds, and the stink of unbreathable ammonia, and a sense that something lay before him, all arms and tentacles, swaying and thrashing about.

The Thing lashed out, reaching for him.

"Uh-oh," said Jason.

Anchors Away

JASON put out a hand to steady himself, but there was nothing . . . no doorway or pass or rock or tree or anything to hold onto as the wind tore at him and threatened to knock him literally off his feet. The world seemed to be nothing but a swirl of mist and cloud and one wailing, angry *thing*.

The only solid thing, it looked like a tall and fleshy flower stalk, with a snapping jaw buried in its top and plenty of vines to catch unwary prey with. It made a noise like a high thin wailing that seemed to be almost out of Jason's hearing range. It swayed as if blindly attracted to Jason.

He jumped away from a whipping tentacle, an orange rope that smelled disgusting and left trails of slime dripping through the air as it moved. A drop touched his arm and stung like a bee! With a yelp he danced out of range and tried to peer into the heavy mists.

The air stank, and he couldn't catch his breath, couldn't breathe whatever was in the wind here. He coughed as he jerked about and knew that, wherever this Gate led, it was not to a place where people could live. He might be on an alien planet somewhere on the far side of the universe, for all he could tell. He scouted about for another moment, just to prove himself wrong, when he heard a scuttling across the rocks.

The thing came after him hungrily, hopping on its one-footed stalk. Jason rubbed his arm, the skin angry and tender, and dodged one, two, now three tentacles frantically searching through the mists for him. Time to go! He put his thoughts back to Trent, wherever he might be, and pulled, *hard.* SssssssNAP!

There was a moment when he had nothing to pull on and another moment when he firmly had Trent in his mind's grip and he boomeranged back where he belonged.

Coughing and choking, eyes tearing with the awful ammonia cleaner smell, he tumbled to the grass at Trent's feet. His friend looked down at him thoughtfully. "I take it that was a no-go."

Jason rubbed his tearing eyes as he sat up and fought for breath. He nodded wordlessly. After a few long moments of coughing and choking during which he realized he would have died inside that Gate had he stayed much longer, not as a victim of orange tentacles but poison air, he was able to take a deep breath. Trent solemnly passed him a handkerchief which Jason used thoroughly and stuffed in his pocket for laundry later.

"I think that might explain why there aren't many Gate-keepers around," Trent added thoughtfully. "Theoretically, if you're opening up doors on universal planes, most of them could be really inhospitable. In other words, it's ugly out there."

Jason snorted. "You think?" He stood, dusting himself off. There was an angry scratchlike welt on his arm where that thing had dropped slime. "If there was only a way to see through a Gate before going through."

"Maybe the other side doesn't exist till you open it. Which, of course, negates everything I just said."

Jason thought about that, then shook his head. "No, because something lived there . . . it just didn't explode out of nowhere."

Trent drummed his fingers on the side of his leg. "Don't tell me this is one of those 'if a tree falls in the forest and no one hears it, does it still make a sound' conversations? 'Cause I swore I'd never get into that."

Jason nodded. "Close, huh? But seriously, I thought I'd fallen into *Star Wars* or something. And whatever it was, it was real." He showed his arm to Trent.

"That's like a burn." Trent grimaced in sympathy.

"Hurts like it, too. I'll have to put something on it later. And I couldn't breathe for all the ammonia or whatever." He took another deep breath and it felt good, California smog or not. "Ready to go again?"

"Sure. I've got the easy part, I just sit here and wonder where you disappeared to." Trent grinned at him.

"Won't be so easy if I disappear for good. You'd have a lot of explaining to do."

Trent's smile faded, and he looked solemnly at Jason. "Just don't do that."

"Right. I won't." They both knew it might not be that easy, but it was reassuring to make it sound that way. Jason put his hand on Trent's shoulder, cupped his crystal, and found a new facet, a new angle inside its beauty to focus upon. Within a moment, he saw a threshold, and stepped through. . . .

Nighttime. Wild countryside. Late autumn chill in the frosted ground below his feet, and Jason shivered in his short-sleeved shirt. A moon overhead lay very low in the sky, just barely clearing the treetops, like a great yellow pumpkin, and he marveled at it for a moment, so large and clear. It seemed larger than any harvest moon he'd ever seen before. He took a halting breath, carefully, but it smelled only of the night, a little moist. Some faint night flower perfumed it along with the scent of the grass and trees, and there was the chill of the crackling frost on the ground. He had a sensation of dream time and shook it off. This was real. This was no dream where all he had to do was wake up to return to reality. What existed here could and would hurt him if it seemed dangerous.

Still and all, this was promising. From the brilliance of the many stars in the sky, he realized there were no city lights nearby to diffuse their strength. No traffic sounds or noise reached him. It was not quiet, by any means; he could hear the rattle of tree branches and the chirp of many crickets, and the sound of a brook flowing nearby. The nightscape was rocky and rather bare, but it was obviously nearing winter. Many of the trees were leafless, their branches shaking in a slight night breeze. He looked about, trying to imagine what it would be like to have a Haven here. They could bring a tent, perhaps, something salvaged from one of the family garages, and pitch it permanently.

It might do. It might indeed. Smiling, Jason turned around and started off over a little knoll to get a better look around. His foot hit a stone, and it rolled downhill a bit, then bounced off a boulder, and clattered noisily down a slope where he felt the brook might be. It sounded louder than it was, because there wasn't much other noise around to muffle it. He didn't hear a splash follow it, though. A few more clatters echoed as if smaller pebbles had also been dislodged and were rattling down the incline.

Then silence fell. Complete and total silence. The crickets stopped. The wind held its breath. And Jason felt a stab of fear.

A howl sounded from not very far away. Another joined it, and then a third.

Jason turned slowly. His blood went icy with recognition. It seemed he had been unlucky enough to find the world which was home to wolfjackals! He raced back to the spot at which he'd opened the Gate, and palmed his crystal, seeking Trent's anchoring presence.

It was there, but thready, fading in and out like a cellular phone transmission with a battery going dead. He could feel his friend, and then he could not, all faint and watery feeling. He didn't know much about Gates except that they had a very real base and he couldn't run, or he'd lose this one. And if he didn't run, the wolfjackals were likely to pull him down!

The howls grew stronger in the night, and he looked across the ridge. By the light of the low, yellow moon, he could see three massive wolfish bodies racing fast across the disk's illumination. Another few jumps and he would be able to see their ivory fangs gleaming in their jaws, altogether way too close!

Jason rubbed his crystal. He tore his gaze from the ridge and looked down into his crystal, barely visible in the evening, his hands shaking. The scar on his left hand began to throb painfully, almost a match for the burn on his right arm. If only Trent could focus, too, from his side.

But his friend couldn't, and suddenly Jason questioned his suitability for what Jason had chosen him to do. He should have waited for Bailey. Or even Rich and Stefan. Anyone but someone with no Magick. He drew his crystal close, his breath exhaling in a white mist about it. *Just think, Trent, harder and harder—or I'm going to lose you and . . . me!*

His hands trembled, and he dropped his quartz. It bounced into the stiff and spare grasses about his feet and abruptly winked out of sight. Jason dropped to his knees, searching frantically. Nothing met his touch. He ran his hands through the brittle, frost-dried tangled grasses and found nothing. Chilled and dirty, he began to search even more desperately. Wonderful if it had bounced away and he didn't hear it.

Howls rippled nearer. He wouldn't look up. He was lost without his crystal, and it didn't matter if the wolfjackals got him or not then. Panic began to well up in him. He had to find it. It had to be here somewhere. He dug across the shale and grass tufts frantically.

Nothing. Gone. It was gone.

It couldn't be gone. He'd *feel* it if it was gone. Like . . . like a hole in himself or something. *Think, Jason, think.*

At camp when they'd been introduced to the crystals, the tables had been covered with trays. Crystals, quartzes and rocks of all kind were laid out, and they'd been told to look them over very carefully, and not touch unless very very sure of what they were doing. His had held a kind of warmth that drew him, a fuzzy kind of tingle.

He wasn't just looking for any ordinary rock in the dark. Jason took a breath to steady himself and calm his racing thoughts and put his hand out, palm down, and tried to feel for his crystal. That faint warmth that was for him and him alone.

A chorus of howls nearby shattered the air again. He could hear their hot pants, the click of their nails on the rocky slope as they bounded up. Something warm grazed his fingers, he grabbed for it.

Jason blinked in surprise. Crystal it was, but not *his* crystal. This was bigger, and absolutely transparent, with a bold lavender color to it that shone in the dark. How he'd not seen it before, he couldn't tell. Before he could stand in puzzlement, his other hand found a steady warmth and reached for his own crystal, secure, wrapped in fallen autumn leaves and damp from lying on the ground.

He turned, a crystal in each hand and made fists, as the wolfjackals bore down on him. It was now or never for him to find Trent. Otherwise, he would have to open another Gate and just fall through.

He squeezed his hands. Trent's tuneless humming filled his mind. With a shout of relief, Jason anchored on him and pulled through just as the first wolfjackal leaped.

23

Surprised Party

TRENT blinked as Jason tumbled to the grass in front of him, pale almost beyond belief, arms stiff at his sides with his hands knotted into fists. He bent over his friend immediately and felt the icy cold radiating from him. Jason smiled stiffly up at him, teeth chattering, lips blue around the edges.

"Oh, man," Trent breathed. "That doesn't look good at all! Come on, come on, get up!" He pulled Jason to his feet, half-surprised his clothes didn't explode into frozen splinters. Jason continued to shake, jaws clattering, and he hugged himself as if trying to hold what little warmth remained inside him. "In the house. Come on." He pushed and pulled at Jason, got him upstairs—thank goodness the inquisitive sister and overachieving stepmom were out at some lesson or other—and he steered Jason up to the trapdoor ladder leading to the attic bedroom.

Once there, Jason toppled over onto the bed. Trent piled blankets and quilts on top of him. He ran downstairs and microwaved a steaming cup of hot tea, raced back up and fed it to Jason who tried to sip it, shaking so hard he spilled more of it than he drank and finally waved the mug away. Trent plunked down at the computer desk, and watched. It got worse, until Jason shook all over with helpless chills, but the color slowly came back to his face, and he finally stopped shaking. He melted into his bed, and unclenched his teeth, and drew his hands out, uncurling his fingers slowly. He sat up, and not one but two crystals fell from his fists onto the coverlet.

They both stared in astonishment.

"I . . . I . . . d–d–d–didn't imagine it," Jason got out.

"Two crystals? How'd you manage that? And what happened? You stumble onto Antarctica or something?"

"N–n–n–nothing like that." Jason stumbled onto his feet, and the two brilliant crystals tumbled to the bedroom carpet. "Did they come through with me?"

"The rocks? Yeah. We were just talking about that." Trent stared, baffled. He pushed Jason gently back onto the bed. "Just sit there till you warm up. I'm not so sure you're not in shock or something."

"N–n–no. I'm fine. I d–d–didn't know I was so c–c–cold." Jason pulled his blankets tighter around him. He reached out and picked up his own crystal, shoving it deep into his pocket, and then picked up the second. Crystalline, completely transparent, with a faint, pure lavender color throughout its many facets. He held it so that Trent could see it, too. "Look at this."

"I'm looking." Trent sighed faintly. A slight note of envy crept in, and he flushed a little.

Jason said immediately, "I'm sorry."

"Don't be. You didn't do anything. Where'd you find it? Are you Bonded, do you think? It *is* one of those rocks, isn't it?"

"I think so, and it was there, where I was. The Gate area looked like Earth this time, only out in the country, the wilderness. Nighttime, and out on the . . . the . . ." Jason tried to search for a word to fit the landscape. "Moors? Countryside. Slopes and rock and trees gone to winter. Everything very dark and still, with this huge harvest moon hanging in the sky. It looked really promising until I heard the wolfjackals. And then I dropped my crystal."

Trent looked stunned. "No way."

"I couldn't find it in the dark." Jason inspected his hands. They looked like he'd been digging in the dirt, grubby and scuffed and even bruised. "I combed the ground . . . I could hear them coming after me, howling, running across the hill."

"They knew you were there?"

"They always do." Jason shuddered. "I didn't think I'd make it back."

"What did you do?"

"I stopped trying to dig out . . . my crystal has a warmth. I decided to find that, you know? And it came to me. This strange one. I found it first, then the other, but they both just kind of answered me. One minute I had nothing, the next I had two." Jason held the lavender gem out to Trent.

He took it carefully. It hadn't been polished or faceted, but it looked like a handful of faintly purple diamond. "This could be valuable. Some gemstones are priceless, like diamonds." It held no heat for him. Disappointed, he passed it back. "You look better. Warming up?"

"Yeah." He bounced the new crystal in his hand for a moment. "I could hardly feel you. I don't think I would have made it back without this second one."

"Really?"

Jason nodded.

"Awesome."

Jason laughed then. "You're stupid."

Trent grinned. "Hey! You made it back. Don't complain!"

"Yeah, yeah. I'll have to show this to Gavan, see what he thinks of it. It could be I am bonded."

"And the problem with that is . . . ?"

Jason looked at him. "It came from the Haven where wolfjackals roam. I've no idea what kind of energy it could hold . . . who might have had it before. Think about it, Trent. This could be big trouble."

They both looked at it in solemn silence. Trent finally broke the silence. "I don't think," he stated, "that anything about you could be evil." He cleared his throat. "Some people just have this quality about them. You're one of 'em. You can't even tell a lie to save yourself." He stopped awkwardly, then started again. "Now Bailey, on the other hand, would cheerfully kill both of us if we missed the party."

Jason's jaw dropped. "The party! I nearly forgot it. Let me get cleaned up and then go find Dozer for our ride." He shed the blankets and comforter like a cocoon, and the two of them tumbled downstairs.

San Francisco was hazy and cool, with a stiff wind coming in over the bay where the airport sat, far outside the city actually. Her uncle and his family came to meet them, and they rode to the city in his van, filled with his children and their conversation, mostly in English with an occasional string of Mandarin wrapped around it. Ting sat, surrounded by it all, smiling when she could. Her mother seemed cheered by her brother's presence and attitude. It was not, as Ting had feared, like going to a funeral. Grandmother might be seriously, dreadfully ill . . . but no one seemed to think they were going to be burying her soon. That made everything something to look forward to.

When the van finally neared the city and its neighborhoods, they all grew a little quieter, only her uncle and mother in the front seats talking, their voices pitched so softly that it was very hard to hear them. When they neared her grandmother's address, it was impossible not to know. Asian faces filled the streets. Chinese calligraphy lettered shop windows and billboards, even the great banks at the corners, as well as small eateries. She could smell delicious, smoky odors as they drove by . . . garlic, ginger, other spices she couldn't name. She thought of FireAnn, the Magicker cook and herbalist with the fiery red hair, and how she could probably reel off every aroma floating from restaurants and home kitchens alike.

She saw many elders walking the streets in their quilted jacket and trouser outfits, very Old World, and yet not at all strange here. Then, at last, they pulled up to the house, hidden behind its circular driveway. When Ting got out of the van, she tilted her head back and stared briefly at the bronze dragon coiled along the roof's edge. The chrysanthemums were a brilliant orange-red, like the ripest of persimmons.

Her uncle paused next to her, his arms full of baggage. "I painted the flowers for her birthday," he said. "Enameled them, actually. You like?"

Ting beamed at him. "I do!"

He nodded. "So did she. Come inside. I imagine she has lunch waiting."

They entered the house. Actually, with Uncle and all the nieces and nephews, it was more like an invasion. Her grandmother appeared in the small, very formal living room, dressed in a flowered Chinese red dress that made her appear very tiny, very pale, and very old, her formerly dark hair now almost entirely silver. Ting could not remember her grandmother's glossy black hair going gray, but it obviously had.

Pleasure spread over her grandmother's face as she opened her arms to embrace them.

And indeed, she had luncheon ready. The great, round kitchen table was spread with two kinds of rice, duck, Buddha's delight with tofu squares in vegetables and brown sauce, two green bean dishes, and one big heaping platter of chicken cooked in a gingery, garlicky sauce. Ting's stomach growled in spite of herself as she sat down, and her grandmother smiled. She sat next to Ting and hugged her shoulders.

"I am so glad you could come to help me." Little was said

beyond that as everyone took out their chopsticks and practically fell on the lunch.

Ting noticed that her grandmother ate little, although she nursed a cup of egg drop soup, and a fine porcelain cup of tea throughout the meal. She looked up to meet her mother's gaze and realized Jiao had caught that as well. She shook her head slightly at Ting. Now was not the time. There would be many days ahead.

After the meal, Uncle Han took his boisterous family and left them alone. She helped her mother put away the leftovers and clear the table. Then they cleaned the kitchen. Grandmother lapsed into a silence, her lips pressed in a pained line, as if exhausted by it all. They worked around her gently, trying not to disturb her, and then Jiao fixed a pot of fragrant jasmine tea, and they gathered together again.

She took her mother's hands in hers as Ting poured them all cups.

"I am glad you came," the old woman said, her voice very thin and tired.

"I am glad you told us we could come." Jiao kissed her mother's forehead. "We will see this through."

"My fortune and house is a strong one."

Ting sat down quietly.

"As for you." Her grandmother's almond eyes turned to her. "I am sorry to take you from your school and friends."

"I'm happy to be here. And I can go to school here, and well . . . I can help here."

"But still . . ." Grandmother signaled Jiao to sit. She took up her teacup. "Ting. I have only seen you once since the summer, but I know you have changed. You have begun to walk a new path."

Ting looked into her dark, rosy tea. What did her grandmother mean? She didn't want to think. Was she going to have to sit here and listen to a lecture about growing up? She peeked at her mother. Jiao gave no sign of anything in her expression. Ting tried not to sigh, and settled on the hard rosewood chair, prepared for a lesson she was not even sure she would understand, steeped as it would be in old Chinese proverbs.

Her grandmother said firmly, "Look at me, please."

Embarrassed, Ting raised her gaze.

"We know," her grandmother said, nodding to Jiao and then looking back at her. "We know your secret."

"Know what?" Ting felt totally baffled. Then it began to creep in fearfully. Know . . . *what?*

Her grandmother stretched out a hand. It was still an elegant hand, for all the age showing in her knuckles and slightly wrinkled skin. She moved, and a fan filled her fingers, snapping open with a second graceful movement. She dropped the fan, made another gesture, and her hand filled with silk flowers. She dropped that bouquet on top of the fan. "On the mainland, my father was a magician. He was known for his talent and his wisdom, but as you know, true wizardry is not sleight of hand."

Ting thought her heart would stop. Oh, no! The Oath of Binding crept into her throat. Even if she wanted to, she could not speak! She stared at her mother desperately. *Oh, please, don't ask me anything!* she begged silently.

Her grandmother waited, watching her face. Then, after long moments in which Ting thought her heartbeat ticked as loudly as the old clock on the wall, she sat back in her chair. She reached out and took Ting's wrist in her hand, and turned it, showing plainly the bracelet with its caged bit of crystal in it. She tapped the crystal.

"We know," her grandmother repeated quietly.

Now there was no doubt about it. Ting's secret of being a Magicker was no longer secret!

Henry and Bailey were walking the mall near the pizza restaurant when McIntire dropped the two boys off. Jason and Trent bailed out of the truck, waved good-bye after a few instructions on when and where to be picked up.

"Is she here yet?"

Bailey shook her head. "Any minute now, I bet." The evening sky had begun to darken, and shoppers thinned out as dinner elsewhere called them. The atrium ceiling of the mall showed stars already, their silvery blue twinkle bright in a dark October sky. Only the costume shops were still doing a brisk business, their storefronts filled with mannequins in wizard and witch costumes, and satin cats with sequined masks. There was a werewolf in the far corner, fake fur costume bristling in gray-and-black stripes. Henry let out a shudder as they passed it, and Trent and Jason swapped glances. *Test*, mouthed Trent at Jason, and Jason nodded. If Bailey noticed, she didn't show it. She paced up and down the mall, her face scrunched up. Finally, she disappeared into the public phone kiosk.

She came out, flailing her arms in exasperation. "She's not coming."

"What?" Henry's round face collapsed in disappointment and he rubbed his nose. "Not coming?"

"She's not even in the same county any more."

"Ting?" chorused Jason and Trent together.

Bailey gave an emphatic nod. "How," she demanded, "can we have a surprise party without the honored guest?"

Truth or Dare

"TING'S gone?"

"She's already left for San Francisco. In fact, she was up there by lunchtime." Bailey crossed her arms over her body. "I talked to her older sister, who says she called and left a message at your house yesterday, Jason, but somebody forgot to pass it along."

He winced. "I didn't get it."

"Obviously." Bailey tossed her head.

The only one he could think of who might have thoughtlessly forgotten it would have been Alicia. He made a mental note to ask her about things like that more often. Just in case. "Sorry."

Henry let out a discouraged sound, drawing Bailey's attention. Jason kept his mouth shut, happy the other distracted her.

Bailey nudged Squibb, softening. "Hey, it's not like we can't talk to her when she gets her computer set up again! After all, we've been e-mailing Danno even though he's an ocean away from us now."

His round face brightened a little. "True."

"Well, then. We're all here anyway. Let's go order a pizza and talk. You guys can tell me all about the game you've been running."

Henry fell into step with her, Jason and Trent trailing behind. "It's been great. You ought to join. Hey, guys," he threw back over one shoulder. "We can fit her in, can't we? Pick up an elf along the way or something?"

Bailey waved her hand. "No, no. My mom won't let me online that long. We have to keep the phone line clear, in case she gets a call from work or something. Sounds like fun, though. So what do you play?" and she ducked her head, listening intently, as Henry happily told her all about his halfling alter ego, filled with cheerful larceny. She laughed as they made their way to the pizza parlor.

They ordered two, because all three of the boys professed to being starving, and Bailey wanted to make sure she'd have some for herself. And a pitcher of root beer to go around for everyone but Henry. "I don't drink soft drinks any more," he apologized. "Not since I got back from camp. Something about sugary, fruity tasting things . . ." He quivered. "Water or iced tea, no sweetener, for me!"

The Draft of Forgetfulness had been a berry concoction Fire-Ann stewed for days at the back of Camp Ravenwyng's kitchen. No one knew what it was at first. Henry had been one of the first to drink it, and seeing him go . . . blank . . . had been devastating. Later, the other campers being sent home because of the Brennard attack would drink it, too, except for the handful Jason had rallied and hidden away. He'd had plans of his own! Jason had thought the Draft incredibly harsh, but the others had insisted it was best. He still didn't think so.

By the time the pizzas arrived, bread crust steaming on round aluminum pans dripping over with melted cheese, they had their table covered with maps and graphs and character descriptions, and lists of treasures and magic items recovered so far. They talked of orcs and dragons and enchanted swords and crafty adventurers. Curious onlookers from nearby glanced over from time to time, smiling, as tales of a fantasy world swirled around their table.

Only once did Bailey sigh and sit back, saying she wished Ting were there. Henry reached for her hand to pat it, and instead found himself holding a furry creature as it darted down Bailey's sleeve. He let out a squawk, and then shut his lips, face reddening in embarrassment.

Bailey grabbed for Lacey who had evidently decided she'd waited long enough for pizza crumbs! The little kangaroo mouse chittered in annoyance as Bailey stuffed her back in her pocket.

Henry reached for his water. He gulped down half a glass and nearly choked on an ice cube. He lowered his voice. "You picked up a rat!"

"Mouse!" hissed Bailey back. "Well, kangaroo mouse . . . a pack rat. Don't you remember my pack rat from camp?"

Henry shook his head as Trent and Jason muffled their amusement and each reached for another slice of pizza.

"Well, she haunted our cottage. Stole things right and left, much like your halfling. We found her, though, and she was just too little to put back in the wild. What if something ate her? So she's mine now."

"And hungry, too, it seems." Henry scrubbed at an eyebrow. He pinched off a bit of cheesy dough and passed it to Bailey. "Maybe that'll help."

"Couldn't hurt!" Bailey said cheerfully and stuffed it down her pocket. Her shirt rumpled and rippled and there was a tiny, contented chirping sound. Henry's eyes grew a bit rounder behind his circular glass lenses.

Trent pushed aside an empty pizza tin, gathering up some of his papers. "Enough about D & D. How about some truth and dare?"

Jason leaned on his elbows. "Secrets?"

"Sure." Trent waited while everyone stored away the paperwork they had brought. "Everyone has secrets. Like Lacey."

"Well . . . okay." Bailey wiped off the table in front of her carefully, poking another small bread crumb or three down into her pocket and settled down, watching Trent.

Henry took off his glasses solemnly and cleaned them. Trent nudged him, saying, "Relax! This is supposed to be fun." Henry bobbed his head, brown hair waving up and down. "Who wants to go first?" Trent looked round the table.

"Me," Bailey said with a definite nod of her head that sent her golden-brown ponytail bouncing.

"Okay. Hmm. Let me confer with my associate." Trent grinned and leaned over to Jason. They talked for a moment. Trent straightened up. He gazed at Bailey a moment before saying, "Is it true you prefer Brad Pitt over Justin Timberlake and would kiss either to death if you had the chance?"

"Trent!" Bailey gasped, her face glowing pink.

"Truth or Dare?"

She babbled for a moment, then shut her mouth and said firmly, "Dare."

"Ooooh." Trent grinned. "Gotta be a good one."

"Conference," suggested Jason, leaning over.

"Righto."

They talked for a few minutes, and then Trent pointed at Bailey. "Three times around the restaurant, making chicken noises as you go."

"We'll get thrown out!" Bailey stared at him.

"You chose the dare." Trent sat, unmoved.

"I can't do that." Bailey glanced around the parlor, which was still fairly full of diners. A sports team of boys their age reigned at two whole tables in one corner although their talk and laughter wasn't loud enough to be disturbing.

Trent just stared at her.

"All right. All right." Bailey stood slowly. She put her hands back and tightened the scrunchie on her hair, and took a deep breath. Deliberately, she walked to the center of the room. "Ladies and gentlemen," she said loudly, but not too loudly. "In praise of the barbecued chicken pizza!" And she began to trot around the room, arms bent at her elbows, begawking and clucking every few steps.

Trent rolled against Jason, laughing. Jason tried not to explode in mirth but couldn't help it. "Thank goodness we don't have live chickens in here!"

Trent turned red at that. "They'd all be following her!"

Bailey tossed her head, ponytail bobbing. "Begawk! Bock! Bock!"

Diners turned and laughed. Her face got pinker, and the cooks came out of the kitchen, watching curiously. As she drew near the end of her third circle, Bailey threw up her hands and said, "Chicken pizza so great I just had to squawk about it!"

She bowed all around to applause and chuckles, then raced back to their table amid cheers and claps. She poked Trent. "So there!"

"Well done. Your turn." Unabashed and unflinching, Trent grinned at her and gave her a tiny salute.

Henry looked at her in total awe. "That was great, Bailey. I'd have never thought of anything like that."

"I am a genius." Bailey gave another little bow. She leaned over, adding, "And I didn't get us thrown out either!"

Jason looked across the room. "I wouldn't say that." They all stopped talking as the manager began to approach them. He stopped at their table, envelope in hand.

"I don't know what brought that on, but it was one of the nicest endorsements I've ever had." He passed the envelope to Bailey and left.

She opened it slowly, then began to giggle.

"What is it?"

"A coupon for a free barbecued chicken pizza! I'll bring Ting when she gets back." Laughing, Bailey tucked it inside her backpack. "Okay. My turn!" She looked around the table. "Jason," she announced slowly.

"Rut roh," commented Trent as Jason sat up straighter.

Ignoring Trent, Bailey continued levelly, "Who would you rather kiss . . . Jennifer or Eleanora?"

Jason's jaw dropped for a moment as he tried to think of an answer. But he didn't have to give one, because he was interrupted.

Henry spluttered. "Eleanora! Jason can't kiss her!" he blurted out. "She's . . . she's . . . she's beautiful. And older. She could . . . she's got Magick . . . she could turn you into a toad if she wanted to, Jason!" He took his glasses off again and rubbed his eyes as if totally embarrassed by his outburst.

He didn't notice the looks they all exchanged round the table. "Calm down," Bailey said quietly. "It's just a game." She rolled her eyes as nearby tables looked over curiously, then looked away again and the murmur of other conversations rose around them.

"Actually," Jason said truthfully, "if I had to kiss anyone right now, it would be you, Bailey. Thank heavens I don't have to!" He grabbed Henry. "Henry, do you know what you just said? Do you?"

Henry's hands shook so his glasses fell to the table with a clatter. His face whitened. "I . . . I . . . I . . ." His words ground to a halt, and they could all see the cords in his neck tighten.

Bailey scooted her chair over. "It's all right, Henry," she said quietly. "It's all right."

"I'm not crazy," he said finally, in a squeaky, forced, and scared voice. It was barely audible.

"No way. None of us are." Trent picked up his glasses and handed them back.

"You don't know what I mean."

"Oh, I think we do," Jason told him. He pitched his voice low so as not to be overheard, whether everyone thought they were still talking about their gaming or not. This was a public place, and they would all do well to be wary. Still, things had to be said. "We all do. We're all Magickers, Henry. And it looks like you still are, too."

"A . . . a . . . what?"

"Magicker," Jason, Bailey, and Trent all repeated to him simultaneously.

He looked very pale. Trent nudged a glass of water over to him, saying, "Drink it slowly."

He did so, every last drop, and looked much better when he set the glass down. "All of you?"

"All of us," Jason said. "Including you."

Henry made a sound of utter relief. "Thank goodness," he added. "I really thought I'd lost it." He squirmed in his chair. "I wanted to ask about it, you know . . . there are these big, blank spots about the camp which I ought to have known but didn't, even coming home early like I did. And nightmares. I've had some awful nightmares. Not about you guys, though!" He shook his head.

"About Jonnard?"

"How did you . . . well, of course you know. You remember."

"He stole your Magick, Henry," Bailey said in a rush. "No one thought you'd ever get it back, so they made you drink this juice drink, called the Draft of Forgetfulness, and they sent you home. But you were stronger than that, and Jason was right all along. He didn't want any of us to forget about you."

"What did you think?" Henry eyed Jason.

"I never thought they should send you home, and I think you're getting stronger every day. Which is good—and bad."

"Bad? How?"

Trent tapped the table, talking for Jason. "One, you're not

trained well, none of us are, but you've missed a lot, and two, you're in danger because of it."

"What else could possibly go wrong?" Henry stared in disbelief at them.

Jason felt the hairs at the back of his neck prickle. The scar on his left hand gave a twinge. He moved in his chair, and looked around the mall restaurant. "Plenty," he began.

"Oh, look," someone said. "Someone's wearing that werewolf costume from the shop!"

There was a sound of chairs rattling as people moved to look. He looked.

He stood, grabbing Henry and Bailey by their jackets and yelling for the one friend he couldn't quite reach. "Trent!"

The werewolf-looking creature peered into the windows of the pizza parlor and let out a low, rumbling growl.

"That's no costume."

Moonstruck

"WOLFJACKAL!" Bailey's face went dead white even as she grabbed up her things.

Jason reached for his crystal as Trent joined the other two, and he searched the room for another way out as the wolfjackal sprang to the doorway, blocking it. He found one, marked Emergency Exit Only, and pulled them all that way, muttering, "If there was ever an Emergency . . ."

No one argued. Henry hit the door's big chrome bar first. His chunky body came to a halt. They piled up behind him. Jason turned and saw the wolfjackal come through the pizza parlor entrance, huge and snarling. A woman turned, looked, and screamed, her voice shrilling through the noise of other diners and the row of game machines in the corner. "It's real! George, it's real!"

The room dissolved into crashes of chairs and screams.

"Go, go, go!"

"I'm trying!" Henry grunted. He struggled to push the heavy bar with Bailey throwing her shoulder against it as well. The two suddenly plunged through, setting off loud alarms everywhere. Lacey poked her head out, squeaking in terror, her tail hanging out, black tuft jerking about. She dove back into safety, only her tuft twitching, as they all stumbled into the back street outside the pizza parlor.

"This way!" Jason spoke a word as he pushed through, and his hand filled with the golden lanternlike illumination from his crystal, and they dashed away, with a growling snarl just a leap behind. He could hear the animal grunt as it gave chase and crashed into the closing door. Above it all, the loud thin alarm of the Emergency Exit shrilled through the air.

"Run," he yelled, "as fast and hard as you can."

They didn't need his encouragement.

As golden light from his hand spilled out into the black alley, revealing dark looming shapes from huge trash bins, and skittering paper trash that the October wind swirled about as they raced through, they heard the low, haunting howl of the wolf-jackal. It had gotten outside after them.

Henry managed to pant, "I don't remember that. Somehow, you'd think I would!"

They swerved around a low block wall that marked a delivery dock for the back of the big department store that took up most of the space at this part of the mall. Debris scattered about them as they ran. Trent muttered, "Hurry, hurry, hurry," while the golden light from Jason's crystal spilled out like a fountain from a Fourth of July sparkler. Cars were scattered throughout the lot, parked and empty, and great overhead lights tried to thin the darkness without much success. Their sneakers slapped the ground at a frantic pace, because they knew that no doorway or nook could be ducked into, for the sharp nose of the wolfjackal would not be easily fooled. It was a chase, a chase until someone dropped or was cornered or the wolfjackal could be attacked hard enough to frighten it away.

They swung around the lower edge of the mall and found

themselves heading uphill where it was harder to run. They faced less traffic, fewer cars, as the only building they approached was a store that had gone out of business. The building was huge, dominating the whole upper end of the shopping area. It lay in front of them like some petrified giant beast.

Vast store windows were boarded over with plywood nailed securely for protection, decorated only by the trash wrappers clinging to them and the occasional spray-painted graffiti. The quiet in this section of the shopping park made the chase seem more ominous. There would be no unexpected help coming their way.

Bailey wobbled. She bumped shoulders with Henry unsteadily, then turned and threw a desperate look at Jason and Trent. "I can't run much longer . . . not on a stomach full of pizza."

"Not running is not an option!" Trent shouted back at her. He grabbed her elbow to steady her.

"I . . . can't . . . help it." She let out a belch of despair and Jason felt badly for her.

The only stand they could make was with one of them shielding and the other attacking. Trent couldn't do it, and Henry had no crystal nor training . . . if his Magick was even strong enough yet to attempt it. That left Bailey and she was good, but he feared her Magick still wouldn't be enough. Although Trent and Henry could grab something, a box or stick and whack away at it. Holding their ground seemed impossible . . . unless. . . .

The sound of tires squealing reached him. He looked out into the empty parking lot of the abandoned store and saw headlights racing closer. A vehicle careened toward them. Teens, accelerating and skidding through the open lot.

Jason swerved abruptly into the loading dock bay, pulling the others in with him. He went to one knee. "Bailey! Shield. Trent, protect Henry." He cupped his crystal, snuffing out the lantern light. Next to him, Bailey dug under her jacket and sweater, and grabbed her pendant. Its white light flared out and into an umbrella over them. She burped again, rolled her eyes, and said, "Remind me never to eat and run again." Her shield light flickered, then grew stronger.

Trent drew Henry next to him.

Jason rubbed his crystal gently, calling on the Magicker beacon. He could not feel an answering warmth. "Beacon's off again."

"It can't be."

"Well, it is! Someone's either blocking it, or it's gone out or . . ." Words failed him as the wolfjackal sprang onto the asphalt in front of them, crouching, eyes glinting, and ivory fangs gleaming from lips drawn back in a snarl. The beast put his head back in a triumphant howl.

"Yup," said Henry. "I would have definitely remembered this!"

"Good news," muttered Trent. "There's only one of 'em."

Another snarl ripped the air as a second wolfjackal padded around the corner of the building, its skulking body slinking into position next to its pack mate.

"Bad news," Trent added. "I can't count." He pulled his crystal out for Bailey's benefit. Dull and opaque even on the best days, it stayed that way now. "Even worse news, I've got the Curse. Crystal is deader than a doornail." He shoved it back into his sweatshirt pocket and reached for a length of wood, part of a splintered loading pallet, lying against the block wall of the dock. "Grab one, Henry, and make yourself useful."

Henry took up a thick piece and waved it in his hand like a club. He followed Trent's advice not a moment too soon as both wolfjackals bunched their haunches and then sprang at them!

Jason sent a beam slicing through the air, not unlike a laser sword. It sizzled as he wielded it, white-hot light cutting at the beasts. One wolfjackal yelped and curled about, biting at the beam and snarling. His pack mate hit the ground rolling and came up snapping at Henry and Trent. The creatures' hot breath steamed the cold night air. Trent fenced with one wolfjackal while Henry clubbed at its dancing feet. Bailey held steady, shielding them as well as she could, although the power of the wolfjackals slashed into her barrier again and again.

Jason turned, taking a long sweep at the beast facing him. Foam whipped from its jaws as it spun about, tracking him. His beam landed, the impulse rocking into his arm and shoulder, but the wolfjackal barely faltered. He jabbed and sliced again, his crystal sharp against the palm of his hand as he held it tightly. Jason could feel his power, holding the creature back but not really harming or driving it away. Eventually he'd weaken, and the wolfjackal would lunge through Bailey's shield. His pack mate yelped as Trent clipped it on the head, and the beast went rolling. It scrabbled for purchase on the slick, dark pavement as it did, amid the squeal of tires from outside the loading dock, and Jason got an idea.

"Drive 'em out of here and stay clear!" he said.

Trent and Henry surged forward, swinging their wooden slats and quickly fell back behind Bailey as the wolfjackal snapped, and Henry's wooden sword splintered in its jaws. The second one drove in, grabbing Trent and shaking him like a doll and not letting go till Trent beat it on the head with his jagged wooden board. He staggered back, into Henry and Bailey, with a curse, sweatshirt ripping as the beast let go. "They ain't budging."

"Try another plan," panted Henry.

Jason had one. But he wasn't at all sure it would work.

"Hold 'em here, then!" he cried out, and took a running start. He catapulted over the shoulders of the nearest beast, barely clearing it, and hit the ground in a dash. Both critters whirled with howls and scrambled after him. He knew they would, of course. Well, not knew, but hoped!

"Jason!" cried Bailey sharply in warning, and he swerved. A heavy body lunged just past him, and he could practically feel its foaming jaws as it did. It smelled of hot beast and something fearful he couldn't identify, something no natural creature smelled of. He swerved again, sharply, dodging into the parking lot.

They all collided: joyriding teens, Jason, and raiding wolf-jackals. The car's headlights blinded him for a moment, the squeal of brakes filling his ears as it skimmed past him, and the heavy thud as the vehicle hit a beast, sending its limp body rolling and rolling. Wild yipes suddenly went quiet. The second wolfjackal let out a mournful howl, took a leap over its pack mate's body, and disappeared into the night.

The car skidded to a halt. Jason bent over, hands on his knees, breathing hard. The crumpled, bloody form of the remaining wolfjackal wavered as if in a mirage. Then it disappeared from sight. The asphalt where it had lain showed not a trace of its existence. Dead, yes. Gone where? Back to its own element? Or had its sender called it back?

Car doors opened and four teens piled out.

"What was that!"

He looked up. "Man, you hit my dog!" Straightening, he pointed a hand into the night.

"Oh, man. How bad is he hurt?"

"He ran off."

"Oh."

"Can't be too bad if he ran off. Come on, let's go." One of the passengers tucked at the sleeve of the stocky driver.

"What about my bumper?"

Jason stared angrily. "What about your bumper? Could have been *me* you hit! What are you doing driving out here like that, anyway?"

They sneered uncertainly. "Come on, let's get out of here. Then, almost as one, they turned and piled back into their car.

As quickly as it had spit them out, the car swallowed up the four teens. Its engines revved and it squealed away into the darkness. The upper level of the mall went pitch-black as its lights faded away.

"That was close," Trent said at his elbow.

"Yeah."

"Guys? I've gotta get back . . . it's time for my mom to pick me up," Henry said, abashed. He dropped his board and dusted his hands free of grime and splinters. Then he grinned. "And I'm even more afraid of my mom than whatever it is we just faced."

Bailey giggled, in spite of herself. She cupped her crystal, and the glow faded. Jason's felt white-hot to his hand as he put it away, wincing. "We'd better hurry," he suggested. "There's still one out there, maybe. Even one wolfjackal can do a lot of damage."

They gathered themselves to hurry Henry back to his rendez-vous point.

Game Plan

THEY grouped together under a faintly shining streetlight, its amber glow nearly obscured by the evening air and a foggy mist that threatened to grow stronger. After a few deep breaths and shaky laughs between them, Jason managed, "Everyone all right?"

"I'm fine, but I think my sweatshirt is totaled."

Bailey tossed her head, cheeks apple rosy even in the dim glow of the streetlight, her golden-brown ponytail bobbing. "I'm great, but Lacey is buried in my pocket somewhere, shaking so hard she probably won't come out for two days."

"Or till she's hungry." Trent grinned at Bailey.

"Maybe a cookie." She nodded. "How about you?" She watched Jason. "They were after all of us, but I'd say you were the target."

"This thing is burning a hole in my pocket!" Jason pulled out his crystal, and it glowed in the night like a fallen star.

"Wow." Bailey leaned close. "Ever do that before?"

"It's done some odd things, but nothing quite like this."

She touched hers. "Mine is cold. Like a battery or something . . . it gets drained sometimes. Then it goes all icy." She shivered as though she shared the chill with her crystal.

"That's exactly what it is, Bailey. A battery gone dead. You have to recharge." Trent shrugged into his sweatshirt, and examined his sleeve for a moment, looking at the small, jagged tears. "That's about as close as I want to get to a wolfjackal for a long time."

Jason frowned. "He didn't break skin, did he?" He rubbed the scar on the back of his left hand absently.

"Noooo." Trent pushed his sleeve back, then shook his head emphatically. "A smack here and there, and Bailey's shield . . . I'm okay. Henry seemed to be, too, although we hustled him into his mom's car so quick it was hard to tell. A lot of good the alarm beacon did us."

"But that proves it isn't working," noted Bailey. "We've been wondering about that, and now we know. Unless that's some kind of response making your crystal glow, but I don't see what that helps and it never did that before, unless Gavan or someone is feeding you power to break the Curse."

"Maybe."

"I think we're out of range now." Trent cast his gaze around. "We can't stand out here all night, it's getting late, and we've got to get back. Focus, and see what's up, if you can."

Jason nodded absently, already cupping his crystal and beginning to look into its myriad depths. He rubbed his hands together, rolling his focus between his palms. He blinked, then looked up. "I don't know how . . ." he stopped in mid-sentence.

Bailey stomped her foot. "Stop that right now, Jason Adrian. How, what, when and where!"

"Someone's imprinted a message in my crystal."

Trent glanced at Bailey. "You missed Who."

"Oh, shush." She stared at Jason. "I didn't know that could be done."

Jason shook his head. "Me either. Hold on, let me see . . . I mean, I don't know how to retrieve it or anything. This is not an answering machine." He cupped his hands, looking down into his focus.

"It is now," returned Trent. He tried not to shiver as the cold, dark wind swirled around them, making it more than ever like a Halloween night. It wasn't, of course, but with wolfjackals and rogue Magickers after them, it might as well have been.

Bailey stood on one foot and then the other, hunched into her jacket. "Who is it?" she asked several times, getting no response from Jason as he concentrated heavily on the crystal he gripped.

"Bailey!" he finally snapped.

She looked at Trent, rolled her eyes, and fell silent after muttering, "That put frost on the old pumpkin." She folded her arms over her chest and shut her mouth tightly.

Jason's lips were moving slightly as if that helped him see or concentrate on what he was revealing hidden inside the crystal, a message as slow to appear as snail tracks on a sidewalk. Tired from the long day, the chase, and the battle, Trent thought of napping while his friend worked through the message, then as quickly dismissed it. *Dark Hand,* he thought, *still trying to muddle my mind and reactions.*

Then Jason gasped! "It's from Fizziwig!"

"It is? No kidding? The guy Gavan's been looking for?" Bailey gave a bounce.

"Who?" Trent stifled a yawn.

"Yes, but it looks like he's found me." Jason frowned and gripped his crystal tightly. "He's the Magicker who's been missing, Trent. He's been on some sort of assignment for the Council and he went missing before camp even started."

Trent whistled.

"He's sent this message and engraved it inside one of the

quartz walls, but it disappears as soon as I read it. All but this last word."

Bailey had uncrossed her arms. "Which is. . . ?"

Jason shook his head. "Can't say it until we're ready to go, because it'll bring us to him. It looks like some kind of hyperlink. It activates when I say it. He says he's found something of great importance to the Gatekeeper."

Bailey rubbed her nose. "Didn't you tell me he knew something about Gates?"

Jason nodded to her.

"Then let's go!"

Jason hesitated again. "Bailey, there're some urgent questions here. Like, should we tell Gavan and the others about the attack first? But if we do, are they going to rein us in?"

"And," added Trent, "how does this Fizziwig know about you? Since he hasn't been seen since last spring. If he's been missing, I would assume he's had no contact with anybody."

Their gazes met. "True. That's a very good point, Trent."

The other bowed.

Jason looked back into his hand and crystal reluctantly. "It could be a trap."

"Something to think about anyway."

"Let's think about what Fizziwig said." Bailey peered at Jason. "What exactly did he say?"

"Desperate times mean desperate measures. I have found something of great importance for you, Gatekeeper. Speak and find me, elder Fizziwig." Jason cleared his throat. "That's about it."

"He has that flair. Victorian or something, like Eleanora. It could be a genuine message." She considered Jason's words. Trent merely shrugged.

He looked at the two of them. "Are we going, then?"

"I'm about charged up." Bailey rubbed her crystal pendant, hidden under the flap of her jacket.

Trent grinned. "I'm as charged as I'll ever be. And we've still got some time before our rides home"

"All right, then." Jason opened his hand and said, *"Come!"* His figure wavered and started to thin, like mist.

"No!" Bailey grabbed for Trent's wrist. "Jason, no! We're not joined!"

Too late, as his body disappeared altogether into fog and the wind threatened to shred even that away. Bailey gripped her pendant hard, yelling, *"Follow!"*

"What are you doing?" Trent gawked at her.

"Following!" Her expression was fixed in concentration as she held onto his hand tightly.

And they did. There was a moment when the night whirled around them, and they felt as cold and indistinct as a wet wisp of fog, and then with a *thump*, they appeared inside a thickly carpeted hall, well polished oak panels surrounding them, and a door just closing ahead of the two of them.

"Someone's house," Bailey murmured.

"You think? Actually, it seems to be more of a mansion. Maybe even a castle," Trent commented.

She nudged him. Her hand fell away from her pendant. "I don't like the feel of this. It stinks of wolfjackal and the others." She looked up and down the hallway uneasily.

He didn't either but wouldn't say so because his feeling came from entirely different senses than hers. "This is where your rock led us. Let's just find Jason and get out of here. *If* it worked. We could be burglars or something if it didn't." He pointed at the door. "That looks like the best bet."

She arched her neck, squinting back down the long corridor. "I know there're times when it's just not wise to go barging around. He's here somewhere, I feel it, but . . ."

"Gotta start someplace." He put his hand on the knob, turning it slowly, and pushing the door inward. It creaked with all the theatrical noise of a Hollywood horror movie. "After you."

Bailey stood in the doorway, her back to the jamb. "I think I'll keep one foot in the door, thank you."

Trent moved past her. "Well, someone has to go in."

Bailey tossed her head, ponytail swinging, and answered firmly, "It doesn't have to be me. And Jason is already in there." She looked into the amber-shadowed room, and saw the silent figure of their friend standing by the side of a great wing chair that faced an immense fireplace with brass firedogs at either side.

Trent frowned. Of course, Jason was already there! And if he'd been attuned to his crystal, he would have known that. Many more mistakes like that and the whole world would know he wasn't fit to be a Magicker. He thumbed the opaque rock hanging from its watch fob as he stopped at the center of the room. "Jason?" His voice echoed in the vast library, and sort of hung there, although he swore he could hear pages ripple as if an opened book were disturbed.

A very long moment passed during which Trent seriously wondered if he and Bailey could even be noticed by their friend. Then Jason stirred and looked up, his face pale and stricken. "I've found him," he said slowly. He put one hand on the brocaded chair. "And he's dead."

He pushed on the chair, and it swung around slowly, revealing the body of the late Fizziwig, dressed in dark suit and smoking jacket, thin white hair all tousled, with a surprised expression on his still, dead face. He'd been a spry old man from the look of him, and there wasn't a mark on him aside from his surprised expression.

A door shut with great authority. Bailey moved into the room, her face angry. "That does it." She gestured furiously. "We know it's the Dark Hand, this whole place reeks of their Magick."

"We don't know that they killed him."

Trent pointed out, "We know that they were here, and he's not alive."

Jason unclenched his left hand slowly. He looked at the two of them, first Trent, then Bailey. "We don't know what happened here. We don't even know what he thought it was important to tell me."

Trent slowly pivoted in a circle, surveying all the bookshelves built into the library walls and running from floor to ceiling on three sides, leaving only the massive fireplace and a few paintings on the fourth wall. He touched a shelf, a massive book whose spine read *Ars Magica and Secularus*. His fingers tingled, and he drew his hand back hastily. "If it's a book, we've got a long search."

"I don't intend to stay in here with a dead man long enough to look. We have to tell the elders and the authorities." Jason shifted uneasily. "We should have contacted Gavan and the others before coming."

"That's great. Not only am I out later than I should be, but I found a body." Bailey wrinkled her nose.

"We found it," Trent corrected her. "Normally, I'd vote for calling 911, but . . . this time . . . I think maybe we should get hold of an elder."

Jason nodded. "My thoughts exactly."

Bailey lifted her chin defiantly. "We've got to tell the others, warn everyone . . . and then get ready. It's us against them now, and they've given us no choice. Opposites attack."

The Dark Hand Closes

"THE first thing we do," Tomaz said calmly, "is get you kids out of here. Then I call in Dr. Patel to get the body. We take care of our own, and no stranger will touch Fizziwig." He frowned, his weathered face showing deeply etched lines. "None of you should be here. What happened?"

"Fizziwig sent me a message." Jason tapped his crystal. "I thought it was important, so we came."

"You knew he was a Magicker?"

"Yes, I remembered the name." Jason shifted. "We wouldn't have come otherwise, Tomaz, but he etched a message inside my crystal. I've never heard of anything like that before, and it seemed important. I never thought . . . I never thought I'd find him like this." Jason gestured helplessly. "Look, we know it's dangerous now."

"Dangerous is not a strong enough word for it, and I don't want to have to be rescuing any of you from situations you shouldn't have been in, in the first place. Do I make myself clear?"

"We'll be careful!" Bailey promised.

"Good." He dropped a hand on Jason's shoulder, and squeezed slightly. "Brennard's searching for you. We cannot be sure why, but we assume it's because the handful of you seem to be the most Talented. The others are scattered to the four winds, unaware and untapped, and they'll stay that way till we have an academy to offer them safety, but you . . . all of you are at great risk. It comes with great ability." Bailey flushed, pleased, but Tomaz barely paused in his speech. "That confers extra responsibility on you. We expect many things of you. Don't disappoint us."

Jason felt the failure of Camp Ravenwyng, like a heavy burden on him. "We won't," answered Jason, with Bailey and Trent echoing him faintly.

"Good." Tomaz took a deep breath and without any of them even blinking, they were *gone,* swept away with him.

A blink of nothingness and then all stood in Gavan Rainwater's office at Camp Ravenwyng, stopping the Magicker in midpace, electric lights flaring in the room, and his dark cloak swirling about him. He pivoted on one heel. "Tomaz! Got them all, have you?"

Crowfeather nodded, and released his grip on Jason's shoulder. "They will tell you the tale. I have to take Anita back."

"It's true, then?" Sadness veiled Gavan's face. "You found Fizziwig?"

Tomaz nodded.

Gavan sighed before gesturing. "Better hurry, then. I don't know what the Dark Hand will make of these circumstances, but let's not give them a chance."

"It will be done." Tomaz was there, and then he was not.

"Whoa." Bailey let out her breath. "I'd like to be able to do that! He's fast . . . I have to think and think . . . it's like the hare and the snail."

Trent blinked. "You meant the tortoise and the hare."

She looked at him. "I meant what I said!" She gave an of-
fended sniff.

Gavan smiled slightly and perched on the corner of his great
desk, looking at them all. "Teleporting comes with focus and
knowing exactly where you're going. The more certainty, the
quicker you come and go." The beacon crystal sat on a filing
cabinet in the corner, its clear crystalline facets sparkling in the
light. "Practice, Bailey, practice." He rubbed his palm over the
pewter wolfhead of his cane. "Are you all right? All of you?"

"That," Trent told him, "was my first dead guy."

Gavan winced. "We had no way of knowing, but we would
have spared you all that if we could. I had hoped beyond hoping
that Fizziwig was all right, just buried in some research of his
own." He coughed. "Perhaps buried is a bad choice of words?"

Jason laughed nervously.

"It's okay. He didn't look bad or anything. Just very, very
still. I mean, for a minute or two, we all wondered if he was a
dummy or something." Bailey put her hand over her pocket,
stilling her pet for a moment. "He was in a library, a huge one."

"Tell me what happened then," the Magicker said, and stood
back as the flood of words began, prompted now and then by a
question from him, until all three finally grew quiet as the last
words spilled out of them and faded away.

Gavan shook his head. "To lose him, and to have you find
him, is a double tragedy for us. I have to ask you to not say
anything to anyone, which makes it harder. But if it bothers
you at all, I want you to contact one of us, to talk, all right?"

"I'm okay with it," Trent said. Jason and Bailey quickly
agreed.

Gavan nodded several times then, as if considering. "I hear
there have been wolfjackals about on other occasions, as well.
And Dark Hand."

"They're stalking," Jason told him. "I don't like it."

"They are getting more aggressive," Gavan agreed. "I'm not

sure what we can do about it. The beacon doesn't always work. They may have found a way to circumvent us or . . ." His words trailed off. He thumped his cane on the floor smartly. "Be that as it may, it only points out the need to keep you safe. We need the Academy, a Haven where the blink of your mind can bring you to safety and give you the opportunity to learn all you need to know, but it also means we may have to reveal ourselves. I am finding much opposition. I'm bringing the Council together again in a few days. I'll gather you up then, so be prepared."

"A war council!" Bailey glowed at the thought, her cheeks apple red and her ponytail bouncing.

"Well . . . not exactly."

"I'm with Bailey, sir. I think we need to start hitting back." Trent ran a hand through his curly hair.

"We've already been through a war," said Gavan quietly. "We know the devastation, and that there can be no winners."

"They're counting on that! They're counting on no one fighting back! Can't you see?"

Gavan looked sadly at Bailey. "You have to trust us, lass. You have to trust that we know what we're doing."

She looked down at her sneakers and squeaked. Or, that is, Lacey squeaked, even though it sounded like it was coming from Bailey. She put her hand over her pocket flap.

"Any other complaints?"

No one answered.

He stood. "Away with you, then." He passed his palm over the wolfhead and first Trent disappeared, and then Bailey. Gavan aimed his brilliant blue-eyed gaze at Jason, hesitating. "You seem troubled. You're not ready to do battle?"

"There are things that could be better." Jason shoved his hands stubbornly in his pockets, as reluctant to be analyzed by Gavan as by Statler Finch. "I can handle it." He touched crystal with both hands in his jeans pockets and remembered what he'd almost forgotten.

"Of course you can. We will be asking even more of you soon." Gavan started to move his palm over his cane.

"Wait! Wait . . . there is . . . something." The weight of the second crystal reminded him, and he drew it out. "I wanted to ask about the crystals, and the bonding . . ."

"You've got a second? Already? Astounding. Where did you find it?" Gavan stepped to his side, and extended his hand, over but not touching the gemstone in Jason's palm. Its pale lavender hue shone in the office light. Fire glittered as Jason turned it, showing Gavan all its facets. "Incredible. It is a beautiful stone, my lad."

"But you can bond to more than one, right?"

"Of course, we all have and do. Sometimes a crystal fractures under stress, or burns out, and we have to replace it. Occasionally they get lost, or even stolen. Most of us have several favorites we keep on us or near us at all times. Did you worry?"

"A little."

"I won't say it's usual to get another Bond so early in your training, it's not. It can be difficult to learn your crystal, and it requires study and focus. Now your attention must be split, between this one and the other. However . . ." And Gavan looked keenly into his face. "These things are not coincidental."

"What?"

"I mean it happens for a purpose. That rock was meant to come to you, or it wouldn't have." Gavan reached out and closed Jason's fingers over it.

"No one will take it away?"

"No. Why would you think they might?"

Jason felt a keen reluctance about telling Rainwater where he'd found the crystal, and why. He just shook his head.

"None of us will. Let me put it that way." Gavan opened his hands, and then cradled them about his pewter wolfhead. "Look at this crystal closely, and tell me what you see."

Jason leaned over to look at the gemstone held in the wolf's jaws. It was brilliant, he'd noticed that the first time he and the Magicker met, but more than its diamondlike quality, he'd never really been able to see. He narrowed his eyes to look into the great, uncut gem. "It *is* a diamond," he said finally, without tearing his gaze away.

"Of a sort. It's called a Herkimer diamond, and it came from these shores to my home in England not long after the colonies were first established." Gavan scratched at his jaw absently. "It's quite flawed at the heart, if you can see it in the light. I was advised by many not to take this stone and make a focus of it as it would never allow a Bonding."

Jason peered closer. "It's like . . . it looks like a teardrop or something inside."

"Precisely. Not a teardrop, actually, but water, yes. Trapped within the heart of the gem. A bit of life, if you would, in stone."

"How did that happen?"

Gavan smiled then, and shrugged. "I am no creator, I've no idea. As the minerals came under intense heat and pressure, this bit of water became trapped and so it stayed. And it may make the stone very fragile and subject to shattering, but it's held for me. We've been through a lot, we have."

Jason straightened up. "The Bonding is really important, then, and personal."

"Yes, it is. As we learn our crystals, we learn ourselves. It's not the only important thing, but it can prove crucial. You'll have to split your studies between them. I'll consult with Eleanora. Perhaps she or Aunt Freyah can work with you on it."

Sharp-eyed Freyah might not be pleased at all when she heard where he'd found it, Jason thought. On the other hand, Gavan's disclosure had revealed a lot. It *had* come to him, even under unusual circumstances. He put the lavender stone back in his pocket. "Thanks."

"Any time. Any more surprises about you?" Sudden humor twinkled in those startling blue eyes.

"I hope not." Jason smothered a sigh, and Gavan laughed.

"The weight of the world is a heavy one, hey, my young Atlas? Just remember that you're not the only one holding it up. We're all here with you." Gavan made a face. "Come to think of it . . . it is heavy!"

Jason couldn't help laughing. He took a deep breath. It would be later than it should be, and he hoped there'd be no trouble getting his and Trent's ride home, but compared to other problems, it seemed a minor one. "I'd better go now."

"No sooner spoken, than gone." Gavan whispered in his ear, and then he was back in the mall. Lingering in his mind was the whisper: *And someday soon you'll have to tell me where you found that crystal, lad.*

Jason felt his face flush.

A few shoppers brushed past him. He looked around and saw that Trent and Bailey were both gone. He checked the large clock by the information booth and was relieved that not nearly as much time had gone as he'd feared but he was late. He called McIntire for a ride home. His stepfather did not say much till they were halfway home, then he commented, "It's a little later than we planned, Jason."

"Sorry. We had so much to talk about."

"There's a certain amount of trust in letting someone your age go off on his own." McIntire looked briefly at him before turning his attention back to the road.

"I know." What was he supposed to say? He didn't want to lie.

"I'm not accusing you of anything. I just want you to know I'm paying attention."

Jason began to nod, then said, "Okay." He added, "Ting couldn't make it, she had to fly up early this morning, but

Henry Squibb was there and we were talking about camp and games and stuff. I'm sorry we ran a little over."

"I understand." And he must have, because not another word was said until they arrived home, and Alicia met them at the doorway.

His stepsister was pretty, like her blonde mother, but a lot harder to take. He frowned. "I had a phone call yesterday from Ting?"

"Did you?" Alicia looked thoughtful. "Oh, that's right. You did. I am sorry. I completely forgot. Sort of like you forgot to do the breakfast dishes."

He scowled. "I would have done them after practice."

She tossed her head, hair swinging. "By then, I would already have been in trouble. Mother likes a clean kitchen."

"Still . . . the message was important."

"Oh, all right! I won't forget again."

Jason curled his hand about the lavender crystal. It felt slightly warm and soothing in his palm. "Please try not to?" It grew hot in his hand as he talked to Alicia.

She looked at him, her face suddenly going expressionless. She blinked slowly, then said, "Whatever you want, Jason."

That surprised him. She gave him a pleasant, if blank smile, and wandered off. He let go of his crystal hastily. He hadn't done that, had he?

Upstairs, in his room, he sat down at his desk and took out the lavender gemstone to examine it more carefully. He had been, he decided, distracted by its beauty and by the fact he'd found it where he had. He had to look beyond that . . . into it. Unable to tell Gavan of his true worry over the intrinsic nature of the stone, whether it was good or evil, he realized he had to discover that himself. He rested his elbows on the desk, his chin in his hands, and looked into it. It was much clearer than his first stone and yet more complicated in its way, with more facets and planes.

He didn't know if a crystal could be good or evil, or whether it was like a pitcher that held water to be filled or poured, with no value but function. He only knew that he couldn't afford to be wrong. He cupped the gem in his hands, bringing it closer to his eyes.

Jason stared very, very deep into the pale lavender stone. Something wavered buried in its heart, an image. He held his breath, narrowing his eyes to sharpen his vision and found himself looking into dark eyes the color of rich ale, an unlined face crowned with unruly curls of silver-gray, and a clean-shaven chin that looked as if it had borne the brunt of many nicks getting that way. The image was so clear it looked as if the man might speak to him! He dropped the stone.

Bailey had been trapped in her stone once. Had he found something cursed? Panting, Jason opened his desk drawer and swept the gemstone into it. He'd have to think. He might yet have to reveal his secrets to Gavan and Eleanora and risk their anger.

Secrets

THE trouble with secrets, Ting thought, is that they had
to be kept that way. She sat in the atrium garden of her
grandmother's house, her schoolbooks spread upon the patio
table, sun pleasantly warming the back of her neck, as she
read over her homework. Her grandmother napped in a
chaise across the table, her voice making cheerful sleep
noises as she breathed deeply. She'd had chemo that morning, and the peaceful expression on her face now hid the
pain that had been there earlier from the illness. Ting's
mother was in the house, quietly making chicken rice noodle
soup and other delights to tempt Grandmother's fading ap-
petite. Ting worked quietly to keep from waking her, using
the calculator only when she absolutely had to. She was not
to disturb her grandmother's much needed rest, but sometimes she wondered how asleep the older woman really was.
An abacus lay on the table as well, but only her grandmother
knew how to make the counting beads fly as rapidly as her
electronic calculator.

Those sharp button eyes had already flown open once to catch Ting focusing on her charm bracelet of crystals. They had not shared more words about what had been brought up, but Ting felt more and more pressure regardless. Should she tell them? They were her family. Would it make it easier for them all, or bring them all under great danger? She'd read Bailey's excited account of what had happened Saturday, and it bothered her a lot. They had all thought that the creatures needed immense mana, or power, and stayed near Gates and storms of wild mana. What if wolfjackals came to San Francisco after her? How could she keep all of them safe, especially with her grandmother fighting cancer?

Ting found her hand on her bracelet, cupping the huge central rose quartz that made up her crystal, as if seeking comfort or answers from it. It did give her comfort, knowing it was there.

Her grandmother's eyelids flew open. Ting looked up to see her watching. Flushed for no real reason, Ting caught up her pencil again and returned to diagramming sentences.

"Secrets," her grandmother said slowly, "can be very powerful."

Had she been reading her thoughts? Ting looked back at her. "Grandmother, you know I love and honor you very much." She hesitated, unsure of what else to say.

"But you cannot tell me." Her grandmother sat up, straightening her quilted silk jacket about her. "That is the way it should be. Granddaughter, let me say this again. I understand what it is to have magic. As I grew older and saw nothing of it in my children, I became very sad for losing what was in our blood. Seeing it in you fills my heart and heals me as none of this medicine could possibly." She held her arms out. Ting went and knelt by her chaise lounge and hugged her tightly. Her grandmother was even tinier than she remembered and she held back her strength, afraid she might hurt her.

"Maybe someday I can tell you," she whispered in her grandmother's ear. "And have you meet the others."

"That would be both good and wise." Her grandmother smiled. "In the meantime, if you have a question, without revealing your secret, perhaps I have an answer or two."

"That would be wonderful. Someday." Ting pulled back reluctantly. "Now I have sentences to diagram."

Her grandmother shuddered. "English," she muttered. "An impossible language! And American is even worse."

Giggling, Ting settled back into her seat and picked up her pencil.

Despite what Gavan had promised, days dragged by without Jason hearing anything. Halloween weekend drew close. Soccer practice got harder, and Jason was afraid his ankle might start hurting, the old sprain acting up. It rained once, making the grasses slick, but the dirt stayed firm below, and he and Sam slid about the field, laughing even as they tried to take shots at the goal net. After practice they hurled insults at each other and let those of Brinkford and Canby roll off their backs as they dressed to go home. They could say anything to each other, but no one else had that right.

"What are you doing for Halloween?" Sam asked as he hoisted his backpack over one shoulder.

"Dunno yet for sure, but I think Joanna has some charity Haunted House we have to run. She's been trying to decide if I'm still too short to dress up as the Grim Reaper."

That made Sam laugh. "Better than dressing up like some wizard wannabee," he added, snickering. "They're gonna be all over the place."

"What's wrong with wanting to be a wizard?"

"Please," snorted Sam. "I want to live in the real world!" He pulled his sweatshirt jacket out of his locker and kicked it shut. "See you tomorrow!"

Jason watched him go. "Yeah. Right." He could hear the footsteps of Sam and one or two other stragglers jogging out of the P.E. building, and the clang of the metal door banging shut. He found himself holding his breath. How close he'd come to finding a way of telling Sam what he was! And what would have happened if he had? He'd have broken a vow to the Magickers, and all he would have done would be to set off his friend's scorn. Sam wouldn't have understood at all.

He got up off the wooden bench, gathered the last of his things, and closed his locker slowly. He had almost made a total fool and oath breaker of himself. It saddened him a little. It was like finding out your best friend really wasn't, and he wondered how he could have misjudged Sam that way. Not liking magic? How could he feel that way? Sam was always the one saying, "I wish" or "if only." Not that Magick worked that way, but there were possibilities Sam could only dream of, and Jason had them at hand.

There wasn't anything he could do about it, and it wasn't like he didn't have Trent, Bailey, Ting, and the others. He guessed it was that he didn't have anyone that stayed close in his life for long. No one that went all the way back to the beginning, and he missed that. He missed belonging.

If you belonged, then you could trust—no matter what. He wasn't sure how he fit into the McIntire household, and if Statler caused enough trouble, Jason wasn't sure he would even have a home. What if they decided to foster him out as some sort of troubled youth? Could they, would they, do such a thing to him? He didn't know and he never wanted to find out. His mom had been lost so long ago he had only bare memories left of her, usually ones he found in dreams. His dad . . . well, he couldn't help what happened to his dad. Car accidents took people every day, no matter how you wished that away. It had just happened, and he'd just been left behind.

Jason shouldered his gear securely before going out the gym door. They'd stayed really late, and he'd lingered, so it was nearly dark, the sky going into the deep gray-purple of dusk. Daylight savings time had gone into effect, and Halloween was just around the corner, and five-thirty in his neighborhood meant nightfall. He ought to hurry.

Outside the big gym building, he could see that the middle school campus looked deserted. The teachers' parking lot had one car left in it, and that probably belonged to one of the janitors. The cold air hit him. As he shivered slightly, he decided a slow jog home would be the best way to keep warm. He angled across the grounds. It was his own fault for thinking too much, and he had science lab and math homework waiting for him after dinner. That meant no television tonight at all, and maybe a half hour at most for the computer. If he hurried, he might be able to stretch that, because he wanted time to play with Trent and Henry, as well as time to talk with Bailey and Ting and anyone else on the network of Magickers.

His sneakers thudded rhythmically over the blacktop as he left the physical education area and neared the social studies wing where his footfalls made odd noises echoing off the breezeway. So odd that, for a moment there, he thought he heard two sets in a running tempo. Past the buildings and crossing the driveway, with only the physical plant building which provided energy for heat, lighting, cooling, pumped water, and had the trash bins lined up against its walls between him and the way home, Jason stopped dead in his tracks.

He could hear the tattoo of something racing after him. Then it stopped.

His heart thudded. Not shoes. Not sneakers. He began walking, then broke back into his steady jog, listening. After the briefest of pauses, that slightly out-of-place echo joined him. He was being followed.

By who? . . . or . . . by what?

He drew close to the physical plant. He could hear the generators and pumps inside humming away, doing whatever it was they did. The building almost radiated a comforting heat. As he swung toward it, a howl sounded sharply just behind his right shoulder. Wolfjackal! And unbearably close.

Jason swung around and grabbed his crystal from his pocket. It almost jumped into his hand as if knowing it were needed, filling his palm with a barely felt warmth. He summoned the alarm beacon. He caught a brief, mind-filling glimpse of the great crystal ball in Gavan's office, turning, scintillating with red-orange rays of alarm, and then it went dark. He blinked, his own sight and thoughts jolting back to the dusk shadowing his school.

No alarm beacon again! Yet he had triggered it . . . he'd seen it! It was as if something or someone had snuffed it almost immediately. He had no more time to consider it as a black-and-silver form came slinking across the open parking lot, growling and heading for him.

Jason backed up. Here, in the open, was no place to use his crystal. Not where he could be seen by anyone who still might be hanging around the school, despite the fact it looked abandoned.

The beast grinned, red tongue lolling from between its great ivory fangs as if it knew Jason were cornered. "Mine," it growled, shuddering and quaking as if forming a word took great effort and left it in greater pain.

"No way," Jason said. "Not today. *Not ever.*" He looked about. The janitor's car still sat in the deep purple shadows across the diagonal. He hated to do it . . . but it was the only option he could think of.

Jason turned quickly and ran to the trash bins. He spotted

the least full one with a lid half open, took a running leap, and dove headfirst into the metal shape. The lid clanged shut over him not a second before it shook all over as a heavy body collided with it, growling and snarling.

Jason's nose ran and his eyes stung with the stench of the container. Trash pick up was a day or two off, which meant the thing was pretty ripe and awful. Usually when Brinkford and Canby tossed him in, it was the day after trash collection. On a scale of awfulness, it wasn't all that bad, really, except for the humiliation. And today he had jumped in on purpose!

The wolfjackal clawed at him from the outside, toenails clicking and raking down the side. It thudded against the metal again, heavily, the bin shaking from side to side on its iron wheels, and then, suddenly, he could hear the growling overhead. Something hot dripped down on him. He looked up through the gap in the lid and saw part of the wolfjackal's snarling face, dripping saliva down on him.

He had two choices. One, to use his crystal, but after the failure of the beacon he was afraid to depend on it . . . or two . . .

Jason grabbed his soccer shoes, heavy and studded, out of his gear bag. Yelling at the top of his lungs, he began to beat them against the side of the trash bin. The racket nearly deafened him, but he kept yelling and pummeled his soccer shoes till his shoulders ached. He couldn't tell what the wolfjackal was doing because the whole container rumbled and quaked all around him, rocking as if it had a life of its own.

Suddenly, yellow-white light flared in, blinding him, as someone threw the lid open, shining a flashlight in. He blinked as he stuffed his shoes back into his duffel and stood.

The janitor, flashlight in hand, peered down curiously. "What are you doing?" he demanded.

A second visage leaned in for a look. Statler Finch's nose wrinkled from the stench. "Curious behavior, Jason. I thought

you hated being trash canned and yet I just saw you dive headlong into one. We'll be talking about this on Friday, I think.
Oh, yes. We'll have a nice long talk about the difference
between being bullied . . . and pretending to be bullied for
attention."

The Hidden

THE look of disappointment on Joanna's face was almost more than he could bear. He was used to seeing worry and concern there, for she attempted to be nothing less than a perfect parent. But this betrayal of his had stung his stepmother to the core.

"Oh, Jason," she murmured. "How could you? I thought we had everything settled with Mr. Finch."

"We did." He stared at McIntire, whose tanned, line-etched face actually seemed to be easier to look at. His stepfather had been in his offices, working on plans for the big development which had once been the McHenry estate, although the old mansion seemed to have survived demolition, and had appeared when Joanna let out a cry of dismay and called for Jason. The Dozer's wishes for a back road were even now being carved through the foothills, and his clothes were dusty with the digging of it. He looked steadily at Jason, though, and said to his wife, "Things aren't always as they seem. What's going on, Jason?"

She interrupted. "I'll tell you what's going on. Mr. Finch seems to think Jason is some kind of . . . some kind of lying psychopath! All this for attention." She put her hand to her mouth, her hand trembling, as if she might break into sobs. "I know it's hard for you, Jason, no mother and no father, but I do try. I do. And I thought talking to Mr. Finch might give you an outlet outside the family. But it appears I've failed! He says you're shamelessly manipulating all of us."

McIntire put a great arm about his wife's shoulders. "Now stop that," he said mildly. "Jason hasn't done anything wrong, that I've seen. Finch is in a new program at the school, and he strikes me as the overeager sort. The kind who might make a reputation anyway he can. I have no intention of letting him run roughshod over any of us."

She sniffled. "But . . . what happened?

Jason exhaled at finding an unexpected ally. That put him in a spot, though, which he wasn't quite sure how to get out of. He shifted uneasily. "I can tell you it wasn't what it looked like." He bit his tongue before he could add *trust me*. There was no such emotion on Joanna's immaculately made-up face. And no tears yet, either, although they seemed just around the corner.

She sighed. "All right, then. But no Internet tonight. Do I make myself clear?"

"Yes, ma'am."

"All right then, hurry on upstairs, dinner's a little late tonight. You may have time for homework before I call you."

"Yes, ma'am." Jason turned and pitched out of the living room before anyone whatsoever could think of anything else. He took another shower and set his clothes aside to be washed after dinner, unable to bear even the faintest reminder of the garbage bin. Then he sat down, shoved the computer screen aside so he wouldn't even have to look at its darkened face, and did his science lab.

Alicia wasn't in for dinner, having gone to a friend's house after dance practice, so he was spared her knowing and accusing glances at the table. He announced he'd gotten his science lab done already and only had a page of math problems to do after dinner. Joanna's red mouth thinned to the barest of lines, and she repeated firmly, "No Internet."

"Yes, ma'am." Sometimes there was just no moving a mountain, and he knew when to not even try. He stifled a yawn and dug into the lime jello and carrot salad that also served as a kind of dessert for the evening. He cleared the table and loaded the dishwasher before heading back upstairs.

While he did his math, his mind worked on the real puzzle. How was it Statler had seen him but hadn't seen the wolfjackal? How could that be?

Or had he seen it and not believed it? Or had he decided it was merely an overly bold coyote.

Neither option made Jason feel very comfortable. He tucked his math papers inside his workbook and stowed everything back in his backpack, ready for the next day.

And even if he were all right, that did not mean the others were. He broke his word and went on the Net long enough to send e-mail to everyone, warning them anew, especially Henry. He took his time over Henry's letter, mulling about what to say without frightening him half to death and yet urging him to be very careful.

He flipped off the computer when a floorboard creaked behind him, and he spun about in his chair guiltily. He'd been caught!

Gavan Rainwater sat down on the edge of Jason's bed, his cloak puddled about him like great, dark wings, his chin resting on the head of his wolfhead cane. He smiled as Jason gulped once or twice. "Sorry. I should have knocked, but I hate creating a fuss."

Jason pulled up his trapdoor for privacy. "I bet you do. What's wrong?"

"It's time," Gavan said simply. "Come with me?"

Of all nights to be called away from home. Jason looked at his trapdoor. It was not to be helped, he supposed. What to do?

He wrote a quick note reading "Do Not Disturb (sleeping)" and lowered it out of his room on a string, and then pulled his door up and shut tight. Just in case, he fixed his bed and Gavan stood, watching him with his mouth twitched to one side.

"The old pillow under the blanket trick?"

"I'm in a little bit of trouble," Jason told him.

"Ah. Covering your tracks, then. Let me help." Gavan gestured and the room steeped in darkness, and he could hear the very very faint sound of someone in deep sleep. Gavan dropped his voice to a whisper. "There," he said. He extended a hand to Jason. "Shall we be off?"

And they were, in what Aunt Freyah often referred to as two twitches of a lamb's tail.

Ting put the finishing touches on her English essay and printed it out. She heard the sound of the walker in the hallway, and her bedroom door eased open. "Ting," her grandmother said. "Your mother is out getting groceries, and you have a visitor. I believe you have something to do tonight."

Puzzled, Ting followed her out to the kitchen, where Fire-Ann sat with a cup of Chinese tea in her hand. "There you are, lass! I'm to bring you to a meeting."

Her grandmother hugged Ting. "We had time for a little chat," her grandmother explained, smiling widely.

She looked from the flamboyantly red-haired Magicker and cook of Camp Ravenwyng to her grandmother. "You . . . talked?"

"Indeed we did," answered FireAnn with her lively Irish accent. "Why didn't you tell me your grandmother was one of the Hidden Ones? Things could have gone a lot smoother!"

"Hidden Ones?" Ting repeated, feeling totally lost.

FireAnn bounced to her feet and took her hand. "I'll explain later. It's a good thing," she said. She hugged Ting's grandmother as if she had known her all her life, and then rubbed her crystal and *whoooosh!* Away they went.

It's a wonder, Bailey thought, they all didn't bump into each other on whatever plane it was they traveled through. She and Trent popped out of nowhere into the Council meeting room at Ravenwyng just ahead of Jason and Ting, like corks popping out of champagne bottles. Even so, it looked like the Council had been in session for a while before they got there.

Her excitement at seeing Ting so unexpectedly bubbled over in spite of everything. "Ting!" she cried out and grabbed her friend and did an excited swing. They grinned at each other. "You missed the best farewell party!"

"Without me?"

"We thought of you a lot!" Bailey teased. She hugged her friend tightly. "How is your grandmother?"

That sombered Ting's expression. She flipped her dark hair back over her shoulder. "She has a lot of healing to do, but she surprises me every day." She looked at FireAnn who gave a slight nod, before adding, "She *knows*, Bailey."

"Knows? Knows what?" Then Bailey's mouth snapped shut for a moment as thoughts tumbled. "You don't mean—"

"I do. FireAnn calls her one of the Hidden Ones."

"Wow. What's that mean?"

Eleanora put her hands on their shoulders, saying quietly, "Ladies. Shall we sit and let the Council continue?"

Ting blushed faintly as the two of them found their chairs. Bailey leaned over and whispered, "I wanna know everything!" before lapsing into dutiful silence. An empty chair with a black wreath upon it sat at one end, for dear old Fizziwig, she supposed. Eleanora tucked herself demurely into her own chair, and smiled at Gavan. She fixed her gaze on Gavan, and Bailey followed suit. She'd been at enough meetings between her mom, her dad, and the divorce lawyers, to know when something important was being discussed.

Gavan cleared his throat. "Here we are, all concerned who were asked for, and all safe."

"What about the other two . . . the skinwalker and the rather ordinary Magicker who follows him about?"

"Unable to get away without being missed." Tomaz leaned forward on the table, the beaten silver disks of his Indian jewelry gleaming. "I will fill them in later."

"All safe and accounted for," Gavan repeated firmly.

"Not good enough," snorted the one known to the children as Allenby from Gavan's wicked impersonations of him and occasional tirades. They watched him in fascination. He frustrated Gavan because of his tight-pocketed attitude, although Rainwater himself was the first to admit a good accountant could be worth his weight in gold and Magickers couldn't find a way to have money fall out of a tree. Yet.

"The fact remains that because of your actions, young Magickers are exposed and at risk. Better to have found them, one at a time, and apprenticed them, kept them close and safe, rather than to have them scattered to the four winds as they are now. The world we live in is more dangerous for all of us now, and even more so for those of Talent but without training. If found, they will be misused. Think of the days of the Inquisition, Rainwater, and you have a glimpse of what worries me." The dark, disagreeing voice issued from a man wrapped in shadows, and his words were even darker.

"Who's that?" Ting whispered into Bailey's ear. Bailey answered, "I think that's Khalil. Very mysterious."

Gavan stood at the table's end, his cloak swirling about him.

He looked angry, and the flash in his eyes was echoed by a glint stabbing outward from the crystal held in the jaws of his wolf-head cane. "This is not the Old World," he said finally, and then closed his mouth tightly as if there were many, many more things he would like to have said.

Jason sat back in his chair. Trent tapped him on the arm, drawing his attention, and he looked at his worried friend. He shook his head, once, and then looked back to Gavan. Jason took a deep breath, trying to relax. Perhaps Trent was right; now was the time to listen, not to protest. It wasn't easy, though.

"The children . . . the young Magickers . . . are more at risk than ever. Surely you can see that." Khalil sat in his chair, quiet, inscrutable, his Moorish features hidden by his head-to-toe dark clothing. "This is the same argument we had but a few weeks ago. You need us to help anchor and ward this school. But you've made no progress in finding a Gated Haven to put it in. Why do you bother us? You want action, yet you hesitate to take the first step!"

"I would be a fool not to admit that I've bitten off more than I can chew. Together, we can protect them. Educate them. I need your combined wisdoms and talents. With Fizziwig's death, we know the Hand will stop at nothing. Can we survive yet another disaster? I don't think any one of us wants to find that out." Gavan put both hands on the table and leaned forward, his gaze sweeping all assembled: Council, young Magickers, and elders from all around the world. "Gregory and Brennard were masters of the arts. When they fought, they did so to destroy each other, not the world around them. They contained the havoc they wrought. I don't know about Brennard today, but I can't muster that kind of control. I don't ever want to be brought into that kind of fight. So we fight by guile, as we must."

"If, by calling this meeting, you are hoping to bring pressure to bear on us and force a hasty, perhaps unwise decision, you will fail, Rainwater." The tall, elegant woman, wrapped in dark crimson satin, sat catty-corner from the end of the table where Gavan stood and Eleanora stayed quietly, as if biding her time. The two women looked at each other, then away, as if something unspoken had passed between them. She tapped her fan, of dark watered-silk crimson that matched her gown, on the table's edge. "You will call me Isabella, children," she said imperiously, before looking to Gavan. "You have a Gatekeeper! Open Gates. Choose them wisely, and then and only then, can we work with you. You might remember that some Gates lead only to havoc and chaos."

Gavan's hands turned white around the knuckles as he leaned on them. "I need protectors for my Gatekeeper. We may well lose him, if not."

Jason went cold. He stared at Gavan. Lose? What did he mean by that?

"We've lost two candidates already," Eleanora spoke up. "Henry Squibb, fallen to betrayal by the Dark Hand, and Jennifer Logan, who was one of our more trained recruits."

"Not Jennifer!" protested both Ting and Bailey in unison before clapping their hands over their mouths and turning pink.

Eleanora smiled sadly. "Jennifer has retreated. She's renounced her Magick, and although I am working with her, her crystal has been shattered, and I'm not sure she'll ever be able to take up a new one. It happens sometimes. She won't tell me what she was attempting or what went wrong, but she is frightened. Terribly, desperately frightened. I'm doing all I can."

Both Ting and Bailey let out small breaths, and grabbed for each other's hands, and held them. Lacey poked a whiskered nose out of Bailey's pocket, then dove back in, followed by a small crunchy, munching sound.

"We'll lose more like that, too, if we don't move," Gavan

his real last name, but he liked being called something that sounded like it came from Dickens with just a little twist . . . Fizziwig was a classmate of Gavan's. They were trained together, and came forward together."

"Oh, Gavan," said Ting. "We're sorry! You must have known him well." Her brow creased in sympathy.

"We didn't know, when we found him," Bailey added.

Jason echoed with an "I'm sorry" of his own.

"That's not the point, guys," Trent cut in. "I think the point is," and he looked right at Gavan, who seemed to be studying the crystal embedded in his cane without responding to any of their kind words, "the point seems to be that they were classmates. In other words, the same age. But we found an old man."

"Not that old," snapped Freyah. Her dark eyes glared a hole through Trent.

Gavan sighed. "Old enough." He looked up. "Trent has cut the Gordian knot again and gone right to it. Fizziwig was, or should have been, my age."

Bailey let out a small "Meep" . . . or maybe it was her pocket that squeaked. "He couldn't have been."

"Trust me, he was." Absentmindedly, Gavan pushed a shock of dark brown hair from his forehead. He did not reveal any creases by doing so, nor was there a single thread of gray in his hair. His eyes were the same, piercingly clear blue they'd always been, with only a very few fine lines at the corners.

Jason shook his head in disbelief.

Trent cracked his knuckles. "It makes sense," he said. "Magick has a price, it always does, and all the wizards and sages are old, wise. Bearded. So it takes youth, maybe even the life force itself, to use."

Aunt Freyah fastened her gaze on the back of his head, her apple cheeks blazing, her silvery hair a corona about her face. Trent didn't seem to notice.

"For all we know," he continued. "They could be the ripe old age of twenty or something."

Bailey snickered. She put her hand up to muffle it. Eleanora smiled faintly, shifting gracefully inside her lacy dark dress. "I would be hurt," she said softly. "But I know you mean well, Trent."

"Are there things you should be telling us you're not?" Jason sat forward in his chair. "Is that what killed Fizziwig? The Curse of Arkady? Do we face aging incredibly if we use any mana?" He looked at all of their faces, and no one would look back at him except Aunt Freyah.

"We don't know what killed Fizziwig," Gavan said finally. "I wish we did, but we haven't a clue. His heart just stopped. As for the Curse, well, I don't think it would have applied to Fizziwig at that point in his life." He tapped his cane lightly on the floor in a mild, uneasy rhythm, his fingers gripping the pewter wolfhead tightly. Bare glints of the massive crystal the wolf held could barely be seen.

"Will we ever know?"

"Probably not. FireAnn is working on it, but she's not found any answers yet in herbology and Dr. Patel had seen him first, of course. There doesn't really appear to have been a reason for it, despite what you think of his aged appearance. Up till the last, he was hale and hearty, as he should have been." Gavan stood. "A lot of issues have been thrown about the table today, and I guess it's time to answer one of them." He looked at Jason. "I had hoped for you to have more time, more training, more understanding before I showed you this." He extended his hand. "Gatekeeper. Are you ready to glimpse the futures?"

Gates

TRENT shot him a look, but Jason shook his head slightly as he put his own hand out to meet Gavan's. Now was not the time, he thought, to be telling the others they'd done a little exploration of their own. Definitely not the time. He'd played dumb, he'd stay that way.

Trent stood, too, as Jason rose to take Gavan's hand. He asked quietly, "Do we all get to see or is this private?"

"I think we're going to need the help of all those here, who can stay to help. Jason is the Gatekeeper, but I think part of the phenomena of your Talents . . . all your Talents . . . is that you support and draw on each other." Gavan wore a wistful expression. "Perhaps if we'd been raised with that spirit of cooperation instead of competition, Brennard might never have fought Gregory. We shall never know."

Allenby pushed away from the Council table with a new sheen of nervous sweat dappling his egg-bald head. "I have appointments and work to do. We have investments we need to keep up to date and accountings to be made. I am, as always, at your disposal, Rainwater, if you need information on the finances. Good day, ladies, gentlemen." He bowed stiffly to the Magickers sitting around the table before taking out his watch from his vest, snapping open the silver cover to expose a brilliant crystal, glancing into it, and disappearing.

Trent let out a low whistle. "He makes it look easy."

Dr. Patel considered the spot which had held Allenby. "Never underestimate any of us," she said finally. She straightened her sari about her petite frame, the silver bracelet on her dusky wrist chiming as she did so.

"Ready, Jason?"

"Yeah." He slid his hand into Gavan's, aware that he was not yet full grown and his hand felt even smaller inside the other's grasp. Rainwater, like McIntire, had strong, callused hands although his stepfather's hands could be called massive. His own, while not those of a child, still had a ways to go. Gavan closed his fingers slightly around Jason's.

"I suggest that everyone else who's coming link to Eleanora. I'd like to be able to concentrate on the Gatekeeper and start with Iron Gate."

A coldness swept around the two of them. Jason had a last impression of Trent touching him, gripping his shoulder, before being drawn away from his friends and hurtling into a storm-dark nothingness, towed after Gavan.

After a long moment in which his feet did not touch anything, he could feel gravity again, and see ground below him as the nothingness they'd been in parted, and he and Gavan settled onto a rocky pass, looking down into a vale. At their flanks were the rusting iron gateposts, and a flag showing wear and tear at its edges as it fluttered in a faint breeze. Jason touched it. That banner had been made by Trent, and the flagpole was actually a crudely whittled wooden lance, to battle wolfjackals with if necessary. Instead, he had buried it into the ground to mark and claim the opening of Iron Gate.

He could feel the presence of others at his back as the gathering caught up, though they did not materialize. Gavan nodded at Jason, reading the expression on his face.

"They're here, but Eleanora is holding them back. Now, then." Gavan took a deep breath. His cloak slowly settled about him like a sail that the winds of the travel had kept unfurled, and let fall only now that he had landed completely. "These are the Four Great Gates which control the elements, that we know of. The Iron Gate, the first one, you found and opened here. We were hoping that the opening of that one Gate would lead us to what we needed, but we feel now that is probably not the case."

"Why?"

"It's not stable. The only thing we've put here, that has stayed here, has been this." Gavan tapped the flag. He smiled faintly. "We've laid a foundation twice down there, and it disappeared, shifted elsewhere, overnight."

"Wow," Jason breathed. "Where?"

"We've no idea."

"That would be cool, but I think I know what you mean. We can't have an Academy drifting in and out of realities."

"No, we can't. Think how hard it would be to assign homework." Gavan winked.

Jason laughed, though his nerves were twitching and his stomach felt a little queasy. "What about the others? Do you know?"

"We . . . think we do. Mist Gate, Fire Gate, and the last is the Bone Gate." Gavan may have tried but could not conceal a shudder at the last naming. "Those are the elements that must be mastered to bring other lands into balance. There may be others, hidden, that we don't know of."

"So, even trained, I'm not fully prepared."

"No."

Jason nodded. "That's why it's so dangerous. There's no way of knowing what to expect."

It was Gavan's turn to nod. "Sometimes, it's better to be intuitive about Gates, finding them by your own best feelings, and opening them that way. There are schools of thought about doing what it is you need to do, and no one agrees. It's a very individual thing."

"How did Fizziwig do it?"

Gavan smiled sadly. "I've no idea. He usually did it alone, and he only opened one or two successfully. He helped Aunt Freyah open and maintain her small Haven, but that's not really a Gated area, that's more of a . . . hmmm . . . how to explain it?"

"A pocket beyond the boundaries."

"Yes. She can have incursions, though she's managed to keep them harmless and to a minimum, but she expends great energy in doing so. We can't have a school on that basis. It has to be solid, well grounded, and self-sufficient. We'll have our energy drained by many, many other things."

"No floating candlesticks?"

"Hardly. Think of the tapestry and banner liabilities alone." Gavan's expression flickered with humor.

"So what is it you can train me to do?"

"I'm not sure. I was hoping Fizziwig would be around to do it." Again that sad smile. "Jason, there are procedures. I can show you how to open a Gate or two that isn't right, and deal with what we find. I can show you how to defend yourself, and cover your tracks, and slam a Gate shut, if you need to. What I can't do is show you how to find the right ones. The Great Gates. It's a Talent, and a rare one, and although we can often describe a Talent like that later, after working with it for years and years, we can't really explain what makes it work. A Gate-keeper just . . . does."

"You don't know."

Gavan shook his head slowly.

"But didn't Fizziwig ever tell you? Even a little?"

"He tried once. He might have been speaking Mandarin Chinese for all I understood, and believe me, I tried although I had no idea how important it would become later. And, truthfully, I can't say that it was the Gating which aged him. That seemed to happen all on its own, unrelated to anything we had done or planned to do. It was almost as if the centuries we were thrown through . . . which we skipped . . . were bound and determined to catch up with us."

Jason looked at Gavan. "Are you aging?"

"A little. Not like he did. But." Gavan pulled his cloak about him, straightening the shoulder seams and correcting its hang, a bit uneasily it seemed to Jason. "Once I was a rather shy and awkward lad, who developed a great crush on this Magicker lass, a woman really, just grown and in her prime, with a blush to her cheek and music in her hands. Then came the Happening, and when I awoke and we met again, she hadn't aged at all. Not a day. But I had found a decade or so, and wore it, and had become a man. I thank the disaster for that, she could look on me as her peer and perhaps entertain my suit. When we're not bickering."

There was a noise from the misty clouds behind them rather like a snort.

"Not," Gavan added hastily, "that anything has ever come of it, thank you for grounding me, Aunt Freyah." He gave an ironic bow.

Jason, however, was not quite sure it had been Aunt Freyah who'd made the stifled noise. The cloud at their backs boiled a little bit as if a storm or wind pushed at it, but it stayed in place. He looked into it, wondering if he could make out Bailey or Trent but could not see them although he could feel their presence. It was uncanny.

He turned and looked down into the valley below, with its backdrop of dragon-spined mountains the color of red-orange spires like something out of a wind-sculpted desert rock. Once, he'd seen a dragon lying there, just like that spread of peaks, or so he'd thought. Now, he didn't know exactly what he'd seen, but surely not what he'd thought he had. The pool of water looked more blue than ever, a long thin waterfall trickling down one of the cliff faces, feeding it, its borders a luxurious and verdant green. He wanted to jog down the small pathway into the valley and taste that water . . . run through the grass and get a closer look at the spine of mountains, see how close or far away they really were, and if they could be such a thing as a petrified dragon.

He lifted his foot to take a step or two. Gavan caught him by the elbow.

He glanced up at the other. "Looks perfectly fine to me."

"Well, it's not," answered Gavan grimly. "Eleanora, might you have another brick about?"

A red clay brick came sailing out of nowhere and landed with a thud at Gavan's feet. He picked it up. A small imprint at the corner read Firehouse Station Queens 12. "An excellent vintage," remarked Gavan. Then he said firmly to Jason, "You stay here." Without explanation, he marched down the winding pathway until he reached the flat valley floor. Then he shouted back, "Here will do." With his bootheel, he scrapped out a small patch of dirt, then firmly implanted the brick there. "This will make a fine cornerstone . . . if it stays." Gavan straightened back up, dusting his hands off, and returned up the path to Jason. "Won't take long," he said confidently.

"What won't?"

"You'll see." Gavan leaned against one of the great rocks forming the pass out of Iron Gate Haven. He whipped a handkerchief out of his pocket and began to polish his cane with great care.

Jason stared downhill. The brick was so far away now, it looked little more than palm-sized as it lay in a tiny square of dirt. He watched it for a long moment, then flinched as something itchy, crawly, seemed to be going down the back of his neck. He squirmed and threw his arm up so he could scratch at it, but again Gavan caught him by the elbow.

"It's not an itch," he said.

"The heck it's not! It's a bug or something." Jason fairly danced with the need to scratch at it. "Let me go so I can get at it!"

"No," said Gavan. "It's this . . ." and he pointed downhill at the brick which lay in the sun. Jason stared as the object wavered slightly, seeming to jump and quiver upon the ground, ever so slightly and yet detectable even from where he stood. "Earthquake?"

"Confined to one tiny patch of ground? Don't be ridiculous." Gavan stared expectantly downhill now. "Wait for it."

Right elbow held tightly in Gavan's grip, Jason threw up his left arm and began to scratch furiously at the back of his neck, even as he watched the brick. It began to dance upon the dirt, vibrating, jumping up and down with enough vigor that he knew he couldn't be imagining it. "What is it doing?"

The itch wouldn't go away, the scratching wasn't helping, so he dropped both arms to his sides. He stared at the brick, which could have been a marionette on strings for all its wild activity now, standing on end and flip-flopping from side to side. Then a dull pop assaulted his ears, and the brick exploded into a chalky red cloud of dust which slowly disappeared.

Jason blinked.

He heard Bailey whisper, "Wow" out of the misty fog behind them.

Gavan sighed.

"What happened?"

"We're not quite sure. It has to do with the compatibility of the planes. Ours and this one . . . Eleanora?"

Her soft voice drifted out of nothingness. "Think of your world as a tuning fork, Jason, vibrating to a certain pitch or sound. Then think of someone else striking another tuning fork, vibrating to another note. They are not compatible, they're just pitches of noise and one will rule the other out. Everything molecular has its own pitch, its own song. If the forks are conjoined, one vibration will eventually rule the other, or both vibrations will cease to exist. In this case, the brick . . . ceased."

"But we don't belong here either." The back of Jason's neck had stopped itching but now his nose did. He rubbed it. "Could that happen to us?"

"I hope not. It is a possibility we've considered."

Jason felt itchy all over. "Worse than that can happen through other Gates?" Considering what he'd just seen, he and Trent had been incredibly lucky.

"Wrong Gates? Much, much worse."

Jason nodded. "Okay. When do we start training?"

Tiger, Tiger, Burning Bright

J ASON woke in the middle of the night, staring at his port-hole window which framed a great yellow slice of moon. For an uneasy moment, he couldn't quite remember where he'd been, other than sleeping, for it seemed he'd been somewhere, doing or thinking of something important. Then he remembered the Council meeting and sank back into his blankets, temples throbbing with a slight headache, and worry.

They had discussed Henry briefly before everyone dispersed, news the Council had not heard though Gavan had been told days ago. It seemed to hearten them a bit, to hear of a Magicker regaining lost powers since such a tragedy was often thought irreversible. The Council broke up on a positive note, each member determined to go through his or her own notes and journals for anything that might help Jason in his quest.

Afterward, all he could remember of his uneasy dream was Mrs. Cowling, Aunt Freyah's niece, both ladies so much alike with their apple cheeks and bright-eyed gazes and soft curly hair although Aunt Freyah's was definitely silver and Mrs.

Cowling's a soft brown with blondish tones . . . well, all he could remember was his old English teacher reciting a poem to him. " 'Tiger, tiger, burning bright, in the forests of the night.' That's Blake, Jason. Remember it."

Burning tigers. He scrubbed at his face. Back to sleep or wake up? He was in that in between where he could easily do both, and it seemed silly to wake up in the middle of the night.

He should have been dreaming of Gates. Gavan had refused to start his lesson on the spot, saying that he had obligations to return Jason, but that lessons would and must start . . . soon. In the meantime, Jason had to look within himself for that was where he would begin to find the Gate desperately needed to help anchor the Haven they wanted for the Academy.

In other words, it was all on him. Without a clue or book to help him, without a lesson or a Magicker versed in such things, it rested on his shoulders. No wonder Gavan had called him Atlas, the man in ancient mythology who carried the world on his back, and told him not to let the worry squash him. He didn't tell him not to worry, just not to be squashed.

Jason grinned at that. Rubbing his face again, he slid back down into his bed, watching the great yellow moon outside as it slowly edged past his porthole window. Once or twice, he thought he saw a crow wing across it, but that could have been his imagination. Better a crow or raven than a burning tiger, he yawned to himself sleepily, just before burrowing his head into his pillow with his eyes shut.

Earlier in the evening, however, others had been just as busy. Henry had evening chores and baby-sitting after dinner while his parents and all his siblings but the youngest went to a planning meeting. It took him a while to get his baby sister sleeping happily in her crib. He made sure the sides were up, for she was a toddler now and had climbed out once or twice. It was something that worried his mom, and so it worried Henry. He'd already decided he was never going to have kids when he got older, as it seemed totally not worth the hassle. Not even when his sister gave him a sloppy hug and snotty kiss.

He was taking the last sack of house trash out to the garage barrels when the shadows moved. Henry let out a stifled noise that would have been a yell except he couldn't breathe, and he threw the trash bag at whatever it was, preparing to run.

Dr. Patel emerged from the shadows. "Henry. Are you quite all right?" She bent over and picked up the plastic sack, handing it back to him. "Did I frighten you?" Her anklet chimed softly as she stepped forward, wrapped in a bronze-and-gold silken sari with a shawl folded over her arm, her smile gentle.

"Dr. Patel! N–n–no. No. I was just . . . just . . . startled." His face turned red hot as he took the trash from her and hugged it as if it could hide his embarrassment.

"It's all right, Henry, I understand the wolfjackals have been about lately. I do not blame you for jumping. Have you a moment for a visit?"

He looked back toward the house. "A quick one. Everyone's gone except me, but my sister's asleep. Would you like a . . . a cup of tea or something?" He hugged his trash sack tighter and something inside belched. He bolted into the garage, lobbed it into the trash can, and came back out, his face hotter than ever.

"Tea would be most pleasant, but I cannot stay long." Anita Patel smiled at him. Hardly taller than he was, and with soft, dark eyes, she didn't appear very intimidating. She put her hand to the crystal at her throat, worn almost like a cameo.

"R–right." Henry led the way to the kitchen's back door. He used the microwave to boil the water, and soon had two cups of his mother's most fragrant orange-and-spice tea on the table, putting out cream and sugar.

Dr. Patel made her tea like the English did, he thought, as he watched her use a lot of cream and sugar, making the cup look almost like coffee with milk, caramel colored. He almost spilled his mug watching her fix hers, and his face stayed hot just when he thought it might cool down a bit. He must look like one of his mother's garden tomatoes in August!

If his face was incredibly red, the Magicker who was also a physician did not seem to notice. She sipped at her cup a few times before settling back in her chair with a pleased sigh. "Thank you for your hospitality, Henry."

He nodded happily. "Any time."

"Do you know why I am here?"

"Well." He twisted his body about on the wooden kitchen chair, considering. "No."

"I came by to see how you were doing, and to congratulate you. I heard the good news about your Talent returning this evening."

"Oh! That." Henry beamed, pleased. "I'm hoping I can go back to camp next summer and start lessons again."

"Oh, no. Time is too precious. Each Magicker gets a guardian of sorts, who visits and gives private lessons throughout other seasons."

"You're my guardian?"

Dr. Patel set her cup down, surrounding it with her small, neat hands. "I don't know yet, Henry, but I'll ask if you'd like. You have a great deal of potential."

"That would be terrific! I need someone calm, I think."

She laughed softly. "Couldn't hurt."

"What would we do?"

"Oh, lessons at home, mostly, perhaps a field trip now and then. Gavan is working very hard to get Ravenwyng established as the Iron Mountain Academy."

Henry felt his eyes get rounder behind his glasses. "An academy?"

"So we all hope. Anyway, I should go. You have duties here, although . . ." and Dr. Patel paused, listening. "Your sister sleeps well."

"I should hope so."

Anita stood and put her hand on his head. "This is a time when you need to be most careful, Henry. You are very vulnerable."

He looked up at her. "I know," he said, and his voice broke, to his further embarrassment.

She took off a wraparound bracelet, which he saw when she handed it to him was a snake which curled upon itself so that its own jaw clamped to its tail. Small crystals made up its eyes. "If there's trouble, break this, and I will know and come immediately to help."

"Break it?"

She showed him a tiny line. "It is meant to be undone there, by breaking it open. There is a hidden hinge inside. You're not actually breaking it. But it is a magical circle and when that is changed, I'll know it, and I'll know immediately that you did it."

"All right." Gratefully, Henry shoved it deep in his pocket, where he could feel its heavy weight against his skin even through the cloth. "Thank you."

"I expect it back when you've a new crystal and can defend yourself." Anita smiled encouragingly. "Until then, the cobra, which is also a guardian of my country, will watch you." She smoothed her sari down, and brought her shawl up about her shoulders. She raised her hand, palm out, in a kind of wave and as he blinked, she was gone.

Only the half finished tea proved she had even been there. That, and the bronze bracelet in his pocket. He finished his quickly and put everything away in the dishwasher. To his disappointment, neither Trent nor Jason were on-line for some quick game time, so he picked out a book and curled up in the old chair in his bedroom and read till everyone got home.

Jason stirred and woke again, from a dream that was really a memory of camp, from their lessons learning how to bring a lanternlike fiery glow to their crystals. Henry had set his on fire . . . twice . . . singeing his eyebrows as flames fountained upward, and the only thing protecting his hands had been a pair of FireAnn's oven mitts. It had been both funny and scary, scattering campers and adult Magickers alike. They said that in every Talent, there was a leaning toward certain elements. Obviously, Henry's had been fire.

With a sigh, Jason swung his legs over the edge of his bed. Dawn was still an hour away, school another two hours after, but it was plain the night held no more sleep for him. Too much depended on him, and he had no idea what to do or which way to go. Or perhaps he did.

He dressed quickly and as quietly as he could, although the deep rumbling snore that always accompanied McIntire's sleep thundered gently throughout the house. He left his lavender crystal behind, tucking it away in a corner of his desk drawer under a soft piece of cloth he kept for polishing his original focus.

He held up his original quartz and gently spoke a word, and it glowed with a steady golden light. He held it close with both hands, and thought of Iron Gate. In a moment, it stood before him where his bedroom wall had been, and Jason stepped through.

For all that Gavan had shown him how unstable it was, he felt good when he stepped into the dale. The sun had risen here, and although the small valley was still a bit chilled by late autumn, he could feel warming rays on his back. He put his crystal into his pocket after quenching the lantern spell, and stepped down the pathway, not exactly sure what he was here for, but knowing here was where he needed to be.

Here was where he needed to bring all the Gates to open and anchor this Haven. So . . . this was where his clues should lie. Shouldn't they? He yawned slightly, and as quickly covered his mouth. No sleepiness on the job! He needed to be keen and observant. And quick, if wolfjackals showed up again.

As he descended to the pool of water which formed from a thin veil of a waterfall issuing from the rusting mountains, a thin spray of mist dappled his face. It felt icy and left him shivering. He looked at the rim of encircling mountains which, from high up where the Gate swung open, always looked to him like a great, dark orange dragon slumbering. Once, he thought he had seen just that. But only once.

He sat on a flat slab of rock that bordered the small pond, and slid his hand into his pocket where his fingers curled comfortably about his crystal. He should not stay, in case another quake or shift struck the valley, but he liked it here. Something scampered over the toe of his sneaker, paused while he glanced down at it, and then skittered away, slithering through the grass. A small salamander, or fire lizard. His shoe even felt a trail of warmth where it had been. Jason grinned at the tiny lizard which moved so quickly and hid itself so well.

He leaned back, tilted his face skyward, and let the sun chase away the icy veil of mist. For a moment, he felt just like the salamander, basking in the sun and wondered how a dragon might have felt, if the Iron Mountains had ever once been a great winged beast.

"Why don't you ask me how I feel?"

The voice rumbled out of the very ground, its timbre deep and yet light. It was like no voice he'd ever heard before. Jason opened his eyes. Very, very slowly, he turned his head because it seemed to be all that he could move.

He wondered that he hadn't seen it before, for it was clearly visible now, its dark orange-and-rust body lying against the foot of the mountain range that mimicked it. But perhaps, like a chameleon, it could only be seen when it moved or willed itself to be seen. At any rate, a dragon rested not far from where he sat, golden amber eyes watching him. He could feel its heat and smell its coppery blood. The immense creature could only be dwarfed by the mountains themselves, and he asked himself yet again how it was he hadn't seen it!

"Sometimes one looks too hard," the dragon provided. It curled up a forepaw and considered its magnificently taloned foot. "Or so I find it."

Jason managed to inhale. "How . . . how do you feel?"

"Lazy. I am still greedily absorbing all the sunlight I can, and I am feeling drowsy with it. You?"

"Grateful. The water is very chilly."

"It will ice over in a week or so."

Jason vaguely remembered reading that one wasn't supposed to look into a dragon's eyes, but it was too late now; he was already staring directly at the great, luminous amber eyes. "I don't mean to disturb you," he said finally, feeling rather lame.

"Not at all, not at all. I rather enjoy company. Company is so much better than the stray dinner or two which often bolts past, right under my nose. Dinner, if it knows it is a repast, seldom stays to chat."

"I'm not dinner?"

"Of course not." The dragon rumbled in what must have been draconic laughter. "You're literate. Do you eat books for lunch? I think not!" He stretched his wings out, the great bones and spines in them nutmeg-colored shadows under the russet-scaled skin, and folded up again. The dragon peered at him. "You *are* literate?"

"Sometimes I wonder, myself. As a race, I mean. As people who live on the face of the Earth . . ." Jason halted. "Hard to explain." He thought of recent events, and stopped talking altogether.

"Hmmm." The sound came out as a grating rumble, heated and raspy. "This could be awkward. I think you should decide whether you are or not."

Jason winced. "Or I could be lunch?"

"That seems to be the way of the worlds." The dragon bared its many sharp teeth in what could have been a smile or a snarl.

"I'm afraid it isn't a snap decision. I think being literate, or civilized, is something that takes a while to happen. It's realized after the fact. It might take me a whole lifetime of living to prove whether I am or not," Jason concluded sadly. "Or one awful deed could do the same."

"Weighty thoughts."

"No kidding."

The dragon stretched again, rather like a serpentine cat. "Is that why you came here?"

"No, actually, I came to think about the Gates."

A long, amber blink. "The Gates? Is that all?"

"All?" Jason twisted about on the rock slab to better look at the talkative dragon. "Seems important to me."

"Well, yes, it would. You're a Gatekeeper, but haven't they trained you? It should be as easy as roasting a sitting duck. Think of what you are, and what you need. No other Gatekeeper at all?"

Jason shook his head. "There only seems to be me at the moment."

"Hrmmm. Bad luck, that. And no wonder I've not had more company."

"Yes."

"Seems to me that finding and opening Gates would be a . . . hrmmm . . . an instinctual thing. Rather like flying, once you get a bit of strength and practice."

"Could be. Or . . . falling off a log."

"Rather like that." The dragon flexed his talons.

"Would it upset you, if I got all the Gates opened for here?"

"Not at all. This is only my sunning spot. I get here rather like you do. My own place is a Gate away. I can say this, it would be rather amusing having a bunch of you running around here. I would be asking myself constantly if you were appetizers or apprentices."

Jason grinned.

The beast got off its belly, and rested on its haunches, straightening its forelegs. Again, he was struck by the catlike quality of the dragon. "A word of advice. It is easier than you make it. It is right in front of you, and all you have to do is look at it. Three more Gates have you, each as elemental as it can be. I shall repeat, think of what you are and what you need. Think too much and you will Open that which should never be touched!" With that, the beast reared up, roaring with a sound that began like deep bass thunder and rose in volume and pitch until it keened into a screech. It leaped skyward, stretching out its wings, and was airborne in a heartbeat or two, leaving a wake behind that rolled him about as if a giant hand shook him, throwing him off the rock.

He flailed out to catch himself, the Haven tilted and shifted, and his stomach wrenched as everything *changed,* and he was thrown headlong back through Iron Gate.

He shifted uneasily on his chair. "I didn't have anything to do with that," he said earnestly. "Honest."

"Maybe not, but what I told you originally stands. If you can't make practice regularly, you're off the team. Your teammates deserve to play with someone who works as hard as they do, and is reliable. Not only that, but with these three, he's not leaving me with much of a team! I can't have that."

Jason tried not to clench his hands. "What does he want?"

Coach shook his head. "All I know is, I'm to send you over. This is your last chance, Adrian. Straighten these meetings out, or I will drop you from the team. Understood? You've ability, but if I have to drop you to save more players from getting caught up in your mess, I will."

Jason gulped. "Yessir." He jumped to his feet. "I'll be back as soon as I can!"

Halfway outside the P.E. building, Sam caught him by the elbow. "What's up? What was Coach so mad about?"

Jason had one tight-lipped word for him. "Finch."

"That perv."

"I have to go see him."

"I thought your appointments were Friday mornings."

"Exactly. Coach says if I miss any more time from practice, he's dropping me. And you're gonna get hauled in, too."

Sam breathed in and out indignantly. "Can he do that?"

"Yeah, he can. Listen, I've gotta go, I'll be back if I can."

Sam nodded, and watched Jason with a forlorn expression as he trotted off across campus.

Students still milled around in the hallways, going through their lockers or bunched in small groups talking, classroom doors banging open and shut as he made his way to the cubbyhole Statler Finch called an office. No one seemed to be inside as he peered cautiously through the doorway. Relief flooded Jason. He'd come back later, at his regular appointed time then. . . .

No I in Team

"WE made a deal," Coach said, his square face creased in a heavy frown. "Three weeks ago, and this is what I get. I won't have this, Adrian. Either you're a player on my team or you're not, and this tells me you don't want to be."

The long night had turned into a long day, and Jason's baffled feeling about being called in turned into out and out worry. "I don't understand—"

"Statler wants to see you. Now." Coach tapped a piece of paper on his desk. "I thought we had this worked out. Not only does he want to see you, but he's told the vice principal he wants to see Canby, Brinkford, and your friend Sam. He feels a need to interview them about you, and possibly add them to counseling as well."

"We did make a deal. I've been to every session. He wants to see me now?" Jason's chest felt heavy. First a home meeting, now more meetings at school. What did the man want of him?

"Now," repeated Coach flatly. His face wrinkled even more till he reminded Jason of a thundercloud about to burst rain and lightning.

"Ah, Jason! Go on in, I'll be right there. Just getting a cup of coffee from the staff room!"

Jason whirled. Statler stood behind him, coffee mug in hand, blocking the corridor, a most curious expression on his face. He gestured through the air with the empty cup. "Go on, go on. I'll just be a minute."

Trying not to sigh, Jason ducked his head and went into the office he'd grown to hate. He plopped down on the visitor's chair, tucked his feet around the side rungs, and waited, thinking.

His gaze swept the office. Everything was compulsively neat, what little there was of books and files. The only picture on the wall was a poster comparing a wizened chimpanzee face to an elderly Albert Einstein. Wrinkling his nose at that one, Jason turned back to the desk. He curled his fingers about his crystal, holding it close, running through his focusing exercises, feeling the anger and resentment drain away. This wasn't fair . . . but then, many things weren't. He'd get through it, and once he did, it would be a small victory. Any triumph could be enjoyed later.

"Here we go." The counselor slid into his desk chair. "Thank Coach for me, for letting you out."

"I'm off the team if I miss workouts again," Jason told him.

The counselor said, without expression. "And how do you feel about that? About getting that kind of attention?"

"I feel like it's your fault, and I don't like getting into trouble for it." Jason stared back at him.

"Do you enjoy assigning blame?"

"I enjoy making a deal and sticking to it. We agreed on Friday mornings."

"As long as your behavior warranted it. But what I saw the other night convinced me that your case is a great deal more complicated than I thought." Statler wrapped spindly hands about his coffee mug and laced his fingers together. "What would you like to tell me about that? The . . . trash bin . . . incident."

"I saw a coyote trotting around the parking lot. It looked mean and hungry, so I dove into the can and made a lot of racket to chase it away." Jason was glad his words stayed even and did not give away the lie, and he leveled his gaze on the counselor's face.

"Did anyone else see the coyote?"

"Apparently not. But they are pretty hard to see, especially since it was nearly dark."

"Not a stray dog?"

He considered it. "Maybe. I thought it was a coyote. They come out of the hills, you know. It's been a dry year for them, and my stepdad says construction always chases them around a bit until they can resettle."

Statler drank about half his mug of coffee in one gulp. "Interesting reaction. Why didn't you try to outrun it? Or go get help?"

"Everyone seemed gone, and if you try to outrun things like that, you only attract their attention. They'll chase, if that's their gig. Chase and bring down."

Statler opened a desk drawer, reaching inside for his notepad and pencil. As he pushed through an assortment of writing instruments looking for one with a sharpened point, Jason saw deep into the drawer. Surprise hit him.

Crystals. Statler had focus crystals in his desk drawer. One, large enough to fill the man's thin hand, and two smaller ones. They glinted dully at him as the counselor pulled out what he needed and then shut the drawer tightly, and made a few notes as if deciding that Jason had finally said something worthwhile.

Jason watched. Why crystals? Why hidden? Did Finch know what they were for? Did he have an inkling of why and how they could be used? And if he did, where had he learned? An uncomfortable feeling prickled up the back of Jason's neck. He began to talk about soccer and why he loved it and why he wanted to stay on the team, not letting Statler get more than a word or two in edgewise. When he finally rambled to a halt, Statler had long since stopped scribbling whatever it was he wrote in his notebook and drained his coffee mug dry.

"And that is why," Jason finished, "I can't come to any more afternoon sessions."

Statler's eyebrows went up. "You're hardly in a position to dictate when you'll be here."

"You'll ruin everything."

"Blame again." Statler smiled thinly. "That's an interesting issue we should discuss tomorrow morning, Jason." He waggled his pencil at him. "Your usual appointment and I'll see you bright and early."

Jason took his leave, trotting back through now deserted corridors, wondering what he was going to do. A door swung open in his path. He went nose to nose with a chart covering the inside door of the science lab. "Composition of the Human Body," it read. "Seventy percent water." Without further thought, he swung past the door, listening to the grumbles and laughs from kids who'd stayed behind to finish a lab or work on a science fair project. He got his things from his locker and headed for home, shoulders hunched against a cold, dry wind. What *were* crystals doing in Statler's desk? What were the odds he merely liked pretty rocks?

Jason didn't think it could be that simple. Brennard's forces had sent a spy deep into the camp at Ravenwyng. They could do it here, too . . . to watch and break him, if they got a chance. Or was he just beginning to think as crazily as the counselor thought him to be?

Coach grabbed Sam by the scruff of the neck as he started out of the P.E. building. Sam looked up, feeling his eyes go wide.

"Come with me," the teacher said. "We have an appointment with Statler Finch."

Sam's heart sank. Just as Jason had warned. And, unlike Jason, he wasn't a stellar student and if any inkling of trouble reached home, his parents might ground him. He sighed un-happily as the coach marched him toward the offices at the front of the school. He wasn't any happier as Coach sat him down inside the office and said, his voice tight and annoyed. "I want to have a word with you, Finch."

Statler Finch got to his feet. Sam watched him, thinking all the while of Ichabod Crane. He even has a bird name like the character, he thought, as the two men went out and down the hallway. He could hear Coach's voice rising with every step.

". . . Trying to . . . ruin . . . my team?"

Sam looked around. He wasn't exactly sure why he was there or what he should say. Sure, he wanted to help Jason, but at what cost? He couldn't very well lie either till he knew what was going on!

He stood. Finch had left papers scattered across his desk. He craned his neck to look at them.

"Dear Student. This is an official notification that your loan package has been turned over for collection. As stipulated in original loan applications, all student's loans come eligible for repayment six months after leaving classes, whether graduated from a program or not. Your loans for the Masters program have been forwarded accordingly, and a payment program will be set up. . . ."

Something crashed down the hallway. Backing up guiltily from the desk, Sam jumped. His elbow hit the cubicle wall and a picture frame fell down. He almost caught it. Almost.

The frame cracked slightly, losing its tension, and the glass fell out. The diploma behind it slid out as well. Sam frantically tried to gather everything up, but as he did, the gold-embossed seal on the diploma flaked off and sailed through the air.

With muffled curses, he set the framing down on a chair seat and managed to get it back together, and the glass in place, with only a tiny nick in the corner of it. As for the diploma, Sammee looked at it as he retrieved the fallen seal. It just looked . . . well . . . fake. And besides, Finch couldn't have graduated with a Masters if the letter on the desk said he'd dropped out. So how could he have the diploma?

He could hear a shout and footfalls coming back his way. Hurriedly, he licked the golden seal and managed to get it stuck back on the diploma and the whole thing back together and on the wall.

"Do what you gotta do," the coach practically bellowed. "But if you take my team apart for the sake of one kid, I will see this program of yours stopped." He paused just outside the open office door and then stomped off. A pale and shaken Statler Finch stepped inside.

He blinked at Sam as though he'd forgotten he was there. Then, he took a deep breath and sat down. "I'll make this very, very brief, Samuel."

"No, it's Sam."

"Whatever. Very brief." Hands shaking, the counselor swept his papers into his desk drawer and then drew out a notebook.

Sam appeared to be looking at Finch as the man started asking questions, and he started answering. But in reality he was looking at the diploma on the wall, and thinking about his friendship, and the team, and what everything meant.

Oh, Henry

HENRY got up early, readying himself for school. He always liked the last day of the week, even though it invariably meant tests in English and Math and often small quizzes in History. He liked it because he loved to sleep in on Saturdays, which his mother let them all do, because she liked to sleep in on Saturdays. If any of them did get up, they were under the strictest orders to do so quietly and stay that way, so as not to disturb the peaceful rest of anyone else. So he had only one more day to wait until Saturday, when his time was his, to be spent (in the morning anyway), any which way he could so long as it was quiet.

He'd decided to take charge of his destiny. And, although it might be just as well to wait a day or two, today was probably as good as any time to begin. There was a shop on the way home from school, a little store carrying candles and crystals and incense and stuff. He didn't intend to spend his time wondering if a wolfjackal or a terrible Magicker stood in the shadow waiting to steal his powers again. No. He'd get a crystal of his own, and he'd fight back!

The morning sun shone brightly in the backyard, and Henry took the opportunity to box his shadow around, showing it who was boss! He danced about in proper kung fu style, kicking and jabbing. It felt good to have Jason and Trent, Bailey and Ting all believing in him again. How could he have forgotten them? Well, he'd been enchanted to, but still! And to become a full-fledged Magicker again? He could hardly wait. If only he had his crystal!

He wouldn't have the summer back, but he had days of it in his mind, vivid and happy. With the exception of Jonnard who'd betrayed all of them, the memories he had seeping back were good ones. Magick lessons and campfire sing-alongs and warm days canoeing on the lake and afternoons playing sandlot base-ball. He'd never been happier. Who'd want to forget that?

He punched and kicked at his shadowy self who deftly danced and twisted out of range. In the house and upstairs, he could hear his siblings clattering out of the house for school. One more good kick box . . .

Henry.

He halted in his tracks. The thick, unruly hair on his head stood on end. Something—someone?—hissed at him from the shadows.

He turned, straightening his glasses. The morning sun lay across his backyard in sharp contrast to the early shadows cast by corners, and fencing, and the garage. The yard almost looked black and white, rather than shades of greens and browns, edged and dotted with colorful flowers. This was his home! How could anything have got in?

But he knew better even as he thought that.

Could wolfjackals talk? And if they did, did he really want to listen? Henry pivoted cautiously and began to walk toward his back door. His sneakers swished through grass thick with dew, the bottoms of his jeans going dark purple with the wet-ness. Something trailed behind him. Cautious, slow, but he could hear footfalls.

Henry.

Something panted. It could be him, his chest rising and falling in gasping breaths, unable to call out, but trying to. Or it could be the something behind him, or the something in the shadows flanking him, or the something in the corner by the kitchen door waiting. . . .

He made it through the back door, lunging quickly in at the last second and slamming it in the face of whatever pursued him. He heard a low whine, and a frantic scratch. Wood and paint splintered, by the sound of it. Still panting, he stood for a moment, then grabbed up his book bag with Henry Squibb neatly stitched across the back of it. Something bronzed and heavy fell out as he hoisted it and clattered over the kitchen floor, coming to rest under the lip of the cabinet. He bent over quickly to retrieve it.

Dr. Patel's cobra bracelet! He didn't know how he could have forgotten it so quickly, but he had. Its surface felt cool as he rubbed it between his fingers. Just break it, she'd said.

He couldn't go off and leave danger so close to home. It was up to him to make sure everyone was protected.

Taking a deep breath, Henry broke the bracelet.

His feet left the ground in a dizzying motion. His body soared upward even though his eyes appeared to be shut tight, and he had no idea where he was going or how. He moved through the air with great speed, as though a tornado had picked him up and carried him off. Everything whirled around him. He could feel his backpack straining from its strap, and his shoes tugging at his feet, laces untying and flying about like spaghetti. His ears roared so loudly that, for a few moments, he seriously wondered if it *was* a tornado.

Then everything stopped as suddenly as it had begun. He hung suspended, suddenly aware that he was no longer moving, and the roaring noise had finished, and there was nothing but the sound of silence and his own squeaking breath. Wherever he was traveling to, he'd arrived! But nothing met his feet, and it was impossible for him to stay hanging in air much longer.

"Gaaaaaah!" cried Henry and he fell.

He fell short and hard, tumbling onto an old linoleum floor that was glazed almost golden yellow with years of wax. The fall thumped the breath out of him. Henry knelt on hands and knees for a minute before getting shakily to his feet. His backpack slipped from his shoulder and fell to the floor. As he looked down, he saw that he held half a bronzed and twisted cobra in each hand. He hadn't just broken it open, he'd snapped it in two. Henry winced, hoping that Dr. Patel either wouldn't mind or could fix it.

That was probably the least of his worries, he thought, as he looked around. He was in Gavan Rainwater's camp office, and he knew that Ravenwyng was a considerable distance from anything he could even remotely call home. Furthermore, he seemed to be here alone.

"Hello?" He twisted around. The place looked as if Gavan were here often, but not this morning. No one was about this morning.

He put the pieces of jewelry in his backpack, hoping the Magicker doctor would not be angry with him. She had given it to him to use when there was trouble, and a wolfjackal at his back door meant a lot of trouble to him.

Pulsating color caught his eye. A great crystal on top of a wooden filing cabinet in the corner moved and shimmered as if alive. Amber rays shot out from it every now and then, and it revolved on a base, as if it turned about on its own. Henry hesitated. Then he licked lips gone terribly dry and moved toward it, just to look. This, he knew, belonged to Gavan. It must be the alarm beacon Jason talked about, the one that didn't always work. It seemed to be working now.

He stepped to its side and tentatively waved his hand through a ray, and amber color flowed over his hand like water, but he didn't feel it, just saw it.

"Wow." Henry dipped his hand in again. Golden waves dappled him. He grinned.

"Henry? What are you doing here? Is there a problem?"

He spun about guiltily at the voice, flinging his hands up, and backing clumsily into the file cabinet. His face lit up, though, with welcome. "Dr. Patel! We had trouble, a wolf-jackal."

"Indeed? Does anyone know you're here?"

He shook his head.

"They will." Smiling, she stepped forward with a very faint chiming of the belled anklet she wore, and something snarled from the corner behind the desk, leaping over at both of them. He caught a last glimpse of the alarm beacon crystal, as he fell into the cabinet and it flew off its base, arching through the air and shattering as it hit the floor. He grabbed for a shard of it, thinking of Jason as he did. Dr. Patel was reaching for him. Then he hit his head, hard, and found only darkness.

Jason paused halfway to school. A feeling arched through him, like a shock wave of warning and dismay and terror, and it seemed to call out to him. He blinked. It was like . . . like a disturbance in the Force, corny as that sounded, but this must have been what that felt like. Something was terribly wrong somewhere. His hand went immediately to his crystal. His friends and family ran through his mind, but he found nothing but pleasant warmth when he thought of them. Except for Henry.

He found an icy cold when he thought of Henry.

Darn it! He'd known all along Henry was the most vulnerable of all of them. He didn't even have a focus he could use to help stave off the Dark Hand if they came after him.

Jason looked down the street. His early Friday morning appointment with Finch loomed. But the crystal in his hand told him Henry was in trouble, somehow, and he needed to find out why and where. He took a deep breath, turned about on the sidewalk, and headed back home.

Everyone was gone but McIntire when he came back in. He entered the study hesitantly, unwilling to disturb him, for McIntire sat with his desk covered in blueprints and sketches, and a heavy frown on his face. He looked up. "Oh. Morning, Jason. Problem?"

"Sir. You know, we talked about trust?"

"Indeed we did. Used to be, when I started out in business, you could shake a man's hand and that would be the contract, his bond. Trust. Now, you need a fleet of lawyers on both sides, and why? Because people break their trust."

Jason cleared his throat uneasily. "I know I have to see Mr. Finch and get things straightened out, but I just can't do it today. I need to . . . I need to miss my counseling appointment this morning and maybe a class or two."

"You intend to ditch some classes and you're telling me about it?" McIntire stared at him.

"Yup. Look. I need you to trust me on this. I've got to help someone out, it's this project."

"No drugs."

"No, sir." Jason swallowed tightly. "Nothing like that."

"Anything to do with Halloween?" McIntire watched his face steadily.

Tonight was Halloween night. The irony of Brennard striking out at all of them like the vampire he was hit Jason with irony. "It might, I'm not sure yet."

The Dozer put down his pencil. "You know, Jason. I never hesitated asking Joanna to marry me because of you kids.

Bright, good kids, both you and Alicia. I'm proud to be your
father. Stepfather." He coughed slightly. "You haven't given me
any evidence otherwise, so . . . all right. Let me know when
you're back then. I've got trouble with the McHenry house coming out my ears. I'll be on the cell phone. And I'll handle your
mother when she gets home. But—" And McIntire pointed at
him. He paused as if searching for the right word. "Be careful,"
he finally said.

"Yessir! I'll try!" Jason darted out of the door and upstairs to
the safety of his room. He pulled his trapdoor shut after him
and got first the lavender crystal out, and then his own. Cupping them closely, he summoned the alarm beacon and found
no answer. Not again! Not now, not this time!

Jason closed his eyes and called on Gavan with all his might.
His thoughts went ebony and then crimson with intensity, then
suddenly, he conjured the image of Rainwater in his mind.

"Jason?" came a faint response. "What is it, lad?"

"Trouble."

Gavan suddenly strengthened in his thoughts as the other
Magicker threw his own power into their conversation. The
head and shoulders image of the man stared through Jason's
mind. "What kind and where?"

"I don't know! It's Henry. He's just . . . well, he's gone cold."

"Jason, that's not enough to . . ."

"And the alarm beacon is out."

"What? I was just in my office. I had some matters to take
care of, about Fizziwig. The crystal was fine. What the hell is
going on?" Gavan shook his head. "Let me get some of the others. We'll follow up on Henry and let you know."

"Okay."

Then, as quickly as he'd been watching Gavan's face grow
concerned and angry, the image was gone and his thoughts
were empty.

Jason sat back in his chair. There was really nothing more

he could do. He booted his computer and left quick messages for Bailey and Trent, not knowing if he would catch them before they left their homes. Rich and Stefan had auto-messages on their e-mail stating that the team was out of state for a middle school football tournament, and they were gone for a long weekend in Texas. He didn't even leave mail for Ting. There was no sense in frightening her.

Jason checked his watch. His session with Statler Finch was nearly half gone. Gavan would contact him, when there was anything to know. He decided to face the music and go to school anyway.

By the time he got there, the campus was crowded with students clustered around, waiting for regular morning classes to begin. He wouldn't have to deal with missing first period then, for which he could be grateful, if he wasn't so worried about Henry.

Sam caught him in the main corridor by their lockers. "Man, where have you been?"

"I got up late. I haven't missed anything yet."

"Nothing but your appointment with the psycho-ologist."

"That's not funny, Sam." Jason sighed. His friend pulled at his arm.

"It will be." Sam stuffed a folder of papers in his hand. "Listen, he was all over campus looking for you this morning. So he'll haul you out of first period soon as he finds out you've shown up. But this . . ." Sam tapped the folder. "This is your ammo, bro."

"What are you talking about?"

"I got hauled in last night to talk to him."

"Oh, man. I'm sorry, Sam. Really, really sorry."

Sam hit him in the shoulder. "Shut upppp! Let me finish. Coach brought me, and they went down to the teachers' lounge and yelled at each other for a while. So I poked around a little. Looked at the diplomas on the wall and stuff. He had mail on his desk, Jason, about repaying a student loan. Then I came home and looked everything up on the Internet." Sam shook Jason. "Jason. He didn't finish his Counseling Masters. He dropped out. The diploma is a photocopy."

Jason opened the folder. He looked at what appeared to be a list of graduates. "Doesn't exist? He's not in here?"

"Nope. That creep is a fraud. A fake. He shouldn't even be working here at the school! So when he comes after you . . . just point that folder at him and slap him down." Sam grinned. "I put copies on the principal's desk. He'll see 'em in a day or two, I'm sure."

"Wow. He's a fake? His credential is no good?" Jason tried to take in all the implications. He was free!

"Yup. I can get a better diploma from the grocery store and fill in the blanks." Sam slapped him on the shoulder as the bell rang.

"Sam . . ."

"Yeah?" Sam turned back to him.

"Thanks."

"Are you kidding? That's how friends take care of each other. Even if you are a Potter geek."

"Soccer geek!"

Sam laughed. He raised a hand as the warning bell sounded and trotted off to class.

Jason clenched his folder. He slipped into Home Room and sat through the morning's bulletins, and wasn't at all surprised when his teacher looked up, motioned him forward, and gave him a pass sending him immediately to Finch's office. Nor was he surprised at the look of cruel triumph that flashed across Statler's face.

"Breaking appointments won't do you much good, Jason." Statler practically crowed as he gestured Jason into the office.

"I'm not staying long," Jason said. "I volunteered for these sessions, and now I'm not."

Statler's thin mouth tightened until it all but disappeared. "Sit down, young man, and be quiet."

Jason stayed in the doorway. He shook his head. "No, sir. You can't hold me. I'm going back to playing soccer and making practices and doing anything else I need to, just like any other student."

Statler moved to the far side of his desk, and began to slide open a drawer. "I think," he said, "you have no idea of what you're dealing with."

Jason waved his folder. "I think you thought you were too smart for your papers to get caught. But they're fakes, and so are you. I don't have to stay here for classes with you, and I don't intend to. You're twisted, Statler, and you're caught."

"You can prove nothing."

"Copies of this are on the principal's desk right now. I don't have to prove anything. I think you're the one who needs to answer the questions."

Statler snarled. His face contorted and reshaped, and Jason could almost smell the hot spittle, just like a wolfjackal's growling snarl. He stepped back, suddenly frightened in spite of himself.

Statler reached in and grabbed a large, blood-red crystal. "You have no idea what you're dealing with!" He let out a short howl of hate.

"You're mine!" And the jaws in his face had trouble saying the word.

Jason blinked, staring into the gullet of a rapidly transforming wolfjackal. "You came after me specifically." His hand throbbed with a white-hot pain, searing through his scar. "They planted you here!"

"Cleverrrr lad," the beast managed. Its clothes disappeared as if they had only been a veil of illusion.

No wonder Statler hadn't seen the wolfjackal . . . he *was* the beast.

Rescue

H E stumbled into Gavan's empty office seconds later, his heart still thudding from his escape from Statler Finch. One hand was knotted about the folder, clutching it, and the other about the crystal so tightly, it left its imprint in his palm. He slid the folder into his backpack and zipped it tightly, then looked about into chaos.

The massive desk was overturned. Amber shards were strewn everywhere . . . the alarm crystal had shattered and been rendered useless. Jason swept his gaze over the room and the destruction. Chairs, overturned. The wood filing cabinet had nearly gone, too, but it leaned heavily on a small table. Its drawers hung open, papers overflowing from it. The office looked like the aftermath of an all-out brawl, especially with broken glass lying around.

Jason shifted uneasily. Under the lip of the overturned desk, he could see Henry's backpack. Lying next to it was the prone and dead form of another wolfjackal, an amber sliver of the broken crystal through its flank. He shuddered. One close encounter too many.

"Oh, Henry," he sighed. Whatever had happened to Henry, it had begun here. He put a hand to the back of his neck, and rubbed it. He thought of Khalil's last words during the Council argument. *You have a betrayer in your midst.*

He didn't even dare think who. But he knew why. And if Gavan, Tomaz, Eleanora, and whoever else had gone after him had not yet come back, he had a lot of thinking to do about that, too.

He righted Gavan's leather chair, worn and cracked in places, and plopped down in it to wait.

After an hour, he stretched fretfully. Then, he *knew*. And knowing what he knew, he could wait all day. He scrounged around in his backpack and found the two nutritional bars he kept there for emergencies and energy. He also fished out the water bottle at the bottom and drank that, and then he napped. He got up when he woke, and left the office, wandering out of Lake Wannameecha Gathering Hall, then watched the sunset over the lake itself. It was incredibly beautiful.

An owl hooted and drifted silently over the pines. It was time. He went back to Gavan's office. Halloween Eve.

He palmed his crystal and sent for Trent, and then Bailey. Trent appeared, his jaw dropped, and then he gave a yelp as he saw where he was. He was half shrugged out of his sweatshirt and quickly pulled it back on. "What happened here?"

Bailey popped in next, blinking in astonishment, and then let out a snort. "Bachelors! Can't keep anything clean!" She put her hands on her hips. Lacey poked her head out as if to see what the commotion was about.

"Bailey!" both boys said in unison. She tossed her head. "Oh, all right, I see there's trouble and that starts with T and that rhymes with B and stands for Brennard."

Jason's jaw joined Trent's in the down position. Trent slowly shut his mouth and shrugged. "She's right. It's gotta be Brennard's doing. This is not because someone didn't get the trick or treat they wanted." He looked about at the shambles.

"And what was your final clue? The dead wolfjackal under the desk?"

Bailey's eyes got big as saucers as she looked, but Trent only frowned slightly. "What are you talking about?"

"Beast body on the floor." Jason pointed.

Trent shook his head. "I don't see a thing."

"But it's there!"

"Look. I've had enough of those things breathing down my neck! I see nothing. This one's invisible!"

Bailey sidled over and put out her foot and nudged the still form with the toe of her sneaker. "Feels like a wolfjackal," she observed. She crossed the room warily. "They can be killed, right?"

"Right. Although the bodies often don't stay here. They're not stable or something, I guess." Jason considered it. It had been there all day, remarkably unchanging. "Poke it, Trent."

"I can't even see it," Trent protested. Grumbling, he picked up a cane in the stand by Gavan's doorway. He make a show of waving it and poking it through the space under the Magicker's desk.

A ripple ran through the body, distorting it, and then it . . . disappeared. Bailey, who obviously had been able to see it, let out a shriek and jumped back against the wall.

"Very interesting." Jason took a deep breath. "Or as Alice would say, Curiouser, and curiouser."

Trent surveyed what was left of Gavan Rainwater's office. "I'd say this was really serious or you wouldn't have yanked us here. Better be, 'cause I had plans for tonight."

Jason rolled his eyes. "I know you did, 'cause they were with me!"

Bailey got in between them, her face pale under her freckles. "What happened?"

"I found it like this. They took Henry."

"Poor Henry." Bailey shuddered. "When?"

Leaving out his troubles with Statler Finch, Jason told the two of them about Henry and his probable disappearance, and what he knew of it, and his contacting Gavan. And then finding this when he hadn't heard.

Bailey whistled low. "I'd say our rescuers need a rescue."

"She has a way with words." Trent shifted uneasily.

"But she's right."

"Okay. What'll we do? What can we do that Gavan and Tomaz and whoever else was here . . . couldn't?" Trent stared at Jason, not angrily, but his eyes locked on Jason's face. "And why have you waited all day?"

"I don't know what we're going to do." Jason reached down and picked up Henry's backpack and looked at it briefly. "I don't think we're going to have any trouble finding him," Jason replied at last. "I think Henry was bait, and I think the wrong people took it, the first time. The trap was meant for us, not the elders. Wherever he is, they are. And they're all still waiting for us. I had all the time in the world, so I took it to do a lot of thinking."

Trent let his breath out with a hiss. "Then we can get in. But we might have a lot of trouble getting out."

Bailey let out a worried sound. Then she put her shoulders back. "We might take the bait, but who says we have to go into the trap like mice?"

"Exactly. With a little planning, we can cause a lot of trouble, I think. And don't forget, if they're still alive," and Jason swallowed hard at that thought. "If they are, Gavan and Tomaz probably only need a distraction or two to break loose."

Bailey put up a second chair and set it down properly, and rested on it. "I can send Lacey in for a look around, wherever it is. She's little and she's fast."

"You can do that?"

She nodded. "I've been training her. Sometimes," and Bailey blushed at this, "sometimes I see what she does." She looked at Trent. "Remember, I said I could follow her?"

"Okay," said Trent. "That officially makes you weird, Bailey."

"I know," she huffed. "But helpful, too!"

He punched her shoulder. "Did I ever say you weren't?"

Bailey's face turned even redder.

Jason ran his hand over the backpack embroidered with Henry's name. There was a vibration, a faint path there, to be read, leading him onward. "I know where he is," he said, in sudden realization. It seemed inevitable.

"Where?" Two heads turned to look at him.

He waved the backpack. "This is an invitation to the McHenry house." And just as suddenly, just as inevitably, he desperately didn't want to have to go there.

"We're the cavalry, Jason," Trent said quietly, as if reading his reluctance. "Let's get a game plan."

So they huddled close, and made their plans and crossed their fingers. They linked arms and Jason took them to the doorstep of the McHenry house. Night had settled in, and it was dark, pitch-black with a moonless sky.

Trent looked up. "Figures," he commented. He lit one of the old camp lanterns, and handed a second to Bailey. The house looked derelict and abandoned, as if it had never even been wired for electricity.

The front door was open the tiniest crack. Bailey leaned over, fetching Lacey from her pocket, and nuzzling her gently, whispering to her. She put the little pack rat down on the porch step and Lacey cautiously went inside, her long, black tufted tail disappearing in little jerks until suddenly it was gone.

They all stood, very quiet, keeping a sharp eye out for wolfish figures loping over the rolling front lawns of the estate . . . if any could be seen in the dark. After long moments, Bailey rubbed her temple.

"She's in," she whispered. "Lots of people in the back. Gavan! Tomaz . . . long frilly skirts . . ." She let out a sigh. "They've even got Eleanora."

"Alive?"

"Everyone, so far."

"Okay, then. We know what we have to do."

They all nodded, and Bailey started for the door.

Abruptly, Jason said, "Wait a minute." He looked at Trent. "I think we'd better tell her."

Come into My Parlor

"JASON, this is not a good time." Bailey put her hands on her hips, facing them. "Whatever it is you want to tell me, I think it can wait."

Jason shifted. "Ummmm. No. I don't think it can."

Trent nodded in agreement. "You're right. It can't wait."

She tossed her head, eyes rolling. "All right! Hurry up, then. Lacey is all alone in there!" She stabbed a finger at the looming McHenry house.

"This is important." Jason put a hand on each of Bailey's shoulders to still the impatient bounce. "Listen to me. Trent is a Magicker without Talent. Not an ounce of it."

Trent nodded again, solemnly. "Not a Magickal bone in my body."

She looked from one to the other. "Oh," she said slowly. Then, "This is sooooo not funny. Look, I'm sorry I ragged on you, but this is NOT funny."

"Bailey, I'm not joking, Trent isn't joking, we're not pulling your chain, this is not meant to be funny. He can't do anything you and I can."

Her jaw dropped. "How . . . what . . . how . . . ?" She stared at Trent in total amazement.

Trent shrugged, his face getting slightly red. "I'm good at faking? I know all the moves? I've read all the magic books ever written? I know how it should go? I want it really badly? I dunno. But I'm not and Jason's been carrying me, and so have you, and . . . it might be really, really important inside there to know what we're dealing with."

"You can't go in with us."

"Oh, yes, I can. A wolfjackal can take a boot in the gut from anyone. And it's the three of us now, right? If I don't go in, who'll protect your backs while you're focusing on your crystals? You need me as much as I need you." Trent inhaled. "I hope."

Jason dropped his hands from Bailey, but not before he could feel how cold she seemed, and the slight shivers running through her. "I need you," he said quietly. "We know this is a trap. First Henry was bait, now Gavan and Eleanora and the others are bait. We're the ones Brennard wants, and so they're expecting us with whatever they can throw at us. What I'm counting on." And he halted, and looked into each of their faces. "What I'm counting on is that the traps will be aimed specifically at Magickers."

"He hasn't a chance, Jason," Bailey said earnestly, her face knotted in a frown. "I don't know if I can protect him."

"Listen to Jason," Trent pleaded. "Just listen. I belong here, if I belong anywhere!"

"I can protect him, and even more so, I think he can protect us. He won't be affected by Magicks aimed specifically at Talent. He might very well be able to get through what we can't." Jason watched Bailey closely.

"Oh. Ohhhhhhh." Bailey chewed on her lip. "Well, if he can't, it's a little late now!" She rubbed her temple as a faraway look came into her eyes and her attention was taken from them as if she was listening to something else. "Lacey says there are books everywhere, and people everywhere. She's found them! Eleanora and a round-headed boy, and Gavan and Tomaz and Dr. Patel." She gave a shaky laugh. "That's Henry."

"They're in the library, then. Figures. I've been in there before, they know I know the way. It's in the center of the house. We go in there, and we can be effectively surrounded."

"Anything else?" Trent asked as Jason's voice trailed off in thought.

"Like what?" Bailey looked at Trent, puzzled.

"Anything. Anything could be important."

Bailey got a distant look on her face again then, and again rubbed her temple slightly as if her very thoughts hurt. "Pretty things everywhere. Wax . . . cold."

"Candles?"

"Maybe. Cold, though." Bailey shrugged. "I'm not good at this yet."

"Call her back to you," Jason said. "Ask her to look at one on the way back. Soon as you scoop her up, we'll go in." He touched his first crystal, and then his second. *Armed,* he thought, *to the teeth.*

Long moments passed, and then a tiny furry creature shoved its way through the crack in the door, scampering up Bailey's jeans and into the palm of her hand. Bailey nuzzled the pack rat with her cheek before tucking Lacey away into her pocket. "Candles," she said firmly. "Everywhere. In great boxes and on every table, chair, and ledge imaginable."

"Strange." Trent scratched at the back of his neck.

"Candles burn," said Jason in an odd voice, before pulling the door open and stepping inside quickly. He didn't want to face the Fire Gate of his nightmares, yet it seemed inevitable. The itching, the nearness to a Gate waiting for him to discover and open it seemed unbearable. Not now! Not tonight, not without training. Not here. The other two tumbled after him.

At night, the old mansion seemed as cavernous and dark as

any haunted house. Although electric lights burned through it in dim corners, their illumination seemed very pale and weak. Trent craned his head. "Low, low watts. Just barely enough to almost see by." He stepped around a pile of crates, reading their labels. "Someone's buying fancy floor tile. Pretty, cold things. But definitely not wax."

Jason paused at a nearby pallet of crates. "This is. Candles by the dozen. It's marked for a shop," and he read aloud, "The Flickering Flame."

"I know them!" Bailey's face brightened for an instant. "They've got the coolest shop in the county. More than candles, kind of New Age, with aromas, herbs, meditating music, that kind of thing. They said they were expanding. They must be putting a shop in here."

"Could be. Place isn't even renovated yet, though. Moving stock here is kind of jumping the gun."

"Maybe they needed storage room." Trent looked around. "Watch out for spiders."

"Spiders?" Bailey scooted to one side quickly.

He grabbed her by the sweatshirt. "Don't move."

She stood in place, eyes getting bigger.

Jason froze and looked about, carefully. "What do you see?"

"Webs. Silvery strings. Just kind of out of the corner of my eye, but the whole foyer is full of 'em."

"I don't," said Jason, even as he eyed the entryway again, "see a thing. But that doesn't mean you don't."

"What are webs for?"

"Trapping food. And the strands quiver when the prey touches and struggles in them, alerting the spider . . ." Trent stopped.

" 'Come into my parlor,' said the spider to the fly," quoted Bailey.

"The strands must be energy. An energy net, like. The minute we brush one, they know we're here."

Jason said quietly, "I think they already know we're here. I'm suspecting the webs are a lot worse than that. Take the lead, Trent, and try not to touch one." He waited for Trent's lead and wondered if Brennard had somehow gathered up and corrupted ley lines, the natural flow of the Earth's various energies.

Trent took Bailey by the hand, moving her away from the shadowed foyer wall, and began to walk to the lighted square of a door at the other end. Jason followed, but it was difficult because Trent took a very odd path through, casting right and left, ducking low, then stepping over things that Jason could not begin to see. They would have looked very peculiar, if there had been security cameras on to see them, but those awaiting them had chosen to depend on Magick for their surveillance.

Trent and Bailey stood in the golden arch and he had nearly reached them when something stung across his left arm, his bicep, as if he'd been lashed with a fiery whip. He let out a yelp of surprise and pain.

"I told you to duck!" Trent fretted as Jason wheeled sharply to the right and then took a side step to join them. "Is it bad?"

Jason rubbed his arm gently. He pulled the sleeve of his sweatshirt around, certain it must have been ripped open, but there was nothing . . . nothing but a faint, charcoal burn mark that smelled of singed cloth, but was cold to the touch. He rubbed his hand over it and felt the powdery grit of residue.

"What did that thing do?"

"It was like . . . like a whiplash or something. Stings like crazy. It must have been the web or something. Don't touch any strands." The moment was over, but he felt a little queasy and who knew how he'd feel if he'd hit more than one of those things, whatever they were. "See any more?"

"Not as many but they're everywhere, Jason."

"I wonder if a creature makes them. Some big scary Dark Hand spider." Bailey shivered all over.

"Let's hope not. We've got enough trouble with people and wolfjackals." Jason gestured at Trent. "We need to go that way, and through the door."

"Follow me then, and do what I do, very carefully."

They crossed the inner parlor, its room nearly empty except for alcoves with unlit candles in them, and boxes scattered about. It looked bigger, and older, and dustier than he remembered. The second-story floor overhead creaked, once, as if someone or something had taken a firm step. They all froze, and listened. Lacey stuck her head out of Bailey's pocket, whiskers trembling, but making not even a squeak as if the tiny pet sensed the danger. They all held their breath for a few long heartbeats, then Trent jerked his head.

"Old houses creak," he said. "And this one is plenty big and old."

"It must have been grand once," Bailey whispered in awe. She looked upstairs to a landing, all paneled in deep, rich wood.

Jason nodded in agreement. "Dozer calls it settling noises." He breathed in and out a few times to settle himself. His left bicep finally quit stinging. He set off after Trent and Bailey, casting glances around and behind them, wondering when the first attack would come. After that came other thoughts, wondering what kind of battle it would be, and if it would be to the finish.

Was he prepared for that? Could he even begin to do something like that? He didn't think so. But he would do what he had to in order to get his friends and the elders out of there. Even if he had to open a Gate to do it, a way through which the Dark Hand could not follow.

That thought sent a thrill right through him. The answer! He could. Yes, he could. Open a Gate, draw everyone with him through it, and snap it shut right in the faces of the Dark Hand. All he needed to do was find one, sense it, and focus on it, while Bailey and Trent distracted Brennard's efforts.

Of course, that might be a lot harder than it sounded, and it sounded impossible.

Charge!

"WE'RE going in," Jason told them. "I want you to know who you're going to grab when I say, 'Do it now!' I've got Trent. Each of you has to grab two people."

"Eleanora and Henry," Bailey claimed.

"Gavan and Tomaz."

"All right. Once I've done what I'm going to do, I can grab Dr. Patel. I'll be linking arms with Trent, so we both have our hands empty. Bailey, you'll have to stow your crystal when I yell. Everyone understand that?"

"Yeah," said Trent, and Bailey nodded. "Sorta," she answered. Then, "No. What are you going to do?"

"Something spectacular and hopefully unexpected." Jason felt excitement build in him. He could do it . . . he could! He grinned at her. "Opposites attack!"

She took a deep breath. Lacey poked her head out of the pocket, let out a tremorous squeak and dove back in, only her tail hanging outside. "I'm ready."

"You're sure."

She nodded, ponytail swinging. "Nearly sure, anyway."

"In that case . . ." Jason reared back and then kicked out hard, the doors falling open and inward under the blow. "Charge!"

The library doors slammed open with a Bang!

"JASON!" shouted Henry. His glasses sat sideways on his round face, one of the lenses broken, and a long scratch underneath it, his brown hair standing nearly straight up. One sleeve of his sweater hung in unraveled strands.

"Jason, go back!" cried Eleanora. Her pale face turned to him, dark curly hair in a disorderly mass about her face. She sat in a Victorian chair, her wrists neatly tied to the wooden arms, her long skirts tumbled about her.

"Jason, lad, think very carefully what it is you're going to do." Gavan Rainwater spoke last, bound elbow to elbow with Tomaz, who kept his silence. Even as Jason looked toward the two who stood against the bookcases, dark shadows enveloped them, and he lost sight of them. The veil, he was certain, was only illusion.

The trap was sprung.

"I can't quite see them," Trent told him in a very low whisper. "But I can see the wolfhead cane. They're still here."

Brennard stood in front of the great mahogany desk which seemed to brace him as well as set him off. Shadows held other figures which Jason could not quite see as he came to a halt in momentary dismay, then he realized it did not matter if the Magickers he hoped to rescue were tied or not. Easier, perhaps . . . a package deal!

Trent whispered behind his left ear, "Room is filled with webs. The only straight path is right for that guy."

Jason looked straight at "that guy," and said, "I believe this is the first time I've actually met you . . . Antoine Brennard."

"True. It seems our knowledge of each other has only been in dreams."

"Nightmares," Bailey snorted. "Afraid to come out in the open? Jason's not scared of you."

"Oh, but he should be." The Magicker looked at her. The expression in his dark eyes seemed to be one of amusement. When it changed, and it would, Jason thought, she would be in deadly danger.

"The Hand seems to be here, too," Jason commented.

"You can see them?" Brennard's eyebrows arched in his slender, elegant face.

He shook his head, even as Trent whispered softly to him, "One behind the desk behind Brennard, two to your left corner rear and one in the right corner rear . . . I don't see a fifth." Why show all your cards? It disturbed Brennard enough that Jason could even sense them.

Brennard relaxed slightly then, leaning back against the massive desk. He wore a dark velvet coat showing ruffles at the cuffs as he crossed his arms over his chest. "A proposition, Jason. A trade."

"I'm listening but not for long. Tell your Hand in the left corner to stop trying to flank us." Jason put his chin up and shifted his position to guard Trent, who had again relayed the enemy's movement to him. He grinned and repeated Trent's whispered comment. "Or maybe he's just a Finger?"

Total surprise flared over Brennard's face and disappeared as suddenly. He raised a hand and gestured and something Jason could almost but not quite hear ceased to happen. Anita Patel looked with concern toward Brennard. She alone seemed unbound. Bailey stared at her for a very long time, as did Henry, who seemed to have begun to twitch, and his eyeglasses now dangling even more precariously from his face. His mouth worked soundlessly.

"This need not be as unpleasant as it could," Brennard stated. "I want—"

"We know what you want," Jason interrupted. "You want the three of us. You used Henry for bait for them, and all of them as bait for us." He took a deep breath. "You're not getting any of us."

"I don't think you see the situation clearly," said Brennard. One corner of his mouth twitched, showing that he was still amused.

"I see it far better than you think I do."

"Hand moving on the right," Trent whispered quickly.

Jason looked to the right and said, "Hold it right there."

Anita Patel swung about in astonishment, and Brennard jerked an impatient thumb. "Do not force things yet," he said quietly, and again that almost noise he could almost hear stopped.

Bailey cleared her throat. "Let's play . . . Red Rover." She smiled brightly at Brennard.

The Magicker looked at her. "Red Rover?"

"Yes. Red rover, red rover, won't you please send Henry Squibb over?" And she put her hand out for Henry.

Brennard laughed. "She thinks it's a game."

"Not hardly. And you're not playing with children." Bailey held her crystal up, and a thin white light lanced across the room, smoking. It sliced across one arm of the chair Eleanora was bound to, and then she pulled on her bindings and the ropes parted with a faint *twing!* Quickly she reached over to undo her other wrist, but Brennard gestured with a harsh word that seemed to darken the room. The Magicker went limp in her chair, and Bailey went to her knees, motionless. Lacey let out a pitiful squeak.

Gavan growled from the shadows that veiled and held him. "I will kill you for that, Brennard!"

"She only sleeps. Do you think I would harm a hair on her head? And the same goes for the girl."

"No," Jason said, a little sick to his stomach, "you wouldn't hurt anyone as long as you had a use for them."

"Oh, I have uses." He held up a woven sack and scattered its contents about the room. Bones and teeth went scattering. "I need a body or two."

"What is that for?" Jason stared, not understanding that one.

"Evidence," Brennard said. "To cover your taking. Your families will grieve over these, all that will survive in the ashes." He gestured. "Get the old ones out of here. Treat them to the delight Fizziwig felt when he disobeyed me!" He stood. "Enough talk. You are well and truly mine. You are mine!" He waved his arm in a grand gesture. *"Inardesco!"* shouted Brennard.

"Burn!" whispered Trent in his ear. "It's Latin for start to burn or ignite."

What? Jason pondered. Burn? Latin? "How on earth do you know that?" He turned his head back toward Trent in total amazement.

"Harry Potter," muttered Trent, and blushed.

"Good grief." Jason turned his attention back to Brennard who had regained his cold smile.

"It is your choice, Jason. Come to me freely, and they go. Or I will take you anyway, and they will stay here . . . to their deaths." Brennard lifted his gaze, across the library room, through the open doors at Jason's back. "Candles burn so well. The whole place will go up like tinder. An All Hallows' Eve prank. No one will prove any different, nor will anyone come after you, thinking you still alive."

Jason could smell the hot wax. Crates and crates of very flammable paraffin candles spread out downstairs and up, no doubt. His nightmare of facing Brennard and burning walls was coming true. . . .

And so was his need for a Gate. Not just any Gate. Fire Gate. He understood now, what it was all about. The McHenry house and his dreams had been trying to tell him for weeks.

He locked his eyes on Brennard's face. He curled one hand about his lavender crystal, and felt it answer to his touch, the only way a cold stone could, by warming. "Let them go."

Brennard laughed, and as in Jason's dreams, it was a sound without true joy, nor did it light his eyes. "Do you think you can coerce me? A mere boy? You don't even have chin hairs yet!" He straightened, and his voice got stronger till it roared out of him, like a banked fire awakening and leaping into roaring sound. "I am the master of anyone in this room. Anyone! Don't fool yourself into thinking you can put enough steel in your voice to make me think twice!"

While Brennard's voice boomed, Trent said in his ear, "I still have clear sight of Gavan's cane. I know where they are, I'll get them."

Bailey said nothing, but her linked arm tightened. She stayed with her head bowed, feigning unconsciousness.

Jason set himself, and began to pull forth what he knew about opening a Gate. He could smell the smoke beginning to pour into the room. By the time the flames reached them, it would be too late. They would already have suffocated. Bailey coughed once or twice harshly, as if confirming that. Smoke would kill before the heat. So the flames of his Fire Gate would have to be in his mind, a thousand thousand candles, ringing all of them.

"Let me help," said Anita Patel, moving forward to Jason, her small, slender hand outstretched. Henry went into a fit of twitches and stammers and fell over in front of her, his heels drumming on the floor.

Trent said, "She's got no ropes on her."

Eleanora, who appeared to have reawakened as Brennard's concentration was focused on Jason, tossed her head, dark eyes on Trent, and she managed a nod, going very pale then as if it took all her strength.

"Jason. Take my hand. You'll need strength for the Fire Gate!" The doctor reached for him, her voice soft as silk, her gaze intent, the bells on her anklet chiming as she drew near.

Traitor! He stared at her as she tried to step around Henry's form, and Henry thrashed back and forth attempting to block her. His glasses finally fell off completely, and Anita's heel crunched them to bits, and she didn't even stop. It might as well have been his head she stepped on, her dark eyes focused only on Jason.

Too eager for the Fire Gate. The Dark Hand wanted them, all of them, through a Gate and out of this world, so they could do with them whatever they pleased. They were driving him to it.

It hung in his head, a Gate wrought of twisting orange-red flames with blue centers, straining to open so that they might escape through it.

The fire came. He could hear the fine, old wood of the McHenry house scream as it exploded into inferno. Window glass burst outward with the heat. Smoke curled in, stinging his eyes. Deadly, it rushed toward them, and only he could lead any of them out. The Gate must be him, what he was made of, and what he needed and knew was right . . . the giant salamander had told him. Dracos infernos. Dragon. Dragon of flame-colored scales and wit and insight. The Gate must be what he was made of. Incongruously, he thought of a school lab door falling open. The human body was made of . . .

Jason *pushed*. The Gate of Flame fell open, inward, smelling like ozone and hot metal. He grabbed up Henry and wrapped his hand around Trent's wrist instead of grabbing Dr. Patel.

"Do it now!" he yelled above the din and chaos.

Trent's vision overlaid his own for a moment. That was all he needed. He pulled on his friends as they reached out for the others, and he knew in a split second when they were all connected. He looked deep into the crystal, the Herkimer Diamond, caught in the wolfhead jaws of Gavan Rainwater's cane. Water, the nemesis of Fire.

And he opened a second Gate, a Water Gate into the tiny drop held in the heart of the flawed diamond and plunged them all into cold, cold wetness . . . and life.

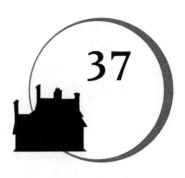

Lucky Guess

THEY popped up out of the pool in Jason's favorite valley like buoyant apples bobbing up in a Halloween dunking tub. Noisier, though, Bailey said later, all of them spluttering and coughing and poor Henry finally found his voice and was screaming to all who could hear that Dr. Patel was the one who'd kidnapped him and watch out!

He quieted after Trent ducked him a second time, while everyone else was hurrying to climb out, for the late October weather and water were cold, cold, cold. Gavan said a word, and his cape steamed as it dried. He wrapped it about Eleanora who forgot to levitate so she would be inches higher as she leaned quietly into his embrace. Tomaz gently made sure that little Lacey hadn't drowned while in Bailey's pocket, holding her in his hand and softly stroking the little creature's flanks until she coughed up spittles of water and finally began breathing evenly on her own.

Jason kept his arm linked with Bailey's, trying to send her reassuring feelings about Lacey and the whole mess while Trent

eventually helped a much calmer if spluttering Henry out of the
lake. They all straggled up the hill and through the Iron Gate,
and Gavan took them home to Ravenwyng, where—after making sure that they all got messages to their families that would
give them acceptable alibis for not being home—they had tea
and cookies and talked while the world around them celebrated
haunts and ghosts and evil running wild, only to be reined in
by the morning's dawn. Jason thought he would never look at
Halloween the same way again.

"How did you know?" asked Rainwater.

"I didn't. I guessed."

"Come, lad. Life and death don't ride on guesses." Gavan
watched him, his cape still wrapped about Eleanora and her
chair pulled very close to his.

"Well, then . . ." Jason stared down at his plate which now
held nothing but crumbs and pushed the china toward Bailey.
There was a pause, then a little chirp, and Lacey came out cautiously and hunkered down to steal the cookie bits. "Let's say,
it came together. They wanted that Fire Gate. I realized that
they'd probably already had it open once, preparing it to receive
all of us . . . like a prison or concentration camp, or something."

"Why?" Tomaz rocked back in his chair, coffee mug settled
deep in his hands. "How did you figure that?"

"Fizziwig. They'd got a Gate out of Fizziwig. It's probably
what killed him, the strain. Even if it didn't, that's why they
wanted him and took him."

Pain crossed Gavan's face. "Of course. I should have realized
that." Jason stopped, and he gestured. "Go on."

"For weeks I've been pushed toward a Fire Gate. In my
dreams, waking, the McHenry house, they made sure it was
centered in my life. The wolfjackals were herding us toward it,
and Brennard was piling the pressure on in ways you don't even
know about yet, so that I would just have to discover it and

open the Gate, for us all to escape." He looked around the table. "They didn't figure on all of you going after Henry, just us."

Tomaz snorted. "No credit for good sense. But it was quite a trap, and we were caught."

"That still doesn't explain why you suddenly went for water."

"The fire would have claimed or killed us. I'd been advised that Gates are within yourself, and I . . . well, it's silly . . . all I could think of, was that I'm seventy percent water. It suddenly became the only thing I could do. It had to be a Water Gate. The only drop I could find in that whole room to focus on was buried in your Herkimer diamond."

Gavan lifted his cane, smiling at the wolfhead figure with the gemstone in its jaws. "I've always been very fond of this. Now I have a reason."

Eleanora said something, muffled, and he tightened his hold about her shoulders. She quieted, smiling.

"You managed to control Brennard after all."

Jason nodded to Tomaz. "In a way. Actually, all I wanted to do was make him really angry because when you're angry, you can't think. I didn't want him following us."

"I felt a push," murmured Eleanora. She tucked some wayward hair behind one delicate ear. "What did you do, Jason?"

"I had this." He pulled the lavender stone from his pocket. "It seems to have a Talent for persuading." He grinned, thinking how nice Alicia was every time he asked her to do something while he had the stone in his hand.

"But you couldn't persuade him to let us go." Henry's voice was squeaky from too much shouting. Now he had barely said a word and looked as if he didn't want to say much more.

Jason shook his head. "I'm not strong enough for anything like that. I was standing there looking at all of you tied up like turkeys for a roasting, and I knew I couldn't outwrestle him. I persuaded him to get angry. And it worked." He kept grinning broadly.

"May I see that again, Jason?" Gavan put a hand out for it.

"Sure." He dropped the lavender crystal in Rainwater's palm.

"Where did he get that?" Eleanora stirred, sitting up straight. She put her hand over Gavan's and peered at the stone.

"I was . . . hmmm . . . well, I was practicing opening Gates."

Gavan's eyebrows went up, but he said nothing. "Were you now? I don't seem to remember you telling me." Eleanora was practically tucked under his chin, looking at the new focus, and he seemed to be enjoying her proximity, despite his concern over Jason's behavior.

"Gavan," said Eleanora quietly. "Look deep into it. Really focus."

"It's Jason's stone," he reminded her.

"Oh, I know it is! Just look."

He did. Then he looked up at Jason. "Lad . . . do you see an image inside this?"

"Sometimes."

"I cannot see it well. Describe it."

Eleanora leaned back against Gavan's chest, visibly trembling.

Jason told them of the silvery-haired gentleman, with a warm smile and humor and youth despite the color of his curled hair. He stopped as Eleanora spoke a name. "Gregory!"

Tomaz rumbled, "None other. I would say it was no accident Jason found that crystal, and even less of an accident he could use it against Brennard."

"*The* Gregory?" Trent piped up.

Bailey kept quiet, busy feeding small bits of cookie to her near-drowned Lacey.

"None other. My father," Eleanora returned. She handed the crystal back to Jason. "Use it well and wisely."

Jason stared at it as if it had become a hot potato. "He's not . . . he's not trapped in there. . . ."

"Oh, no. Nothing like that." Eleanora laughed then, a bit of color coming back into her cheeks. "Just an enchantment or two of his in there. He knew things none of the rest of us did, including, I think, what Brennard was capable of."

"It's a good thing that came into your hands, lad," Gavan said, "and we'll discuss later the appropriate discipline for trying something daft like that without a backup."

"Trent was there!"

Gavan looked at Trent, and said nothing.

"What about the others? Think they got out?" Bailey picked up Lacey and was coaxing her back into a pocket, but the pack rat seemed determined to keep an eye on everyone about the table and their cookies.

"No doubt they used their Fire Gate. I imagine the house was lost. It was meant to be. They planned a devastating fire to cover up their taking you four. They had teeth, bones . . . to scatter in the ashes." Tomaz grunted. "We underestimated them. Won't happen again."

"Well," said Bailey. "All's well that ends well."

"It's only just begun, Bailey."

She tucked Lacey back in her pocket. "I know that! We've more Gates to get open, more Magick to learn! As long as we get to that ending well part."

Trent sat back. "Since dessert is a good ending any time . . . I could use a bit more. After all, it is trick or treat." He looked about the table hopefully, and Henry hoarsely seconded him.